THRILL KILL

ALSO AVAILABLE BY BRIAN THIEM:

Red Line

THRILL KILL

A MATT SINCLAIR MYSTERY

Brian Thiem

CROOKED
LANE

NEW YORK

Published in the United States by Crooked Lane Books, an imprint of The Quick Brown Fox & Company LLC.

Crooked Lane Books and its logo are trademarks of The Quick Brown Fox & Company LLC.

Library of Congress Catalog-in-Publication data available upon request.

ISBN (hardcover): 978-1-62953-766-5
ISBN (paperback): 978-1-62953-781-8
ISBN (ePub): 978-1-62953-782-5
ISBN (Kindle): 978-1-62953-783-2
ISBN (ePDF): 978-1-62953-784-9

Cover design by Andy Ruggirello
Book design by Jennifer Canzone

Printed in the United States.

www.crookedlanebooks.com

Crooked Lane Books
34 West 27th St., 10th Floor
New York, NY 10001

First Edition: August 2016

10 9 8 7 6 5 4 3 2 1

For

My brothers and sisters in blue who dedicate their lives to protecting and serving our communities.

And all often, give their lives in the process.

Chapter 1

Oakland homicide sergeant Matt Sinclair stopped fifty yards from the small stand of trees. Silhouetted against a gray sky, the body of a naked woman hung by a rope from an oak tree. The toes of one foot barely touched the ground, while a second length of rope suspended the other foot level with her head, as if someone had posed her in a modern dance move. A cheap blue tarpaulin had been tied in the branches above the body by the responding officers to prevent the crime scene from getting any more soaked than it already was. Three men wearing black Gore-Tex raincoats and navy-blue baseball caps with the Oakland Police Department patch huddled under the tarp.

Sinclair stood on an asphalt pathway that ran from the parking lot, past a set of bleachers that overlooked a little-league baseball field, to a basketball court at the back of the park. He reached into his raincoat pocket and pulled out a stack of assignment cards, obsolete forms the size of archaic computer punch cards. Although they hadn't been used in years for their intended purpose, the department continued to stock them for officers to use for taking notes in the field, specifically in rainy weather that would dissolve the paper of a legal pad.

Sinclair snaked his hand under his raincoat and suitcoat and fished a pen out of his shirt pocket. He glanced at his watch and wrote on the top card: *Dec 4, 0658—Arrived at scene (Burckhalter*

Park). Cold, dawn, overcast, rain. He hated murder scenes in the rain. Not only did the rain wash away critical evidence, but it also forced him to be more of an asshole than usual to get the uniformed cops out of their dry cars to scour the area for witnesses and evidence.

He heard a car door slam behind him and turned to see a woman dressed in a tan raincoat open an umbrella and head up the path toward him. Maybe it was a man thing, but Sinclair could not fathom a cop, even when in plainclothes, using an umbrella when doing police work. Cathy Braddock and Sinclair had been partners for just over a year, and although Sinclair had had his doubts about her when she was first assigned to him, she proved herself during their first case together and helped bring down the serial murderer the media had nicknamed the Bus Bench Killer.

"I like the hat," she said. Braddock was forty years old—three years older than Sinclair. She was five-foot-six and well proportioned, with chestnut-colored hair worn in a fashionable bob. Under her raincoat, she wore a stylish black pantsuit that allowed her to conceal her gun, handcuffs, and other tools of the trade. In the year they'd worked together, she'd transitioned from a mix of Berkeley frumpy and New England preppy to a San Francisco sophistication that conveyed authority and professionalism—she definitely didn't look like a rookie anymore.

"Keeps my head dry." Sinclair tapped the brim of his gray fedora, causing water to cascade onto his shoulder.

"You just get here?"

"Two minutes before you. Just taking in the sights."

Braddock looked past him toward the victim. "Jesus. The desk officer said it was a naked woman hung from a tree, but I was hoping that was just his early-morning sense of humor." They walked down the path, trying to avoid the puddles. "You okay, Matt? You look beat."

Sinclair had heard that on every call-out back when he drank. Since he had gotten sober, he seldom looked as if he'd been up all night, even when the frequency of murders cut into his sleep. But sleep was hard to come by these days for Sinclair nevertheless. "I'm fine."

Although his raincoat covered his uniform and hid the sergeant strips on the sleeve of the shortest man of the three standing under the tarp, Sinclair recognized the area supervisor by the bright smile that seldom left his face.

"Hey, Matt. Hey, Cathy," said Sergeant Duane Boone. "Great morning for a murder, huh?"

Boone had been on the department for ten years, four years fewer than Sinclair, and was promoted to sergeant last summer, which explained his assignment to the midnight shift with Tuesday, Wednesday, and Thursday as his days off.

"No place we'd rather be," said Sinclair.

"Who's got the honors?" Boone asked.

"I'm up," said Sinclair. "Braddock had a mom and pop Friday night." Homicide investigators in Oakland worked in pairs and were assigned what was termed "standby," where they were the on-call team for every murder that occurred during the week. The two partners took turns assuming the responsibility of being the primary investigator of new cases.

"I heard about it," said Boone. "Dude was stepping out on his old lady, and she took a butcher knife to him as he slept."

"She was still holding the bloody knife when the first patrol officer got there," said Sinclair. "Said she wasn't a damn bit sorry."

"I take it you don't have the suspect on this one waiting for us in the back seat of a patrol car," said Braddock.

"Let's get out of the rain," Boone said, stepping under the tarp alongside two officers, both in their midtwenties and about eye-to-eye with Sinclair's six-foot frame. "The tech already processed the ground around the body and found nada. We have the caller in a car down in the parking lot. He was walking his dog and saw the vic and called it in."

Sinclair stepped under the tarp and looked at the corpse. A heavy yellow nylon rope was tied around her neck, looped over a branch fifteen feet above the ground and tied to the trunk of a smaller tree about thirty feet away. Sinclair pictured a very strong man pulling the rope over the branch until the woman was suspended, wrapping it around the other tree trunk, and tying it off. Another length of rope, tied around her right ankle, was looped over the same branch and tied to the trunk of the oak tree. She was naked except for a soggy piece of cloth hanging from her crotch. Sinclair estimated her at around five-foot-eight, slim build, probably about 130 pounds. Her long, blonde hair hung over her face like a stringy mop. He pulled an assignment card from his pocket and jotted down some more notes.

Sinclair looked around the area. Grass covered the ground except under the tree where the sun couldn't reach. He knew there'd be no footprints in the grass even if it hadn't rained all night. "Any signs of footprints where the ropes were tied off?"

"Nothing," said a voice behind him. Sinclair turned to see Joyce Talbert, one of the department's civilian crime-scene techs. She was in her midforties, short and squat. Her black raincoat extended to her knees, and her bleached-blonde hair was stuffed under a baseball cap with the OPD patch on the front.

"Hey, Joyce," said Sinclair. "How'd I get so lucky to get you as my tech?"

"You know how much I love working outdoor scenes in the winter, so when I heard the call of a DOA over the sound of rain pounding on the roof of my car, I jumped at the chance to handle it."

"Everyone says we need the rain," said Sinclair. California was in its fourth year of drought, but more than three inches of rain had fallen in the last week, and even the Californians who had been forced to let their lawns die because of water rationing last summer were starting to complain.

"It's those cute little weather girls who don't have to work in it that say we need it," Talbert said.

"Have you found anything interesting?" Sinclair asked.

"Only this," she said, stepping under the tarp and opening a black garbage bag.

Sinclair looked inside as she opened a paper bag containing a can of Aqua Net hairspray and another paper bag containing a green plastic lighter. "And this is connected how?"

"I found them about twenty feet down the path," Talbert said. "Come around this side and it'll make sense."

Sinclair and Braddock walked to the other side of the body. A piece of burned cloth hung from the victim's crotch. The skin on her upper legs, abdomen, and lower chest was charred and blistered.

Braddock crouched and looked closely. "Oh god, are you telling me some asshole . . ."

"That's my guess," said Talbert. "That's the sleeve of a cotton sweater. I found the rest of it in the parking lot. It looks like someone soaked it in gasoline or lighter fluid—I could smell it when I first got here—stuffed the end of it into her vagina, used the hairspray and lighter as a blow torch, and lit her on fire."

"That's one sick motherfucker," said Sinclair.

"I only hope she was already dead when the asshole did it," said Braddock.

"I'm sure the coroner will be able to tell us. Speaking of the coroner—" Sinclair turned to Boone.

"I called them as soon as you drove up. They said they're on their way."

"What about the canvass?"

"Two officers are still out knocking on doors, but I don't expect much. The park is pretty isolated, and with the cold and rain, I doubt anyone was outside or had their windows open to hear anything."

Although it was a relatively low-crime neighborhood, Sinclair had handled a few calls in this area when he worked patrol years ago. Burckhalter Park was a small community park between the 580 Freeway to the north and Edwards Avenue to the west. A chain-link fence and heavy vegetation separated the park from homes with spacious backyards on the other two sides. Edwards Avenue was a busy thoroughfare during commute hours when drivers exited the freeway and took the winding two-lane road down the hill to MacArthur Boulevard and into the heart of east Oakland, but it was a quiet road at night. It was a perfect place to dump a body—easy access to a freeway for a fast escape, yet dark and isolated once the sun went down.

Sinclair pulled up the collar of his black London Fog and trudged through the rain to the parking lot with Braddock. The engine of one patrol car was running, its wipers flicking back and forth intermittently. Sinclair tapped at the window. The officer behind the wheel lowered it a few inches and said, "Morning, Sarge."

"You took the statement from the man who found the body?"

The officer handed two sheets of paper to Sinclair, which he tucked under his raincoat to keep dry. "Sir," Sinclair said to the man sitting in the passenger seat, "why don't you join me in my car."

A gray-haired black man got out of the patrol vehicle and followed Sinclair. Sinclair opened the passenger door for him, and Braddock climbed in the back. Sinclair grabbed a handful of paper towels from the glove box and dried his hands and the sleeves of his raincoat to prevent water from dripping on the statement. "Beautiful weather, huh?"

"I've seen worse," the man said.

"I'm Sergeant Sinclair and behind you is my partner, Sergeant Braddock. We work homicide."

"Bobbie Hines." He held out a calloused hand. A firm grip.

"Give me a minute to read your statement, Mr. Hines."

"Take your time."

The statement contained the basics: Hines left his house on Sunkist Drive at 5:10 AM and walked his dog to the park. He saw the woman hanging from the tree and called 9-1-1. He checked for a pulse and determined she was dead. He waited in the parking lot until a fire truck, ambulance, and police cars arrived. He escorted them to the woman. They checked the woman and confirmed she was dead. The officer asked him to wait, so he called his wife, who came and took their dog home.

"I see here that you're retired," said Sinclair, looking at the information on the statement form.

"I do some volunteer work, but no longer have to work for a paycheck."

"Isn't it a little unusual to be walking a dog at five in the morning in the rain?"

"The Navy taught me to be an early riser. I'm awake by five every morning. Never need an alarm clock. Buster's bouncing up and down and spinning in circles the moment I put my feet on the floor. I get dressed, start the coffee, and out the door we go, rain or shine. We walk straight to the park, where I let him off leash. I know it's against the law, but we're alone this time of the morning, and I always carry some poop bags just in case Buster decides to do his business in the park."

"So, you were walking through the park and saw the woman?"

"Not exactly. We walked through the parking lot and Buster stopped to sniff that wet sweater I pointed out to your CSI lady. Then we walked down the path going toward the basketball court. Buster was off in the trees, sniffing and peeing on bushes like he always does. He picked up something, maybe some sweatpants or something. There's always abandoned stuff lying in the park. I told him to drop it, which he did."

"Where was that?" asked Sinclair.

"To the right of the path, maybe ten or twenty feet. It was dark, so I don't exactly know."

"What happened then?"

"We continued up the path. We normally walk through the old basketball court, then loop around the rest of the park back to the parking lot, where I put him on the leash for the walk home, but he started barking up ahead of me. That's not like him. I ran up to him and shined my flashlight. I saw the woman hanging there. I checked her pulse. She was cold and I knew she'd been dead a while."

"You seem pretty sure," Sinclair said.

"It might've been years ago, but the Navy taught me real well."

"Have you ever seen her before?"

"I didn't get a look at her face."

"Fair enough. What about any suspicious people or activities around here recently?"

"This is Oakland. There's plenty of that going on, but we're far enough from the flatlands that it's not as common up here. This morning, I didn't see anyone."

Sinclair plucked a business card from the case he carried in his shirt pocket. "Here's my card. Call me if you think of anything else."

Sinclair walked Hines back to the patrol car and asked the officer to take him home just as the coroner's van drove up. The rain had slowed to a drizzle. Boone and two of his officers exited their cars, while Coroner Investigator Charlie Dawson and his partner unloaded the gurney. Dawson had been working for a mortuary transporting bodies when he was hired by the coroner's office nearly four decades ago, back in the days when coroner investigators did little more than pick up bodies and transport them to the morgue. The three uniforms led the procession up the path, and Sinclair and Braddock brought up the rear.

"Any ID on her?" Dawson asked.

"No," said Sinclair. "We'll need to roll her prints and hope she's in the system." Even though the days of rolling a victim's inked fingers onto a fingerprint card had given way to electronic fingerprint readers that transmitted prints within seconds through the county system to the state and FBI if necessary, the terminology had stuck, and Sinclair had always been an old-fashioned detective.

"What about missing persons?" Dawson asked.

"None that fit her description," Braddock answered.

"Who found her?" Dawson continued.

"The RO can give you all of that once we get her back to the parking lot," Sinclair said.

Although Dawson understood protocol dictated that the reporting officer was his source of information, he'd been picking up bodies for twenty years already when Sinclair came on, and he felt that his experience made him the equal of homicide investigators.

Dawson and his partner gloved up and spread a white sheet under the body to catch any trace evidence that fell when they moved her. "Do you want us to untie the rope or cut it?"

Sinclair had already examined the knots in the hope they would tell him something about the killer. If the knot at her neck was an authentic hangman's noose or a properly tied bowline, it might tell him who he was looking for, but these were all sloppy granny knots. However, he also knew that rope was a great medium to collect skin cells that could contain the DNA of the person who handled it. "Let's cut the rope."

Sinclair reached under his raincoat to his suit coat pocket, pulled out a Spyderco folding knife, and snapped it open with a flick of his wrist. Its four-inch blade was serrated at the base and designed to cut through seatbelts to extract people trapped in cars during traffic collisions. With its razor-sharp tip, the knife was also the perfect last-ditch weapon.

Sinclair donned gloves and cut through the rope holding up the leg. Both coroner investigators hoisted the body, and Sinclair cut through the rope around her neck. Dawson arranged her on the sheet and wiped her wet, stringy hair from her face.

"She's in full rigor, so time of death was at least four hours ago," Dawson said.

The onset of rigor mortis was a very rough estimate, but it did tell Sinclair that she was likely killed last night rather than that morning.

Dawson pointed at her forehead. "Looks like the cause of death might not be the hanging."

Sinclair stood over the body and saw a small hole surrounded by dried blood in her forehead. He looked more closely at her face. "Oh, shit."

"What?" Braddock said.

"Our victim's name is Dawn Gustafson."

Chapter 2

Of all the hookers Sinclair had arrested in his early days in vice-narcotics, Dawn was one he would never forget. Ten years ago, he was the new guy in the unit and often got stuck as the undercover on street prostitution details, or "trolling," as they called it. He was the bait the vice unit dragged around the city, hoping to get a bite from one of the hookers. He would drive along the streets where the prostitutes worked, called the "ho stro" (short for "whore stroll"), in an undercover car and pull over when a likely working girl waved at him or gave him "the look." They would agree upon a sex act and an amount, normally around twenty for oral sex and thirty or more for a half-and-half, sex that began with oral sex and ended with intercourse. She'd jump in the car and direct him to an isolated spot for a car date or to a cheap motel for more involved acts. Two other undercover cars would follow him. Once he'd driven out of the area, he'd say a code word that the hidden microphone would transmit to the undercover officers in the follow cars, and they'd direct the arrest team to swoop in and arrest the prostitute. Sinclair would then drive to a different spot and troll through fresh waters. On a good night, he could land fifteen or twenty keepers.

The night he met Dawn, Sinclair had just arrested a working girl who offered him a half-and-half for fifty dollars at her motel room. He was heading to West MacArthur when he spotted a tall, pretty white girl a block west of where the veteran street hookers normally operated. It was a warm evening, and she was wearing a tight miniskirt that barely covered her butt cheeks and a hot-pink halter-top. She smiled at him as he cruised slowly by, so he pulled to the curb. She leaned in the passenger window, displaying deep cleavage and a smile with perfect teeth, and swung her waist-length blonde hair over her shoulder.

"Are you dating?" she asked.

"Are you working?"

"Girl's gotta pay the rent. You're not a cop, are you?"

Sinclair laughed. "Do I look like a cop?" He'd only left uniform a month earlier, so his dark-brown hair was just beyond regulation, but he had grown a thick beard to blend in better on the streets.

"You're too cute to be a cop." Her eyes were the color of deep water. "What're you looking for?"

"Whatever you're offering."

"I can give you head in the car for fifty or plenty more if you have the time and money."

"The plenty more sounds good."

She got in and told him to make a right on Market Street. "How much money do you have?"

Sinclair pulled a money clip from his pocket and showed her the hundred dollars his sergeant had given him earlier that night. "About eighty."

She counted it. "You've got a hundred there. Can you hit an ATM?"

"Not until payday."

She was silent for a moment. "Have you ever been to the hot tubs?"

"What are *the* hot tubs?"

"A place in Berkeley where you rent a hot tub for fifty an hour."

"That's a lot of money to sit around in a hot tub with a bunch of strangers."

"No, silly. You get your own hot tub in a private room. People go there to fuck."

"This is all the money I got."

She looked into his eyes and smiled. "No problem."

"That would only leave you fifty. You can make that much with a five-minute blowjob."

"Like I said, I think you're cute. Do you wanna go or not?"

Flashing red-and-blue lights filled his rearview mirror. Sinclair pulled to the side of the road. One officer came to Sinclair's door and asked for his license and registration—all part of the ruse—while another officer ordered Dawn from the car, handcuffed her, and put her in the backseat of their marked unit. That officer returned Sinclair's money clip with the hundred dollars and said, "Sarge told us to make the arrest even though you didn't give the signal yet. I think he was afraid you were falling in love and forgot you were working."

He never saw Dawn again—until she called him three years ago.

★

"How do you know her?" asked Braddock, crouching down to get a better look at the bullet hole.

"I arrested her for six-forty-seven-B when I was working vice. Seventeen-year-old kid who ran away from somewhere in the Midwest to find fame and fortune in San Francisco. That would make her around twenty-seven now." The same age he was when he'd arrested her on that warm summer night.

"You've got a great memory for names, Sarge," Dawson remarked.

"It's hard to tell looking at her right now," said Braddock, "but I'll bet she was a darn pretty girl."

Sinclair watched as the coroner investigators wrapped her in the sheet and lifted her into the body bag laid out on the gurney. Sinclair walked through the wet grass alongside the path as the others made their way to the parking lot. He spotted a pair of black leggings at the base of a tree. Behind it was a soggy nude-colored bra and lace panties. He crouched down to see if there was anything under the clothes.

Talbert walked up the path. "Find something?"

"The witness said his dog had grabbed some item of clothes around here. Probably this stuff."

"I'll photo everything and collect it."

"Appreciate it."

"You okay, Sarge?"

Sinclair straightened up. He hadn't slept well in weeks, and his nerves felt ragged. Stuff that used to roll off his back was now weighing him down. "I wish she would've stayed in Minnesota and had a normal life."

"You can't save them all," Talbert said.

"It just seems like we hardly save any of them anymore."

Back at the parking lot, a heavyset man was loading camera equipment into the hatchback of a Honda CRV. Sinclair recognized him as a stringer who often showed up at fires, accidents, and crime scenes. He sold his photos and video to whichever news organization would pay.

The man slammed the trunk. "Sergeant Sinclair, what can you tell me about this one?"

"Nothing much," Sinclair said. "Woman found dead in the park."

"Cause of death?"

"That will have to wait until the autopsy."

"Hanging by her neck from a tree. I can guess she didn't die from drowning."

"But if you guess wrong . . ." Sinclair let him ponder the repercussions to his reputation. "Did you get any good shots?"

"Got some good stills of her silhouette hanging there. Can't tell she's naked, especially in black and white, so the papers could use it. The video didn't turn out as well, but who knows, maybe it'll be a slow news day. Is she anyone famous?"

"I don't think so."

"She's a hooker, right?"

"What makes you say that?"

"It's Oakland, man. In this town, the odds are a man gunned down in a drive-by is a drug dealer and woman stripped of her clothes and hung from a tree is a hooker. Looks like it's just another number in Oakland and nobody cares."

"I do," Sinclair said as he turned and walked to his car.

The rain had stopped, and Sinclair threw his hat in the back seat. He remembered the words from his first homicide partner, Phil Roberts, when they stood over the body of a young drug dealer killed in a drive-by, one of Sinclair's first murder cases: *You and I are the only two people in the world who care about avenging the death of this young man.* Phil said it was their job to speak for the dead, but to Sinclair, investigating the death of a human being had an even higher purpose—to bring the killer to justice. If people were allowed to kill with impunity, the fragile sense of civilization that existed in urban communities like Oakland would collapse. It was his duty to prevent that from occurring.

★

It took less than twenty minutes to drive to the address on Tennyson Road in Hayward where the DMV showed Dawn Gustafson living as of two years ago. The rain had started again, speckling the surface of the apartment-complex swimming pool like hundreds of tiny bullets being fired from the sky. Sinclair and Braddock walked through the courtyard and up the stairs to apartment 238. A twenty-something Hispanic woman wearing jeans and a sweatshirt opened the door. Sinclair swept his open raincoat aside to show the badge clipped to his belt. "We're with Oakland police. Does Dawn Gustafson live here?"

"I think that's the name of a previous tenant," she said. "My husband and I have lived here for over a year, but we still get mail for her."

"What kind of mail?"

"Bills, junk mail."

"Any idea where she went?"

"The rental office is open at noon today. Maybe they can tell you, but I heard she was asked to leave."

"Any idea why?"

"I don't pay attention to rumors, but Rachel in two-thirty-two might be able to tell you. I think they were friends."

Rachel answered her door wearing a tank top and yoga pants, wiping sleep from her eyes. Sinclair introduced himself and said, "Can we talk to you about Dawn Gustafson?"

Rachel was in her midthirties, with a jet-black pixie cut and tattoos of Chinese characters on both pale shoulders. "I haven't seen her since she moved out two summers ago."

"May we come in?" Braddock asked.

She opened the door and walked into the living room. "I just woke up. I'll be a minute." She disappeared into a bedroom, and Sinclair and Braddock took off their raincoats and draped them over a chair in the dining nook. A minute later, the toilet flushed and Rachel reappeared wearing a cobalt-blue velour robe. "I'll be glad when this rain stops and the sun comes out."

She sat in a chair in the living room, and Sinclair and Braddock sat on a sofa across from her. "Did you know Dawn well?" Sinclair asked.

"Not really. She lived here maybe two years and I'd run into her and chat. Sometimes we'd be at the pool together and talk about boys and stuff."

"Did she have a boyfriend?"

"Not just one. She was a party girl. I saw all kind of men coming and going from her apartment. And I mean all kinds."

"How's that?" Sinclair asked.

"Young, old, black, white, some in jeans and T-shirts, others in suits."

"Did you two ever talk about that?"

"She said she liked men. Said most of them were her clients. She was an accountant and worked out of her apartment doing people's business books and taxes and stuff."

"But you had your doubts," Sinclair said.

"We'd be out at the pool. She had a killer body and gorgeous long hair. Guys were always coming on to her. Really cute guys. But she just ignored them. Said they weren't her type."

"These clients of hers, did you ever catch any of their names?"

"No, they didn't hang around once they left her apartment. A neighbor once said they recognized a really muscular black man who used to visit. They said he was an Oakland Raider who was on the kick-off return team or something like that."

"How about any other friends?"

"I never saw any of her girlfriends, assuming she had any."

"Why'd she leave?"

"She said the manager found out she was using her apartment for commercial purposes, you know, running her book-keeping business there, and that was a zoning violation." Rachel tucked her legs under herself on the chair. "What did she do?"

"She got herself killed last night in Oakland," said Sinclair.

"That's too bad," Rachel said.

He copied Rachel's full name and contact information, the last phone number she had for Dawn, and the phone numbers for the manager. He handed Rachel his card as he left.

On their return drive to Oakland, Braddock said, "It looks like Dawn was operating an in-call business out of her apartment. I think Rachel knew it, too, but didn't want to come out and say Dawn was a call-girl."

"At least it gives us a direction."

"And a few hundred possible johns who might have killed her."

"Piece of cake," Sinclair said. "All we have to do is find the last trick she was with."

Sinclair dropped Braddock off at her car at Burckhalter, and while she headed back to the station, he drove to the coroner's office.

Chapter 3

Sinclair dressed in a cloth gown, paper cap, safety glasses, and booties and pushed through the double doors into the morgue. The ventilation system in the ceiling hummed, but the smells of decaying flesh and disinfectant still hung in the air. Three bodies lay on stainless-steel tables, and Dr. Gorman, one of the pathologists, hovered over the body of an elderly man.

Gorman looked through his plastic splash-protective visor. "Good morning, Sergeant Sinclair. This gentleman can wait. I'll return to Ms. Gustafson for you."

Sinclair gestured to the elderly corpse. "What's his story, Doc?"

"He lived alone and was found dead by his son. He hadn't seen a doctor in years, so there was no one to sign off on the death certificate. I'll probably discover his death is of natural causes resulting from one or more undiagnosed medical conditions."

"As long as you don't find a bullet in him."

"If I do, it belongs to Fremont PD, so today will be your lucky day."

"I'll see if that's true after I hear what you have to say about my victim."

Gorman moved to a flat-screen illuminator mounted on the wall and attached several x-ray films. "You can see here," he said, pointing to a dark object at the base of the skull in the image, "we have a single projectile that passed through the anterior portion of the skull, the thick frontal bone, and came to rest at the back of the skull without penetrating the parietal bone. I see no fragments, so it appears the projectile remained intact, which should aid in the ballistics examination by your crime lab."

Gorman flipped off the light of the x-ray viewer and walked to the table where Dawn's body lay. Her skin was pale white except for black soot and charred skin on her upper legs and abdomen. Her hands rested alongside the torso, the manicured fingernails short and covered with clear nail polish. The head was propped on a hard plastic rest. "I've already done the external, but I wanted to point some things out to you before I proceed." He pointed to a white line running through the lightly charred flesh on her stomach. "This is a Caesarian scar."

"She had a baby?"

"There's no way to know if she gave live birth or not, only that she had the surgery," Gorman said, as if it were obvious. "It's well healed, so her pregnancy could have been a number of years ago. If you look at the neck, you can see some abrasion of the skin, apparently caused by the rough fibers of the rope that was used to suspend her from the tree. But what you don't see is more interesting."

"The absence of ligature marks?"

"Precisely. The abrasion marks might appear to be ligature marks to the uninitiated, but they are clearly postmortem. She was hung after she was dead. There is some bruising on the neck, which is consistent with manual strangulation, but it's doubtful that was the cause of death. I'll know more when I open her up. I also examined the burn marks on her body and concluded they occurred after she was dead as well. They occurred when the body was in an upright position, as indicated by the rising flame marks in the skin that are pointing toward the head. Therefore, my preliminary assumption is there was some degree of struggle, at which time she was manually choked. She was then shot in the head, which caused her death. Next, her body was suspended from the neck, and finally, it was burned."

Sinclair watched as Gorman opened the chest cavity with a Y-shaped incision across the chest. He stepped aside to let his assistant move in and cut through the ribs and breastbone with long-handled pruning shears. Even though Sinclair had attended countless autopsies, the crunch of bone still made him wince. Gorman lifted off the breastplate, took blood samples from the thoracic cavity, and removed the organs. He examined each one carefully before cutting off pieces and placing them in marked containers. He used the shears to cut through the pelvic bone and spent several minutes examining that area.

He recorded long medical descriptions into a recorder that hung on a swivel above the table, then turned to Sinclair and summarized. "She was in excellent physical condition. Excellent muscle tone and low body fat indicates a healthy diet and some sort of vigorous exercise program. Liver, heart, and lungs appear healthy. There's no damage to the outer layer of the vaginal canal or mucosa, despite the insertion of the piece of clothing several inches into the canal. I conclude that no instrument was likely used, because if one had been, some tearing would have been likely. I found no indication of semen, but I'll collect samples for examination. The burns in the pubic region definitely occurred postmortem."

Gorman cut into the neck tissue along the line where the rope had rested. "As I suspected, there's no underlying tissue damage, which means the victim was dead when the constriction around the neck by the rope occurred." He cut into two purplish bruises on the front of her neck and slowly dissected the windpipe, closely examining the throat and neck region. "Someone strangled her with their hands. Most likely from the front, with the thumbs pressing into the larynx and thyroid cartilage, which fractured the hyoid bone. That injury may have eventually led to her death if the muscles and tissue swelled and cut off her air supply, but it appears the bullet ended her life before that occurred."

He looked at the bullet wound with a magnifying glass and snapped a half dozen photographs with a digital camera equipped with a macro lens. "There's no indication of fouling in the tissue of the wound, nor any on the skin around the wound. I do, however, see signs of stippling on the skin."

No experienced pathologist would estimate the range of a gunshot based on his examination of the body alone, but Sinclair could tell from the wound that it was not a press contact, where the gun muzzle was touching the victim. Likewise, the absence of fouling—soot or residue from burned gunpowder—indicated that the gun was probably at least six inches away, assuming the weapon was a medium-powered handgun. Stippling, also called tattooing, resulted from unburned gunpowder embedding in the skin around the wound and seldom occurred beyond two feet. But without knowing what kind of gun and ammo was used, he could only estimate the distance from which it had been shot as somewhere beyond a few inches and less than two feet.

Gorman took a scalpel and made several deep incisions through the scalp, pealed the back of the scalp over the corpse's face, and stepped back as his assistant cut through the skull with a high-speed electric rotary saw. Gorman carefully removed the skullcap, set it in a stainless-steel pan, and made a few cuts through the membrane to remove the brain. He probed the soft brain tissue with a finger, plucked out a copper-jacketed lead slug, and placed it in a plastic container. "Your firearms examiner can tell you for sure, but it appears to be a nominal thirty-eight caliber jacketed hollow point."

Sinclair knew that could mean a 9mm, .38, .357 magnum, or .380, all very common calibers for handguns. Gorman took a stainless-steel probe and slowly worked it through the wound track in the brain until it came out the back. He held the brain up, shifted it until it was level, and looked at Sinclair. "From the location of the entrance wound, the bullet track, and where it came to rest at the back of the skull, I'd say the victim's face was perpendicular to the barrel of the gun as well as close to ninety degrees laterally."

Sinclair liked the manner in which Gorman explained his findings. Doctors with less experience would try to conclude how tall a shooter was based on the wounds or the direction the person was facing, but there were too many variables to come to quick conclusions. A shot that went directly into a victim's forehead could result from both the victim and shooter facing each other or the victim being on her knees and the shooter standing and shooting from the hip, or it could just as easily result from the victim lying on the ground and the shooter standing directly over her and shooting downward.

"So, she was looking right at the gun, and it was up close and personal," said Sinclair.

"That's about all there is for you to see. If I discover anything else significant, I'll give you a call. Good luck, Matt."

★

Braddock was sitting at her desk typing on her computer when Sinclair walked into the homicide office. The office consisted of a large room containing eighteen small metal desks that had been purchased by the city when the Police Administration Building, or PAB, was opened more than fifty years ago. Walls were lined with metal file cabinets. A few windows overlooked Washington Street and the county court building across the street. On the opposite side of the room were two glass-walled offices, one of which belonged to the homicide lieutenant. The other had been converted into a soft interview room, a casual place to talk with family and cooperative witnesses. A table with chairs, a green vinyl-covered sofa, and a small end table with a cheap table lamp that had not worked in years filled the room. Toward the back of the main office were two metal doors that led to the other interview rooms—small six-by-eight rooms where Sinclair had spent countless hours trying to convince witnesses and killers to tell the truth.

"Was she alive when the killer lit her on fire?" Braddock asked.

Sinclair hung up his raincoat and suitcoat and poured himself a cup of coffee. "She died from the gunshot to the head and was hung and torched sometime later."

"Thank God for that."

"Before the gunshot, she was manually strangled hard enough to fracture the hyoid," Sinclair said. "The gunshot was within a few feet."

"Sounds like it was personal."

Sinclair had come to the same conclusion. Other strangulation murders he had investigated were normally crimes of passion—committed during a sudden rage—rather than premeditated. But the firing of a bullet into Dawn's head didn't necessarily fit unless the killer just happened to have a gun on him and his anger totally engulfed him. Sinclair began running other possibilities and motives through his mind and finally realized how futile it was with the limited information he had so far.

Sinclair wrote the number ninety-two on a piece of paper from a memo pad, added today's date and his and Braddock's initials, and pinned it to the bulletin board. With only a few weeks left until the end of the year, it looked like the city would tally under a hundred murders for the year, something that had only occurred a few times in the last four decades. "I'm guessing the shooting took place somewhere else, and she was transported there and posed," he said.

"I was thinking the same thing," Braddock said. "The way she was arranged seemed symbolic."

"Is the RO gone?" Sinclair asked.

"Yeah, I reviewed his report and approved it. With only one witness, there wasn't much to it. I ran out our victim. Her history begins with her juvenile arrest for the B case you put on her ten years ago. She was counseled and released to her parents by juvenile hall two days after the arrest. It appears they flew to

Oakland and signed for her. I have their address in Minnesota, but I don't know if it's any good after all these years."

"I'll let the coroner's office contact them. I doubt the parents will be able to shed any light on her recent activities."

"You just hate talking to family."

"You blame me? All they do is babble and blow snot and tears. And for what? If Dawn was close enough to her parents for them to know what she was up to, she probably wouldn't have been involved in whatever it was that killed her." Sinclair was angry. Angry not only because she was dead, but angry with her for not staying out of Oakland when she had the chance.

Braddock continued, "She had one other arrest for soliciting six years ago. The report says it was an operation run by the PSA due to citizen complaints of overt prostitution activity on Market and West Mac. Case was dismissed in the interest of justice."

In one of many departmental reorganizations over the last ten years, the vice unit was disbanded, and the responsibility for street prostitution enforcement fell on the police service areas, which were responsible for all general police services in their sector of the city. At times, the special victims section, the investigative unit that handled sexual assaults and child abuse, conducted prostitution enforcement. But with all their other responsibilities, these units didn't have the time or resources to do many undercover prostitution operations. As a result, the numbers of street prostitutes and the brazenness with which they flaunted their wares in public had increased dramatically over the last few years.

"Anything in LRMS?" Sinclair asked, referring to the law records management system.

"Only two field contacts for looking like a hooker in a high-hooker area. The last one was a stop by the beat officer two years ago at Brockhurst and San Pablo. She gave the officer the Tennyson Road address. She never did a change of address with DMV from that one."

"Vehicles?"

"A two-year-old Chevy Camaro is registered in her name. No leaseholder or bank is listed, so she bought it outright."

"You don't often see a girl working the stroll with a brand new car."

"She's only had one traffic ticket. That was five years ago. She was driving a BMW three series, which was registered to her back then. I don't know of many street prostitutes who own cars like that."

"Maybe she was primarily doing outcalls and only hit the streets when her phone didn't ring," Sinclair said. "That would explain how she stayed below the radar most of the time."

"I wonder if she worked the circuit. That could explain her limited contact with the police in the Bay Area."

"Is that still going on?"

"When I worked the special victims unit, we investigated a ring that rotated girls between Salt Lake City, Tucson, Reno, Sacramento, and Oakland. Some worked the street, some had in-calls arranged for them in apartments provided by the managers of the operation. The girls liked it. They got to spend summers in Salt Lake City, winters in Tucson, and a week here and there in Reno for conventions."

"They were living the dream," Sinclair said.

"The rental office of the Tennyson Road apartments called when you were at the coroner. She moved there four years ago. No mention of her reason for leaving and no forwarding address. They did a credit check on her and she looked good. Her rental application said she did public relations for an entertainment company, made five grand a month, and provided the name of her supervisor, a Helena Decker, and a phone number. They made a note on her application that they spoke to Ms. Decker, who gave Dawn a positive reference. I checked the number and it comes back to a Verizon cell phone."

Sinclair called the number and got a voicemail message: "Hello, this is Helena. Leave a message and I'll return your call."

Sinclair left his name and number and said he was inquiring about Dawn Gustafson, but didn't mention that she was dead.

Sinclair and Braddock spent the next two hours driving the whore strolls from the San Pablo area in West Oakland to MacArthur Boulevard in East Oakland. The rain fell steadily, punctuated by several five-minute-long pounding torrents that emptied the streets. When it finally transitioned to lighter rain, they saw a few hookers and showed them Dawn's driver's license photo. None admitted to knowing her. Sinclair couldn't tell if they were lying or not. Not many johns cruised for prostitutes on normal Sunday afternoons, and with the cold and rain, only the desperate girls or those with demanding pimps were out looking for business.

They returned to the office, and Sinclair drafted a press release—a requirement on every homicide call-out.

NEWS FROM THE OAKLAND POLICE DEPARTMENT

On December 4, at 0548 hours (5:48 AM), Oakland police officers and emergency medical personnel were dispatched to a report of an unresponsive person in Burckhalter Park on Edwards Avenue near the 580 Freeway. Upon arrival, they discovered an adult female with a single gunshot wound. Paramedics pronounced her dead at the scene. The victim, whose name is being withheld pending notification of next of kin, has been identified as a twenty-seven-year-old woman whose last known address was in Hayward. Anyone with any information is urged to call Sergeants Sinclair or Braddock of the Oakland Homicide Unit at (510) 238-3821.

Sinclair e-mailed the release to the twenty people on the distribution list and put a hardcopy on the lieutenant's desk and another on the desk of Connie, the unit admin. He returned to his computer and started typing his investigative log while Braddock began combing the Internet and other public systems the department subscribed to in an attempt to learn more about Dawn.

A half hour later, the door to the office clicked, and John Johnson walked in. He'd worked the crime beat for the *Oakland Tribune* for forty years and was the only reporter who had free access to the PAB. Johnson poured a half cup of coffee into a Styrofoam cup and pulled a desk chair alongside Sinclair. He studied his BlackBerry for a few seconds and then said, "You kept the press release pretty vague."

"We don't know much yet."

Johnson showed Sinclair a photo from his phone of Dawn hanging from the tree. "The editor wants to put this on the front page of tomorrow's paper."

"She's no one famous, John. All that picture's going to do is invite a lot more attention to this case than it probably deserves."

"Won't that help? Maybe get people to come forward?"

"It'll cause the mayor and the chief to get involved in one of my cases again."

"Not if I mention that she was a prostitute. Then the pressure will be off because everyone assumes her chosen occupation led to her demise."

"Who said she was a prostitute?"

Johnson smiled.

"I sure wish other cops would stop blabbing about my cases," Sinclair said.

"I'd find it out tomorrow anyway when I check court records and see the prostitution conviction."

Sinclair grinned. "Nice bluff, but your sources are wrong. It was a juvenile arrest, so it's sealed and you couldn't get it. Besides, your editor knows better than to print a juvenile arrest record."

Johnson pulled his spiral reporter notebook from his pocket, flipped it open, and studied a page. "I'll bet if I scoured the jail logs, I'd find another arrest and get someone to confirm she was working the streets."

"When the media says my victim's involved in criminal activity, it infers she got what she deserved and that her life is less important than someone else's. I need cooperation from friends and family to solve this, but when they read your paper, all they see is the cops badmouthing her."

"It won't be you saying it. Besides, if I run it by the PIO, you know he'll say that it's important for the public to think average citizens are safe so long as they're not running the streets."

The department public information officer's purpose was to portray the department and crime in the best light possible. It looked better to City Hall when murder victims weren't righteous citizens. "It probably won't make much difference," Sinclair conceded.

"The hanging's obvious from the photo," Johnson said. "What should we say about the burning?"

"I'd like to withhold that."

"Okay. Do you mind if I talk to Dawn's parents?"

"You're going to print her name?"

"The coroner's office already notified the parents, Eugene and Cynthia Gustafson of Mankato, Minnesota. Eugene manages a John Deere dealership there."

"Go ahead."

"What about an occupation I can attribute to her?"

"You mean other than 'lady of the evening'?" Sinclair said. "I talked to a friend in Hayward who said she was an accountant. I haven't verified that through an employer or anything."

"I'll put it down. No one will complain if it's not true. Is there anything you can tell me—any great quote about how you're going to catch her killer?"

"I met Dawn about ten years ago when she was seventeen and had just moved to Oakland. She was a sweet kid, mature for her age, very pretty, and optimistic. She didn't deserve what happened to her."

Johnson wrote feverously in his notebook. "You worked vice-narcotics back then, so I imagine you don't want to say under what circumstances you met her."

"You know we seldom meet people in Oakland when their lives are going well."

Chapter 4

By the time Sinclair finished his report, it was dark outside. The rain had turned into a light mist, so the sidewalks along San Pablo Avenue were full of working girls trying to make up their lost income. Sinclair pulled up to a street corner. Upon seeing his unmarked car, three girls scurried down a side street. One remained in her spot and waved. Tanya had been working that corner longer than Sinclair had been a cop. She was about five-foot-six, dark skinned, and had shoulder-length straight hair that was undoubtedly a wig. Tanya was known for her large butt, which she swore was natural and more perfectly formed than Kim Kardashian's.

Braddock lowered her window, and Tanya looked past her and smiled at Sinclair. "How ya doin', honey?"

"I'm good, Tanya." He pulled a photocopy of Dawn's DMV photo from his portfolio. "You know this girl?"

"That's Blondie. She okay?"

"No, she's not. What can you tell us about her?"

"Business is slow out here. Buy a girl dinner and I'll talk with you."

Sinclair bought Tanya a bacon cheeseburger, fries, and a chocolate shake, and coffee for him and Braddock, at the Carl's Jr. drive-through on Telegraph Avenue. He parked in the BART lot across the street. Sinclair looked at his watch: 7:00 PM. On weekdays, trains rumbled overhead every five minutes and deposited late commuters from San Francisco and other parts of the Bay Area who were lucky enough to get a parking spot at this station. But on Sundays, trains only ran every thirty minutes, and the lot was nearly empty. Sinclair pulled a Macanudo Robusto cigar from his breast pocket and held it up. "Do you mind?" he asked Tanya.

"Baby, a man buys me dinner, he can smoke crack while I eat if he wants."

Sinclair lowered the front windows, turned the heat up a notch, and lit the cigar with the old Zippo lighter he'd bought at the Army PX in Baghdad five years ago. "When did you last see Blondie?"

"Maybe last summer. On this side of the street between Thirty-Third and Thirty-Fourth."

"Is she out there much?" Sinclair asked.

"These days just to visit. I remember when she was fresh off the farm in Iowa. She comes out here, watches the pros, and in a week, she's got the walk and the talk down. Then she's gone for a year, then back a few months. After a while, we girls figure out she's mostly doing regulars and calls."

"When was this?"

"I don't know—a while ago. I just remembers she was working the stro more nights than not. Sometimes for just an hour, then her phone rings and she says she gotta go—she got an appointment, gots to go home and freshen up for some real money."

Sinclair puffed on his cigar and blew the smoke out the window. "You think she got those calls from regulars?"

"Oh, yeah, she had regulars. Sometimes tricks pull up and I think they want some of Tanya's sweet chocolate bubble butt, but they ask for Blondie."

"It's been a while since I worked the girls and dope, but do johns call you all for dates these days?"

"You know, Sinclair, some girls just like the street. I pick my hours and pick my johns. Don't nobody call me to suck his dick when I'm off duty. But most girls dream of being escorts or call girls. They give out their numbers to tricks all the time, hoping to score enough regulars so they don't need to work the corner."

"You think that's what happened with Blondie?"

"I think she so movie-star pretty that some john paid to keep her, like Richard Gere did with Julia Roberts. But that movie's a fairy tale. Rich men might pay to keep a ho for a while. But pretty soon, she stop being a ho for the man and think she a lady. If a rich man wants a lady, he don't come to the stro looking for one or dial one up from an escort service."

"How long's it been since she worked the corner?"

"Four, five years, maybe more." Tanya stuffed the last bite of cheeseburger in her mouth, wadded up the wrapper, and threw it on the floor. "Blondie was always chirpy happy. Never a bad day. A sweetie pie. Always get along with everybody. I think that even when she had lots of regulars and was making plenty of money, she came out here for fun. You know—the thrill of a new dick. Just like with you, Sinclair. I bet when they make you chief of police, you still get in your po-lize car and come out here."

"You don't have to worry about me making police chief," Sinclair said with a grin. "Who else might know what she's been up to recently?"

"Talk with your friend Jimmy."

"Jimmy?"

"Yeah, you know. Sheila's old man."

"I thought Jimmy was still in Santa Rita."

"He been out at least a month."

"Where's he hanging?"

"Down here or maybe at the Palms."

"What will Jimmy tell me when I talk to him?"

"He might tell you that he knows Blondie ever since she got off the bus. He watched over her back then. When Blondie stopped working the corner and she still come out here, most the time it was to check on him. Couple years back, Jimmy was tweaking bad, shooting a hundred dollars a day. Blondie makes some calls and gets him into a thirty-day program in Napa. People say she paid for it."

"So Jimmy was her pimp back in the day?"

"Maybe at first, but she probably went independent quick."

"Did she have any problems with anyone, anyone who would want to hurt her?"

"All the girls loved her. There was no competition. Some men like her Barbie look, some like full-figured dark meat. Never heard a trick say she didn't treat him good. But you know, Sinclair, sometimes a john can go off."

"Have there been any weird or rough tricks around lately?"

"No more than usual." Tanya loudly sucked the last of her milkshake through the straw and threw the cup on the floor next to the wrapper. "I didn't ask because I know you homicide, and if you asking about Blondie, it means she dead. How'd she die?"

"Someone shot her and hung her from a tree out in East Oakland."

"Honey, that's some cold shit. You gonna get whoever did that?"

"Oh, yeah, I'm gonna get him."

They dropped Tanya off on her corner and headed up Market Street. "You were awful quiet," Sinclair said to Braddock.

"I know better than to interfere when you're working your Sinclair charm with the ladies."

"Yup, buy a girl dinner and they put out for you."

"Is the Jimmy she mentioned the famous CI I've heard so much about?"

"Jimmy Davis, confidential informant extraordinaire. I popped him for a two-eleven strong arm when I worked robbery. He was a tennis-shoe pimp, running two or three old worn-out whores at Thirtieth and Market and supplementing his income by robbing tricks. I had three robbery cases on him. Needless to say, none of his victims were too thrilled about testifying. Who'd want to admit that when you're getting head from some skanky whore, a guy yanks open the car door and rips your wallet out of your pants? But I told Jimmy he was looking at five to ten with his past record. He came up with the names of the crew that was responsible for twenty bank jobs in the Bay Area. I had one of the cases—three guys all wearing masks who hit the Wells Fargo. The FBI coordinated the cases from eight different cities. They had no leads, but Jimmy's info was enough for me to get a search warrant. From there, I had enough evidence to arrest the suspects and clear all the cases. Of course, the FBI tried to take credit for it."

"Did Jimmy walk on the strong-arm robberies he committed?"

"I could have gotten him a pass, but he was out of control and needed to go away for a while, so I asked the DA to offer him six months."

Braddock smiled. "And thus the relationship was formed."

"He's called me with tips ever since, and helped me solve three murders. If anything's happening along West Mac or the San Pablo stroll, Jimmy knows about it. But it's a tradeoff between the info he provides and his menace to society. He was all coked up last year and nearly beat some tweaker to death. It wasn't a strong case, but everyone knew Jimmy needed to do some time, so they let him plead to a bullet in Santa Rita."

"One year with no good time?"

"That's what it was supposed to be, but it sounds like he got out early."

"Do you believe what Tanya said about him being Dawn's pimp when she first arrived in Oakland?"

"Jimmy was different before he started shooting heroin and smoking crack. He was smooth and quite the charmer, even when high, so I guess it's possible."

Sinclair pulled into the parking lot of the Palms Motel. The Palms had been around before the 580 Freeway existed, when MacArthur Boulevard was the main thoroughfare from the San Francisco Bay Bridge through Oakland and to cities beyond. It was among a dozen motels where travelers stayed back then, but for the last forty years, the Palms and other motels along West MacArthur mostly catered to prostitutes, drug dealers, and occasional out-of-towners who didn't know any better.

Sinclair flashed his badge to the elderly Indian man on the other side of the bulletproof partition that separated the tiny lobby from the office. He handed Sinclair the registration cards. Sinclair shuffled through them but didn't see Jimmy or Sheila's name. "Do you know who Jimmy Davis is?" Sinclair asked.

"Yes, I know Jimmy. He's not registered here now."

"I see that," said Sinclair. "But has he been around?"

"I haven't seen him. And if he's not registered here, he's not staying here."

"Of course not."

Sinclair and Braddock walked through the parking lot and up and down the sidewalk in front of the motel, asking people about Jimmy and passing out their cards. A few admitted to knowing him, but no one said they'd seen him recently, which didn't surprise Sinclair. He knew no one would call, but the word would get back to Jimmy that Sinclair was looking for him.

Chapter 5

Sinclair leaned back in the recliner, adjusted his earphones, and closed his eyes. The memory came slowly at first, bits and pieces. Then he was there.

"What do you see?" Dr. Jeanne Elliott asked.

He screeched to a stop in the middle of the street seconds after the gunshots. Rolled out of his patrol car, gun in hand. Screams, people running, smoke, the smell of burning gunpowder hanging in the air. The Sig Sauer .45 caliber pistol heavy and slippery in his sweaty hand.

"Bodies," Sinclair replied. "Three of them. Blood."

"Any sounds or smells?"

"People yelling: *That way—he went that way.* I smell the blood. And sweat—my sweat. I smell my fear."

The words poured from Sinclair's mouth, uncensored, as if someone else were speaking. He felt as if he were in two places at once, part of him sitting in the plush chair in the therapist's office, the other on Telegraph Avenue twelve years earlier. The tones sounded in his ears at one-second intervals. *Beep, beep,* left, right, left, right. The beeps acted like a sort of audible pendulum.

"What's happening now?" Jeanne asked.

"I'm running. People point into the theater. I run into the theater."

Sinclair's breathing was ragged, his heart ready to leap out of his chest.

"Slow down," she said. "What are you feeling?"

He didn't need to search for the words; they rolled off his tongue. "Anger. Sadness. Fear."

"Should we stop?"

"I need to go on."

"Okay, but slowly," Jeanne whispered.

At the theater door, he rushes inside. It's pitch dark. His left hand reaches for his belt, feeling for his flashlight. He touches the leather holder. Empty. He freezes.

"What's happening?" she asked.

"My flashlight . . . I left it in the car. He's there. In the dark. Waiting. I have to get him." Sinclair's voice quaked as tears squeezed through his closed eyes and down his face. He tasted the salt as they rolled over his lip. "But I can't move. I'm too scared. I'm a coward."

"That's enough," Jeanne said. "I want you to return to your safe place." She described the mountain lake, the birds singing, and the smell of pine trees.

Sinclair felt his breathing level out. The image of the dark X-rated-movie theater where the murderer had fled slowly dissolved.

"When you're ready," she said, "I want you to open your eyes."

Sinclair opened his eyes and removed the headphones.

Jeanne leaned back in her chair. "You did very well today. I can tell you're beginning to trust the process."

The process she referred to was called Eye Movement Desensitization and Reprocessing. When Sinclair had first met with her two weeks ago, she explained how patients can bring up memories of traumatic experiences and then process them through EMDR, which reduces the emotional intensity of the feelings and the lingering symptoms. For at least a year, Sinclair had suspected he had PTSD to some degree. He'd known many police officers and soldiers who'd experienced a fraction of what he had over the years who had been diagnosed with it. But much like his alcoholism, which he hadn't dealt with until the department forced him into treatment after he crashed his unmarked police car two years ago while driving drunk, he didn't do anything about his PTSD until it smacked him across the head.

A month ago, he'd stayed late one night to return several phone calls. The final call was to a Napa Valley phone number. The man told Sinclair that he and his wife had adopted a baby boy from Alameda County foster care after the boy's family was murdered. Ben was to turn thirteen in January, and the family was planning his bar mitzvah celebration. The man hoped Sinclair would attend, but especially hoped he would join the family for dinner the night before. That was when his parents intended to tell Ben about his life before they adopted him. Sinclair knew the story all too well.

The boy's parents had been pushing him down the street in a stroller when a crazy man ran out of the back door of a theater, shot both of his parents in the head, and snatched Ben out of the stroller. The man ran through the streets, cradling Ben like a football, and holed up in his small room in a transient hotel. The hostage negotiators reported the man had no grasp of reality and was going off on a tirade about having killed the devil's disciples. Next, he had to sacrifice the devil's child. A police sniper team had eyes on the man pressing a pistol against the infant's head through a window, but didn't have a clear shot.

The police incident commander ordered an immediate SWAT entry to save the infant, giving the four-man SWAT team that was stacked outside the door the green light. Sinclair was first in the stack. He stepped through the door and saw the man holding the baby in his arms and a gun in his hand. Sinclair snapped his M4 rifle up, and when the red dot of the close-combat optics was within the imaginary triangle formed by the man's two eyes and nose, he pulled the trigger. The man collapsed in a heap to the floor as Sinclair rushed forward and caught the baby before he hit the ground. News photographers and videographers swarmed him as he stepped into the sunlight. Within twenty-four hours, his picture—a serious-looking man decked out in body armor, ballistic helmet, and goggles, holding a small infant in his arms alongside an M4 carbine—graced the front page of every newspaper in the country.

Sinclair had told Ben's father he would call him back with his answer. He then sat at his desk with rivulets of sweat rolling down his armpits and tears welling in his eyes. His whole body shook and his breaths came fast and shallow. He hardly slept that night as memories of that day came back to him, followed by other memories—dead and injured people, times when he pulled the trigger and took lives, times when he faced death but evaded it. A few days later, he called the department's employee-assistance program, and they referred him to Jeanne Elliott, PhD, Clinical Psychologist.

"I'd like to explore one of the last things you mentioned," Jeanne said. "Your feelings are valid, and I don't intend to challenge them; however, you said you were a coward because you didn't chase a killer into a dark building without a flashlight."

"I know that's illogical," Sinclair said. "But the man got away because I was afraid to pursue him, and he killed two more people."

"And you blame yourself for that?"

Sinclair shrugged his shoulders.

"Did you ever consider that Ben is alive today because of you?"

"He's probably traumatized, even more screwed up than I am."

"If you decide to attend the bar mitzvah, you might learn that's not so."

"Maybe."

"Do you realize that millions of people who heard the story thought you were a hero?"

"That was the media's spin."

"I suspect Ben's adoptive father thinks you were responsible for his son seeing his thirteenth birthday."

"I wish that day never happened."

"Burying traumatic incidents might work for a while, but eventually, as you've experienced, they come bubbling up at the most inopportune times."

Sinclair looked at his watch.

Jeanne continued. "How's your medication working?"

"I'm on homicide standby this week and have to be available when the phone rings, so I haven't been taking the trazodone at night."

"Are you sleeping?"

"Not well."

"I'm not a medical doctor, so I don't want to give you medical advice. However, you know you're not the only police officer I treat, and my experience is that trazodone will not prevent you from waking up and functioning when you need to. It's not a sedative or depressant."

"Okay."

"And as I offered previously, I can work with your department and get you time off that won't count as vacation or sick time."

"You know I can't do that," Sinclair said. "People will know."

"Your department is prohibited from taking any adverse actions against you."

The way the city's employee assistance was administered ensured that no one, not even the police chief, knew the names of those who used it. But the moment he hit off sick or with a so-called on-duty injury diagnosed as PTSD, the word would be out that he was mentally and emotionally incapable of handling the job, and he'd find himself at a desk.

"I'll let you know," he said.

Chapter 6

When Sinclair entered the office, the other nine homicide investigators in the unit were at their desks, busy pounding away at their computers, talking on phones, or reading reports. Braddock looked up. "How'd it go with your insurance agent?"

Sinclair hated lying to his partner, but he had told her he was meeting with his insurance agent about reimbursement for when the Bus Bench Killer firebombed his apartment last year and destroyed everything he owned. "I just had to sign a bunch more forms."

"The lieutenant wants to see us when you're ready."

Sinclair filled his dark-blue coffee mug, which had an outline of a dead body on one side and "Homicide: Our Day Begins When Someone Else's Ends" on the other. Lieutenant Carl Maloney was in his late forties with thinning hair and a flabby middle. Sinclair and his fellow investigators had had their doubts about Maloney when he was assigned to command the unit, fearing that he had gotten the coveted job because of his previous position as one of the chief's hatchet men in Internal Affairs, but Maloney turned out to be a good boss. He had never investigated a homicide, and although that didn't stop most command officers from micromanaging their subordinates, Maloney never pretended he knew more about murder investigations than the sergeants under him. In addition, despite the fact that he could be reassigned in the blink of an eye, he still stood up to the chief and defended his investigators even if it was politically expedient to do otherwise.

Maloney dug out the *Oakland Tribune* from under an assortment of papers. "I'm sure the chief will have some choice words to say about her being a 'sweet girl' when I see him later this morning. Is there anything else I should know?"

Braddock said, "The unnamed source the *Trib* quotes, who we all know is the PIO, said she was a prostitute, which should balance out Matt's attempt to humanize her."

"Not to City Hall," Maloney replied. "To them, it sounds as if we're not on the same team."

Sinclair and Braddock briefed him on what little they knew at this point. When they got up to leave, Maloney said, "Matt, hang on a minute?"

Once Braddock left, Maloney leaned forward in his chair. "How are you doing?"

Sinclair chuckled. "Fine, and how are you doing, Lieutenant?"

"You know I'm not good at this, so I'll come right out and say it. You don't look so good. You came in late today, and that's not like you."

"I told Braddock and I left you a note that I was pushing back my shift and working nine to five today because I needed to meet with my insurance adjuster."

Maloney paged through a stack of paper in his in-box. After a minute, he gave up. "Are they still denying stuff from your apartment?"

"It's working out; they just require more documentation."

"You're still sober, aren't you?"

Sinclair had been subject to a last-chance contract, where he had to submit to random urinalyses for a year after the department reinstated him as a sergeant and returned him to homicide. "Even though the contract expired over two months ago, I know damn well I'm an alcoholic and if I drink I'll risk losing everything again."

"I'm inquiring as a friend, not as a boss."

For years, Sinclair had butted heads with Maloney, but their relationship changed after the Bus Bench killings when Sinclair came to realize that Maloney had never been the enemy. "I'm still going to meetings and still have a sponsor."

"If there's anything, you know you can talk to me."

"I know," Sinclair said.

★

Sinclair swung his car into the Palms Motel parking lot and accelerated toward a mixed-race man standing out of the rain under the second-floor landing. The man was in his midthirties, five-foot-eight, and wore dirty black jeans and a black canvas jacket. Sinclair and Braddock jumped out of the car and triangulated on him.

"Hands behind your back!" Sinclair shouted.

The man complied. Sinclair handcuffed him, patted him down, and stuffed him in the backseat of his car. Sinclair turned the car around and sped out of the parking lot onto West MacArthur Boulevard.

The man grinned from the backseat. "Thanks for the *Starsky and Hutch* move, Sinclair. Don't want folks to think I'm snitching."

"How've you been, Jimmy?" Sinclair asked.

"You know. Just trying to make a living. Who's the lady, Sinclair?"

"Jimmy, meet my partner, Sergeant Braddock."

"Nice to make your acquaintance, Braddock. You look like that lady detective on *Castle*. You watch that show?"

"Hi, Jimmy," she said. "No, I don't watch cop shows."

Sinclair bought three coffees at the McDonald's at Forty-Fifth and Telegraph, drove a block down Forty-Fifth, and parked under the 24 Freeway to get out of the rain. He pulled Jimmy out of the car, removed the handcuffs, and handed him a coffee. Sinclair watched as Jimmy emptied eight sugar packets into his cup—classic junkie.

"Do you want to sit back in the car where it's warm?" Sinclair asked.

Jimmy bounced from one foot to the other, stopping only long enough to take small gulps of his coffee. "Been sitting too much. Can we talk out here?"

Sinclair pulled up the collar of his raincoat. It was still in the low forties, and as long as the rain continued, they'd be lucky if it topped fifty today. Braddock buttoned her coat to her throat and thrust her hands into her pockets.

"I guess you wanna know about Blondie." Jimmy pulled a pack of Kools from his pocket and lit one with a plastic lighter.

Sinclair set his coffee on the hood of the car, clipped the end of a small cigar, and lit it with his Zippo. "You heard what happened?"

"It's in the paper and all over the street."

"You know who did it?"

"Shit, Sinclair. You get right to the point, don't you?"

Sinclair puffed on his cigar. Jimmy looked healthier and probably twenty pounds heavier than the last time Sinclair saw him, but three squares a day in the county jail and no drugs will do that for a man. Braddock picked her coffee up from the hood of the car, took a sip, and wrapped both hands around the paper cup.

"I'm gonna find out for ya," Jimmy said.

"I'm sure you will, but in the meantime I need to know where she was living and who she was hanging with."

"She was private."

"She have an old man?" Sinclair asked.

"Old man, as in pimp? Come on, Sinclair, you know girls out here don't really have no pimps. You don't see no Cadillacs with fancy-dressed assholes driving around Oaktown, do ya?"

"How's Shelia and the kids, Jimmy?"

"Doing good. That apartment is sweet. She really appreciate you pulling strings to get her Section Eight."

"And how was her Thanksgiving?" Sinclair sipped his coffee and stared at Jimmy.

"I should've told you I was out." Jimmy looked at his brown sneakers. "What you did was real nice."

Sheila had four kids, and although Sinclair had never asked, he assumed Jimmy was the father of at least a few of them. Sheila had worked the streets off and on ever since she was sixteen. When Sinclair found out Jimmy was in jail last Christmas, he submitted Sheila's name with the ages of her kids to the police officer's association to have a food basket and toys delivered to her a few days before Christmas. He did the same for Thanksgiving two weeks ago, so Sheila received a turkey and all the other trimmings, more than enough for a family twice the size of hers.

"I help Sheila because I feel sorry for her," Sinclair said. "And because she deserves a man who takes care of her and the kids. I don't do it in exchange for your information. So I don't like you talking to me like I'm a chump."

Jimmy studied his shoes again while he took a deep drag on his cigarette. "Sorry, man. A black man's not used to having cop friends. I known Blondie since she left the farm in Nebraska. In no time, she finds some rich regulars. One even buys her a condo and takes care of her. She'd come by the stro and visit, showing off new cars and nice clothes. But after a year or two, she leaves him and disappears. When she come back, she's working for some escort services. Make lots of money, but she still come out here. Sometimes she helps me out. I haven't seen her since I went to Santa Rita."

"Is she still living in that condo?" Braddock asked. "Where is it?"

"That was like a 007 pad. She never tells no one where it was. She takes me to her apartment a while ago. Different than her condo. She makes me dinner and helps me do tax returns.

Never did that before." Jimmy took a deep drag of his cigarette. "Did you know that for people who got no job and no
income, the government gives you money for just sending in
tax forms?"

"Was that apartment in Hayward?" Sinclair asked.

Jimmy finished his cigarette, flicked it to the street, and lit
another one. "She says she just moved from Hayward, but this
place is in Oakland."

"You know the address?"

"No, but I can show you."

Jimmy directed them down MacArthur Boulevard and
around the east side of Lake Merritt.

"I'm having trouble picturing you and Dawn as BFFs,
Jimmy," said Braddock.

"It wasn't like that. In all that time, I never touched that
girl. When she first come to Oakland, she was like one of them
little deer with the big eyes—nice, trusting. I watched over her
so she didn't get eaten by the big bad wolves. But she was smart.
The vice squad got her once early on, sent her to juvie, then
home to Nebraska. When she come back, she was smarter and
had big plans."

"What plans?" asked Sinclair.

"You know, get off the street, make some real money, invest
it, and live happy ever after."

Jimmy pointed out a three-story tan stucco building on
Athol Avenue, about three blocks from the lake.

"You know her apartment number?" Sinclair asked.

"No, but I can show you. Second floor, go right out the
elevator, third door on the right."

"We need to handle it alone from here," Sinclair said. "Let's
run you back to the Palms first."

"I can walk. You do what you gotta do here."

Sinclair pulled two twenties out of his wallet and handed
them to Jimmy.

Jimmy stuffed the bills in his pocket. "I ain't doing this for no snitch money. Blondie didn't deserve this. You get the motherfucker who killed her."

"I will. You keep in touch and call me if you hear anything."

"You know it." Jimmy bounced out of the car and sauntered down the hill in the rain.

Chapter 7

A petite Chinese woman with wire-rimmed glasses perched on a beak-like nose leaned against the open doorway of the manager's apartment. Sinclair and Braddock flashed their badges. "Do you have a tenant named Dawn Gustafson?" Sinclair asked.

"Unit two-oh-eight," the gray-haired woman said. "Is there a problem?"

"She was killed yesterday. We need to take a look in her apartment."

"Oh, my goodness." She stepped into her apartment and returned with a key. "What happened?"

"That's what we're trying to determine," Sinclair said as they walked to the elevator. "What kind of a tenant was she?"

"Quiet, always paid her rent on time. A nice, polite young lady."

"Did she live alone?"

"Yes. She sometimes had friends visit, but it was never a problem."

"Male or female?" Sinclair asked.

"I never paid attention," the woman said, leading them to the elevator.

"Did she have a boyfriend?" Braddock asked.

"Maybe. She wasn't here much, so she may have been spending nights with a man."

"You didn't pay attention if her guests were male or female, yet you know she wasn't here much," Sinclair said.

"If I came through the garage around nine or ten at night, her car was normally gone. When my husband left for work at six the next morning, it still wasn't in her space."

"Is her car here now?" Sinclair asked.

"We can check." They took the elevator down one level. As soon as the door opened, she said, "Nope, it's not here."

"What kind of car did she drive?" he asked.

"A red sports car."

"A Camaro?" Braddock asked.

"I think that's what it was." The manager pressed the button for the second floor, and the small elevator bucked upward. Sinclair and Braddock followed her down the hall to 208, where she stuck a key in the upper lock. "Huh, the deadbolt's unlocked."

"Is that unusual?" Braddock asked.

"We don't have many problems here, but it is Oakland, and I don't know anyone who doesn't use their deadbolt."

After she turned the key, Sinclair said, "Wait out here, please," and gently brushed past her.

Although he didn't expect the killer to be there, the unlocked deadbolt raised the pucker factor a notch, so he swept his coat aside and rested his hand on the butt of his gun. Braddock followed him inside and did the same. Sinclair scanned the combination living room, dining room, and kitchen. The drapes were closed and the lights on. All the cabinets in the kitchen were open and cushions on the sofa were flipped over and askew. He glanced at Braddock. She nodded, understanding they would do a quick sweep of the apartment to ensure no one was present.

Sinclair opened a closet next to the front door. One coat on a hanger, a vacuum cleaner on the floor, and some shoe boxes on the shelf. He led the way down a hall and opened an accordion door to a linen closet. Sheets, towels, and a few rolls of toilet paper. The bathroom was empty. They stepped into the bedroom. A king-size bed was covered with a cherry-red satin bedspread and a pile of red and pink pillows. Sinclair peeked under the bed and opened the closet. Hanging inside was an assortment of lingerie that looked like the back wall of a Victoria's Secret store: lace teddies, satin slips, see-through bustiers, and cutout corsets.

"Looks like we found where she works," Sinclair said to Braddock.

They returned to the front room and told the manager, who was patiently standing in the hallway, they would notify her at her apartment when they were finished. He jotted down some notes and opened the drapes. The view was the roof of a large, old house on the next lot and another apartment building beyond it. The windows were intact and locked. He went back to the front door and examined the lock and doorjamb. Nothing indicated forced entry—no scratches on the strike plate or the locks and no impressions in the wood door frame or the door itself.

The living-room furniture was arranged as a sitting area on one side and a desk, filing cabinet, and bookshelf on the other. It was nothing fancy. The desk could be bought for a few hundred dollars, and the living-room set would go for under a grand at a dozen Bay Area stores. On the desk was a computer keyboard and flat-screen monitor. Cords hung over the back of the desk to an imprint in the carpet where a computer tower had apparently been. The bottom drawer of the filing cabinet was open and empty.

"I wonder what was so important in the computer and paper files for someone to take them," said Braddock.

"Maybe something they didn't want us to see."

"I don't see any signs of a struggle."

"Doesn't look like she was killed here, but we'll need to process the apartment anyway. If nothing else, we might find some prints of whoever searched the place."

"Should we get a warrant?"

Normally, a search warrant wasn't required at a homicide victim's residence, the assumption being the only person whose privacy was being invaded was the victim. A murder victim would want the police to find her killer. If the suspect also lived there, courts might determine he had a right to privacy, and any evidence the police found that connected him to the crime could be thrown out if they didn't get a warrant. Braddock had a more conservative take on the rules of search and seizure. Sinclair appreciated that. During their time working together, she had kept him from making rash decisions more than once. "The manager says she lives alone, and we didn't see any clothing that would indicate another person lived here," he said, verbalizing his justification for forgoing a warrant.

"You're assuming the lingerie was hers," Braddock said. "What if other girls used the bedroom and one of them is our suspect?"

"Possible, but unlikely. What do you make of the office setup?"

Braddock's fingers traced the books on the shelf. "These are mostly school books, subjects like business management, accounting, and taxation. She's got a thick user's manual for QuickBooks, and a copy of *QuickBooks for Dummies*. Maybe she really is an accountant. What if we discover evidence when we search that she worked with someone else here and he's the killer?"

"So to be on the safe side, we should get a warrant?"

"If it were my case, I would," Braddock said.

★

Three hours later, Sinclair returned to the apartment with a copy of the warrant. It hadn't been a difficult affidavit to prepare, but to Sinclair, it was nothing more than a legally mandated waste of time. The four-page affidavit summarized his training and experience, the crime and his investigation, the evidence he was looking for, and the legal justification for the search, to include identifying the suspect, the motive, and the location of the murder. It took Sinclair an hour of roaming the courthouse to find an available judge so he could watch her read his documents before he was asked to raise his right hand and swear to their truthfulness.

Since Sinclair had called Braddock as soon as he had the warrant, the crime scene processing was well under way by the time he returned to the apartment. One evidence technician was twirling a brush and spraying fine black graphite powder on the file cabinet. The other, a woman dressed in the same dark-blue utility uniform, was taking a photo of a latent print on the desk. She then applied tape to it and placed it on a card.

"They've already photoed all the rooms," Braddock said. "I figured I'd have them start with the office area since that's where we probably want to look first."

"Good idea," Sinclair said.

"I had a uniform secure the apartment, and I started a canvass of the building when you were gone." She opened her notebook and paged through a legal pad. "No answer at half the doors. I left my card with a note to call. None of the other tenants really knew Dawn. Those who did knew her by first name only. The consensus was she was a very nice, quiet tenant. They mostly saw her afternoons and early evenings. I couldn't find anyone who saw her leaving for work in the morning, so everyone figured she went to school and worked irregular hours or that she slept somewhere else. She had occasional guests, normally men, but no one could remember anyone specifically or provide a description. The officer's continuing to knock on doors on the first floor."

"All finished here," the male tech said. "We'll do the bedroom next."

Sinclair pulled on a pair of latex gloves and opened each drawer of the file cabinet. Empty. "No reason to have a file cabinet if you have no files."

"So whoever took her computer grabbed the files as well," Braddock said.

Sinclair sat at the desk. Brass desk lamp, electronic calculator, a two-hole punch, computer monitor, and a wireless keyboard and mouse on a leather desk blotter. Very neat and organized. The desk drawers were filled with typical supplies: ruler, paper-clips, scissors, tape, an assortment of pens and markers, pads of paper, and envelopes. Two small boxes of business cards were in the top drawer behind an assortment of power cords.

Sinclair placed the boxes on the desk and removed a card from the first one. A headshot of Dawn wearing a conservative blouse and "Dawn Gustafson, Business and Personal Bookkeeping" followed by a phone number and Gmail address.

Braddock leaned over his shoulder. "It's looking more and more like she's a bookkeeper. Did you have this number and e-mail for her?"

"I had nothing." Sinclair pulled out his phone, hit speaker, and called the number.

It went immediately to voicemail: "You've reached the number for Dawn Gustafson. Please leave your name and number and I'll return your call."

"No landline here," Sinclair said.

Braddock removed an iPad from her handbag, powered it up, and entered the phone number into the Safari search engine. "It's a Verizon cell phone. Nothing else comes up, so she probably doesn't list it on a website or anywhere else on the web."

"We should eventually do a warrant on it," Sinclair said. "I'd like to see all of her call and text records and any locator data the account shows."

"Verizon will take at least a week to return info unless we can justify exigent circumstances."

"Yeah, and another half a day wasted typing when we should be investigating. I'll put it on my to-do list along with writing a warrant on Google to get her e-mail info." Sinclair slid a few of her business cards into his pocket and opened the other box. Sadly, he wasn't surprised at what he saw. A photo of Dawn wearing a lace negligee and a provocative come-hither smile took up the left half of the card. On the right, it read, *Blondie, Special Ladies Escorts, San Francisco & Bay Area, www.specialladies .com*, followed by a 415 area code phone number.

"She was such a pretty girl." Braddock sighed. "It's so sad she allowed herself to be exploited like this."

Sinclair put a few of the cards into his pocket. "It's not like someone shanghaied her, dragged her to California, and forced her into a life of prostitution."

"The coercion and influence that lead girls into this life is more subtle than that—abuse in their childhood, lack of opportunities," Braddock said.

Sinclair didn't buy the bad-childhood and no-job excuses for crime. He and Braddock had had this discussion before. Her stepfather was an ultraliberal professor at UC Berkeley whose worldview was the polar opposite of Sinclair's. Sinclair had quipped with Braddock many times, only half-joking, that after four years at UC Berkeley, the Peace Corps, and social work jobs, her leftist brainwashing was nearly complete, and even with the harsh realities of the real world she saw as a cop, she had a tendency to slip toward the dark side when he wasn't watching.

"Even if some of those factors got her into the life, she had plenty of opportunities to get out," Sinclair said. "Don't forget, when I busted her the first time, she was sent home. But she came back. On her own. She got out of the business a few years after that, but here she was again."

"She got off the streets a second time?" Braddock asked. "When did that happen?"

Sinclair hesitated for a moment and then said, "I'm just assuming that, based on what Jimmy said and the rough timeline I have in my head about her life."

Braddock studied him. He wondered if she was trying to read his mind or trying to get him to say more. "Okay then," she said, obviously willing to let it drop. "Maybe that's why she was studying to be an accountant—to change her life. And it looks like she was paying her bills—at least some of them—with her bookkeeping business."

"So she might've been in the process of changing," Sinclair said. "All I'm saying is most people don't commit crimes because they have no alternative. They make a choice to sling dope or sell their bodies on the corner because it's easier than getting up every morning, working at an entry-level job, and busting your ass to move up to something better."

"I still feel sorry for Dawn."

"So do I," he said. "She didn't deserve this, and the only person I blame for her death is the one who killed her."

Braddock returned to her iPad while Sinclair went through the bookshelf, fanning each book and hoping a piece of paper with something relevant would drop out. Nothing did. When he was finished, he looked over Braddock's shoulder as she swiped through the pages of the Special Ladies Escorts website. Dawn was one of about fifty women advertised. Each had a short bio designed to play into men's fantasies.

The techs returned from the bedroom. The female tech said, "We're done in here, if you want to have a look. We went through all the clothes and checked them with the ultraviolet light. We didn't find any blood, semen, or other secretions, so they were probably washed before being put away. We went through all the boxes in the closet, photographed the contents, and put them back for you. When you're done, we'll collect them as evidence in case you want to have the lab examine them for DNA later."

"What's in the boxes?" Sinclair asked.

The female tech grinned. "You'll see."

The bedroom furniture was made of honey-colored oak, heavy and sturdy. The top of the dresser was clear. The top drawer contained some bras and panties, sexy, but the kind of underwear any twenty-something woman would wear. Two conservative sweaters and two sweat suits were in the next drawer—clothes someone would wear lounging around their home. The other drawers were empty, as were the drawers in both nightstands.

He pulled two boxes off the closet shelf and opened the first. Inside were an assortment of leather restraints and plastic handcuffs. The second box held a dozen satin blindfolds and a vast array of vibrators and dildos.

Sinclair looked at Braddock. "How many boxes of this stuff do you have in your bedroom?"

"My only sex toy is my husband," she said. "What about you, Sinclair?"

"I'm saving myself for marriage, remember?" Sinclair replied with a wry smile.

Sinclair went into the bathroom and slid back the shower door. Not even a bar of soap or shampoo. The drawers below the sink were equally sparse, containing a toothbrush and tooth-paste, a few brushes and combs, and some dental floss.

"She didn't live here," Braddock observed.

"And I doubt she entertained any clients here either," said Sinclair. "Wouldn't a call girl need to shower and clean up between clients?"

"I'd think so, and a woman would have all kind of toiletries if she even stayed here overnight."

In the main room, the techs were on their hands and knees, crawling along the carpet and stopping occasionally to examine different locations. "We saw some spots," said the male evidence tech, "but it wasn't blood."

Sinclair went through the kitchen cupboards and drawers. A basic set of glasses, dishes, eating utensils, and cookware. A Mr. Coffee coffeemaker, a can of coffee, and a bunch of bananas beginning to turn black were on the counter. In the refrigerator were four containers of yogurt, a carton of cream, a package of deli turkey, and a bottle of salad dressing.

Sinclair stripped off his gloves. "What do you think?"

"She's not living here," said Braddock. "She uses it as an office for her bookkeeping, but that's it. She probably eats lunch snacks here, but the kitchen doesn't look like anyone's cooked in it."

"Stealing her computer and files could mean the motive relates to her bookkeeping stuff rather than her prostitution."

"Unless she's an accountant for the mob, bookkeepers aren't killed for what they do," Braddock replied. "Maybe the killer thought she had trick information on her computer and in the file cabinets and grabbed everything."

"Then we're back to assuming she was killed over her prostitution activity." Sinclair scratched his head. "But we've decided she's no longer using this apartment as a hooker pad."

"Maybe she never was," said Braddock.

"You think?"

"She moved from the Hayward apartment a year ago. What if she just moved her bedroom stuff and living-room stuff here because she had to do something with it? If she had been using the sex toys, wouldn't she unpack the boxes and put the stuff in drawers where she could get at it easier? Wouldn't some of her lingerie be dirty and in a laundry basket?"

"Most escorts only do outcalls," said Sinclair. "When I worked vice, we hardly ever ran across girls who took customers to their own place, and let's not rule out something to do with the streets. She never fully broke away according to Jimmy and Tanya. What are the rest of the tenants like in this building?"

"Quite a few middle-aged and elderly Asians, the rest a mix of young professionals of every race, but mostly single women."

"Not the kind of place you'd bring tricks, especially when you've already been kicked out of one apartment complex for it."

"No," Braddock said. "So she set the place up to look like she's living here, with a bedroom and all, but she's only using it as an office."

"She wants to give the outside appearance that she works out of her home, but she's living somewhere else and either hooking there or just doing outcalls."

"Or maybe she's gotten out of the business."

"Anything's possible, but I'm not convinced." Sinclair turned to the techs. "Did you find anything to indicate she was killed here?"

"Nothing," the man said. "Although someone searched the place, they didn't really tear it apart. No signs of a struggle, so maybe she wasn't abducted from this location."

"We think this was an office for her," Sinclair said. "And she was already dead when someone came back here to take information that could be incriminating."

Chapter 8

"What are you thinking?" Sinclair asked Braddock as he started the engine. The rain had stopped and the sun was fighting to break through the clouds.

"The truth?" She laughed. "I'm trying to figure out what to buy Ryan for Christmas."

"How can your brain jump from figuring out a murder to shopping for your husband?"

"Multitasking. We women have superior brains. Did you want to discuss the murder some more?"

"Hell, we've talked it to death." Sinclair eased the car into the street and drove toward Lake Shore Drive.

"Good. There are only nineteen shopping days left. What would a man want for Christmas?"

"Jeez, Ryan's married to a homicide cop who leaves him home to take care of two kids while she hangs out with me looking at blood and gore all day and night. With his forty or more hours a week at work, he obviously doesn't have time to have any fun, so that eliminates all kinds of cool things like a road bike, golf clubs, or a motorcycle."

"He's not getting a motorcycle until the kids have graduated high school and their college is fully funded."

"You both wear OPD badges for a living and you're worried he'll hurt himself riding a motorcycle?"

"What about you and Kayla? Are things serious enough to exchange gifts for Christmas?"

"I ended it a few weeks ago."

"Why didn't you tell me?"

"There was nothing to tell. We lasted a month, had fun for a while, and then she got clingy and wanted to make plans for the future."

"And you got scared and ran."

Sinclair thought about what Braddock said. The longest he had dated anyone since his divorce almost four years ago was the six months he and Liz were together. That ended more than a year ago when she was nearly raped and murdered by the Bus Bench Killer and subsequently took a position as a news anchor in Chicago. He'd lost track of how many women he'd gone out with since then, but knew none lasted longer than a month.

"It wasn't like that," he said. "I knew from the onset that she wasn't the kind of woman I would settle down with. But she knew how to have fun. She was still into the party scene, though, and I'm just not into that anymore."

"It's got to be hard when you don't drink."

"I don't mind going out with people who have a drink or two, but when the sole purpose of going out is to drink . . . Being around drunk people when you're not also drunk isn't much fun."

"You're not alone." Braddock pulled out her phone and began texting as she talked. "These days, I start getting sleepy halfway through my second glass of wine."

"It wasn't just the partying. Kayla just wasn't right for me."

"If the right woman appeared, would *you* be ready for her?"

"If you mean am I ready to buy a house with a white picket fence and have a couple of little rug rats? I think I have a ways to go." Sinclair glanced at Braddock. When she looked up from her phone, he continued. "But if you mean am I ready to give up the serial dating routine, then yes. I'm getting so tired of that."

Braddock read something on her phone and put it into her purse. "Can we stop by ACH on the way back to the office? I need to pick up some paperwork on an old case."

★

A patient yelled for more pain meds from one of the rooms as Sinclair and Braddock walked down the long hallway. Alameda County Hospital—ACH to cops—housed the regional trauma center and one of the busiest ERs in the Bay Area. Every cop wanted to be brought here if they were shot or seriously hurt, but as soon as they were stabilized, they'd want to be moved to a hospital with nicer rooms, a higher class of patients, and nurses less calloused by the workload and the worn-out facility.

A tall, thin white man with a ponytail and a stethoscope around his neck said hi to them as they slipped past the nurse's station into the break room. A nurse dressed in purple scrubs got up from a seat at a chipped Formica-topped table. She smiled and gave Braddock a quick hug. Alyssa Morelli then stood there for a few seconds staring at Sinclair.

"Matt," Alyssa said as she finally opened her arms and embraced him.

Sinclair's chin touched the top of her head as she pressed her body against him. He was certain she could feel his heart pounding in his chest by the time she stepped back and looked up at him. Her hair, pinned up loosely on top of her head, glistened in the sunlight streaming through the window. The sun had finally peeked through the clouds that had blanketed Oakland for the last two days.

"You look good." Her enormous brown eyes scanned him from head to toe. "I was afraid that you'd turned into some ruddy-faced bozo with a beer belly and blood-vessel-covered nose."

Sinclair had been a long-haired, unshaven narcotics officer when he last saw Alyssa nine years ago. She was one of the nurses who hung out with a group of patrol officers that Sinclair used to work with. The nurses and cops skied together in the winter, boated and hiked together in the summer, and met at the Warehouse, the local cop bar, most nights after work. After months of being just friends, Sinclair and Alyssa had gone out on a few dates, but their relationship fizzled after that. She didn't return his calls and stopped associating with the group. Sinclair heard she started dating a doctor. Shortly thereafter, she became engaged and left ACH for a hospital where the patients were cleaner, the workload lighter, and the pay better.

"You look the same," he said.

"I'm hoping my wrinkles deepen so patients stop thinking I'm one of the student nurses or high school volunteers." She laughed—a real laugh.

Alyssa's Mediterranean ancestry showed in her olive complexion, and her hair was such a dark brown it appeared black under certain light. "We should catch up," Sinclair said.

"I'd like that," Alyssa replied.

Just then, another nurse poked her head into the break room. "We've got a trauma coming in. Car accident with two victims."

"I have to go." Alyssa took both of his hands in hers, rose onto her tiptoes, and kissed his cheek.

Sinclair felt his heart racing again.

"We'll talk," she whispered into his ear.

She hugged Braddock, and Sinclair noted a conspiratorial smile between them as they left the break room.

Sinclair waited until they were back in their car before he spoke to Braddock. "You set me up."

Braddock laughed. "She's wanted to see you ever since she learned we were partners but wanted it to be a surprise."

"To watch me make a fool of myself?"

Braddock smiled. "It was funny to see you at a loss for words."

"I had a wicked crush on her back in the day."

"Duh! I've known about you two for years. Alyssa was working pediatrics at John Muir when I took Ethan there for an ear infection five or six years ago. We recognized each other from Oakland and became pals. She's probably my best non-police friend. And she had a crush on you, too."

"I don't know what happened. She got scared or something, and the next thing I knew, she married some pretty-boy doctor."

"You had that bad-boy thing going full speed back then. She saw you on self-destruct mode and couldn't stand to watch it. She wanted normal. The intern she married was that."

"What happened? There's no ring on her finger."

"Once her husband finished his residency and started making the big bucks, he got into the country club scene and wanted her to quit nursing, have babies, and become a Stepford wife. Last year, she finally decided she couldn't be that kind of woman and filed for divorce. She got bored with the routine of working a floor at John Muir and came back to ACH last month."

"How's she doing? She looks great."

"She loves being back in the ER and is happier than she's been in years. She ran the San Francisco marathon last summer and teaches Pilates classes at her health club."

"You have her number, right?"

Braddock turned in her seat to face Sinclair. "Like the rest of the world, she knows about your divorce, you and Liz, and your pattern of one-night stands. Alyssa is all goodness, and that's rare in people who deal with the same slime as we do on a daily basis. Don't disrespect her by using your Sinclair charm on her while you're still dating other women. She's not just another girl for you to screw and run from when it gets too real."

Sinclair pulled out of the hospital parking lot. Braddock's words stung. She knew his game. He wanted to tell her to mind her own business—that Alyssa was a big girl and could take care of herself. But he knew Braddock was right. Alyssa was smart to distance herself from him back then. He wondered if he had actually changed much since.

He turned onto Fourteenth Avenue, deciding to avoid the freeway since it was approaching rush hour. Braddock stared out the window silently as he drove.

"I was pretty hard on you," she said, breaking the silence.

"I know. Why'd you set this up, anyway, if that's how you feel?"

"Matt, I love you like a brother. I trust you with my life."

"But not with your best friend?"

"You're an awesome guy. You just don't know how to do relationships. I don't want to lose either one of you. And I don't want to see either of you hurt."

"Maybe this was a bad idea."

"She hasn't been with anyone since her divorce and isn't ready to date. She enjoys outdoors stuff—running, kayaking, hiking. When we get off standby, and if this rain ever lets up, maybe the four of us can go hiking or something."

Braddock went back to staring out the window.

Sinclair remembered hiking up Mt. Diablo years ago with a group of cops and nurses, watching Alyssa's tight butt in a pair of hiking shorts. Although Alyssa might be all goodness, as Braddock said, she was still damn sexy.

Chapter 9

Sinclair listened in as Braddock placed a call from her desk phone. She was much better at getting people to talk to her on cold calls than he was. When Sinclair did it, people all too often got pissed off and hung up on him.

"Special Ladies Escorts," said a woman with a husky smoker's voice.

"This is Sergeant Braddock, calling from the Oakland Police Department," she said, pausing to let the woman take in what she said and reconcile it with the caller ID that surely appeared on her phone.

The woman's tone changed from friendly and flirtatious to cold and professional. "How may I help you?"

"One of the women who works for your agency was murdered in Oakland Saturday night, and I'm trying to gather information on her."

"Do you have a name?"

"She's known as Blondie on your website. Her actual name is Dawn Gustafson."

Sinclair heard the clicking of keys on a computer keyboard. A moment later, the woman said, "I can't confirm or deny that Dawn Gustafson is an employee of the company."

"Is there someone there who can?" Braddock asked.

"Hold please." A Rihanna song, "The Monster," beat over the phone for several minutes until the voice came back. "I'm sorry, but there's no one here with that authority."

"Do you have a number where I can reach the owner?" Braddock asked.

"I can pass on a message to her."

"What's her name?"

"I'm not at liberty to reveal that. Would you like to leave a message?"

Braddock gave her the office phone number and repeated her name. "When can I expect her call?"

"I wouldn't know. I will pass on your message." The woman's voice lost a touch of its edge. "If I may ask, how was she killed?"

"She was murdered and hung naked from a tree in East Oakland."

"I'm very sorry to hear that. I'll pass your message on immediately."

Braddock hung up. "Do you think she'll call?"

"I wouldn't hold my breath," Sinclair said. "These escort services are tough to crack."

"Didn't vice used to work them back when you were there?"

"We worked a few, but they were labor intensive. I was one of the UCs on a few operations my first few months there, but then I went over to narcotics."

"Undercover in an escort operation. Every guy's fantasy."

"Yup. Sitting in nice hotels, drinking room-service wine, and waiting for sexy women to come to my room, take off their clothes, and tell me what kind of kinky things they want to do to me."

"And then you'd arrest them," Braddock said.

"And offer them a way to stay out of jail if they flip on the higher ups that make all the money."

"Did vice ever make any cases?"

"A few actually got some prison time," Sinclair said. "But most cases fell apart somewhere along the way. Usually, the agency shut down and reopened under a different name. When the department disbanded vice, didn't SVU pick up that responsibility?"

Braddock huffed. "In theory. But when I was assigned to the special victim's unit, we couldn't even keep up with the rape and child abuse cases, so there wasn't much time to take on major investigations like that."

It still riled Sinclair when he thought of how the department had been decimated by budget cuts and reorganizations demanded by the Oakland City Council over the years. When he came on, vice-narcotics had three squads, one totally committed to prostitution and gambling enforcement. A half-dozen investigators out of the youth services division handled child abuse cases, and another four sergeants handled sexual assault cases out of the criminal investigation division. Today, the responsibility for all those crimes, as well as domestic violence, fell on the newly created SVU with half the personnel.

"Since you didn't have time to work them, what did you do when you came across information about escort services or major prostitution rings?" Sinclair asked.

"We passed on the info to Intel in the hopes they could coordinate with the Feds and take down the organizations."

"Did they ever get the owners of the escort services?"

"I don't think the department's targeted anything but street-level prostitution in years."

"If the department wants to address the problem, they need to do more than a couple of operations a month picking up the girls who are dumb enough to solicit an undercover," Sinclair said.

"What about the johns?" Braddock asked.

"Bust them, too," he said. "They're half of the problem. You remember when we used to do the john sweeps? We'd put a female officer that wanted to play hooker for a night out on the corner and snatch up every dude that solicited them."

"I loved watching other officers I worked the streets with hang up their uniforms and slip into their hooker getups in the locker room. They made bets on who could snare the most johns."

"I never saw you out there."

"Not my kind of thing, but I respect the gals who did it."

"I think the record was something like thirty-four johns in one night."

"That was Jane Oliver," Braddock said.

"Where's she working now?"

"Still patrol in East Oakland. You'd never know how hot some of our female officers are when you only see them in uniform."

Sinclair's desk phone rang.

"This is number seventy-three in radio," a dispatcher said. "We just received a nine-one-one call from a woman who said her name was Tanya and she's helping you on a murder case."

"Yeah, well, sort of," Sinclair said.

"She said some really sketchy dude just approached a few of the girls at Thirty-Third and Market, showed off a gun in his waistband, and asked if any of them wanted to take a drive to Burckhalter Park and party. Isn't that where your murder occurred?"

"Yeah. Did she give a description?"

"Male, Hispanic, twenty-five to thirty, five-ten, slim build, driving a black Camry, partial plate six-four-three."

"Did you broadcast it?" Sinclair asked.

"I assigned two units to check the area. The caller said she wouldn't talk to uniformed officers—only you. She's waiting inside the Cajun restaurant in the thirty-one-hundred block of Market."

Sinclair hung up the phone and said to Braddock, "Let's go. Tanya might've spotted our killer."

Chapter 10

Sinclair cruised north on San Pablo Avenue, scanning left for the black Camry, while Braddock scanned right. The sun had set more than an hour ago, making it difficult to distinguish car makes and models through the rain-streaked windows. The wipers beat rhythmically, ending with a squeak at the bottom of each sweep that reminded Sinclair that they were far beyond their useful lifespan. He could drive out to the city corp yard and wait an hour for a city mechanic to do the five-minute job, or stop at an AutoZone and change them himself as he usually did. He took a slight right onto Market Street and pulled to the curb in front of a fast-food restaurant that advertised Cajun chicken and fish. Tanya waved at them from inside the door and trotted to their car with short high-heeled steps.

Braddock lowered her window and Tanya leaned inside. "I think he the muthafucker."

"The man you described to the dispatcher?" asked Braddock.

"Yeah, the Mexican."

"Did you see a gun?" asked Braddock.

"He put his hand on it under his shirt."

"But you didn't actually see it?"

"No, but I know when a dude's packing."

"What did he say, Tanya?" asked Sinclair.

"He said he wanted to take me or some other girls to the park and party like he did with Blondie."

"Let's get a better description." Braddock opened her notebook and poised her pen. "You told the dispatcher that he was Hispanic—"

"Yeah . . . there he is!" Tanya shouted, pointing at a dark-gray car creeping past them on the street.

Sinclair yanked the shift lever into drive as Braddock grabbed the radio microphone and said, "Thirteen-Adam-Five, we see the possible one-eighty-seven vehicle southbound thirty-one-hundred block of Market."

Sinclair pulled from the curb, cranked the wheel to the left, and punched the accelerator. The big Crown Vic spun in a 180 on the wet pavement. The gray car ran the light at San Pablo. Sinclair flipped on his emergency lights and siren and took off after him.

"Code thirty-three," the dispatcher said. "Thirteen-Adam-Five is in pursuit of a possible one-eighty-seven vehicle southbound thirty-one-hundred block of Market. Confirm this is the Toyota Camry, black, partial plate six-four-three."

"It's actually a dark-gray Honda Accord," said Braddock. "I'll get you a plate when I can. Turning westbound on Twenty-Sixth."

Sinclair braked hard and felt the chatter of the ABS that prevented the Ford's wheels from locking up and sending them into an out of control slide on the wet pavement. The Honda fishtailed in the turn. It then straightened and sped down Twenty-Sixth Street. Sinclair powered out of the turn, finessing the gas pedal to keep the car below the speed where it would break loose. Within a block, he gained to within three car lengths of the Honda.

"California license Five-George-Lincoln-Henry-Six-Four-Three," Braddock said over the radio. "Turning north on Chestnut."

The Honda took this turn more slowly. Sinclair stayed right on its tail.

"Plate shows a ten-eight-fifty-one reported stolen out of Dublin today's date," said the dispatcher. "Speed and conditions when you can."

Braddock knew the liability game they were forced to play as well as Sinclair did. If they were honest and said they were going fifty in a twenty-five mph zone with heavy early evening traffic and people on the street, some patrol supervisor or commander more concerned about lawsuits than catching murderers would order them to abort the chase. "Forty in a twenty-five, light traffic, no pedestrians," Braddock said as they zipped past two people standing next to the stop sign that the Honda sped through without slowing.

Sinclair followed the Honda to the next street, where it turned right. It ran the stop sign at San Pablo. A truck going southbound screeched to a stop to avoid hitting it. Sinclair weaved around the truck and onto San Pablo. He then shot across the four-lane road just in time to see the Honda turning left onto Market. It was going too fast to make the turn. The Honda spun around and slid onto the sidewalk and into a low chain link fence that surrounded a vacant lot.

Sinclair slammed on the brakes and stopped two car lengths behind the crashed car. The driver bailed out and sprinted down the sidewalk on Thirty-Second Street. The normal protocol for two-officer cars was for the passenger officer to pursue fleeing suspects on foot, while the driver takes the car around to the next block to contain him. But Sinclair was the faster of the two by far.

Sinclair threw open the door and yelled, "Cut him off!" to Braddock. He then yelled the obligatory, "Police! Stop!" to the suspect and sprinted down the sidewalk, his open raincoat flapping behind him. The man had a hundred-foot head start, but Sinclair cut the distance with each step. He was confident that Braddock was climbing into the driver's seat and advising every unit on the radio that her partner was in foot pursuit, stressing that he wearing a suit and a black London Fog raincoat to prevent a blue-on-blue shooting accident.

The man cut between two parked cars and ran into the street, apparently hoping open ground would increase his chance of escape. Sinclair followed into the street and began gaining even more now that he was off the broken and cracked sidewalk. The man's arms pumped up and down as he ran, and Sinclair could see his hands were empty. If he was armed, as Tanya alluded to, his gun was tucked in his waistband or a pocket, so Sinclair didn't draw his own gun, preferring to keep his hands free.

The man looked over his shoulder at Sinclair, surely surprised to see a cop gaining on him. Although Sinclair had lost a few ticks in his forty-yard dash split since he played wide receiver in high school and junior college, he was still fast enough to stay with all but the most fleet-footed criminals during the first minute or two of a foot chase. After that, most street thugs ran out of steam. Sinclair didn't.

Sinclair heard the roar of the police interceptor V-8 behind him before his car shot past. When Braddock was a few houses past the man, she swung the Ford across the street, flung open the door, and drew her gun.

The man did a stutter step and glanced over his shoulder at Sinclair. It looked like he was about to give up. Instead, he cut left, leaped across the sidewalk, and raced between two houses. Sinclair continued the pursuit, now no more than forty feet behind as they entered the backyard of a house.

As Sinclair pivoted around a rusted washing machine, his leather dress shoes slipped in the wet grass. He planted his left hand on the ground to keep from falling. By the time he was back in stride, he had lost the distance he'd previously gained. Sinclair knew Braddock was racing around the block to the next street and calling in his location so that responding units could set up a perimeter. All Sinclair had to do was keep the suspect in sight.

The man ran around a detached garage set behind an old, falling-down Victorian. For a second, he lost his visual with the man as he disappeared into the shadow of a large tree. Sinclair stopped. The man could be drawing his gun and lying in wait for him. He wiped the rain from his eyes and scanned the darkness. With his hand on his pistol, he was ready to clear the leather holster and begin a methodical search.

The man reappeared out of the shadows and sprinted into the pool of light emitted by the next house. Sinclair continued the chase. The man ran down the long driveway of a house that fronted Brockhurst Street, the next street north. He was starting to lose steam. Except for the initial sprint, Sinclair had been pacing himself, steadily gaining on the man as he tired. When the man popped out of the yard and hit the street, Sinclair was only thirty feet behind him.

Hoover Elementary School took up the entire block on the opposite side of the street. A ten-foot metal fence, which was topped with outward-facing rods specifically designed to keep the gangsters and drug dealers off the property, surrounded the entire school ground. Had the man been from this neighborhood, he would have known that, too. In the darkness, he nearly ran into the fence. At the last second, he turned and ran up the sidewalk paralleling the school fence. Sinclair was only three steps behind.

Sinclair saw the headlights of a car speeding toward them and heard the unmistakable sound of the police interceptor engine. Braddock shot past them and stopped in the middle of the street to block the suspect's path. The man cut left, ran diagonally across the street, and made a valiant attempt to escape into the backyards once again.

Sinclair burst forward and grabbed the man's left shoulder just as the man's foot hit the slick grass of a front yard. Sinclair pulled him down and back. He finished the tackle by wrapping his right arm around the man's chest, and using his forward momentum, he threw his full weight onto the man's back.

Sinclair heard a "whoosh" as the air rushed from the man's lungs when Sinclair's 170-pound frame slammed the man to the ground. He grabbed the man's right hand and twisted it behind his back. Braddock dropped her knee into the man's back and twisted the suspect's left hand behind his back. They hand-cuffed him and pulled him to his feet just as two marked units pulled up.

The uniformed officers took over, pulled the Hispanic man to the nearest marked unit, and searched him. One officer pulled a rusted, blue-steel revolver from the man's waistband, snapped open the cylinder, and handed it to Sinclair.

"Not even loaded," the officer said.

Sinclair examined the .38 Rossi snub nose. Even brand new, Rossi revolvers weren't worth much, and with the heavy rust pitting the barrel and frame, it wouldn't fetch more than fifty dollars on the street. Even in that condition, though, Sinclair had little doubt the gun would fire. "What're you doing with this?" asked Sinclair.

The man said nothing. The officer continued searching him and handed Sinclair a folded piece of paper he pulled from the man's pants pocket. It was a property receipt from Santa Rita Jail in the name of Eduardo Rodriquez.

"Eduardo, what were you in jail for?" Sinclair asked.

"No speak English," Eduardo replied.

"Bullshit," replied Sinclair. To the officer, he said, "Stuff him in your car. Let's regroup back at the Honda."

Sinclair climbed into the passenger seat of his car. As Braddock drove, he retrieved a wad of paper towels from the glove box and dried his face and hands.

Braddock glanced his way and laughed. "You're a mess. But was it fun?"

Water trickled off his head and down his neck. "Chasing bad guys—that's what they pay us for. Just wish I was dressed for it." His pants and the front of his shirt were soaked. Mud caked the knees of his pants and his shoes.

Another uniformed officer was searching the Honda Accord when they pulled up. Sinclair grabbed his fedora and stepped out into the rain.

The uniform said, "The car was stolen from a parking lot in Dublin between noon and one. I found a wallet with ID in the name of Eduardo Rodriquez under the seat. Picture matches our guy. I ran him out. He just did sixty days for probation violation on a burglary. Was released this morning from Santa Rita. Also a bag of weed and some rolling papers in the car's door pocket."

"Gotta love it," Sinclair said. "Guy gets released, steals a car, finds a gun, and a few hours later he's back in handcuffs."

"I guess that means he couldn't've killed your victim two nights ago," the uniformed officer said.

"I appreciate you pointing that out after I chased the asshole through the rain and mud and ruined a nice suit."

"If you didn't catch him, you wouldn't know," the officer said. "I guess he's just one of the dickheads who likes to fuck with the whores. They think it's some kind of a game."

Sinclair and Braddock stopped at Tanya's corner and told her what happened. When they got to the PAB, Sinclair went straight down to the locker room and stripped off his dirty clothes. He wiped the mud off his suit pants and was glad to see he hadn't ripped out the knees of the Brooks Brothers suit, one of the new suits he'd bought last year with the insurance money from his apartment fire. As he stood under the shower, washing mud and strands of grass out of his hair, he wondered if he should go back to wearing cheaper suits to work.

Chapter 11

It was eight o'clock when Sinclair returned to the office dressed in a pair of slacks and an olive-and-brown plaid sport coat, which he kept in his locker for emergencies such as this. Everyone else had gone home hours ago. Braddock was at her desk eating a taco salad.

"I got you a steak burrito," she said, pointing to a bag on his desk.

He unwrapped the foil, took a bite, and dialed his voicemail. A message from Dawn's parents asked him to call them back day or night. He dialed the number and had Braddock listen in on her line. A man answered with a hello.

"This is Sergeant Sinclair, Oakland homicide. Is this Mr. Gustafson?"

"Eugene Gustafson, but you can call me Gene."

"I'm sorry for your loss, Gene."

"Let me get my wife," he said. A moment later, Sinclair heard the echo-chamber sound that indicated they were on speakerphone. "My wife, Cynthia, is here, too."

"Hi, Sergeant," she said. "I'm sorry we get to meet under these circumstances."

"My partner, Sergeant Braddock, is on the line with us. Before I ask you any questions, is there anything you want to ask me?"

Cynthia asked, "Do you know why she was killed?"

Sinclair replied, "Not yet. I don't know how much you know about Dawn's life out here—"

Cynthia interrupted, "You don't need to tap dance around anything for us. We know she was a prostitute—"

Gene jumped in, "She was in the process of changing her life and putting that past behind her."

"What do you mean?" Sinclair asked.

"She was going to school," Gene said. "Studying to be a CPA. She was doing accounting work and had stopped that other business."

Cynthia said, "Excuse my husband, Sergeant, but Dawn will always be his little girl who could do no wrong. That CPA stuff was a cover. She was still selling her body for a living."

Gene said, "I never said she did no wrong. But she had changed and was making a real life for herself."

Sinclair interjected with questions about their background, which he needed for his report. Eugene and Cynthia both lived in Mankato, Minnesota, where they had been born and raised by parents who were farmers. Gene was fifty-five and managed a regional farm-equipment dealership. Cynthia was a year younger and worked part-time at the local library. They married the year Cynthia finished high school and they had three daughters, one older and one younger than Dawn. Both other daughters had attended college and were married, the oldest living in Minneapolis, and the younger living in Mankato.

"Dawn was the wild one," Gene said. "She always wanted something more than rural Minnesota could offer. We weren't surprised when she ran away at seventeen."

"But to California, of all places, the epicenter of immorality?" Cynthia said. "When we got the call from your juvenile officers, we were heartbroken."

Gene said, "But relieved that she was okay. We flew out there the next day and appeared in court for her."

Sinclair said, "My records show she was released in your custody."

Cynthia said, "That's right. We brought her home. She talked about you a lot."

"She did?" Sinclair said.

"Oh, yes," Cynthia said. "You made quite an impression on her."

Braddock looked at Sinclair with a puzzled look on her face. Sinclair turned his eyes back to his phone. "You mean when I arrested her as a juvenile?"

Cynthia said, "Yes, and—"

Gene interrupted, "We know you only wanted what was best for her, and we're grateful you arrested her and sent her home to us."

"What happened after she got back home?" Sinclair asked.

"She was okay for a while," Cynthia said. "I think the experience frightened her. She went back to school and got her high school diploma that year. She wasn't up for college, so Gene got her a job in the parts department at his store. She was bright and did exceptionally well. That girl could look at a broken piece of machinery and tell you whether it came from a John Deere tractor or an S-series combine."

Gene laughed, "Something I couldn't often do myself without looking at the parts catalogue. And the customers loved her."

"What wasn't to love?" Cynthia said. "She was absolutely beautiful. Every young man in the county wanted to marry her. She had a wonderful way with people—charming, sweet, unpretentious."

"But something happened," Sinclair said.

"One day she didn't show up for work," Gene said. "When Cynthia got home from the library, Dawn's car and all her clothes were gone. She called a month later and said she returned to San Francisco. Said she just couldn't live in our barren farm country another day."

"Did she say what she was doing out here?" Sinclair asked.

"She was vague," Cynthia said. "But I knew she was back in the prostitution life."

"Did she stay in touch?"

"At first she called most Sunday afternoons," Gene said. "She knew we'd be home from church and preparing Sunday dinner. Her sisters were usually here with their families."

"But then the calls became less frequent," Cynthia said. "Soon we only heard from her on birthdays and holidays."

"What did she talk about?"

"Nothing about her life," Cynthia said. "She asked about us and her sisters. And she talked about you."

"Me?" Sinclair said.

"You have to understand Dawn," Gene said. "She thought she possessed some sort of inner sense about how the universe worked. I think of it as fate, but to her it was more than that. For instance, she thought you arresting her was something like God's will—that you were some sort of knight in shining armor who rescued her from the streets of Oakland and put her on the right path."

"But she went back to the streets," Sinclair said.

"My understanding is that when she returned to San Francisco, she became a call girl or escort," Gene said. "Certainly not what we wanted for her, but better than standing on a street corner."

"Did you have an address for her?" Sinclair asked.

"She had a PO box," Cynthia said. "She never would tell us where she actually lived."

"Is there anything else you know about her life out here—a boyfriend, other friends she spoke of, any places she frequented?"

"No, not really," Gene said. "She was very private about her life. She always sounded the same, though, very upbeat, always happy."

Cynthia said, "The only person from out there she ever mentioned by name was you."

Gene cut in, "It was like you were a celebrity—one she'd met and was therefore special to her. She followed your career, which I guess was pretty easy with all the media exposure you've had."

Sinclair said, "The coroner noticed she had a scar from a Cesarean. Did you know she had been pregnant?"

Sinclair heard muffled whispering between Gene and Cynthia for a moment. "You didn't know?" Cynthia asked.

Sinclair kept his eyes on the telephone to avoid a look he was sure Braddock was giving him.

"Three years ago, she just appeared at our front door one day," Cynthia said.

"It was actually three-and-a-half years, because she was a few months along and Maddie will be three next month," Gene said.

"Maddie?" said Sinclair. "So she *did* have a baby?"

"Yes," Gene said. "Madison was a healthy eight-pound, six-ounce, girl. The only thing Dawn said when she came home was she had been in a relationship with a man who turned out not to be who she had thought he was. They had been together for over a year. She was going to school full-time and living in a nice apartment. But when he found out she was pregnant, he wanted nothing to do with it."

"Dawn must've remembered a few things we taught her," Cynthia said. "She was adamant about having the baby."

Sinclair's mind raced—three summers ago—the year after he returned from Iraq.

"She was equally adamant about not telling us who the father was," Gene said.

"Where is Madison now?" Sinclair asked.

"She's with us," Cynthia said. "When Maddie was six months old, Dawn signed over legal guardianship to us and left."

"She left her?" Sinclair said, and immediately regretted his reaction.

"What kind of mother would abandon her daughter?" Cynthia said, choking through sobs.

"She was confused—troubled," Gene said. "She felt her destiny lay in San Francisco. But she came home several times a year to visit Maddie, always for several weeks in the winter to encompass Christmas and Maddie's birthday, and again in the summer. She was a great mom when she was here, but always toward the end of her visits, she grew restless. Said she felt suffocated."

"She felt suffocated!" Cynthia exclaimed. "Anyone can play mom for a few weeks at a time. Try raising three little girls when two are in diapers at the same time, when your husband's gone twelve hours a day, and there's two feet of snow on the ground, and the temperature never gets above—"

"Honey, I know it was hard," Gene said. "But it's the past."

Sinclair caught Braddock's eye. She wrote *postpartum depression / childhood abuse?* on a slip of paper and slid it in front of him. He nodded in agreement.

Sinclair asked, "When did you last see Dawn?"

"She came home the first week of August," Gene said. "The county fair is a big thing out here, and Maddie was finally old enough to walk on her own and enjoy it."

"Did Dawn talk any more about her life or what she was doing?"

"She said she'd be finished with school in a year or so and was working on plans for her future," Gene said.

"You weren't there," Cynthia said, with an edge in her voice. "You were hanging out with the farmers at the equipment demos. Maddie was petting the lambs and baby horses at the 4-H exhibit when Dawn asked her if she wanted to come and live with her in San Francisco."

"That must have been a surprise," Sinclair said.

"I took her aside and told her in no uncertain terms that Maddie was not leaving Mankato to live with a San Francisco hooker," Cynthia said. "I regret my choice of words, but I was angry. I was scared for Maddie. I knew at that point I needed to begin adoption proceedings so she didn't drag Maddie into her demented California lifestyle."

"Honey, I told you that was unnecessary," Gene said. "That we could all discuss it as adults."

"Unnecessary?" Cynthia's voice cracked.

Sinclair heard her crying over the phone and pictured Gene trying to comfort her.

"Unnecessary?" Cynthia said again between sobs. "If we had allowed her to take Maddie, she'd probably be dead, too."

"I think we better stop," Gene said. "Can we talk again in a day or two?"

Braddock spoke for the first time. "I'm very sorry for your loss. I'm wondering if you could send us a copy of Maddie's birth certificate, medical records of her birth, and some of her photos?"

"I'll e-mail it to you," Gene said. "Sergeant Sinclair, I'm sure Dawn is looking down on us right now, knowing the search for justice in this matter could not be in better hands."

Sinclair hung up the phone and kept his eyes on his desk, letting Gene's final words sink in. When he finally looked up, he saw Braddock looking at him intently.

"Is there something I should know?" she asked.

He grabbed his mug and walked to the coffee pot. He pulled out the pot, sniffed it, and put it back, turning off the burner. "She called me from the jail when she was arrested on the B-charge six years ago," Sinclair said, referring to 647b, the penal code section for prostitution. "I was new in homicide and asked her if she had any information on any murders. She said maybe, so I pulled a copy of the report."

Sinclair sat on a desk two rows from Braddock's desk. "The report said that the officers from the area crime reduction team were assigned to an undercover operation on San Pablo Avenue due to complaints about blatant prostitution activity. It said two officers, working undercover in an undercover car, stopped next to a group of four women that they knew were prostitutes based on their appearance and demeanor. There was some back-and-forth bantering until an officer asked the women if they wanted to go to a bachelor party and have sex with the men there for fifty dollars each. They agreed and the officers signaled the arrest team. The arrest team ran the women and found three of them had recent prostitution arrests and the fourth one, Dawn, admitted she had been arrested for prostitution four years earlier as a juvenile."

"Let me guess," said Braddock. "There was no wire, or it didn't work."

"No mention of a recording in the report. I had the jail pull Dawn from her cell and put her on the phone. She said she hadn't worked the streets in years, and that she was just visiting her old friends that night when two guys came up talking shit. She said she certainly didn't solicit them. She admitted to me she was still in the business, but only doing outcalls and wouldn't even consider doing a bachelor party for less than five hundred. I believed her. I talked to the sergeant who ran the operation. He confided that they were playing fast and loose to make an impact and get the city councilwoman in that district off their backs. He suspected the DA wouldn't file charges on most of their arrests. I told him Dawn was an informant of mine. He had no problem with me cutting her loose, so I went back to the jail and filled out the eight-forty-nine-B paperwork."

"But she wasn't really your informant and didn't have any info on murders?"

"No, but it wasn't the first time we cut someone loose on a bullshit arrest that we knew wouldn't be charged in order to cultivate them as an informant."

"Fair enough," Braddock said. "Did she ever come through for you?"

"She'd call me occasionally and want to talk, but I told her I was too busy unless she had something on a case for me. Then she called me one time and said she was in trouble and needed help. When her parents told us about her returning home pregnant, I thought about the timing and figured that was what her trouble was."

"Was the trouble more than just being pregnant?"

"We met and she said someone, or maybe a group of people, were causing her problems. She never mentioned she was pregnant. She wouldn't tell me who this person or persons were or the nature of the problem, only that she was afraid and didn't know what to do. I tried to get her to open up, but she wouldn't. I figured it was over some john or maybe she got mixed up with some major players. I told her maybe this was a wake-up call telling her it was really time to change her life. She said she couldn't go home, that she felt dead when she was there. I talked to her a few more times over the next few days, and I guess she realized it was more important to go home and feel emotionally dead than stay here and end up physically dead. That was the last I saw her until the park."

Braddock crossed the room and sat on the desk beside him. She bumped his shoulder with hers. "Why didn't you tell me?"

Sinclair thought for a minute. "I guess I knew my relationship with her wasn't fully professional. I couldn't really call her an informant because she never provided any info, yet I was helping her out."

Braddock laughed. "So you felt ashamed because you helped out a citizen for no reason other than she needed help? Jeez, Matt, isn't that what police are supposed to do? Not every interaction with a citizen has to lead to the arrest of a bad guy. Maybe you're afraid you're reputation as a tough, law-and-order-only cop would get tarnished."

"There's also what she was."

"In this city, just about everyone we come across is involved in some kind of crime. As long as you're not banging her and then looking the other way when she robs banks or something, what's the big deal?"

"Just the same, I'd prefer you keep what I told you between us."

"Mum's the word. Not that you don't take every case personal, but I've had the feeling this one was more personal than most."

Sinclair nodded in agreement.

"What do you say we call it a night?" Braddock said. "We're still on standby, and the city's overdue for another killing."

Chapter 12

The mansion was quiet as Sinclair wrote a note and left it with his dirty suit and raincoat in the butler's pantry. When he had first moved into the guesthouse, it felt strange having Walt and his wife handling everything from grocery shopping to house-keeping, but Walt insisted it was part of their responsibilities as the caretakers of Frederick Towers's estate.

Walt had first met Fred Towers six years ago when Walt was working a second job as a limo driver and was assigned to pick up Fred at his Oakland office, where he was the CEO of one of the largest corporations in the city, and drive him home every day because he had lost his license after a DUI arrest. Over several weeks, Walt shared with Fred how booze had destroyed his own life fifteen years earlier, and eventually drove him to his first AA meeting and became his sponsor. When Fred's wife and daughter died in a drunk-driving accident a year later, he asked Walt to move into his house to manage the estate and his personal affairs. Walt and Sinclair's friendship had started in a similar way—at Sinclair's first AA meeting.

Sinclair hadn't been too happy about having to attend AA meetings when he got out of rehab nearly two years ago, and seeing people such as Walt, who talked at every meeting about serenity and gratitude, drove him crazy. But when he almost picked up a drink while investigating the Bus Bench murders,

Walt was there with support and needed words of wisdom. Fred and Walt invited Sinclair to stay in their guesthouse after his apartment was firebombed, and what was intended to be a month or so stay turned into more than a yearlong residency. Whenever he looked at the cost of rent for a decent apartment in a halfway decent area, he realized how good he had it here. Still, he dreamed of buying a house again someday, and hoped the escalating home prices in the East Bay didn't outpace what he was able to save while living rent-free.

Sinclair walked through the commercial-grade kitchen and breakfast room onto a rear stone patio. The rain had stopped, but heavy clouds shadowed the light from the full moon above. He made his way down a flagstone path through the lush yard, around the pool, and into the guesthouse through the French doors. Originally a pool house with changing rooms and a large open space filled with pool tables and ping-pong tables, Fred had it converted to a one-bedroom apartment for his daughter when she turned twenty. By default, it became a guesthouse after she died.

Sinclair took a cigar from a drawer in the rolltop desk that sat in one corner of his living room. He grabbed a towel from the linen closet and a down jacket from the closet and returned to the pool area. After wiping down a chair, he sparked his lighter and puffed on the A. Flores Habano until it was evenly lit.

When he'd first recognized Dawn in the park yesterday morning, the first thought that jumped into his mind was that he had failed her—that if he had somehow said the right thing to her when she came to him several years earlier, she would have walked away from her life of prostitution. Maybe if he hadn't been so focused on his own needs and problems. Although he hadn't mentioned it to Dr. Elliott that morning, Dawn's face was one of those that flashed through his mind as he was reliving the shooting on Telegraph Avenue. Dawn was one of those he couldn't save.

As he savored the hint of vanilla and cocoa in the Dominican cigar, he knew the thought that he was somehow responsible for saving everyone was irrational. Nevertheless, it remained. He heard a door slam in the main house and turned to see a man walking toward him.

"I thought you'd be asleep," Sinclair said.

Walt Cooper set two mugs on the patio table and wiped the rain from a chair with Sinclair's towel. He was in his midsixties, short and wiry, with snow-white hair. "I was upstairs reading and heard your car come in. When I looked out and saw you here, I thought you might like some company."

Sinclair picked up one of the cups. "Decaf?"

"Of course."

Sinclair brought the cup to his lips, watching the steam rise into the cold evening air. He puffed on his cigar as they both sat there silently for a few minutes.

Finally, Walt said, "I saw today's paper. The murder of that girl in the park is yours?"

"Yeah." Sinclair didn't want to talk about the murder, and Walt knew enough not to pry. Walt would continue to toss out other topics like a man blindly throwing darts at a board until one stuck.

"How's it going with your therapy?" Walt asked.

Walt had been one of the top psychologists in the Bay Area until his drinking and prescription-drug abuse decimated his life when he was in his forties. He had lost everything and served time in prison for insurance fraud. Now sober for more than twenty years, he could never be licensed to practice again, but he remained well-versed in the field.

"Slower than I hoped," Sinclair said. "This morning, we were into the shooting that got me started with the shrink and I flashed on other incidents."

"That's how EMDR works. Those are repressed memories, and during future sessions you'll deal with them, too."

"I'm worried about how much shit I have buried inside me."

"It'll all come out as long as you don't fight it. Then you can be free from all the barriers that are holding you back emotionally. Has any childhood stuff come up?"

"Sort of, but I know the heavy shit I need to work through is from my Army and police work."

Walt took a long drink of his coffee and turned his chair to face Sinclair. "You might want to mention those early life memories to Dr. Elliott. Sometimes incidents from our childhood form the foundation for how we think and deal with the world. If that foundation was based on invalid principles, it can skew how we function today and in the worst cases, even our moral code."

"There's nothing from those days that I didn't get over."

"The problem is we don't know what we don't know. I had a patient when I worked with the VA who suffered from PTSD. He had plenty of wartime trauma, but one thing that struck me was a report from his wife that he never cried and appeared to be emotionally dead. During a year of weekly sessions, we pealed back the layers. We finally reached an incident from when he was in the first grade—something he had long ago forgotten. He had fallen on the playground and skinned his knee badly. The school nurse was putting tincture of iodine—or whatever they used back then—on his scrape. Of course, he was balling his eyes out. The nurse said to him, 'Stop crying and act like a man.' That was the last time he ever cried. To ensure he never again cried, he stopped feeling. I gave him permission to feel, even if it led to his crying, and his recovery was miraculous."

"The stuff I flashed on was when my little brother was killed," Sinclair said.

"You never told me about that."

"There's not much to tell."

Walt smiled, took another drink of his coffee, and gazed across the pool at the mansion.

Sinclair puffed on his cigar. "I was twelve when my two brothers and I were going to the zoo with our church youth group. My parents told me to watch over my little brother, but you know how it is when you're a sixth grader and you want to hang out with those your age. I boarded the first bus with my friends, leaving Billy to wait for the next bus with the other little kids. A woman drove up and let two boys out of her car. A man, who I later learned was her estranged husband, got out of his car and started yelling at her. I watched through the bus window as he pulled a gun and emptied it at the woman. One of the bullets hit Billy. I ran off the bus and held him in my arms as the life drained out of him. Although my parents never came right out and said it, I knew they held me responsible for Billy's death."

Walt sat there quietly staring at the pool and sipping his coffee for a few moments. Finally he asked, "Has the issue of being responsible for the life and death of other people come up again in your life?"

"What do you think?" Sinclair said. "I'm a cop. It's my job to save lives."

"Saving lives and holding yourself responsible when they die are two different things."

"Can we talk about something else?" Sinclair said.

"I'm sorry, Matthew. I didn't mean to tread into an area that best belongs to Dr. Elliott. Any time you want to talk, I'm here."

"You've been a great friend. Maybe we can talk about this when it's not so late."

"I was at a meeting tonight. People were asking about you."

"It's hard to hit meetings when I'm on standby. Maybe tomorrow if I get off on time."

"Let me know and I'll go with you," Walt said. "Oh, and Betty will take your stuff to the dry cleaners tomorrow, but even with a rush, it won't be back until Thursday. Is that your only raincoat?"

"Yeah, I'll just have to stay out of the rain."

"Fred has an old Burberry trench coat, one of the classic ones. I've been trying to donate it for years, but Fred thinks he'll lose enough weight to wear it again someday. It should fit you perfectly. I'll leave it hanging on the kitchen door."

"Thanks, Walt." Sinclair watched as Walt gathered up the coffee cups and wet towel and made his way back to the mansion to the small apartment on the second floor where he and Betty lived.

Chapter 13

At ten o'clock the following morning, Sinclair and Braddock waited for the elevator on the second-floor balcony of the PAB. "Still not sleeping?" Braddock asked.

She was surely seeing the same the dark circles under his eyes that Sinclair had seen in the mirror this morning. "Woke up early thinking about the case," he said.

The truth was he had woken with a jolt and sat up in bed, drenched in sweat. The clock on his nightstand read 4:38 AM. He went into the bathroom, stripped off his wet T-shirt and shorts and climbed into the shower. The dream was one of several different ones that took turns rotating through his subconscious every few nights. In this one, a faceless man appeared in front of him with a gun. Sinclair drew his sidearm and pulled the trigger. Nothing happened. He pulled the trigger again, harder, and continued pulling it repeatedly until he finally woke up with a cramp in his forearm. After the shower, he dressed, made coffee, and drove to a 6 AM AA meeting in Lafayette, a meeting he had attended regularly in his early sobriety but hadn't been to in months.

"Is there something wrong with your arm?" Braddock asked.

He hadn't realized he was massaging the muscles of his right forearm, which felt like a taut rope. "Too many reverse curls in the gym the other day," he said.

The elevator took them to the fourth floor. Sinclair pressed the button alongside a door marked only by a room number. The intelligence unit consisted of one sergeant and four officers, each of whom had a specialty such as outlaw motorcycle gangs, terrorism, Asian gangs, or organized crime. Officers who were assigned to intelligence seldom took a promotional exam, because Intel had more freedom and perks than any other assignment in the department. A white man in his midforties with shoulder-length hair, wearing jeans and a leather vest, opened the door. Sinclair knew this officer as one of the foremost experts on the Hells Angels in the state. The main office had four workstations, each with double computer monitors. Heavy file cabinets with combination locks lined a wall. Tiny red lights blinked from a motion detection sensor in the corner of the room. The intelligence unit was the only office in the PAB that had a separate intrusion alarm.

A door to their right opened, and a smooth-faced black man wearing a golf shirt, khaki pants, and a huge smile stepped out. Phil Roberts was the sergeant in charge of intelligence and had been Sinclair's partner for his first four years in homicide and Braddock's for her first six months. Roberts had grown up as an Air Force brat, living on different military bases in the United States and England. He attended Boston College for two years until he was accepted to the University of Oxford, from which he graduated with a degree in English Literature. Upon graduation, Roberts got a job as a grant writer for a consortium of nonprofits in the Bay Area, but he hated it within a year. He took the test for police officer at OPD twenty-three years ago and never regretted his decision.

Roberts and Sinclair did the handshake/half-hug routine. Roberts went for a full hug with Braddock.

"Isn't that prohibited in the workplace these days?" Sinclair said.

"We in Intel operate in a covert status and aren't subject to the sexual harassment regs you mere mortals are," Roberts said.

"Do you still like it up here?" asked Braddock.

"What's not to like? Unlimited overtime, no one watching over me, and we're privy to all the secrets."

"Like who's running the escorts services in the Bay Area?" Sinclair asked.

Roberts ushered them into his office and shut the door. The windowless room was twice the size of the homicide lieutenant's office. Two guest chairs faced a large wooden desk. A matching bookshelf filled with three-ring binders and a row of file cabinets covered one wall. A brown tweed couch backed against the other wall. Seated on it was a slim man in his fifties, dressed in a pinstripe suit and a white shirt with too much starch.

"Mark Cummings, IRS," Roberts said. "My old homicide partners, Matt Sinclair and Cathy Braddock."

Cummings rose slowly and shook hands with Sinclair and Braddock.

"CI special agent?" Sinclair asked, knowing there was a huge difference between an IRS agent and a criminal investigation special agent, whose qualifications and authority were similar to those of an FBI agent.

"That's right," Cummings said.

Sinclair and Braddock sat in the guest chairs and Roberts sat in his high-backed desk chair. Roberts looked at Sinclair and said, "When you left me the message about Special Ladies Escorts, I gave Mark a call. We've discussed them and a number of other escort services over the last year or so."

"What do you know about them?" asked Sinclair.

"I need you to agree to some rules," said Roberts. "No notes about our conversation and nothing in your case file attributed to us. IRS isn't permitted to disclose anything about an active investigation to anyone not sworn in federally, and I don't want to be called in to court to testify about what files we do or do not maintain."

Sinclair and Braddock looked at each other and nodded.

"Helena Decker is the owner of Special Ladies Escorts as well as another four or five named escort agencies that operate from San Jose to Sausalito," Roberts said. "The names come and go. Old ones shut down when police scrutinize them too closely or a customer causes problems. New ones with new phone numbers open up, but all of the phone lines go to one answering service. From there, requests are taken and girls dispatched. Money comes in through a number of different credit card accounts. It's really just one company, SLE Services, Inc., which Decker owns. She reports income and pays taxes on it."

"What's the company bring in?" Sinclair asked.

Cummings looked at him blankly. Then he said, "I can't divulge information that's reported to the IRS."

Roberts raised an eyebrow at Cummings. "Let's just say she reports about a half million in income," Roberts said. "But we suspect she nets ten times that."

"Do you have phone and bank records?" Braddock asked.

Cummings shifted on the couch and crossed his legs. "We would need to have initiated a criminal case to subpoena that, and I'm not acknowledging the existence of any ongoing criminal cases."

"Look," said Sinclair. "I don't need all this *Secret Squirrel* shit. I just need to know where I can find this Helena Decker and make her talk to me about a dead hooker."

"That's where we can help each other," Roberts said. "You know how these organizations are. Decker is not going to disclose anything about your murder victim or her clients. Not unless you have a hammer on her. You don't have the resources to mount an operation to get to her, but together we do."

"And why would the Feds want to help us out?" Sinclair said, looking at Cummings.

Roberts said, "Immigration and Customs Enforcement along with the FBI have a loose-knit human trafficking task force. Because a woman was possibly murdered as a result of organized prostitution, the task force can get involved. The IRS has been looking for a criminal nexus to SLE Services for years, and if we can show Decker receives money from illegal activity, it allows the Feds to grab all of her records and bank accounts. They'll then subpoena everyone connected in front of a federal grand jury. Without the criminal nexus, they'll spend years trying to make a case."

Sinclair summarized, "So, we're going to pretend that we're mounting an operation to solve my homicide case, and if it opens up the huge IRS tax fraud case, we just lucked into it?"

Cummings sat there stone-faced.

"Exactly," said Roberts.

"Okay," Sinclair said. "I worked these kinds of operations back in the old vice days. We'd get a few undercovers, set them up in different hotel rooms, call up the escort services, and order up girls. They'd solicit the undercover officers, we'd arrest the escorts, and try to get them to turn on the owner."

"We're way ahead of you," Roberts said. "There's a similar meeting going on in San Jose right now. Their vice squad's providing the undercover officer down there."

"Who are you planning to use for the one we're doing in Oakland?" Sinclair asked.

Roberts slid a manila envelope across the desk. Sinclair opened it and took out the contents: an expired driver's license, credit cards, and other identification in the name of Carlos Gutierrez, Sinclair's undercover name when he worked narcotics.

"Whoa there," Sinclair said. "I haven't worked undercover in almost ten years, and in case you haven't noticed, my mug's been plastered all over the TV and newspapers for years now."

"It's like riding a bike," Roberts said. "You were one of the best back then, and it's not like we're going to parade you around the city. This isn't a deep cover. One woman will come to your hotel room. Even if she saw you on the news at some point, the chances of her recognizing you and putting two and two together is negligible. There's no one else that we can get up to speed in time and who can play the part we need to make this work."

"Convincing a woman to have sex with you," Braddock remarked. "This is right up your alley."

Sinclair gave Braddock a wry smile and turned his attention back to Roberts. "My old ID is expired."

"The law enforcement section at DMV has agreed to a rush for a new driver's license. You have an appointment at the DMV on Claremont at two to pick it up. Our contact in security at Wells Fargo Bank is issuing you a new Visa card right now. I'll pick it up this afternoon. The Feds are working on a clean cell and the backstop of your identity. Everything will be in place by close of business."

The last time he carried the ID of Carlos Gutierrez had been when he was part of a deep-cover operation into a Mexican cartel that was establishing a foothold in Oakland. He was making his third controlled buy, handing over a briefcase with forty thousand dollars in exchange for a duffle bag with two kilos of powder. After the exchange, everyone was supposed to walk away, and surveillance teams from OPD and DEA were to follow the money. But it didn't work out that way. The two cartel henchmen decided to kill Sinclair, take the money, and keep the drugs. They pulled guns and ordered him to his knees. Sinclair knew the surveillance teams couldn't get there in time, so he drew a compact Kimber .45 from under his shirt. When the firefight was over, one cartel member was dead, the other was wounded, and Sinclair had suffered a bullet wound in his left shoulder that would require three surgeries and continued to nag him to this day.

Sinclair thought his undercover days were long over. But this wasn't like infiltrating a drug gang or buying illegal guns from Chinese Triads. All it involved was pretending he was someone else, something he'd been doing most of his life. He was sure Dawn's murder was connected to her work as an escort, and the key to solving the murder was getting into the organization. "When do we do this?"

"We'll meet right here at five to brief and then head to the hotel. Wear your best suit—you're going to be a high roller."

Chapter 14

Sinclair's cab pulled up to the Waterfront Hotel in Oakland's Jack London Square at 6:30. Escort services were not strangers to the hotels in Oakland, so it was reasonable to expect Special Ladies Escorts might have a contact even at the Waterfront, the most expensive hotel in Oakland. He was glad the Feds had the money to run the operation the right way. He had worked too many undercover operations during his time in vice where shortcuts were taken to save time or money. They'd use cheaper hotels and sometimes work through hotel security to get the room free, but often it blew the UC's cover because the hotel management told someone on the staff who tipped off their target.

Sinclair paid the driver, collected his carry-on, and rolled it into the lobby. As he passed the hotel bar, Sinclair recognized two of the FBI agents from the briefing among the well-dressed after-work business crowd.

"Checking in, sir?" a thirtyish woman dressed in a hotel uniform asked from behind the front desk.

"Yes, my name's Gutierrez."

She clicked a few keys on her computer. It printed out a single sheet, which she handed to him. "Welcome to the Waterfront, Mr. Gutierrez. I show you staying one night in a bay-view suite. Please review the information to confirm everything is correct. May I see a photo ID and the credit card you wish to use for incidentals?"

From his pocket, Sinclair pulled a new black calfskin wallet. As was standard procedure, he had emptied his pockets of anything that could be linked to Matt Sinclair and dropped them into a large envelope in Roberts's office. Braddock took the envelope along with his gun and badge. In addition to the wallet filled with ID in the name of Gutierrez, the Feds gave him a new phone and a set of keys that supposedly fit his make-believe home in Bel Air, his make-believe office, and his make-believe BMW.

Sinclair handed the clerk his license and Visa card. He reviewed the registration form. Just shy of five hundred dollars for one night. Good thing the Feds were footing the bill.

"One or two keys?"

"Two, please," he said.

She returned his credit card and license and handed him two key cards in a pocket-sized packet marked with his room number. "Would you like help with your luggage?" she asked.

"I think I can handle it," Sinclair said.

The door opened to the bedroom area of the suite, with a king-size bed, dresser, and two nightstands. Sinclair threw his suitcase on the bed and walked into the living room, which was separated from the bedroom by a partial wall. A sofa faced the window. A table with four chairs took up a corner, while a desk and chair were on the other side of the sofa. The window overlooked Jack London Square, with its assortment of shops and restaurants, and the Oakland estuary, a mile-wide body of water that separated Oakland and Alameda and flowed into the San Francisco Bay. When Sinclair examined the website earlier in the afternoon to make his reservations, he saw there were other rooms with large private balconies that overlooked the waterfront. He imagined staying in one of those rooms during the summer time and watching the sunset from his balcony while feeling the cool breeze off the water.

He unpacked his suitcase. He placed his shaving kit in the bathroom, hung a dress shirt, polo shirt, and jeans in the closet, and placed two sets of underwear, socks, and a workout outfit in a drawer—the clothes a businessman would bring for a two-day trip. Props in case the escort checked. He looked at himself in the mirror. His tailored charcoal-gray suit was a donation arranged by the Oakland Business Association after he had lost his entire wardrobe last year in the fire. He'd only worn this suit to work a few times, knowing that with his luck it would be the day he got into a wrestling match with a suspect. A fitted ivory-colored shirt, dark-blue silk tie, and a stainless-steel Rolex—a gift from Fred last Christmas—completed his look.

Sinclair heard a double knock at the door. He opened it and Roberts, Braddock, and Cummings came in.

Cummings's eyes scanned Sinclair from head to toe. "Clothes are obviously too expensive for a cop to afford."

"I always thought a suit's just a suit," Braddock said. "But you do look fine."

Looks and demeanor were everything when working under-cover. If anything made the girl uncomfortable—if she thought he was dangerous or too weird—she'd walk away. The stakes weren't as high when Sinclair did prostitution undercover work years ago. If the escort didn't come through, they called another agency, and if that escort didn't come through, they didn't make a case. No big deal. Tonight, they not only had to get the solicitation from the escort; they needed to turn her, too. "I'll be on my best behavior."

"Let's make the call," Roberts said.

Sinclair opened his laptop on the table in the living room and brought up the Special Ladies Escorts website. He scrolled through the pages of photos and settled on a blonde showing off long, slender legs in a body stocking similar to what he'd seen in Frederick's of Hollywood catalogues. He dialed the phone number on the website.

"Good evening, Special Ladies Escorts," said a woman in a singsong voice.

"Hi, I'd like to arrange for an escort," Sinclair said.

"Have you used our service before?"

"No."

"How did you learn about our service?"

"I just found you on the Internet."

"Have you looked at our rates and decided on how much time you'd like to spend with one of our ladies?"

"I see you start at four hundred for the first hour. I'd like an hour."

"Do you have a preference for your escort, such as ethnicity or body shape—thin, full-figured?"

"Danielle caught my eye. Is she available?"

"Let me check." Sinclair heard the clicking of computer keys. "It appears she is. When would you like to see her?"

Sinclair looked at his watch. "Around eight would be perfect."

"Would we be sending her to your home?"

"I'm in Oakland on business and staying at the Waterfront Hotel."

"I believe we can arrange that. Let me get some information from you."

The woman collected the same information from him that any normal business would for a credit card purchase. "To avoid any problem with hotel management, please advise the hotel desk that a work colleague named Danielle Jones will be visiting your room."

"I'll do that."

"Thank you. Enjoy your evening, Mr. Gutierrez."

Technology and the ease with which anyone could check someone out had changed a lot since Sinclair last worked undercover. Cummings had warned him the agency would do a cursory background on him. They'd run his cell phone number to see what service it was provided through. If it were a burner, they'd get suspicious, so Cummings had arranged for a phone with a Sprint account. They may have a contact in DMV to verify his license. They'd run his credit card, so Cummings set it up with a thirty-thousand-dollar credit limit and some fake purchases, such as airline tickets and meals. The agency would run him in the state sexual offender database and try to find him in social media and Google, but Roberts assured him Gutierrez was too common a name to single him out.

"Why don't you order something from room service," Roberts said. "It's all paid for by the Feds, and it'll look normal. You should be finished eating and busy working in your room when she arrives."

Sinclair called the front desk, ordering a gourmet pizza and advising them that Danielle would be visiting.

Cummings adjusted Sinclair's briefcase on the dresser, removed the clock radio from the nightstand, and replaced it with another one. "We have cameras that cover the bedroom from two angles."

Sinclair followed them into the living room, where Cummings fiddled with his laptop. "This has built-in cameras on all four sides, so we can cover the entire room even if you close the lid and power it down. The mic on your phone is also activated, so if everything else fails, we can hear what's going on."

Sinclair handed Roberts his extra room card. "You'll need this."

Roberts said, "Let's review the arrest and duress codes."

"Duress is me raising my hands in a surrender pose or saying gun, knife, Phil, or Roberts. If I want you to make the arrest, I say 'room service.' I stay out of the way when you come in unless she rushes for her handbag. Then I grab her or it."

"That's it," said Roberts. "Don't forget, some escorts carry weapons or pepper spray, so if she goes into her purse quick, watch out."

"I've done this before, remember?" Sinclair said.

"It never hurts to review officer safety. If we see and hear enough for the case, we'll come in on our own even if you don't signal. And don't forget that you're on video, too, so play along as is necessary for the operation, but don't do anything you don't want everyone in open court to see. We'll be in the room right across the hall."

When they left, Sinclair put a three-ring binder filled with financial reports and a legal pad next to the laptop and surfed the Internet until a waiter from Lungomare, an upscale Italian restaurant inside the Waterfront Hotel, brought his pizza. Sinclair read about car road tests as he ate the lamb meatball pizza. It had great flavors, but he would've been as happy with a sausage pizza from his regular joint for a third of the price.

He had finished half the pizza when his phone rang. "Our team in the lobby spotted her," said Roberts. "She's on the elevator now."

A moment later, there was a knock at the door, and Sinclair opened it. Danielle had long, blonde hair, probably dyed, green eyes, and a thin face decorated with heavy eye makeup. She was about five-foot-six once Sinclair subtracted her high heels, and she wore a tan raincoat that extended below her knees.

"I'm Danielle." Her teeth looked extra white next to her scarlet-red lips. "Are you Mr. Gutierrez?"

"Carlos," he said. "Please come in."

She closed the door behind her.

"Do you mind if we get the business out of the way first?" she asked.

"No problem."

"Can I see the credit card you used to make the appointment and your ID?"

Sinclair handed her his credit card and license. She studied his license and looked up at him, obviously matching the photo to his face. She reached into an outside pocket of the oversized handbag she carried over her shoulder, removed an iPhone, and compared his credit card number to something on the screen.

She typed a quick text with her thumbs, put her phone away, and smiled. "We're good. Do you mind if I hang up my coat?"

Before he could answer, she opened the closet, removed her coat, and placed it on a hanger alongside his raincoat. He knew she was studying his clothing in the closet. She wore a black halter dress that left most of her back bare. She turned to face him, and Sinclair couldn't keep his eyes from following the plunging neckline.

She smiled, knowing few men would be able to maintain eye contact with her in that dress. "Do you always wear your suit jacket in your hotel room?"

"I just put it on to answer the door." He laughed. "Now it seems a bit silly."

She giggled and stepped behind him. Fingertips with long red nails grasped his lapels and slid his suitcoat off his shoulders. "Just relax. We're here to have fun."

Sinclair flashed back to Dawn's autopsy. Her short nails and clear polish were a further indication she was no longer in the same line of work as Danielle. He turned to face Danielle and saw her eying the jacket's lining.

"Beautiful material," she said. "No label?"

"My tailor in Beverly Hills thinks it's tacky to put his name in another man's clothes."

She hung it in the closet and walked through the bedroom, looking over her shoulder to ensure he was following. "When I was given your name I was expecting someone different."

"Someone more Mexican?"

She chuckled. "Yeah, I guess so."

"My grandfather was born in Mexico, but that's the extent of my Hispanic blood." Although Sinclair was, in fact, a quarter Mexican, it was his maternal grandmother who had been born in Mexico. As a teenager, she crossed the border with her migrant farm-worker parents for seasonal work in California's Central Valley.

Danielle continued into the living room and looked out the window. "Nice room. Are you in town for business?"

"I have a few meetings tomorrow. Then I'm off to Seattle for another meeting the day after that."

"That's a busy schedule. What kind of work do you do?"

"I work for an employee benefits firm. We provide—"

"I think you're more than just a worker," she said, looking at the table containing the computer, assorted papers, and half-eaten pizza.

"I'm a VP for the company."

"That must be very stressful. How can I help you relax?" She took his hand and led him back into the bedroom. "Don't be shy. Tell me what you have in mind."

"Just regular sex," he said. "Maybe you on top."

"That sounds wonderful."

A successful case required her accepting money and agreeing to an act of sex. That was now covered. But to avoid a defense of entrapment, an overt act, such as her undressing or asking him to, was an added bonus.

She untied the halter around her neck and let her dress drop to the floor. Then she stepped out of her pumps, wearing nothing but lace panties. "Your turn," she said.

The door flew open and Cummings and Roberts burst into the room, followed by Braddock two steps behind.

Danielle screamed and grabbed her dress in an attempt to cover herself.

Roberts held his badge in his hand and said, "Police. Just relax." He took her dress, searched it quickly, and handed it back. "Get dressed."

"You," Cummings said to Sinclair, "come with me." Cummings grabbed Sinclair's arm with one hand, scooped up Danielle's purse with the other, and escorted him out of the room.

Chapter 15

The show for Danielle was over once they were in the hallway. Cummings released his grip on Sinclair's arm and opened the door to a room across the hall. The makeshift command post was smaller than the suite across the hall. Seated at a desk in front of two laptop computers, each with split screens showing different camera views of Sinclair's room, was Linda Archard, an FBI agent in her midforties with severely short brown hair and wearing a plain black suit and sensible shoes.

"Forty-six minutes," she said.

She toggled one computer to full screen, showing Danielle sitting at the table in the living room of the hotel suite with tears running down her face. Archard turned up the volume. Sinclair heard Braddock's and Roberts's voices. Although they weren't visible on the screen, he knew they were sitting at the table across from Danielle.

Sinclair followed the interview by Roberts and Braddock on the computer. They told Danielle they were with OPD and that she was under arrest for prostitution. Their questions collected her personal information: Danielle Rhodes, twenty-four years old, lived in San Francisco in a two-bedroom flat with a girlfriend, worked as an interior designer with an established firm in the city.

Meanwhile, back in the command post, Cummings found Danielle's ID in her purse, brought up a federal website on the other computer, and entered her personal information.

"Is there anything I can do to help?" asked Sinclair, watching over their shoulders.

They both ignored him. With a cell phone balanced between her neck and shoulder, Archard wrote on a legal pad: *No warrants, no arrest record CA or NCIC.* She slid the pad to Cummings, who was studying a screen filled with hundreds of numbers. He wrote a social security number on the pad followed by *Occupation Interior Decorator Associate. Last year gross $53,382. Deductions: interest on college loan, total outstanding $84,000. No other claimed income. Previous year gross $46,108.*

Sinclair turned his attention back to the interview on the other laptop where Roberts was still questioning Danielle.

Roberts asked, "How long have you been doing this?"

"This is my first time," Danielle said. "Really."

Fifteen minutes later, she finally admitted she had worked for the escort agency for six months, normally about two nights a week. Sometimes she did up to three calls a night, but most of the time, only one. She made 60 percent of the agency fee, which came out to $240 per call.

Danielle laid out the rest of the financials to Roberts. "If the customer wants a second hour, it's three hundred and I keep seventy percent. I also keep tips. Most clients tip fifty or so."

"How'd you get started?" Roberts asked.

"A friend I knew from a club in San Francisco introduced me to a recruiter for the escort service. I can't remember her name, but she interviewed me and got me set up."

"Who else have you met at the agency?" Roberts asked.

"No one other than some other escorts when we did parties or a client wanted a threesome."

"Twenty-three minutes," Archard said, snapping Sinclair's attention from the interview back to their room.

"I'm going in," Cummings said. "Roberts will never get her to roll in time."

"I should come with you." Archard looked at Cummings and started to rise from her chair.

"We'll stick with Braddock," Cummings said. "You remain here on the computers."

Archard bit her lip and turned her focus back to the monitor.

Sinclair felt useless. His job was already done. Cummings walked out of the command post with his laptop in his hand and a moment later appeared on the computer screen behind Danielle. After some whispering between Cummings and Roberts, Roberts got up from his chair and Cummings sat down.

"You apparently don't know how serious this is," Cummings said to Danielle. "With the video we have, you could be a porn star."

Cummings slid his laptop in front of Danielle and played back the recorded video showing the back-and-forth conversation that Sinclair and Danielle had just prior to her undressing.

Sinclair heard the door open behind him as Roberts entered the command post.

"You did a great job in there, Matt," Roberts said.

"Wasn't much to it," Sinclair said. "She wasted no time getting down to business."

Roberts pulled a chair alongside Sinclair and Archard and watched Cummings interview Danielle on the computer monitor. She was crying and near hysterics as Cummings told her she was going to jail for prostitution and that he doubted her employer, a respected interior design firm, would keep her on the payroll. He said the newspapers might print her name, which would surely ruin her professionally.

"What will your family think?" Cummings said. Without waiting for an answer, he continued, "Do you have a boyfriend? If so, you won't after this gets out."

She continued to cry. Sinclair saw Braddock's hand appear on the screen with several tissues. Danielle wiped her nose and eyes, leaving black smudges on her face. "What happened to Carlos?" Danielle asked. "Is he under arrest, too?"

"You need to worry about yourself, young lady," Cummings said.

"He's a nice guy with a good job," Danielle said. "Don't ruin him, too."

"Danielle, he's one of us," Braddock said. "He was just doing his job."

"No. He can't be a cop. He was too sweet."

"Fourteen minutes," Archard said.

"What's with the countdown?" Sinclair asked.

"When she got to your room and confirmed your ID, she sent a text to the agency," Roberts said. "She then has an hour to tell them she's out and okay. If she doesn't, the agency will try to contact her. If they can't, they send someone—normally a huge, bouncer kind of guy—to investigate."

"In other words, we have fourteen minutes to turn her," Sinclair said.

"Thirteen," Archard said.

"Any report from San Jose PD?" Roberts asked.

"They struck out," Archard said. "Their escort was an old pro and walked out. They don't know if she made their undercover or if something just didn't feel right to her."

"So it's up to us," Sinclair said. "Let me level with her."

"Absolutely not," Archard said. "Undercovers don't interview suspects. And we can't level with her. If she doesn't flip, she'll go back to the agency and spill everything."

"Cummings isn't going to get her to roll by acting like a hard-ass. Braddock and I can get her to cooperate."

"We'll do it our way," Archard said. "This is our case."

"The hell it is." Sinclair scooped up Danielle's purse and barged out the door. Roberts followed but didn't try to stop him. He entered the other room and made his way through the bedroom to the table in the living room.

"What are you doing here?" Cummings said. "Get out!"

"I'm taking over," Sinclair said.

"We have jurisdiction on this case."

"It's a local arrest," Sinclair said. "Danielle's our detainee. You don't even have a federal crime you can arrest her on."

Cummings's face turned red in anger. "You're making a huge mistake, Sinclair."

Sinclair looked at his watch. "Nine minutes," he said.

"Let him try," Roberts said to Cummings. "We have nothing to lose."

Cummings slammed his chair against the wall as he got up. He stormed around the table and stopped when his face was inches from Sinclair's. "If you so much as hint to her about an IRS investigation, I'll have your job," he whispered.

Sinclair met his stare but said nothing. He took a deep breath, moved the chair back to the table, and sat down. He smiled at Danielle. "I'm sorry I had to deceive you. My real name is Matt Sinclair, and I'm a detective with Oakland PD."

She sniffled and wiped her nose with a tissue. "I trusted you."

"I know. I'm sorry. You seem like a really nice girl. Someone I'd like to get to know if we met under different circumstances. I can only imagine how hard it is trying to live in the city on your salary—paying rent, paying off your school loans. I don't blame you for what you do."

"It was easy money. I could make more in one night than I made in a week at my regular job. No one gets hurt. I never did anything dangerous or degrading."

"I understand," Sinclair said. "Did you know Dawn Gustafson?"

"The girl killed in Oakland? I heard about it."

"She worked for the same escort agency as you do."

"I don't believe you."

Sinclair pulled Cummings's laptop in front of him, brought up Special Ladies Escorts website, and scrolled down until he came to Dawn's photo. He turned it around to face Danielle. "She was known as Blondie here, but her real name was Dawn."

"Oh my god!"

"I tried to get someone from your agency to talk to me about her, but no one would. I suspect it might've been one of her clients who killed her."

"Oh my god," Danielle said again.

"We know the owner is Helena Decker. The only way she'll open up her client files is if I force her to. I'm sorry for putting you in the middle, but we need to catch this killer. Not only for Dawn, but also to protect other women like you."

Danielle sat there mulling over her situation. A timer tone sounded from inside her handbag. Sinclair looked at his watch. The hour was up.

"But how can I help?"

"First you need to buy us some time to talk some more. What happens if you don't check in?"

"I need to text within a minute that I'm out or that the client wants another hour."

"Can you say I want another hour?"

"Cash or credit card?" she asked.

Sinclair removed his wallet and pulled out three hundred-dollar bills.

"One more," she said.

He handed her another hundred, fished her phone out of her purse, and handed it to her. He leaned over her shoulder and watched as she texted: *I'm fine. Carlos wants another hour. Just gave me 100 tip and 300 cash for 2nd hour.*

A moment later, the reply came: *OK. Check in again when you're out.*

Sinclair sat back in the chair, clasped his hands behind his neck, and stretched.

Danielle set her phone on the table. "If I help you, you won't arrest me?"

"No," Sinclair said. "All I'm after is the man who killed Dawn."

"And you're not going to let me keep this?" she said, fingering the money in front of her.

Sinclair laughed. "I'm afraid not."

Over the next half hour, Danielle told them how the escort service worked while she ate the remainder of Sinclair's pizza. She identified a photo of Helena Decker and said she was the woman who hired her. Since most clients paid by credit card, Helena would direct deposit her cut into her checking account every other week. If some paid cash, Helena would take her cut and let Danielle keep the rest. If Danielle got several cash-paying clients in a row, Helena would set up a meet, often for lunch, to collect the money. When they met in person, they'd talk about the work, and Helena would give her advice on how to keep her clients happy and how to keep herself safe.

"Does Helena mention specifically that she knows you're having sex in exchange for the money?" Braddock asked.

Danielle looked at her, puzzled. "Of course she knows."

"Yes, but does she say it, or do you say it and she acknowledges?" Braddock said.

Braddock was searching for the necessary legal elements for a pimping-and-pandering case against Helena, which required that Helena must receive money from someone knowing it came from an act of prostitution. Before the DA would charge a case, they needed to get the money transaction and acknowledgment on tape, which wasn't easy, since some pimps—or a madam in this case—were so careful, never discussing sex with their workers.

"Sure," Danielle said. "Helena is more of a mother figure, but she used to be a call girl herself, so she loves talking about what the men like and what I do with them." She looked at Sinclair and pouted. "Sorry, I don't mean to embarrass you."

"He can handle it," Braddock said. "What would it take for you to set up a meeting with Helena?"

"She'd meet if I had a real problem with a client."

"That could make her suspicious," Braddock said. "I mean if you were to tell her that Carlos got rough with you or something."

"She'd want to meet if I collected a lot of cash."

"What's a lot?" Braddock asked.

"A few months back, a client paid for an overnight in cash. The next day, Helena said she wanted to meet for lunch. Guess she thought I'd spend the money."

"How much did you have?"

"The way it works is it's three hundred for extra hours, but we can agree to two thousand total for eight hours if we're just sleeping with the client for most of that. So I had two grand, not including a tip he gave me."

"Did you have to give all of it to Helena?"

"Yeah, but she just wanted to see it. Then she gave me my cut, twelve hundred."

"If you tell her Carlos wants to do an overnight with you, will she want to meet tomorrow?"

"Maybe the next day."

"Could you insist on tomorrow?" Braddock asked.

"It might sound weird."

"Does a client ever ask a girl to go away for a weekend?" Sinclair asked.

"Other girls have done weekends."

"Would that get Helena to meet with you sooner?" Sinclair asked.

"Bet it would. She'd probably want the client to pay something up front, and if he paid in cash, she probably wouldn't want me walking around with it."

Braddock stayed with Danielle while Sinclair, Roberts, and Cummings returned to the command post across the hall. Archard began downloading Danielle's phone data into her computer.

She spoke to Cummings as if Roberts and Sinclair weren't even present. "We can have Danielle send a text that says Carlos wants an overnight and already gave her two thousand in cash. In the morning, we can have her text that Carlos wants her to spend the weekend with him in Las Vegas."

Cummings said, "That should get a response from them."

"Are we going to let her go tonight?" Sinclair asked.

Archard ignored him and said, "As I suspected, the Find Your Phone app is installed on the girl's phone. I'm sure the agency set it up so they can track her."

"I wouldn't have trusted her anyway," said Cummings. "We'll let the girl sleep in Sinclair's suite tonight. With the other two agents outside, we'll have four of us to take shifts watching her. Meanwhile, we'll reserve a suite at a Las Vegas resort in Carlos's name for the weekend and get everything else set up."

"What do you want me and Braddock to do?" Sinclair asked.

"Go home," Cummings said. "It's good that the girl likes you, but with you around, it'll be harder to control her."

Sinclair was about to object, but he'd worked enough informants to know Cummings was right. "I want to be there when she meets Helena. And I get first crack at interviewing her."

Before Cummings could object, Roberts said, "It's only fair. Sinclair turned her, and besides, his murder case is the priority."

"Okay," said Cummings. "But *we* run the operation, and you take orders from us. Go home and get some sleep. We'll meet here at eight in the morning."

Chapter 16

An hour before sunrise, Sinclair jogged down Hampton Road in a light drizzle. It was only two blocks from his house but far enough to get his body warmed up and awake. He spotted a Mazda Miata at the entrance to Crocker Park. Next to the little red sports car, a woman dressed in turquois leggings and a yellow windbreaker was stretching her hamstrings. He slowed to a walk. "Didn't know if you'd come out in the rain."

Alyssa smiled. "A little bit of rain won't stop me from working out."

Sinclair had called the ER yesterday after Braddock wouldn't give him Alyssa's number. The nurse who answered said it was against policy to give out coworkers' phone numbers, but she'd contact Alyssa and pass on his number. Alyssa texted him last night, and after a few rounds of *hi, how are you?*, he invited her to meet him for a morning run at 6:15. When she replied, *OK, where?*, he was excited, yet apprehensive. He knew Alyssa was the real deal, and he didn't want to screw it up with her as he had with so many other women in his past. "All stretched?" he asked.

"Let's start off slow until I get warmed up."

Sinclair trotted down the road with Alyssa at his side. "How far you want to go?"

"I should be back here by seven so I can get home and showered before work."

"I have a nice five-mile loop I think you'll like," he said.

A few minutes later, they passed Piedmont High School, and he sped up to an eight-minute mile pace. "Cathy says you're a marathoner?"

"I ran the San Francisco marathon the last three years, but I don't consider myself a marathoner," she said. "Every year, when it's over, I wonder why I put my body through that kind of abuse and for the next ten months I only run four or five miles a few days a week. Then I get the bug and start training again for the next one."

They turned onto Oakland Avenue, a main thoroughfare in the sleepy little town of Piedmont. The vehicle traffic picked up, so they moved off the street. He fell in behind her on the narrow sidewalk, enjoying the view of her skin-tight leggings and ponytail swinging back and forth in cadence with her stride.

"Cathy told me all about your marriage and the divorce," she said over her shoulder. "I never figured you as the marrying type back then."

"I was getting ready to turn thirty," he said. "Jill was smart, well respected in the DA's office, and had her life together. I guess I figured it was time for me to get married, and marrying her would help me grow up."

They reached the top of Oakland Avenue and turned onto a quiet residential street where they could once again run in the roadway. She dropped back to his side. "Interesting how we both married looking for stability," she said. "Your wife wasn't able to change you, and my husband wanted me to change too much."

She didn't even seem winded. "I've learned a few things since I've been sober," Sinclair said, trying to control his breathing so Alyssa couldn't tell he was sucking wind. "People like me seldom change until the pain resulting from the old behavior gets too great to handle."

"I know you're talking about your drinking. I know other alcoholics and understand about hitting your bottom, but I think people change all the time when they see positive outcomes resulting through change."

"You mean I don't need to be hit across the head with a two-by-four?"

"You don't fool me, Matt. Cathy talks about how much you've changed since you two have been partners. The core you—those things that make you special—are beginning to shine through that rough exterior of yours."

"She's been pretty tolerant of my rough exterior."

"Good friends are," she said.

They finished their run in silence. Every minute or so, she looked over at him and smiled, and Sinclair felt comfortable alongside her without feeling the need to say anything.

★

Sinclair parked his unmarked car two blocks away from Perry's in the San Francisco Design Center. Cummings and Roberts had briefed him and Braddock at the Waterfront Hotel an hour and a half ago that Special Ladies Escorts agreed to Carlos paying four thousand dollars, half up front, plus a round-trip ticket for Danielle to join him in Las Vegas for the weekend. The Feds bought Danielle's ticket on Carlos's credit card, e-mailed the confirmation to Danielle through Carlos's e-mail account, and Danielle forwarded it to the agency. Within a few minutes, Danielle received a text from Helena's phone, asking her to meet at Perry's with the cash.

Sinclair and Braddock walked to a nondescript white van parked on Rhode Island Street at the rear entrance of the three-building complex that housed more than a hundred showrooms. They slid open the door and climbed into the tight quarters. Cummings, Roberts, and a plainclothes SFPD officer were sitting in front of a narrow built-in table that ran the length of the van's cargo compartment. Two police radios squawked simultaneously. One was the SFPD channel for the geographical district they were in, and the other sounded like an FBI surveillance net.

Roberts introduced Sinclair and Braddock to the SFPD officer and said to Cummings, "It's twenty-five after, should we send Danielle in?"

Cummings keyed the radio mic. "Let's send the CI in," he said, using the slang for confidential informant, even though it didn't exactly fit Danielle's status.

A voice that Sinclair recognized as Archard's acknowledged over the radio.

Two minutes later, an agent with the FBI surveillance team that was set up inside the building's atrium whispered over the radio, "CI is at the breakfast bar, getting coffee. Subject still not in sight."

Cummings turned on another radio. Rustling sounds and distant voices, normal for concealed body microphones, came over the speaker.

The surveillance channel crackled. "Woman about sixty with platinum hair entering via front entrance. Appears to be our subject. Carrying an umbrella and a Starbuck's cup. Approaching the CI."

Sinclair heard Danielle's voice over the body wire. "Hi, Helena."

"Danielle, sweetheart, you look lovely," the other voice, which had to be Helena, said. "Did you get any sleep last night?"

Danielle laughed. "Not much."

"Let's get the business out of the way," Helena said.

"This is all of it," Danielle said. "The money for last night and the advance for the weekend."

"The CI handed the subject an envelope," a voice said over the surveillance channel. "Subject placing it into a handbag on her lap. Looking down, probably counting it. Handing an envelope back to the CI."

"Twenty-four hundred," said Helena. "Did you ever dream you'd make this much for doing what most women do for free?"

"Last night was easy money," Danielle said. "But he wanted a morning fuck and it took him forever to come."

Sinclair gave a thumbs-up to Braddock. Danielle was a natural at this. Her mentioning that she had sex with the client, as long as it wasn't followed by an admonishment by Helena, would play well with a jury.

Danielle continued, "I'm a bit nervous about the weekend."

"Nothing to be nervous about, honey," Helena said. "Did you ever go away with a boyfriend?"

"Sure," Danielle said. "A weekend in Napa and Carmel. Once I went to Cabo for a week with an old boyfriend."

"It's the same thing, except Mr. Gutierrez is paying you for your time."

"But when a man's paying me, I feel like I'm required to do . . . well, you know."

"When that boyfriend took you to Napa, did he pay for the weekend?" Helena asked.

"Yes."

"Did you feel obligated to make him happy?"

"I guess."

"Spending a weekend with a client is like that," Helena said. "A normal call is about the sex. An overnight is about the sex as well as companionship. A weekend will be primarily about companionship."

"You think?"

Helena chuckled. "Oh, honey, there's going to be some physical requirements, but no man can fuck continuously for three days. Think of him as a very generous boyfriend whose generosity you want to reward."

"So I should do whatever he wants."

"Sweetheart, you never have to do anything you don't feel comfortable with. I'm sure you'll be going out to dinner and probably lounging around the pool drinking cocktails. He might be a golfer and send you off to the spa. Suck his dick or fuck him once or twice a day. That's all it takes to keep a man happy. The rest of the time, just enjoy yourself."

"We've got enough." Cummings slammed open the van door and jumped out.

Sinclair followed Cummings as he jogged into the building. Roberts and Braddock brought up the rear. They entered an atrium filled with dozens of tables covered with blue-and-white checkered tablecloths. Archard was converging on Danielle and Helena from their right.

Cummings changed his gait to a brisk walk and flashed his badge when he was ten feet from the table. "Federal agent. Ladies, put your hands on the table where I can see them."

Helena reached into her purse. Sinclair grabbed her wrist and slowly pulled her hand out. She was holding a cell phone. Braddock stepped forward and removed it from Helena's hand.

"Are we under arrest?" Helena asked.

"Yes," Cummings said. He then faced Danielle. "Come with us, young lady." He grabbed Danielle's right arm, while Archard lightly took her left and led her toward the back exit.

Helena began to rise. Sinclair pushed her back down.

"What am I under arrest for?"

Roberts's cell phone rang, and he stepped away to answer it. Braddock took Helena's purse away from her.

"We'll talk about it downtown," Sinclair said.

"I demand I be allowed to call my lawyer," Helena said.

"Downtown," Sinclair replied.

Chapter 17

A few minutes after noon, Sinclair and Braddock entered room 201, an interview room at the back of the homicide office. Six by eight feet, the room contained a small metal table and three straight back chairs. Helena Decker stood when they entered. According to the information Sinclair had been able to gather on her, she was fifty-eight years old, five-foot-ten, and weighed 160 pounds. She had a residence address in Sausalito, a picturesque town in Marin County just on the other side of the Golden Gate Bridge. DMV records showed she owned a brand-new Mercedes and a year-old Range Rover. Her only entry in the state criminal history system was for a prostitution arrest in San Francisco thirty years ago.

"When can I make my phone call?" Helena said.

"Soon," Sinclair said. "Let's sit and talk." Sinclair and Braddock sat at opposite ends of the table and had Helena sit between them.

"I know my rights, and I have the right to call my attorney."

"You have the right to make two phone calls when you're booked," Sinclair said. "It can take up to twelve hours for that to happen."

"What are you arresting me for?"

"Sections two-sixty-six-H and I, pimping and—"

"I know what they are," she said. "Danielle's a snitch, huh?"

"I'm not interested in talking about what you did," Sinclair said. "I'm not reading you your rights. I don't even want to arrest you."

"Then open the door and let me go."

"We called your agency two days ago and tried to get you to talk to us, but no one called us back."

Helena crossed her arms across her chest. "I will not acknowledge that any so-called agency is mine."

Sinclair slid a photo of Dawn from his portfolio and placed it in front of Helena. "She worked for your escort service. She was murdered. I want to know who she saw."

Helena looked up in the corner of the room. "Is that camera on?"

"Yeah, it's always on." The department had recently installed video cameras in every interview room and established a policy requiring the recording of all interviews with suspects and witnesses.

"Lawyer," she said.

"I don't want to book you and see you prosecuted for this," Sinclair said.

"Then don't."

"One of Dawn's clients might be the killer. Do you want him to get away with it? Maybe kill another girl?"

"You don't get it. If I were connected to an escort service, which I'm not saying I am, to disclose clients' identities would be the ultimate sin."

"I guess I have to book you and see if sitting in a jail cell changes your mind."

"Let me call my lawyer. Playing *Let's Make a Deal* is part of her job description."

Sinclair and Braddock left Helena alone in the room and returned to their desks. Sinclair called Roberts, who said he was with a team of FBI and IRS agents at the escort service's office and call center in a San Mateo business park, just south of San Francisco. Roberts told him that the Feds had had a major task force poised for action. When Helena uttered the necessary words, Cummings passed it on to agents waiting in the federal building. They added a few lines to a search warrant affidavit. Twenty minutes later, two agents and an assistant U.S. attorney were sitting in a federal judge's chambers. Once he signed the warrant, different teams hit various locations throughout the Bay Area, including the call center and Helena's house. They also sent priority messages to a dozen financial institutions, ordering them to freeze accounts connected to Helena and the escort service.

"That's a lot of resources for the Feds to throw at one woman for tax evasion," Sinclair said. "What aren't you telling me?"

"I'm telling you what I can," Roberts said.

"They're just using me and my murder case, aren't they?"

"I'd like to think of it as a cooperative effort," Roberts said. "We didn't have anywhere near the people and money at OPD to do what they accomplished."

"How'd they turn a prostitution and pimping case into a federal crime?"

"Danielle gave Helena payment for her to travel over state lines to engage in prostitution."

Sinclair didn't know whether to feel angry at how his old partner and the Feds used him or applaud them for their ingenuity, but knowing the Feds had a different agenda worried him.

He explained his stalemate with Helena and asked, "Have you and your Fed friends found any client files that are cross-referenced by escort name?"

"Everything's computerized," Roberts said. "Not a piece of paper in the whole place. When we tried to question the workers, all they would say was 'lawyer.' The FBI's computer forensics people shut down the system and cut Internet connections so no one can remotely delete the data. They'll send the computers back to the FBI lab. Their first step will be to clone the hard drives. Then they'll analyze the data from the copied drives to protect the integrity of the original computers."

"How long will it take for me to get the data on Dawn's clients?"

"The Feds move slow," Roberts said. "Even if they overnight the evidence back east, I doubt they'll start work on it until after the weekend. That is if there's not a backlog or other priority cases."

"Can they make us a copy of the hard drives so we can look at it ourselves?"

"I'll ask," Roberts said.

"What should I do with Helena?"

"Up to you. The Feds won't want to talk to her until they make their case. That will be months, and I'm sure that process will begin with the AUSA who's assigned to the task force talking with her lawyers," Roberts said, referring to the assistant US attorney. "That *transporting women across state lines for the purposes of prostitution* charge is just a placeholder. They'll be focusing on the income tax evasion, RICO, and public corruption angles."

"Public corruption?" Sinclair asked, surprised.

Roberts was quiet for a few counts, and Sinclair could tell he had revealed something he shouldn't have and was formulating a way to backtrack.

"You have to assume some politicians or government officials will show up on the client list," Roberts said.

Sinclair felt like kicking himself for being so naïve. The Feds were after the client list, a gold mine of influential people involved in an assortment of criminal activity much more serious than prostitution. But he couldn't dwell on that now. "So, if she'll deal, you have no problem with me dropping the pimping charges?"

"I'd use it as leverage and keep it hanging as long as you can. In the long run, the DA would probably defer to the Feds and be glad to dump it."

After Sinclair ended the call with Roberts, he and Braddock moved Helena to the soft interview room, a windowed office next to the lieutenant's office. In addition to the metal table and three chairs as in the other interview rooms, the soft interview room also had a sofa, an end table, and a working telephone. "Call your attorney," Sinclair said. "If we can work something out, I'll release you pending further investigation."

Helena looked around the room. "No cameras in here? Is the phone tapped?"

"If I recorded a conversation between you and your attorney, I'd go to prison."

They left Helena alone in the room. Five minutes later, she tapped at the window and Sinclair stuck his head through the doorway. Helena placed her hand over the mouthpiece of the phone. "My attorney wants to know if she comes down here, that there's some place she and I can talk?"

Out of the thousands of people Sinclair had arrested over the years, he could count on one hand the number of suspects he allowed to talk with an attorney before booking. It was a waste of time, because lawyers never allowed their clients to make a statement to the police except in the rare occasions when they were clearly innocent of all charges and the attorney could convince the investigator of that fact. If lawyers wanted to talk to someone Sinclair had arrested, they could visit the suspect in the jail.

"Why should I waste my time setting up your little conference," Sinclair said, "just so your lawyer can tell you to retain your right to remain silent?"

"Because she knows I don't want to sit in jail and we have to give you something to prevent that from happening."

"Tell her yes."

Helena brought the receiver to her mouth. "He says okay. Yes, the homicide office." She hung up and looked at Sinclair. "She'll be here within the hour."

Braddock escorted Helena back to room 201, while he went to the snack bar in the basement of the PAB and got sandwiches for Braddock, Helena, and himself.

Sinclair took his smoked turkey sandwich into the lieuten-ant's office and brought him up to date on the events of the last twenty-four hours.

When Sinclair finished, Lieutenant Maloney said, "Any idea how many client names are on that computer?"

"If the IRS is right about the business netting five million a year, there could be a thousand, maybe lots more depending on how far back the records go."

Maloney picked up his phone and punched in four numbers. "Marlene, I need to see the chief . . . Now . . . I'll be there."

"What's the big deal?" Sinclair said.

"Back in the early nineties, OPD vice did an escort service operation in conjunction with San Jose and SFPD. We col-lected two file cabinets full of records and created a list of all the escorts and customers. Each department got a copy, sup-posedly so they could call whoever was necessary as witnesses to prosecute the operators of the business in the three different jurisdictions. The lists included politicians, prominent athletes, influential executives, even judges. Soon, each DA's office had a list. Copies went to the FBI and state DOJ. Before you knew it, dozens of the customer lists existed, lawyers were filing motions to get certain people's names redacted, and every news outlet was filing Freedom of Information requests for copies of the list. It was a nightmare, with allegations of favoritism and claims of blackmail by police and prosecutors."

Sinclair had heard rumors of the list when he worked vice-narcotics. One of the old-timers bragged that he had a copy, but Sinclair had figured it was just another legend that had evolved over the years. "I'm just looking to identify a killer," Sinclair said. "I don't intend to embarrass anyone."

"Yeah, but it's like commercial fishing with gill nets," Malo-ney said. "You might be trying to catch salmon, but the nets snag all kinds of other fish at the same time."

Chapter 18

Sinclair had finished typing page two of what he knew would end up being a five- or six-page crime report detailing the arrests of Danielle Rhodes and Helena Decker when Braddock interrupted him. "Helena's finished talking with her lawyer, and I put her back in two-oh-one. The lawyer would like to talk with us alone."

Sinclair followed Braddock into the soft interview room. A fortyish white woman with jet-black, shoulder-length hair wearing an expensive dark-gray suit with a knee-length skirt thrust out her hand when they entered. "Sergeant Sinclair, my name is Bianca Fadell."

He detected a hint of a British accent in her voice. Her hand was slight, almost bony, but rendered a firm handshake. She offered a business card on thick paper with elegant, raised letters. Sinclair began, "Ms. Fadell—"

She cut him off. "Please call me Bianca." She smiled, showing teeth that only professional bleaching could get so white. She resumed her seat at the table. Braddock and Sinclair pulled out chairs and sat across from her.

Sinclair asked, "Is Ms. Decker willing to cooperate?"

"She is. I understand you want a list of Dawn Gustafson's clients. I can get that for you if the District Attorney will provide a signed letter declining to prosecute my client."

"That's not the way it works here," Sinclair said. "The DA's office only files charges on cases the police bring to them. If I don't bring them the case, they don't even know about it."

"I can guarantee the DA knows about this case already." Bianca brushed her hair behind her ear, revealing a diamond stud of well over a carat and a heavy gold hoop dangling below it. "I'm sure that you have enormous sway with the DA's office on most investigations; however, I suspect the determination as to how this matter will be adjudicated will be made at their highest level and may have little to do with what's best for your homicide investigation."

"Then why are you even talking with me?" Sinclair asked.

She leaned forward and made eye contact with Sinclair. "You control whether my client goes to jail or goes home today. In addition, certain parties actually desire justice for Dawn's murder, even if those responsible should turn out to be a client of the agency."

Sinclair leaned back in his chair. "Before the DA would sign this immunity letter you're requesting, he'd want to see the full investigation and view all the evidence. That would take weeks, maybe months. The DA doesn't do that lightly. Do you expect me to let your client walk out of here with only her promise of cooperation and wait until the DA grants her immunity? I might as well just wait for the analysis of her computer files."

"I already know the FBI and IRS have the computers," Bianca said. "You may not fully realize what you have gotten yourself involved in. I doubt the U.S. Attorney will allow you full access to the data on those computers."

"You seem like a very capable attorney," Sinclair said. "But I don't play lawyer games. You'll need to do that with your counterparts at the DA and U.S. Attorney's Office. If I don't get something from your client now, I'll book her, type up my report, and see the charging DA tomorrow."

Bianca's dark eyes bounced between Braddock and Sinclair and finally focused on Sinclair. "You have a reputation as an honorable man—someone whose word is his bond. What I'm about to tell you does not necessarily come from my client. She may or may not have any association with the escort services; however, if you release her, I will be able to gain access to the computer data you're looking for."

"How's that going to happen? We both know the Feds have the computers."

"Don't you think that a company would have off-site back-up of their computer files?"

Sinclair had to admit he hadn't thought of that, but of course, it made sense. "And Helena would give me access to the files?"

"I won't reveal privileged client information, but as I said, I will be in a position to get you some information about the clients of the escort service. In the meantime, would you be interested in knowing that Dawn had stopped working for the agency a year ago?"

"Really?" Sinclair said. "If that's true, what good will old client information do me?"

"Maybe none," Bianca said. "But would you be interested in knowing that Dawn first worked as an escort eight years ago and took a sabbatical when one of her clients fell in love with her about five years ago? Would it interest you that a few years later, she approached the agency and asked to return to work because, according to her, she needed the money to provide a future for a baby she had given birth to? Would you be interested in knowing that she saw more than a hundred different clients during her association with the agency, but toward the end, she only saw a dozen or so regulars, and quite possibly remained in contact with them even after she left the business?"

This fit with what they already knew about Dawn and answered some of the questions that had nagged Sinclair. The existence of the apartment on Athol Avenue and the fact that Dawn wasn't living there made more sense.

"Can you get me the names of these regulars and the father of her baby?" Sinclair asked.

"I believe that's possible, but my client will need to be free to orchestrate it."

Sinclair and Braddock stepped out of the room and conferred. He hated releasing someone from custody on just a promise to provide information—you ended up getting burned more often than not. But Braddock pointed out that they had little to lose by releasing Helena. Neither of them cared about a pimping case. Besides, the Feds could slam Helena much harder than the state courts. It was ironic that they had a better chance of getting the information they needed from a suspect and her defense attorney than from fellow law enforcement officers.

Sinclair and Braddock returned to the interview room. He said, "I'll release her, but she has to understand the release is only pending further investigation. If she doesn't come through, I walk the case to the DA, get a warrant, and have a team of blue suits drag her off to jail."

Bianca held out her hand. "Deal."

Sinclair put out his hand. Bianca took it in both of hers and gazed into his eyes. "I appreciate your trust. I can tell that what both Dawn and Danielle said about you is true. You'll be hearing from me soon."

After Bianca and Helena left the homicide office, Sinclair and Braddock returned to their desks. "Whew!" Braddock said. "With all the sexual energy Bianca was putting off, I felt like a voyeur just being in the same room."

Sinclair laughed. "She was just flirting. I'm sure she's accustomed to using her wily womanly ways to get what she wants from men."

"I'm glad you're too strong to be influenced by it," Braddock said. "But that was no act. That lady is seriously hot and she wants you in a big way."

The lieutenant looked up from the papers scattered across his desk when Sinclair entered his office. Sinclair advised him of their decision to release Helena in exchange for her cooperation and asked, "What happened with the chief?"

"Everything's okay," Maloney said. "Sergeant Roberts had been keeping him abreast of everything. It seemed I was the only one not in the loop."

"Sorry, boss. I didn't think it was a big deal."

"It wasn't crime-wise, but politically is a different story. The chief wants to be informed of the names of any clients you discover."

Sinclair agreed, but was worried that if the escort service clients were politically connected, the chief would be tempted to run interference to protect them. It was beginning to sound like politics might trump his murder investigation.

"The chief also said you're to see Mr. Normart at the DA's office for charging or any legal advice on this case," Maloney said.

Normart was the chief assistant district attorney, the number two person in the DA's office. Seeing him to get a mere pimping case charged was completely out of the ordinary. The only time Sinclair even went to the main courthouse, the old, grand building on the east side of downtown, was when one of his murder cases was in trial. OPD investigators did most of their business at the Oakland branch office, which was right across the street from the PAB.

"He's referring to the escort service case, right?" Sinclair asked.

"The homicide, too, since it's connected."

"Doesn't that strike you as pretty fuckin' weird, lieutenant?"

Maloney leaned into his desk. "It makes sense if they want to control what could be a politically charged trial and coordinate jurisdiction with the Feds."

"Well, there's nothing for me to see Normart about because I don't want to charge Helena Decker with anything."

"You might want to give him a call and tell him that."

"When the hell did we start conferring with the DA before we're ready to charge the case? I thought the police investigate and lawyers prosecute. There's no one to prosecute until I solve the case."

"I don't need a lesson about roles and responsibilities in the criminal justice system from a sergeant," Maloney said. "I'm just trying to keep everybody happy."

"I'm just trying to solve a murder and could care less about everybody's happiness." Once he said it, Sinclair regretted the way it came out. Lieutenant Maloney was one of the few people he did care about keeping happy, not only because it made his life easier, but also because Maloney was a good guy who had put his career on the line more than once to protect his investigators and the integrity of their cases.

"Fine," Sinclair said, backtracking. "I'll call him." Maloney picked up his phone, signaling the conversation was over.

When Sinclair got back to his desk, Braddock was online. "Ms. Fadell, or Bianca to you, is an interesting lady," she said. "Born in London to Syrian and Persian parents, she got her undergrad in poli sci from Princeton and graduated from Yale Law School eighteen years ago, which would make her at least forty-three. The girl looks damn good for that age. There's an article from the society page of the *Chronicle* a few years back saying that after she ended an eight-year marriage, she became romantically involved with Brett Green."

"The financier who made a run for mayor in San Francisco?" Sinclair asked.

"That's the guy. She was listed in the twenty most eligible bachelorettes in San Francisco last year and the hundred most influential women in the Bay Area. Here's a photo of her with some state senator at a fundraiser for the United Way, which she's on the Bay Area board of."

Sinclair looked at the photo on Braddock's monitor of a fiftyish man in a tux next to Bianca, dressed in a black gown with a plunging neckline that extended to her navel.

"Anything about her legal work?"

"She's been with Carter, Peterson, and Shapiro for ten years, and a partner for the last eight. It's one of the top firms in the city. They do everything. She's listed as specializing in international business and global human rights."

"Global human rights," said Sinclair. "That sounds ominous."

"Actually, it's huge. Wealthy people pump big money into international nonprofits that work to improve women's lives in third world countries. Bianca's page on the law firm's website lists some she's associated with."

"So her law firm makes big bucks supporting these liberal causes."

"That's not the politically correct way of looking at it, but she must do more than merely earn her keep doing it or else she wouldn't have made partner. She's listed as legal counsel for EHT, that's Ending Human Trafficking, an international nonprofit headquartered in San Francisco, and some other organizations."

"So she works for outfits that are against sex trafficking of women and defends a woman who, many would say, exploits them."

"Lawyers say everyone is entitled to a good defense," Braddock replied.

Sinclair went back to typing his report. At four o'clock, the other homicide investigators left for the day. But Sinclair had a mile-long task list on Dawn's case. At the top of the list—the task most likely to produce results with the least expenditure of time—was to look into her former clients. But to do that meant waiting for Bianca to come through, which probably wouldn't occur until tomorrow afternoon. Waiting wasn't something he did well, but the alternative often meant spinning his wheels on tangents that weren't likely to pan out. He returned to the report he was writing. At least he'd get that out of the way in case a new lead materialized tomorrow while he waited for the call from Bianca.

Chapter 19

The following morning, Sinclair carried his empty coffee mug to the intelligence unit, set it on Robert's desk, and sat on his sofa. Roberts took his cup into the outer office, returned, and handed Sinclair a full cup of coffee and then settled in behind his desk. They glared at each other for a few moments in silence.

Finally, Sinclair spoke. "We used to be partners. I feel like one of our street whores, the way you've used me."

Roberts took a drink from his cup. "This is bigger than your murder."

"If you told me that two days ago, I doubt I would've gotten involved in this."

"You were looking for an inroad into the escort service," Roberts said. "This was it."

"We used to be honest with each other. I sense there's a whole lot you're still not telling me."

"My job's different now," Roberts said. "There's a whole lot I can't tell many people."

"Will I ever get a list of the escorts and their clients?"

Roberts looked at him for several beats. "I don't know."

Sinclair couldn't tell if Roberts really didn't know or that was his way of saying no. "What unit do those FBI agents work in? They aren't out of the Oakland office."

"What makes you think that?"

"I reached out to my friends over there," Sinclair said. "They knew nothing of the op."

"Are you referring to Archard?"

"Her and the two who were in the hotel bar and later lurking around the design center."

"She's assigned to organized crime out of the San Francisco office."

"The other two?"

Roberts said nothing.

Sinclair drank some coffee. "You can tell by looking at them they're not field agents. They were too clean, too bookish to put handcuffs on an actual bad guy."

Roberts said nothing.

Sinclair continued, "I wrote a crime report covering the prostitution solicitation by Danielle Rhodes and the pimping exchange by Helena Decker. I listed Cummings, Archard, and you as witnesses. Under normal circumstances, you each would have to provide a supplemental report."

"You know we in Intel don't like to be listed as witnesses."

"You know we in homicide don't like to be punked out."

"You wouldn't have Decker if it wasn't for the FBI and IRS," Roberts said.

"You didn't level with me from the beginning. In our world, nothing's more important than a homicide, but you guys are withholding evidence that I need to solve it."

"Have you turned in the report?"

"I'm still holding it," Sinclair said. "I don't need to turn it in until I see the DA to get Decker charged."

"Is that your plan?"

"Why should I tell you my plan when you won't share yours with me?"

"Because if I know your plan, I might be able to help."

"Ya know, Phil, all the dealings I had with Intel in years past were just like this. We peon cops pass on everything we know to Intel. They listen, sometimes say, 'Oh, yeah, we knew that,' and then write it down and stick it in a file. The only time they ever passed on anything to us is when they throw us little tidbits because they need something. I thought it would be different when you came up here."

"Sorry, Matt. It's the nature of the job."

"Yeah, well, I'll get my info from Decker and her lawyer. At least they deal with me honestly and openly."

"You should be cautious dealing with them. They might not be what they appear. And I'd appreciate you passing on anything Decker tells you."

"I'm sure you would," Sinclair said as he got up and walked out the door.

Sinclair stopped at the crime lab to see if they had any results from the crime scene or Dawn's apartment. The firearms examiner had determined the bullet recovered from the victim's head was a nominal .38 caliber projectile, which included .38, 9mm, .380, and .357. Based on the weight of the jacketed hollow point slug, 87.6 grains, they surmised it was most likely a .380. The bullet displayed rifling characteristics of five lands and grooves with a right twist. A list of firearms with those characteristics included Llama, Kel-Tec, Walther, and Smith and Wesson. The lab entered it into IBIS, the Integrated Ballistics Identification System, but got no hits. That only meant the gun that fired the round had not been recovered in a crime by any police agency that enters their crime guns into IBIS, or no identifiable bullets from the gun had been recovered at a scene. In other words, the bullet dug out of Dawn's brain was a dead end.

The fingerprint unit examined nearly a hundred latents that had been lifted from Dawn's apartment. Eighteen were identifiable; the others were either partials or too smudged to identify. Twelve of the identifiable prints were eliminated as belonging to Dawn. That left six, which could have come from different people or could have been from different fingers of the same person. They entered them into their computer, which searched prints at the county level, then the state level, and if neither hit, then on to IAFIS, the Integrated Automated Fingerprint Identification System maintained by the FBI. There were no matches, which meant the prints didn't belong to anyone with an arrest record. A friend of Dawn's or even a technician who fixed a broken refrigerator last month could have left them. Another dead end, unless Sinclair identified a suspect to match them to.

No one from the DNA unit had yet looked at the clippings of Dawn's nails for DNA, but Sinclair never held his breath waiting for DNA results, knowing the backlog of DNA cases in Oakland.

Everyone in the homicide office was busy when Sinclair made his way back to his desk. Investigators were talking on the phone or working on their computers. Both interview room doors were closed, indicating witnesses or suspects were in there awaiting their opportunity to reveal details about a murder other than Sinclair's. Everyone seemed to have leads to work on their cases except him. Braddock had a case packet from another one of her open murders on her desk. Even she was working on something other than Dawn's murder.

Sinclair spent the rest of the day typing up search warrants and affidavits for Dawn's phone and e-mail accounts. The longer he sat at his desk, the more irritated he became, not only because he hated clerical work, but also because it meant there were no active leads that could justify putting these mundane tasks on the back burner.

At five o'clock, he shut down his computer and headed out the door, figuring he should join the commute traffic to Lafayette and hit one of his old AA meetings. That was always a good place to dump a load of irritability.

Chapter 20

Friday morning, Sinclair was in Dr. Elliott's office, listening to the tones in his earphones ricochet from one ear to the other. He had called her office at 4:00 AM after he woke drenched in sweat from a nightmare that left his heart racing for the next hour. Although he wasn't expecting her to call until normal business hours, she called a little after six and told him to come right in.

He was back in Baghdad, a special agent with the Army CID detachment assigned to a trial program that would handle deadly attacks on U.S. soldiers as criminal offenses rather than acts of war. Sinclair and his partner had identified the Shi'ite bomb maker who provided the IED that took out part of a U.S. convoy the previous week, and someone a zillion levels above Sinclair decided they should arrest the insurgent and turn him over to the newly formed Iraqi justice system for prosecution. The operations officer for the MP battalion that was assigned the tactical side of the mission detailed a squad of ten MPs to accompany the two CID agents. Sinclair argued a reinforced platoon was necessary, but the captain said their mission analysis determined a squad was adequate. Sinclair was a soldier, and soldiers obeyed orders.

"You're driving out of the U.S. compound in your Humvee," Jeanne said. "What's happening now?"

"It's hot, over a hundred. We're sweltering with all our gear on, but Iraqi citizens are out, going about their normal business. We're headed into a Shi'ite neighborhood, lots of narrow streets.

That's why we're in the Humvees." *When Sinclair had been told by the MP captain that the MPs' larger, more heavily armed M1117 Armored Security Vehicles couldn't get into the neighborhood, his gut twisted again.*

"What are you feeling?" Jeanne asked.

"Tightness in my stomach. This doesn't feel right."

"What doesn't feel right?"

"Not enough soldiers. Four Humvees, only two with crew-served weapons. An M-two-forty, and a Mark-Nineteen," Sinclair said, referring to the light machinegun and automatic grenade launcher mounted on two Humvees. "The MPs think it'll be a cakewalk."

"Do you continue?" she asked.

"I'm a soldier. It's only two clicks out. Hell, I can run two kilometers. The streets are getting narrower. With peddler's carts on one side, there's just barely room for the Humvees to get through. The street opens up into an outdoor market. That's where the bomb maker lives. It's not yet noon. The shops should be open, but they're deserted. No kids playing in the street."

At that point, all the warning signs came together. They weren't equipped and prepared for the mission they were undertaking. This wasn't a lone bomb maker living among innocent Iraqis, but a terrorist living in a neighborhood controlled by insurgents. Sinclair got on the radio and told the MP squad leader to abort the mission, cover the court-yard with the vehicle-mounted machinegun, and withdraw the way they came in. Even though Sinclair was a warrant officer and outranked the sergeant, he wasn't in the MP chain of command, so the squad leader argued with him as the convoy pressed on. By the time Sinclair convinced him of the danger signs, it was too late.

"What's happening now?" Jeanne asked.

"Boom," Sinclair said. "An RPG round hits the lead truck in the turret. It stops. Catches fire. All three dead. Two men, one woman MP. They're screaming, trapped inside the burning truck. Another RPG round hits the rear Humvee. Glancing blow. It's disabled, but the MPs dismount. Rifle fire from windows above us. One MP's hit, then another. I bail out, empty my

M4 at the windows, grab a wounded soldier, drag him to cover. My partner's hit. I blow through another mag. Just shooting at windows. Spray and pray. More explosions from RPGs. Only me and one MP haven't been hit. Everyone else wounded or dead. I sprint to my truck—the Humvee—get on the radio, yell for help, for medivac. The CP already heard. A reaction force is on its way."

"What are you feeling?" Jeanne asked.

"Nothing. No time to feel. Fight. Never give up. Shoot. Move. Shoot more. Save my men." Sinclair began sobbing uncontrollably. "Save my men," he said again between sobs.

"Matt, what are you feeling now, as you sit in my office?"

Sinclair choked on his words and couldn't speak.

Jeanne talked him back from the Baghdad marketplace to the mountain lake, the beeps sounding in his ears. It took a while for the stench of the garbage and the smell of burning flesh to dissipate, but Sinclair eventually detected a faint smell of pine trees. She gently removed his earphones and handed him a box of Kleenex. She leaned forward on the edge of her chair and smiled. "How do you feel?"

"Exhausted."

"That's normal. You just relived one of the most traumatic experiences imaginable."

"It felt real."

"That's good. We've done some great work this session, but we'll have to revisit this incident."

"I'm not sure I want to."

"The next time will be easier. That's how EMDR works. Your emotional discomfort level was a ten going into this, but you're now lower, maybe a seven or eight. That's still intense, but not as debilitating. I think I'm noticing a common theme that surfaces in your traumatic incidents. Do you know what that is?"

"That I failed to save people."

She smiled. "Very perceptive. That feeling that we somehow should've done more is what often allows PTSD to take hold.

Rape victims experience it when they think they should've fought harder against their attackers. Combat medics experience it when soldiers die under their care. And of course, when you surround yourself with violence and death as you have—"

"I know intellectually I can't expect to save everyone, but how do we change the wiring in my brain to understand that?"

She laughed. "Don't be so hard on yourself. Wanting to save people is noble. You don't have to change that part of you. In our sessions, we deal with the past. That will free you up to better handle what you face in the present. And I'm not talking about just traumatic incidents, but everyday life and relationships."

"What's this have to do with relationships?"

"Until you've dealt with the trauma from your past, you'll never be fully capable of the widest range of emotions, which are necessary for deep and meaningful relationships."

★

Sinclair was on his second cup of coffee when Braddock rose from her desk at eight sharp and walked to the back of the office. She did a small curtsy and handed her car keys to Lou Sanchez, marking the formal transfer of the homicide standby duty to him and his partner, Dan Jankowski. Sinclair normally felt a huge sense of relief when standby was over, but the lack of progress on Dawn's murder only produced frustration. Although they had only picked up two cases this standby, his inability to sleep left him as fatigued as the weeks when they were called out every night.

Braddock spent most of the day testifying on an old case, while Sinclair pulled old case files of murdered prostitutes and combed through them, searching for anything similar, with no luck. It was four o'clock when he picked up his phone and punched in the number to Attorney Fadell's office for the fifth time. His previous attempts met with a polite receptionist taking his name and saying Ms. Fadell would return his call when she returned from a meeting. This time, the receptionist put him through. "Ms. Fadell, this is Sergeant Sinclair. How are you?"

Braddock scooted her chair alongside Sinclair and leaned her head into his phone.

"I'll be better if you call me Bianca."

"Does your client have any information for me?"

"She just acquired access to the back-up data and is culling through it while putting out a million small fires in order to save her business."

"Do I need to light a bigger fire under her ass to make her *culling* the priority?"

"That's not necessary. I'll stay on her," Bianca said. "I was actually about to call you. There's an event occurring tonight in Oakland—a fundraiser for a consortium of human trafficking nonprofits. There will be some people there whom you might find useful to your investigation."

"In what way?"

"I'm not at liberty to say, but if I were to introduce you to certain people at the event, you might want to take note of them."

"I'm not into whatever kind of game you're playing. Just come out and tell me who I should be interested in and what they know."

"I'm sorry I can't be more direct. I'm navigating confidentiality issues, so you'll have to do this my way for now. I'm certain that there will be several people at this event who can shed a great deal of light on Dawn's life and may even have had motive to kill her."

"When and where?"

"It's at the Scottish Rite Temple. An invite-only cocktail party beginning at six thirty. I've been invited and can bring a guest. I'll have a car and driver for the evening. Where should I pick you up?"

"I'll meet you there," Sinclair said. "Don't take this personal. It's one thing for me to be seen in public with a defense lawyer, but people would get the wrong idea if I were to drive up with one."

"Ah, and I was concerned for my reputation being seen with a mere sergeant in the department." She laughed. "I'll meet you at the front entrance at six thirty sharp. And Matt, you'll want to wear your best dark suit. I'd hate for you to feel underdressed."

"Are you sure this is a good idea?" Braddock said once he ended the call. "I don't trust her at all."

"Neither do I, but I think she's trying to lead us in the right direction without putting herself in the middle."

"I'd feel better if I were with you tonight."

"Me, too. But I think I'm arm candy tonight, and you would detract from that."

"I wouldn't be surprised if she's trying to show off a new cop she has in her pocket. If there really are some big shots from City Hall and the federal building at this shindig, they're going to do a double-take when they see you with her."

"Good," Sinclair said. "They think they have the escort service's client list controlled at high levels in the city and federal bureaucracy. I want people to worry about me getting my hands on it."

"I sure hope you know what you're doing."

"So do I," Sinclair said.

Chapter 21

At 6:15 PM, Sinclair drove from his guesthouse toward the front gate. He wore the same suit he had three nights earlier when it was his job to meet with a high-class hooker. He recognized the irony.

Fred Towers's Mercedes S550 partially blocked the driveway. Sinclair pulled alongside and saw Walt, dressed in a black suit with white shirt and tie, sitting behind the wheel. Sinclair rolled down his window as Fred exited the house wearing one of his impeccably tailored business suits. "Where're you two off to?" Sinclair yelled.

"Another fundraiser," Fred said with a wry smile. "Part of a CEO's job description."

"Not at the Scottish Rite, by any chance?"

"How'd you know?" Fred said.

"A long story, but a lawyer for someone connected to my case invited me with a promise that it'll be beneficial to my investigation."

"Ride with us," Fred said.

"I don't want to stay any longer than absolutely necessary, so I—"

"I just need to be seen, shake some hands, and deliver a check," Fred said. "We'll leave whenever you're ready. Besides, parking's a beast and Walt can deposit us at the front door."

Sinclair parked his car and jogged up to the Mercedes. Walt held the left rear door for him. "I'm playing chauffer tonight, so you should sit in the back with Mr. Towers," Walt said. Before Sinclair could object, Walt continued, "I know . . . but this is the image we must convey."

Sinclair settled into the soft leather seat as Walt closed the door. Sinclair ran his hand along the real wood trim and stretched out his legs in the long-wheelbase sedan. "You get used to it after a while," Fred said as Walt drove off. "Who are you hoping to talk to at this little affair?"

Sinclair summarized his telephone conversation with Fadell while avoiding details of the case.

Fred whistled. "If one of the clients of Special Ladies Escorts had something to do with your murder, you'll have plenty of suspects at this event."

Even though Sinclair hadn't mentioned the name of the escort service, he wasn't surprised that Fred had heard about the sting operation. "What makes you say that?"

"Matt, I've heard plenty of whispers in the boardrooms around Oakland and San Francisco over the years about that service. Many highly placed men are quite concerned at this moment. It doesn't surprise me that Ms. Fadell is representing the owner."

"Do you know her?"

"Bianca makes it her business to know everyone. I see her frequently on the social circuit, and her firm was engaged in an action against an overseas supplier that PRM was doing business with."

Sinclair could tell Fred was being evasive, but he wasn't about to treat him as a suspect and press the issue. "Can I trust her?"

"Behind those pretty eyes is an incredibly sharp and calculating mind. There's a purpose behind everything she says and does. Even the clients she represents. It's all about advancing her personal interests and her standing in the legal community and on the society page."

"So the answer is no."

"If her agenda is in line with yours, you have a powerful ally. However, even if she's working at cross-purposes, I don't think she'll overtly sabotage you. Preventing the police from bringing a killer to justice only gets points for lawyers who want to do criminal defense work for the rest of their career."

Walt stopped behind a line of cars creeping toward the main entrance of the imposing granite-faced building. The Scottish Rite Masons were a branch of the Freemason organization. When they outgrew their older building on Washington Street, they built this 110-foot-tall building overlooking Lake Merritt in 1927. In addition to the auditorium, the building included a ballroom that could hold 1,500 people and numerous other banquet and meeting rooms, as well as private rooms for members only. Sinclair didn't buy into the conspiracy theories that abounded concerning the Masons, and he was less concerned about their veil of secrecy than he was about the same that took place in the back rooms of City Hall and the Police Administration Building.

A stretch limo three cars ahead of them deposited two elderly couples who climbed the stone steps that stretched across the front of the building. "We can walk from here," Sinclair suggested.

"We should wait our turn," Fred said. "How we make our entrance is important."

The driver of a black Cadillac XTS sedan opened the back door, and Bianca Fadell, wearing a long fur coat—surely faux mink to avoid the ire of animal activists—stepped out. She looked at her watch as the Cadillac drove off to make room for the black Lexus that followed. Once the Lexus dropped off a heavyset bald man, Walt pulled up to the curb, opened the door for Sinclair, and hustled around the car to open the door for Fred.

"I had no idea you two knew each other," Bianca said as Sinclair and Fred mounted the steps.

Bianca turned her cheek toward Fred, who gave her a light peck. "Matt's been staying in the guest house for a while."

"Interesting," she said, stepping toward Sinclair with both hands outstretched.

He extended his right hand to shake her hand and keep her at a distance. A dozen people watched from the top of the steps.

"Despite the rumors," she whispered, "I really don't bite."

She lightly took Sinclair's left arm and led him up the steps. Velvet ropes corralled people into a single line leading toward the huge metal door, which he heard weighed more than a ton. A tuxedoed man with a clipboard stood at the entrance. "Ms. Fadell and guest," he said and made a check mark on his paper. Another man in a tuxedo swung the door open.

Bianca slipped out of her fur and handed it to a coat-check girl just inside the entrance. She was wearing another show-stopper—a form-fitting black dress with a plunging neckline—which she tugged down, showing even more of her cleavage. She snatched a glass of champagne from a silver tray as a waiter approached. "Something nonalcoholic for the gentleman," she said. When the waiter trotted off, she said, "You are still not drinking, am I correct?"

"That's right," Sinclair said.

"Probably wise. You're lucky to have gotten your sergeant rank and your position in homicide back after what happened. As for me, I'm not sure I could live without it."

Sinclair had thought the same in his early sobriety. Even though he knew he could no longer live with it, he didn't know if he could live without it. Old timers in AA said that at some point it would be more natural not to drink than to drink. He looked forward to that day. A hundred people milled around in the palatial foyer. Grand staircases on both sides of the lobby led to a wide balcony. High above that, hand-carved wood ceiling panels painted gold glistened in the light from a massive chandelier. Dozens of eyes swept over Bianca, some trying not to be obvious, others not so discreet.

"Let's work the room," she said, taking Sinclair's arm and strutting toward a circle of gray-haired men. "Gentlemen,

I'd like you to meet Sergeant Sinclair of the city's homicide division."

Each man introduced himself by name, followed by a firm handshake. Before Sinclair could ask their occupation or how they were connected, Bianca said, "So nice to see you, we must chat later," and swept him further into the room.

A waiter handed Sinclair a fluted glass. "Sparkling cider, sir," he said, and he turned toward another cluster of people with his tray. Other waiters made their rounds with trays of hors d'oeuvres: bacon-wrapped scallops, crackers mounded with caviar, bite-size sandwiches, and tiny pastry shells filled with soft cheese. Although he was hungry, Sinclair had never mastered the art of juggling a plate of food, a drink, and a woman on his arm, while keeping his right hand available to shake dozens of hands.

Across the room, Sinclair saw the shaved head of Clarence Brown, the Oakland police chief, towering above the cluster of people around him. Brown's eyebrows rose and then furrowed when he noticed Sinclair, an unmistakable look of surprise followed by disapproval. "I better go and see him."

"Yes, we should," Bianca said.

As they crossed the room, Bianca set her champagne flute on a waiter's tray and grabbed a fresh one in one smooth movement.

"I'm surprised to see you here, Sinclair," Chief Brown said.

"He's here as my guest," Bianca said before Sinclair could speak. "I thought he might meet some people useful in his investigation."

Sinclair said, "Chief, I'd like you to meet—"

"Ms. Fadell and I have met," Brown said.

"Nice to see you again, Chief," Bianca said, extending her hand.

Brown took her hand lightly.

She turned to Sinclair. "I'm sure you know Mr. O'Brien, the District Attorney."

"Nice to see you, Sergeant," O'Brien said. "As you might know, our office has strong partnerships with many of the organizations represented here tonight. We're working toward a common quest to eradicate human trafficking in the county. Not as dramatic as investigating and prosecuting murderers, but every bit as vital."

Sinclair smiled but said nothing.

A tall, thin, white man, probably in his midfifties, but with boyish good looks, extended his hand to Sinclair, and said, "I'm Jack Campbell. We've never met, but your reputation precedes you. I'm a fan of your work."

Sinclair recognized the name. Campbell was the US Attorney for Northern California, a presidential appointee and the likely heir to one of California's Senate seats if Diane Feinstein were ever to retire. "It's an honor to meet you, sir," Sinclair said.

"Perhaps we can talk later," Campbell replied.

"Whenever you wish," Sinclair said.

"You gentlemen have a nice evening now." Bianca smiled and led Sinclair away as a chorus of *Bye, Bianca*s sounded from the men.

"Lots of power in that group," Sinclair said. "Are any of them . . ."

"On the client list?" Bianca laughed. "I wish."

She crowded in close and turned to face him. He could smell the champagne on her breath. Mixed with her perfume, it wasn't unpleasant. He struggled to maintain eye contact and not look down into her deep cleavage, where from his angle, he could probably see her navel.

"The prying-open-of-the-checkbook speech is about to begin," she said. "We should get a better position." She took his hand and led him through the crowd to the top of one of the staircases.

"This is a good vantage point to see and be seen." She leaned into him, her firm thigh pressed against his leg.

Sinclair inched away, and she looked over her shoulder at him and smiled. "As you wish. Public displays of affection are clearly not your thing."

Bianca was beautiful in a sultry sort of way. She would no doubt be totally uninhibited in bed. "I'm a cop and you're a high-priced lawyer defending a criminal I'm investigating. That would make a relationship extremely dangerous and overly complicated," Sinclair said, as much to explain his actions as to convince himself. And despite himself, he couldn't stop thinking about Alyssa.

"First, I'm not proposing a relationship. They're so old-fashioned. Second, I like dangerous. And third, I thrive on complications."

Sinclair slid a little farther from her as a man with a thick mane of silver hair stepped up to a podium at the front of the lobby. "Many of you know me from my role with Cal Asia, but tonight I'm here in a different capacity."

"His name is William Whitt," Bianca whispered. "He's the COO of land operations for Cal Asia."

"The shipping line?" asked Sinclair.

"One of the top three shipping companies between the United States and Asia."

"Tonight, I'm here as the chair of the fundraising committee of Bay Area Businesses Against Sex Trafficking," Whitt continued. "We're a consortium of twelve East Bay corporations that have pledged to match, dollar for dollar, all donations tonight in order to provide much-needed services for victims of human sex trafficking. A number of nonprofits are in dire need of support to provide housing, legal, and counseling services for minors who have been sucked into the life of prostitution. In addition, we need alternatives to the traditional approach of arrest and prosecution for adult women in the sex trade. Everyone who was invited here, outside of the federal, state, and local government leaders with us tonight—because we know the limitations of government salaries"—Whitt paused to allow the laughter to subside, then continued midsentence—"will be contacted by a member of the committee during the course of the evening. We'll ask you to open your checkbooks wide, as the need is great. Thank you all for coming."

Whitt stepped away from the microphone and into the crowd to shake hands and accept envelopes. "Come on," said Bianca as she led him down the stairs. "You should meet him."

Sinclair followed Bianca as she pushed through a line of people waiting to meet Whitt. She glided in front of the first acolyte, an elderly woman wearing a diamond-studded necklace that should have required the presence of a full-time security guard.

"Bianca!" Whitt said. "You look lovelier than ever."

She kissed his cheek and held his hand as she said, "Great speech, William. I'd like you to meet Sergeant Sinclair. Matt's a homicide detective."

"What brings you out to such a do-gooder cause, Sergeant?"

"I have a murder victim who worked as an escort, and Ms. Fadell thought I might meet some people who could shed some light on how she died."

"I'm not sure how we could help with such a sordid act, but feel free to call on me." He handed Sinclair a business card. His eyes turned to Bianca's chest. "Call me. We really should catch up."

Bianca stepped aside and the woman with the diamond necklace stepped up to Whitt with an embossed envelope in her hand. Bianca led Sinclair around the room, trading hugs, air kisses, and handshakes with scores of people, none of whom seemed interested in knowing who Sinclair was. She then directed Sinclair to a man standing alone in the back of the room, scrolling through his phone. Sinclair recognized him as a city council member with whom he had attended police-community meetings on several occasions.

"Good evening, Bianca." Preston Yates held out a limp hand, which Bianca grasped lightly.

"Preston, have you met Sergeant Sinclair?"

"Never formally."

Sinclair took him in as he would any suspect: male, white, forty to forty-five, five-nine, 150–160, slim build, sandy-brown hair, hazel eyes. His handshake was weak. Sinclair was careful to squeeze lightly. "Pleased to meet you, Mr. Yates."

"Please, everyone calls me Preston."

Sinclair smiled to be polite. Politicians liked to pretend they were ordinary Joes to their constituents, but he refused to be drawn into their pretense. Yates was no friend of the department. He sided with every social issue and voted against every budget item or wage hike for police. Following a violent street protest last summer, Yates was the first politician to publicly condemn OPD's use of tear gas to break up the crowd. The following night, when the police chief held the police line back to avoid criticism of police brutality as protesters smashed and burned downtown businesses, Yates criticized the police for not taking action. "Councilman Yates, departmental regulations specify I address you by your title."

Yates maintained the phony smile that was fixed to his face. "I saw your name attached to several recent homicides. Is this indicative of a trend?"

"I leave those predictions to the media and sociologists. I just investigate them when they happen."

"So then, if the primary objective of the police department is crime prevention, how do we justify spending money on a unit such as yours that only investigates crime after it's already occurred?"

"That's beyond my pay grade, Councilman, but if we don't take a killer off the streets, he'll kill again, so I guess that's how I do my part to prevent future crimes."

"Dawn Gustafson, the woman hung in the park, I understand she was a prostitute." Yates pushed his hair from his forehead. "Don't be shocked. It's my job to know about these things."

"She was, at some point in her life. We're still trying to determine whether it had anything to do with her death. Have any of your constituents mentioned anything about the murder or the victim?"

"It didn't occur in my council district, so it's doubtful; however, if I can be of any further assistance, please feel free to contact my staff at any time." The politician smile remained as he handed a card to Sinclair.

"Charming man," Sinclair said to Bianca when they retreated to a corner of the room.

"That he is. His name's being bandied about as the frontrunner in the next mayoral race."

"Am I right to conclude that Yates and Whitt are two people you thought I should meet?"

She smiled and said nothing. A man dressed in a white shirt, bowtie, and black vest approached them and bowed his head slightly. "Mr. Sinclair, Mr. Campbell would like you to join him in the members lounge."

"Where is that?"

"I'll escort you, sir."

Sinclair and Bianca stepped off behind him. The man stopped and turned. "Sorry, madam, but the invitation is for the gentleman only."

"You've met those I thought you should, Matt," Bianca said. "Can I wait around and give you a lift home?"

"I'll be fine," he said. "And thanks for your help."

They took an elevator to the third floor and followed a long corridor lined with paintings and old photographs to a heavy wooden door, which the man unlocked with a large brass key. Two ornate billiard tables occupied the left side of the room. Across the dark-wood floors polished to a high sheen were several groupings of furniture, a few consisting of leather club chairs, while other larger ones included leather sofas. Five men sat in a group next to the pool tables, while Campbell sat with two men who looked like attorneys in a cluster of club chairs at the far end of the room.

Campbell waved him over. "Can you excuse us for a few minutes?" he said to his companions, who quietly rose and headed toward the billiard tables. Campbell motioned to the chair next to him. "Please have a seat, Sergeant." Campbell held up a heavy crystal tumbler. "Would you care for a scotch? We have some of the finest single malts in the world."

"No, thank you."

The waiter who had escorted Sinclair to the room bowed his head slightly and took his leave.

"Sinclair—that is Scottish isn't it?" Campbell said.

"My father was English and Scottish. The exact lines became blurred generations ago."

"Of course." Campbell swirled the amber liquid in his glass and took a sip.

Sinclair could smell the aroma from where he sat.

"And your mother is Latino?" Campbell said.

It was obvious Campbell had been well briefed. "Her mother was Mexican and her father was American. And you, sir, Scottish?"

"Ah yes, both of my parents trace their lines back to the old clans of feudal times. They weren't too pleased when I married a beautiful woman of Austrian-Hungarian descent, but I don't concern myself with such pedigrees as did my parents."

Sinclair wondered if Campbell was truly impressed with his record and wanted to get to know him better or if this was this just preliminary ice breaking, but he wasn't left wondering for long.

"The victim in the murder that prompted your investigation into Special Ladies Escorts was a prostitute, is that correct?"

"That's right," Sinclair said.

"I'm curious as to why you went to such great lengths—mounting an undercover operation into the service and gathering a mountain of information—when wading through it would take an army of analysts and likely get you no closer to solving the murder?"

"Are you asking why I took on so much work, or why I did so for this victim?"

"I've been told about your work ethic, so on that I'm clear, but this victim is not exactly a prominent citizen."

Sinclair fought to control his composure. "She had friends and family that loved her. I don't pick which murders to work based on someone's determination of the victim's worth. I investigate them all, because in my world, people shouldn't be allowed to commit a murder and get away with it."

"So you work as much for society as for the victim. Very noble. I admire that. However, is it practical? In my office, I make decisions about whom to investigate and prosecute daily. Often my decisions have national implications. For example, you're well aware that under the current administration, police brutality is a major issue. My stance doesn't please my law enforcement brethren, but the President and Attorney General are trying to reshape the way law enforcement agencies in our great nation do business. One of the ways in which we are doing so is by using the FBI's civil rights division to investigate excessive force when it falls under federal jurisdiction and by using the US Attorneys to prosecute individual officers when the evidence is sufficient."

Sinclair was well aware of the witch-hunts by the Attorney General. He announced federal investigations into incidents even before the local jurisdiction had a chance to investigate. "Are you saying I'm doing too much because Dawn Gustafson—that's the victim's name, by the way—was just a hooker?"

Campbell took a long pull of his scotch. "What I'm saying is that we all have only so much time, resources, and goodwill. We need to use it wisely. The path you're taking may consume every bit of goodwill you've earned. You must ask yourself if it's worth it, or if it's wiser to save up some goodwill for the future. You're a man of great honor—a noble knight, if you will—but this may not be the battle you want to ride into with sword and shield in hand."

"May I ask you something?"

"Of course."

"Do you have access to the client list?" Sinclair said.

Campbell looked down at his drink for a few counts. He then locked eyes with Sinclair. "What information I have access to is, quite frankly, none of your business. Your question might be more properly posed to your police chief." Campbell raised his hand and snapped his fingers. The waiter who had brought Sinclair to the meeting reappeared. "Thomas here will escort you back to the party. Tread carefully, Sergeant, you're too good a man to have this be your downfall."

Chapter 22

Sinclair met Braddock at the office at nine the following morning. It was Saturday, so he conceded an hour so she could spend some morning time with her kids. When Sinclair had left the Scottish Rite Temple with Fred last night, they'd seen Whitt climbing into the back of a Jaguar sedan, giving Sinclair a perfect opportunity to quiz Fred about him. They both were top-level corporate executives in Oakland, and Fred had served on various boards and socialized with Whitt at various events for more than twenty years. Sixteen years ago, Whitt's wife filed for divorce when she discovered he was having an affair. After a high-profile court battle, which Fred said was in all the papers, they'd reconciled. A year later, she died in a single-car accident. Since then, Whitt had become more active in philanthropy. Fred told him that Whitt and Bianca had dated for a short while a few years ago.

Once he was home, as Sinclair was smoking a Patron Family Reserve cigar next to the pool, he tried to figure out why Bianca would introduce him to Whitt, knowing that he would find out that she'd dated a man who was hiring escorts. She must have had strong suspicions about Whitt to risk bringing her name into the investigation as an associate of his. The presence of a city council member on the client list was another interesting twist, and he wondered if he was one of the people around whom Campbell was warning him to tread softly. By the time he finished his cigar, he hadn't reached any conclusions.

Braddock listened intently as Sinclair briefed her on everything he had learned last night. "Was Bianca trying to tell you Whitt and Yates are on the client list?"

"She might've been inferring they were Dawn's clients," he said. "But we need something more before we drag two men like that into an interview room and accuse them of having a relationship with a murdered escort."

"That's for damn sure," she said. "I'll start working up background info on them. Maybe something will jump out."

Sinclair went back to his chronological log, hoping to find something they could link to either man. He stopped at the entry detailing their search of Dawn's apartment, read the technician report, and scrolled through the photographs of the crime scene. The tech had taken photos of every book in her bookshelf. In one photo, he saw a price tag marked *SF State Bookstore* stuck on the back of a textbook.

Sinclair knew an officer who had retired from OPD a few years ago and took a job with the San Francisco State University police. Sinclair tracked him down with a few phone calls and told him what he needed. Ten minutes later, Sinclair received an e-mail with Dawn's transcripts and class schedule attached. One professor's name kept showing up. Dawn had a class taught by Ruben Bailey nearly every semester, including an internship with him last year. A Google search showed he was an adjunct professor at SF State and a CPA in Oakland.

Sinclair called his office on the off chance there was a night and weekend emergency phone number. A male voice answered. "This is Sergeant Sinclair with the Oakland police. I'm trying to reach Ruben Bailey."

"This is him."

Sinclair paused. "Sorry, but I thought I'd get a recording or a receptionist at best."

"Heck, it's Saturday," Bailey said. "In this office, only the crazy boss works on weekends."

"I'm calling about one of your students at SF State, Dawn Gustafson."

The line was quiet for a few seconds. "I've been expecting this call for years. I was hoping she could finish her degree and get a good position so she wouldn't have to go back to her old life. Where is she, the city jail?"

"When did you last see her, Mr. Bailey?"

"Week before last, but I knew something was wrong when she missed class this week and didn't show up for work. She works for me part-time, if you didn't know."

"Can we talk in person?" Sinclair said.

Fifteen minutes later, Sinclair and Braddock were sitting in a comfortable office in an older commercial building in downtown Oakland. Bailey was a white man in his late fifties and wore a pair of dark-brown chinos and an open-collar shirt. He had an infectious smile and sparkling eyes under thick eyebrows. When Sinclair told him about Dawn's death, his eyes welled with tears.

"What a terrible waste," Bailey said. "She was a remarkable young lady with great potential."

"It sounds like she was more than just a student to you," Sinclair said.

"To be clear, I knew Dawn was a call girl. I would never engage a sex worker, and I would never cross that line with a student. Detective, do you know how much an adjunct professor makes?"

Sinclair shook his head.

"Thirty-six-hundred a semester. That is for forty-five hours of classroom instruction. A good teacher spends twice that much time reading papers and preparing for class. Add in the time it takes me to travel to the university, after taxes, I make slightly more than minimum wage. Do you know what a CPA bills out at?"

Sinclair shook his head again.

"I make that much in two days. I don't do this for the money. I love my students. I get more enjoyment from teaching and interacting with their young minds than any other endeavor. And by the way, my wife of thirty-five years has met Dawn, and we've had her to the house for dinner on numerous occasions. She thinks of Dawn as a daughter. She'll be devastated."

"I'm sorry if I implied anything inappropriate," Sinclair said. "I knew her before, too, and I agree completely with your assessment. Can we start at the beginning, when you first met her?"

For the next hour, Bailey talked about Dawn. Several years ago, she had signed up for an advanced accounting course he was teaching. He immediately recognized her maturity and poise. She also had a hunger that he seldom saw in students. She wanted to learn, but more than that, she wanted to become a successful CPA. Every semester he selected one of his students for a paid internship with his accounting firm. He selected Dawn to intern with him that following semester. He started her with basic bookkeeping but soon gave her responsibilities normally reserved for certified accountants. She had a gift for dealing with clients, people skills that were rare in CPAs.

Although she was vague about what she did, it was clear to Bailey. She spoke of clients and income that was largely undocumented, similar to tips. He also heard whispers from other students. She wanted to get out of her present line of work, but couldn't do so until she was able to make enough to live and pay for school. She shared with him an idea to start her own business handling the personal finances of people who were too busy to do so themselves—simple things such as paying bills, depositing checks, tracking personal investments, and maintaining a household budget. Under Bailey's guidance, she approached a few of her clients. Within a short while, she had twenty personal-finance clients and quit her other job. Each client only required a few hours of work a month, but when combined with one day a week in Bailey's office, it was sufficient.

Over dinner one evening with Bailey and his wife, she revealed she needed a well-paying career so she could buy a house, regain custody of her daughter, and raise her in the Bay Area. They were shocked to learn Dawn had a child, but it explained her focus and drive. Bailey introduced her to a family-law attorney who was one of his clients, who agreed to help her pro bono.

"I'd like to talk to the attorney," Sinclair said.

Bailey wrote the attorney's name on a notepad and passed it to Sinclair.

"Was Dawn's goal achievable?" Braddock asked.

"She finished her undergrad work last May and was due to take her final exams for her first grad semester next week. She was taking a full load and would've graduated in May. I know a dozen companies that would have hired her at close to six figures right out of school. They'd make sure she got the requisite experience and had time to study for the different stages of the CPA exam. Once she was certified, she could name her salary."

"Was she that good?" Braddock asked.

"Let's be honest," Bailey said. "She was runway-model beautiful. I don't know if she was born with it or it was a skill she mastered working in her previous occupation, but she was utterly charming and knew human nature better than most psychologists. People loved her. She had a three-nine GPA as an undergrad, and I'd be surprised if she ever got less than an A in graduate school. She was the whole package. She was exactly what the big accounting firms and Fortune 500 companies are looking for."

"You think she went back to her old profession?" Sinclair asked.

"When you called, that's the only reason I figured the police were asking about her. But actually, I can't imagine her doing so. She had everything going for her. Her future was right on the horizon, and then there was her daughter."

Sinclair told him about not finding a computer or files at her apartment. "I need to talk to her clients, especially since it appears she recruited them from her escort business."

"Dawn used my firm's software for her work. It saved her a lot of money. Her clients' files should be on our server. My wife handles the computer stuff here, and I'll have her look for it. I should call her clients and tell them Dawn is gone. My firm will take care of them until they find someone new."

"Can you give me a few days to contact them first?"

"Sure," Bailey said. "Do you think I could talk to her parents? I'd like to offer my condolences and tell them how very special she was."

Sinclair replied, "I think they would love to hear that."

★

Once they were inside their car, Braddock said, "We need to find who did this and string him up in a tree."

It wasn't like Braddock to talk so strongly of retribution. "And light him on fire?" Sinclair grinned.

"She was a woman fighting to change her life and win back her daughter. I can identify with her."

"We'll get him," Sinclair said. "Or them. I promise you."

Sinclair put his phone on speaker and called the cell number Bailey had given them for the attorney. When he answered, Sinclair told him about Dawn's murder and their visit with Bailey. "What did she come see you about?" Sinclair asked.

"Normally, this is confidential, but under the circumstances . . . Let me bring up the file."

"You're in the office on a Saturday, too?"

"Hell no. I'm at my cabin in Tahoe. The wife and kids are skiing. All the rain we've had in the Bay Area means several feet of fresh snow up here. But I'm stuck inside prepping for trial. Here we go. Dawn was a sweet kid. Such a tragedy. She told me she had a daughter by a man outside of marriage. She signed away custody to her parents and they legally adopted her in Minnesota. Dawn wanted to regain custody. I advised her to first stabilize her life financially to prove she can support a child and positively put her old life behind her. After that, we'd need to find a family-law attorney who practices in Minnesota to petition the court for custody."

"She told you what she did?" Sinclair asked.

"She alluded to it. It didn't take a rocket scientist to figure out she was a high-class call girl and had been the mistress to her child's father. She said she was currently receiving two thousand a month child support and free rent for a nice condo, which was probably valued at another two grand, plus five hundred into a college fund. She made about twenty thousand a year and the father made $76,100."

"She gave you that exact figure?" Sinclair asked.

"Yeah. She wouldn't tell me anything about him or what he did, but I assumed he was a teacher or had a similar government job where the salaries are public information. I plugged the numbers into the California Guideline Child Support Calculator, which showed the father was providing more than required based on the formula. He obviously had another source of income if he was giving Dawn as much as he was. She was disappointed. She asked if the wife of the father counted, and I advised that spousal income is not considered in the formula; however, under some circumstances, a court might determine it is relevant. My advice to her was not to rock the boat. She was receiving more than a court would award."

"I need to identify the father. Did she say anything else about him?"

"Why don't you check her bank records? The money had to come to her from somewhere."

"I will, but that'll take some time. I think the check's going to Dawn's parents and the man may be trying to conceal his identity."

"I wish you luck. Dawn called me again two weeks ago. She asked if it would make a difference if the man's wife made more than a million dollars a year. Hell yeah, I told her."

"I thought spousal income didn't count," Braddock said.

"The court can consider it under extenuating circumstances. Say a child's father was making eight thousand a month and when he remarried, he became the stay-at-home dad in his new family. I'd submit to the court that his new spouse's income is actually family income and at least half of it should be the basis for child support. Here you have a man making a bit over six thousand a month—not exactly a huge salary in the Bay Area— But his standard of living is based on the much larger salary of his wife. I'd propose, once I had more information about their careers and the stream of income, that his job is little more than a hobby and his wife provides the family income, which he shares."

"Would that entitle Dawn to more child support?" Sinclair asked.

"I think a court would agree that ten thousand dollars a month would not be out of line, as well as direct payments for everything from private-school tuition, to piano lessons, soccer summer camp, and things of that sort. Dawn could also get enough money going into a college fund to pay for an Ivy League education for her daughter. I offered to take her case with no money upfront, but she was sure the father would do everything possible to keep the case out of court."

"Did she say what she intended to do?"

"Not directly, but it seemed like she was going to make direct contact with the man and ask for more money. I warned against it and offered to negotiate for her, taking into consideration everyone's desire to avoid court. If I handle the contact and negotiation, it avoids the appearance of blackmail."

"You mean like, *if you don't pay me this much money every month, I'll take you to court and make sure everyone knows you fathered a child with your call girl*?" Braddock said.

"Exactly," the lawyer said. "You don't think that's why she was killed, do you?"

"Certainly a possibility," Sinclair said.

Chapter 23

When they got back to the office, Sinclair called Dawn's parents. Gene answered, and Sinclair told him about his conversation with Bailey.

"I knew she was telling the truth when she said she'd have a masters in accounting by next summer," Gene said. "Please give Mr. Bailey our number. Maybe Cynthia will be open to hearing some positive things about Dawn."

"Tell me about the monthly checks you get for Maddie," Sinclair said.

"Dawn arranged it a few months after Maddie was born. The local bank set up two accounts for us. One's a checking account that Cynthia, Dawn, or I could write checks on. Two thousand is deposited there every month. The other is a college fund that none of us can touch before Maddie's eighteen. Five hundred's deposited into that every month. Even though Dawn said we should take money out for Maddie's room and board, it never seemed right. She's in Dawn's old bedroom, which otherwise would be empty. We got her on my medical insurance, so there's not much in doctor costs. And with Christmas, birthdays, and such, we hardly have to buy her any clothes or toys. I have detailed records of everything we spent from the bank account if you want to look at it."

"I'm sure everything's on the up-and-up," Sinclair said. "Who do the checks come from?"

"I have no idea. It's an ACH deposit the first of the month, sort of like a payroll direct deposit."

"It must have a name," Sinclair said. "The direct deposit into my checking account says it comes from the city of Oakland."

"All it says on the statements is Charles Schwab and an account number."

Gene agreed to send him copies of the bank statements, and Sinclair thanked him and hung up. He would try to identify the source of the money, but he was sure the Charles Schwab investment firm wouldn't give him anything without a search warrant, and they would be the first of many layers he'd have to penetrate to discover the identity of Maddie's father.

An e-mail from Bailey popped up on his computer screen. Attached was a spreadsheet with twenty-four names and contact information for each. The last name on the alphabetized list was William Whitt. The only other name he recognized was Marcus Wright, a fourth-year running back with the Oakland Raiders.

He called Bianca's cell phone. "I want to thank you for the introductions last night," he said.

"How'd it work out with Jack Campbell?"

"I'm not sure whether he threatened to destroy me if I didn't drop my inquiries into the escort service or if he was merely giving me a friendly warning that someone else might destroy me if I continued."

She laughed. "That doesn't surprise me. Jack's a political animal. He doesn't want the Democratic machine's apple cart upset. There are probably some major donors on the list who wouldn't be pleased to find their names made public."

"Why didn't you tell me about you and William Whitt?"

The line was quiet and Sinclair pictured Bianca composing herself. "What's there to tell?" she finally said.

"That you were in a relationship with him, to start."

"I'm not sure I'd call it that. You'll discover—if you get to know me—that I seldom date one man exclusively. The society reporter at the *Chronicle* might photograph me with one man at the ballet and with another at a fundraiser the following evening. Because I'm seen with someone in public doesn't mean we're in a relationship."

"Were you intimate?"

"Gentlemen don't make such inquiries of women," she said. "But considering your occupation, I'll try not to be offended. You probably assume that sexual intimacy implies a particular degree of seriousness in a relationship. I can be intimate with someone without falling in love or even feeling love. It doesn't mean I'm going steady with him, or whatever the modern term for that is. William is significantly older than I. He's a charming man, a sharp business executive, and a great philanthropist. He has a level of stature in the community that is attractive. I was fond of him, so I slept with him on several occasions. It was nice, but he didn't rock my world by any means."

"But then you found out he was frequenting escorts."

"I'm not judgmental about such things. However, William's past indiscretions were well known. Years ago, he had an affair with his son's teacher, which nearly led to his divorce. After his wife's death, he swore he had turned over a new leaf. When it became known that he was using an escort while attached to me in the public eye, I was embarrassed. I feigned anger and much greater embarrassment for the benefit of my own image and severed my relationship with him."

"How did you find out about him and the escort service?"

"How do you find out about anything like that? Whispers around the country club. Innuendo at a cocktail party. Gossip. Then I asked him directly."

"He was one of Dawn's clients?"

"It wasn't my intent to identify anyone by name to you, but since we've come this far—yes."

"And Preston Yates?"

"When Helena and I first conferred, one of my first questions was about the names of Dawn's clients. I needed names to work a deal for Helena. There were too many girls and too many clients for her to know who saw whom, but those two she remembered without going into her records."

"Why them?"

"I didn't inquire. Maybe because of their status. Maybe because they were regulars. I really don't know."

"When can I expect the client list?"

"Helena's doing this alone to shield her employees, and there's no computerized way to sort the escorts by their clients. She's doing it manually, looking at each transaction, and writing down the escort with the respective client's name."

"In Dawn's personal effects was a list of men. Some or all were her clients. Whitt is on the list. I need Helena to check each name in her database and tell me if they were Dawn's clients."

"E-mail it to me."

"I need it soon. If Helena can't do this, I have no reason to keep her out of jail."

"I'll have it for you tomorrow morning."

Sinclair hung up. He wanted to grab the list Bailey had sent him and drive to the first man's address.

Braddock convinced him to slow down. "We don't know all of these men were her escort clients, so if we interview someone and he denies knowing Dawn as an escort, we have nothing to confront him with. We can try the famous Sinclair bluff, but accusing a group of prominent citizens with prostitution without proof will land us in IAD in a heartbeat."

"You know I'm not afraid of IA," he said.

"If we think one of the men on Bailey's list is the killer, we'll only have one chance to interview him before he flees or lawyers up, so don't we want to go into this fully prepared?"

Sinclair knew all this. You always strive to interview the suspect last, because you first want to gather every bit of information possible to use against him in the interview room. Of course, it didn't always work out that way. Once the element of surprise was gone—when the suspect knew the police were on to him—the methodical investigative steps went out the window and it turned into a manhunt.

"I hate it when you're right," he said. "Let's split up the list and start doing background on these guys."

Only two of the men had an arrest record—a DUI ten years ago and a drunk-and-disturbing-the-peace when one man was in his twenties. When they ran out their addresses in a real estate search engine and vehicles registered to them in DMV, they found one common denominator. Each man was wealthy. Not one lived in a house worth less than a million dollars. Mercedes, Porches, and BMWs topped the list of cars they owned. Marcus Wright had both a Ferrari and a Bentley, which Sinclair figured he could afford after signing a seven-million-dollar contract last year.

It was getting dark outside when Braddock pushed away from her desk. She filled her coffee cup and stared at the office bulletin board. "This is where we'll find the seventy-six-thousand-dollar annual salary," she said.

Sinclair got up to stretch and studied the OPD salary bulletin she was looking at. There were four different classifications for police officers, depending on date of hire, and five or six seniority steps for each one, equating to twenty-two different salaries for the officer rank alone. None was $76,100. Sinclair returned to his computer and entered *$76,100 annual salary* into Google. That was the median salary for lawyers in Iowa City and the median salary for physical therapists in Spartanburg, South Carolina. Another webpage showed it was the bottom step for teachers in the Moreland School District, wherever the hell that was. He added *Oakland* to his search. He scrolled down until an entry for the *Contra Costa Times* website caught his eye: *Oakland City Council Members voted to give themselves a 2.4 percent raise Tuesday that brings their annual salary to $76,100 each.*

"Braddock!" he yelled.

Braddock rushed over and looked at his screen. "Homicide investigators don't believe in coincidences, do we?"

"Hell no. What do you want to bet Councilmember Preston Yates is Dawn's baby daddy?"

★

Later that evening, Sinclair was sitting at a table in a church hall in Walnut Creek, about fifteen miles from Oakland. His mind drifted back to the case while a woman read the twelve steps of Alcoholics Anonymous. His first instinct upon seeing the report about the city council's salary a few hours ago was to rush out, grab Yates, and stuff him into an interview room, but this time he didn't need Braddock to remind him that restraint was necessary. They would need more evidence before they went after someone in Yates's position. The soonest he could request the account information from Charles Schwab was Monday, and it might take weeks to trace it to Yates. There wasn't much he could do to build a connection between Yates and Dawn by sitting around the office on a Saturday night. Still, he'd considered calling the friend who'd asked him to speak at the meeting because it felt like he shouldn't live life when the trail to Dawn's killer was warming. Braddock convinced him that was stupid and that he needed a meeting. He hated when people close to him suggested he needed a meeting, because they were usually right.

Sinclair looked out at the forty or so people sitting on folding chairs in front of him and said, "My name's Matt and I'm an alcoholic."

When Sinclair was getting ready for his first speaker meeting a year ago, Walt had told him not to prepare, but to instead just speak from his heart, and whatever was meant to come out would be perfection. Unlike many public figures, Sinclair had little anonymity remaining to protect in AA meetings, because his drunk-driving accident and affair with the news reporter had been all over the print and TV news for days.

The group replied with a chorus of "Hi, Matt," and Sinclair recited his drinking story, beginning when drinking was fun and alcohol worked, as it did at one time for most alcoholics, until the end when it was destroying everything in his life he cared about, yet he couldn't stop.

"If I could still drink without the consequences, I would," Sinclair said toward the end of his twenty-minute talk. "I loved how a few shots of bourbon quieted the voices in my head, took away the pain of what the world was throwing at me, and removed my feelings of fear and self-doubt. But today I know that a true alcoholic can't ever drink responsibly, so I have to deal with life head on without numbing out. But it's hard. My sponsor once told me that we alcoholics stopped maturing emotionally when we began drinking. In some ways, I agree. I'm trying to figure out how to do relationships at thirty-seven and often feel like I'm still seventeen. You who've been sober a lot longer than me say that if I don't drink and keep coming to meetings, I'll learn how to handle this kind of stuff. Thanks for asking me to speak."

People in the audience filled the remainder of the hour sharing bits of their own drinking stories or how their lives changed in sobriety. Sinclair was walking across the parking lot to his car when his phone rang.

"I just got a call from patrol," Braddock said. "They think they located where Dawn was actually living."

Chapter 24

A half hour later, Sinclair and Braddock were standing just inside the front door of a modern two-bedroom condo at the corner of Twelfth Street and M. L. King Jr. Way in Oakland. Sergeant Carter, a patrol sergeant who recently returned to uniform from a stint in IAD, briefed them. "We got a call from a neighbor who saw two men going into this unit. She was friends with the tenant, who she knew as Dawn Gustafson. That was your murder victim, right?"

Sinclair nodded.

Carter continued, "The neighbor hadn't seen Gustafson in a while and thought it was strange, so she knocked at the door. One of the men came out and told her they were surveying the place because they were supposed to start work there on Monday to move the old tenant's property out and clean and paint the place for the next tenant. The story didn't sit right with her. She called nine-one-one, but by the time the units got here, the men were gone. She let the officers in with a key—she and Gustafson had traded keys in case of an emergency—and they saw the blood stain and recognized the name of your murder victim."

"Did your officers search the place?" Sinclair asked.

"Just a protective sweep. Everything else seems to be in order. No signs of a struggle. Looks like the place was lived in. Neat and nicely decorated."

Sinclair looked around the room. What had once been a large pool of blood was now dried and soaked into the Pergo floor next to a round dining table. A sofa and two chairs surrounded a dark-wood coffee table. A matching stand held a fifty-inch TV. A shiny brass cartridge casing lay on the hardwood floor against a wall. Sinclair dropped to his hands and knees and twisted his head to view the head stamp without handling it. It was a .380.

"I'll go back to the office and type up a warrant," said Braddock.

Sinclair started to argue, but she insisted it was her turn and he should be at the scene. Carter pointed to the door of the neighbor, and Sinclair rang the doorbell.

The woman invited Sinclair into a unit identical to Dawn's. She introduced herself as Angela Porter and said she was thirty-eight and worked at the federal building two blocks away in the civilian personnel office. She had bought her condominium three years ago, at which time Dawn was already living here. Sinclair pulled a photo from his portfolio and showed it to Porter.

"That's Dawn," she said. "I saw the blood in there. Is it hers?"

Sinclair nodded, figuring Porter already knew the answer. "She was murdered last Saturday night. Did you see or hear anything unusual?"

"I was visiting my parents for the weekend. I talked to Dawn Friday afternoon. Everything was fine then."

"Did you know her well?"

"We'd have dinner together, you know, two single gals in the big city, once or twice a month. She was really busy with school and work."

"Did you ever see any people visit her, maybe a boyfriend?"

Angela wiped tears from her eyes with the back of her hand. "She kept to herself. When home, she was usually studying. She said she'd sworn off men until she got her degree and had the time to commit to a relationship. The only person I ever saw at her place was her ex-boyfriend, who came by once a month or so. Dawn said she had to remain civil with him."

"Did you ever meet him?"

"She introduced me once, just in passing. A weird name, something like Les or Jess—no, it was Press."

"Describe him."

"He was a mousy-looking guy, not at all the kind of man I'd expect Dawn to be with. A few years older than me, a little bit shorter than you, skinny, with light-brown hair. Not ugly looking, just not very manly."

Sinclair made a quick call to Braddock and asked her to make up a photo lineup containing Yates's photo and bring it back when she returned with the warrant. "Did she ever talk about him?"

"Only that it was complicated and she was trying to put it behind her."

"Is there a manager in the building?"

"Not on site." She handed him a card for NorCal Property Management with a twenty-four hour number. Sinclair copied it into his notebook and said he'd return later to show her photos.

When Sinclair returned to Dawn's unit, Carter was still at the front door. "My two officers are canvassing the building. That leaves the highly paid sergeant to guard the scene."

"Did anyone check the garage for her car?" Sinclair asked.

"They're working their way down, but I doubt they got that far." He stepped inside, grabbed a key ring from the kitchen counter, and tried a key in the door. It fit. "I'm guessing these are hers. Looks like some other door keys and one to a Chevy."

Sinclair took the elevator to the underground garage and walked to the stall with *419* painted on the wall. He pressed the key fob and the red Camaro in the parking space beeped. It was the LS model with a V6 and automatic. Even though it wasn't the high-performance SS, it was still a sharp car that would leave his department Crown Vic in the dust. Sinclair gloved up and popped the trunk. Empty except for a fleece jacket and a pair of sneakers. He sat in the driver's seat and went through the door cubby and center console: tissues, lip balm, an old receipt from Safeway, and some fast-food napkins. The glove box held the owner's manual and vehicle registration. He peered under the seats, found nothing, and locked the car.

At Dawn's apartment, he returned the keys to Carter and asked him to have one of his officers order up a tow with a hold for a technician.

"Will do," Carter said. "One of my guys is taking a statement from a neighbor who might know something. Number four-ten."

A stocky female officer was sitting at a dinette table across from a slightly built man wearing tight black pants and a pink polo shirt in 410. She handed Sinclair a handwritten statement as soon as he entered. "I'm almost done," she said.

The statement said James Dubois heard a loud pop about 10 PM last Saturday night. He thought it might be a gunshot, but since he wasn't sure, he ignored it. A few hours later, he heard commotion in the hallway. He cracked his door and saw two young white men, both dressed in black, pushing a handcart with a tall metal box on it toward the elevator. One was also carrying a heavy cardboard box about the size that would hold files. They were having difficulty keeping the metal box stabilized on the handcart. When they saw him, they said, "Movers," and continued toward the elevator. Dubois didn't get a good look at the men, but they appeared to be in their twenties and were both thin to medium built and average height. That's all he recalled.

"Mr. Dubois, I'm Sergeant Sinclair with the homicide section. This box, how tall was it?"

"Five or six feet. It was like those storage containers you see in the marinas that boaters put all their lines and boat cleaning supplies in."

"Was it big enough to hold a body?"

"Oh, yeah. Lots better than rolling it in a carpet like they always do in the movies."

"I know you told the officer the standard line about you not being able to recognize them. I know that no one wants to go to court and testify, but be honest with me. You did see their faces, right?"

"Look officer, I'm cooperating as much as I can. I'm trying to help you out, but I only saw those men for a second. I didn't look them in the face. This is a nice building, real nice, but it's still Oakland, and in Oakland, you don't look a man in the eye."

"They said they were movers. Did they look like movers?"

"You see all kinds of people working as movers these days, but those boys didn't know anything about moving. They couldn't even keep the dolly going straight. The box almost fell off a couple times."

"If they weren't movers, what did you think they were doing?"

Dubois shrugged his shoulders. "It's Oakland, man. They could've been doing anything."

Sinclair returned to Dawn's apartment, called the number to NorCal, and got an answering service. He told the woman on the phone three times that he was the police and needed to speak to someone from the management company, but she kept asking him what his emergency maintenance issue was and why it couldn't wait until Monday. She said the only other twenty-four hour number she had was for security and agreed to call them.

Fifteen minutes later, a middle-aged, heavyset white man in a navy-blue BDU uniform with captain bars on the collar showed up. Security guards loved their rank. Sinclair gave him a run down. The security officer told Sinclair they had a security camera in the lobby. He made a phone call, and a moment later, he showed Sinclair a video on his phone from earlier in the evening of two men leaving the elevator and walking out of the building.

"I recognize them," the security officer said. "They work maintenance for NorCal, but they shouldn't be doing a cleanout and painting of an individual unit. Each condo is privately owned and would be the owner's responsibility."

"How do we find out who owns unit four-nineteen?" Sinclair asked.

The security officer's dispatch had a number for NorCal. Sinclair called it and told the woman who answered he was investigating a murder and needed the owner's information for that condominium unit. He spent ten minutes attempting to convince her to locate someone in the corporate office who could get him the information. The best she could do, she said, was to try to reach her supervisor and pass on Sinclair's request. Sinclair wouldn't hold his breath waiting for a callback.

"How do I view the security feed from last Saturday night?" Sinclair asked the security officer, who was patiently waiting while Sinclair was on the phone.

"It's gone." The man twirled the cord of his radio microphone around his finger. "It's on a seventy-two hour loop."

"And the only camera's in the lobby?"

"You ask me, they only put that one in so they could advertise they had a security system in the building."

By the time Braddock returned with the search warrant, Sinclair had two evidence techs waiting with him at the door. He and Braddock followed the techs through the condo as they took initial integrity photographs of the rooms—to record the way it was before they began searching. Kitchen cabinets and drawers were open, and spices and boxes of food were lying on their sides. Someone had done a haphazard search. The king-size bed in the master bedroom was still neatly made, but drawers were open, and clothes, probably once neatly folded, were pushed into piles. The clothes in the closet had been shoved to one side, and the contents of two plastic bins were scattered on the floor.

Braddock studied the clothes and touched several items, as if she could feel the fabric through her latex gloves. "Nice stuff. A few items are from major designers, but most of it's the kind of clothes I can afford. Nothing vampy. Lots of jeans and casual wear." Braddock turned toward Sinclair. "This was where Dawn lived her normal life."

Both nightstands were covered with baby photos. Sinclair followed a chronology of photographs, many from holidays and birthdays and ranging from a tiny baby with squinty eyes held by a smiling Dawn to the most recent one of a blonde-haired, blue-eyed girl in a wading pool on a bright summer day.

"She didn't bring men here," Sinclair said.

"Definitely not," Braddock said. "This was her sanctuary. Her daughter was her life."

Braddock stepped out of the bathroom. "Normal women's stuff in the drawers and under the sink. Drugstore makeup. Nothing exotic. No prescription medications other than a container of birth control pills dated a year ago. Only one month's been used, so my guess is she wasn't having sex and had no immediate plans to."

The second bedroom was small. A desk stacked with accounting textbooks was against one wall, and the cord to a laptop's charger hung empty over the desk. A twin bed with a Cinderella bedspread and covered with stuffed animals was against the other wall. "Dawn's parents were pretty clear that Madison had never been out here," Sinclair said.

"Even though Madison never visited, it was still her room." Braddock picked up a pink rabbit, squeezed it, and held it to her face. "This room represented Dawn's dream for the future."

Chapter 25

The morning's first light was appearing in the sky by the time Sinclair and Braddock got back to the office. While the techs had processed Dawn's condo for trace evidence and dusted the printable surfaces, they went through every piece of paper they could find, hoping to find something with Preston Yates's name on it. But much as with Dawn's working apartment by the lake, this one had also been stripped of all incriminating documents. There was no computer and no paper files.

Sinclair made a fresh pot of coffee and began researching NorCal on the Internet, hoping to find someone he could talk to that day who could tell him why Dawn was living rent-free in a condo they owned or at least maintained. NorCal was a major commercial real estate developer in the East Bay. They owned a number of Oakland office buildings, including a twenty-four story building in the city center. Sinclair found an article about NorCal winning the city council bid to develop the huge tract of land that was once the Oakland Army Base. Another article from eight years ago contained a photo of Sergio Kozlov, the president and CEO of NorCal, posing with a past mayor. The article touted the huge contribution NorCal had made to Oakland's redevelopment efforts and how the city gave NorCal a full city block, land valued at more than twenty million dollars, along with tax breaks, to build a commercial office building.

The only corporate officer mentioned on NorCal's website was Sergio Kozlov. There were photos of Kozlov with various members of Oakland's city council, including one where he had his arm around Preston Yates's shoulder while he cut the ribbon that opened the road from the Port of Oakland's shipping terminal to the redevelopment area, which would turn the old army base into a warehouse and logistics center for the port. There were older photos with him next to Jerry Brown when he was the mayor of Oakland and a more recent one with him next to an older Jerry Brown as the state's governor.

Meanwhile, Braddock was on her computer going through the city council agenda reports, which were public information. It seemed Preston Yates had made the motion for the council resolution to select NorCal as the developer of the Oakland Army Base property, and he was a supporter of every development by Kozlov.

Sinclair said, "Yates throws his support for this billion-dollar project to NorCal Development, and in exchange they give him a free love nest for his mistress."

"If we could prove it, that would be bigger than our murders," Braddock said. "Can you imagine? Political corruption at that level. Multimillion-dollar contracts given in exchange for personal favors. Maybe we should tell Phil so he can have his Fed friends look into it."

"Fuck Phil," Sinclair said. "I don't even know whose side he's on anymore. He'll have to give me something from the escort service computer before I give him shit."

Braddock bit her lip and went back to her computer, while Sinclair began researching Preston Yates. Yates had graduated from UC Santa Cruz with a degree in political science and went on to earn a JD from Boalt Hall, Berkeley School of Law. He was the counsel for an assortment of nonprofits and married the owner of one of the largest ad agencies in San Francisco, a woman ten years his senior. He ran for his first public office, a seat on the Oakland School Board, at twenty-eight, winning easily, largely because he outspent his opponents tenfold. At thirty-five, six years ago, he ran for the District 1 council seat and took 60 percent of the votes. The North Oakland council district was one of the wealthiest districts, comprising a 57 percent white population. No one had run against him since.

Sinclair's cell phone buzzed. "Have you got something for me?" he asked Bianca.

"I have information on the twenty-four names and a series of photos you'd be very interested in seeing."

"Can you e-mail it to me?"

"Sorry, but Helena insists on eyes only."

"She's in no position to insist on anything."

"She disagrees. She says if this isn't good enough for now, you can go to the DA and get a warrant for her arrest. She won't budge."

Sinclair thought for a minute. "Okay, where?"

"I'm working at my apartment all day on a settlement agreement that's due tomorrow. Can you come here?" When Sinclair agreed, she said, "Come alone."

★

Braddock didn't like it at all. She told Sinclair so during the entire drive to San Francisco's Nob Hill. Bianca couldn't be trusted. If Bianca didn't intend to give him copies of whatever information and photos she had, it would be his word against hers. If they acted on the information without the documentation as proof, they'd be left hanging and looking like fools at best. At worst, they could jeopardize the integrity of the investigation. She suggested that if he still insisted on meeting Bianca alone, he should at least put their digital recorder in his pocket and covertly record their conversation. Sinclair agreed and left her sitting in the car drumming her fingers on the dash as he entered the high-rise luxury building.

Bianca opened the door to the twenty-eighth floor penthouse apartment dressed in a short silk kimono. Bare feet, loose hair, and probably nothing under the robe. "I'm having a bloody Mary, but I have coffee made if you'd like some."

"Sure," Sinclair said. "Black."

She glided across the gleaming bamboo floor into the open kitchen. Floor-to-ceiling windows covered two walls with a view of the top of the Transamerica Pyramid building. The bottom of the building and most of the city below was hidden by the fog, which gave him the feeling they were floating on a cloud. She set a glass mug on a massive marble coffee table centered in front of a long, white sofa. "Have a seat," she said. "I'll get the file."

He sipped the coffee, a weak brown brew with hazelnut flavoring.

She sat next to him so closely he could feel the heat radiating off her, and she pulled several handwritten pages from a legal-size envelope. "Feel free to look at these and take notes of what's important, but I'll ask you not to transcribe it word for word. Each of the twenty-four names you provided was run through the service's database. You'll see each name written here." She pointed out the names in the left column. "Next to each name are the dates when Dawn provided services for that particular man."

Bianca leaned over the papers on the table, exposing most of her left breast when the kimono, kept together only by a sash around her waist, parted. Sinclair had no doubt that Bianca was aware of it. He kept his eyes on the papers as she continued. "A few of the men only saw Dawn once. Most saw her less than ten times. Preston Yates was a regular two or three times a week for several months. Then nothing. I'll tell you more about that later. William Whitt was one of her regulars from the time she began working for the agency about eight years ago. He last used her services about a year ago. You don't need to count all the dates next to his name. He paid for Dawn's company a hundred and fourteen times. You'll note that there are no dates within the last year associated with any of the men."

Sinclair jotted the men's last names in his notebook, the number of times they had seen Dawn, and their most recent date. "There are huge gaps when Dawn saw no one."

"From what I understand, Dawn first came to work for the agency about eight years ago. For a while, she continued to work as a streetwalker. Some of the girls who started on the street can't seem to give it up. Eventually, Dawn became fully employed with the agency, taking about two or three calls a day and working about five days a week. About five years ago, Preston Yates stopped calling for appointments with Dawn, which coincided with Dawn's request to take fewer calls."

"Let me guess," Sinclair said. "She wasn't the first girl who decided to freelance with a regular and cut out the agency."

Bianca turned sideways on the couch and casually pulled one of her legs to her chest. "Agencies are on guard for that. They had her followed and tracked her to a new residential building near the civic center in Oakland, a unit on the fourth floor. She spent several hours there three times a week, occasionally overnight." Bianca pulled a dozen black-and-white photos from the envelope and spread them across the table.

One photo showed Dawn entering past an apartment door being held open by Preston Yates. Several others, apparently taken through the window with a powerful zoom lens, showed them kissing. A sequence of photos showed Dawn completely naked walking from what Sinclair recognized as the bedroom hallway into the main room of the condo and embracing Yates as he stood looking out the window, followed by her leading him by the hand toward the bedroom.

"These sure look like blackmail photos to me," Sinclair said from the other side of the coffee table.

"I believe the agency showed the photos to both of them at the time and admonished Dawn for cutting out the agency. Preston paid an undisclosed amount of money to make up what the agency's commission would have been, and Dawn promptly quit. Helena later found out Dawn had become Preston's full-time mistress. The next time the agency heard from her was about two years later, when she called begging for her old job back. She told Helena she had made a terrible mistake falling in love with a john. She said she got pregnant, and when she refused to have an abortion, Yates wanted nothing to do with her. Dawn went home, had the baby, but for whatever reason couldn't stay."

"And Helena, being a kind-hearted madam, took her back in."

"Helena's a savvy businesswoman. Dawn was a major moneymaker. Helena kept her on a shorter leash this time around and met her for coffee or lunch every month. Although many of the girls who work for the escort service say they plan to save up their money and get out of the business, Dawn was actually doing it. Helena was all for it. She always wanted what was best for her girls. Dawn was going to school and finally got a part-time job as an accountant. About a year ago, she thanked Helena and told her she didn't need the agency any longer. Helena wished her well."

"She didn't have her followed?"

"Ah, Matt, you think like a madam. Helena learned that Dawn was meeting with many of her old clients, but one or both of them showed up at meetings with briefcases, and often only stayed together for a few minutes. She concluded that Dawn was only doing accounting work for those old clients, and since most of them continued to call the agency for escorts, Helena was convinced Dawn was actually out of the business."

"Who does Helena think killed her?"

"She has no idea. She thinks that if Preston did it, he would've done it when she refused to terminate the pregnancy."

"Did she ever use those photos again?"

"Not according to her; however, between you and me, I think she'd use them to avoid prosecution. She believes Yates can influence your department."

"Are there others she could also use to influence her prosecution?"

"I haven't seen the client list, but she assures me there are others she could go to for help if she has to."

"I'd like copies of those papers and the photos," Sinclair said.

"Sorry, but that's not the deal. If your investigation identifies one of these men as Dawn's killer, I'll make sure you get everything you need on that man. If it's Preston, I'll give you the photos. But if I were to give you any documents or photos now, you'd have to submit them as evidence. After that, too many people in your department and the DA's office would have access to them."

"Then I guess we're done here." Sinclair took a final sip of his coffee and set the cup on the table.

"We don't have to be." Bianca leaned back against a large pillow. "I find you very attractive, Detective Sergeant Sinclair."

Sinclair tried not to act surprised by her directness. "I'm flattered. There's no doubt it would be an experience I'd never forget, but there're a million reasons why it would be totally wrong."

★

"She really propositioned you?" Braddock asked after he finished briefing her on what Bianca told him on their way back to Oakland.

"It's on tape," he said, handing the recorder back to her.

"You have to admire her directness. I'll hang onto this. I doubt she'll want that little indiscretion to get out."

Sinclair laughed. "I have the feeling she could care less."

"What now?"

The thick fog turned into a drizzle, and Sinclair turned on the windshield wipers as they passed Treasure Island. "I want to talk to Preston Yates."

"Are you crazy?"

"Why not?" he said. "We've got a witness who puts two men taking out the body. I guess it's possible that he killed her and called for a cleanup, but I don't see him as the killing type. If he did it, he'll lawyer up in a heartbeat. He learned at least that much in law school. Forget who he is for a minute. This is the natural progression of our investigation. We know he acquired the apartment where Dawn was killed. She was still living there because of their relationship, so for all practical purposes, it's his apartment. Isn't that the next person you'd normally interview?"

"Of course, but we can't ignore who he is."

"He shouldn't be allowed to hide behind his position. What he's concealing might open up this whole can of worms and get us on the right track."

Chapter 26

Fifteen minutes later, Sinclair parked their car in front of a storefront office on Telegraph Avenue. He had called the number on Yates's card and told the woman who answered he wanted to brief the councilman on a homicide he'd previously inquired about. She told him that since it was Sunday, Yates was at the district community office and could see him between meetings.

Sinclair and Braddock entered through a glass door into an outer office cluttered with secondhand tables and desks. This had originally been Yates's campaign office, and Sinclair remembered how it bustled with activity that flooded into the street when Yates was first running for office six years ago. Now it was purported as a place for volunteers to give back to their community. In actuality, politicians such as Yates used the volunteers and the office to keep the citizens in his council district happy and ensure his next election victory.

A trim woman introduced herself as Yates's chief of staff and escorted them to the larger of the two offices in the back of the main room. Yates wore khaki chinos and a plaid button-down shirt and sat with his feet on an old desk, reading a thick binder. He rose and shook Sinclair's hand with the same limp grip as before.

"Councilman Yates, this is my partner, Sergeant Braddock."

"A pleasure." He smiled at Braddock. "Sergeant, please call me Preston. Have a seat."

They sat on two metal folding chairs in front of his desk.

"You wanted to tell me about a homicide." Yates leaned forward in his chair as if he were interested.

"The murder of Dawn Gustafson," Sinclair said. "We spoke of it Friday night. We found the apartment where she was killed."

"It wasn't in my district, I hope."

"The new condos at Twelfth and MLK Way, unit four-nineteen. Does that mean anything to you?"

Yates's smile faded for a few counts and then returned to his face. "Can't say it does."

"That's interesting, because we spoke to a neighbor who was a close friend of Dawn," Sinclair said. "She was introduced to a man named Press, who was Dawn's boyfriend."

"It still doesn't mean anything to me." Yates's smile disappeared.

Sinclair pulled out the photo lineup that he and Braddock had shown to Angela Porter and set the six DMV photos of white males on the desk in front of Yates. "She picked number four as Press. That's a photo of you, Mr. City Councilmember."

Yates jumped up. "This meeting is over."

"Sit down," Sinclair ordered.

Yates marched to the door. "You may leave now."

His chief of staff and a fortyish man with shoulder-length hair poked their heads through the doorway.

Sinclair slammed the door shut in their faces, turned to Yates, and said again, this time louder, "Sit down."

Yates walked meekly back to his desk and sat down. Sinclair grabbed Yates's chair with him in it and rolled it to the front of the desk facing his and Braddock's chairs. Without the barrier of the desk between them, the confidence left Yates's face. He slumped in the chair. Sinclair said nothing, allowing the silence to build.

Finally, Yates said, "Aren't you going to read me my rights?"

"Did you kill her?"

"No."

Had Yates said yes, Sinclair would have been screwed. The confession would've been inadmissible. But it was a risk worth taking. "Then I don't need to advise you of your rights. I'm looking for the man who did. Everyone else is just a witness."

"A witness to what?"

"You tell me," Sinclair said.

"I don't know who killed her."

"Tell me what you do know."

Yates sat there quietly for several minutes. Sinclair said nothing.

"Okay, I knew her," Yates finally said.

"Tell us about it. From the beginning." Sinclair's phone buzzed. He looked at the screen: Maloney. He pressed a button, sending the lieutenant to voicemail.

"You don't need to do this," Yates said. "I can be of great benefit to you."

"It sounds as if you're offering me something in exchange for me to not do my job. You know what that is, don't you?"

"I'm not trying to bribe you. That's not what I'm saying."

"Tell me what you are saying."

Sinclair's phone buzzed. A text from Maloney: *WTF are you doing?* Sinclair ignored it and put his phone away.

"What crime did I commit? Engaging in prostitution? The DA doesn't prosecute men for that. Even if your department catches them in a sting, the most they get is a fine and court probation."

"I'd rather not arrest you and make you go through that."

"Where's your case? If it was with that girl, she can't testify. Where's your evidence?"

Sinclair's phone buzzed again. He ignored it. "We're not in court and I'm not here to argue a case. I'm here to solve a murder. Tell me about your relationship with Dawn Gustafson."

"You know that if this gets out, it'll destroy me."

"Then tell me everything, and I'll see that it doesn't get out."

"How can I trust you?"

"You've got no choice. I have the dates when you paid Special Ladies Escorts for Dawn's company. Two or three times a week for a few months. I'll eventually track how you paid. I know about the photos and your payoff to the agency. I know you played house with her in the condo where she was killed. I know your friend, Sergio, owns it. I know about the baby."

Yates put his face in his hands. He rocked back and forth, breathing heavily. After a few minutes, Sinclair pealed Yates's hands away from his face.

"I'm not after your career or your reputation, but right now, you're between me and the truth. Trust me, Mr. Yates, I will bulldoze over you or anyone else who tries to keep me from the truth."

"If my wife finds out—"

The door swung open and Chief Clarence Brown appeared in the doorway. If looks could kill, Sinclair would have been a dead man. "Sinclair, Braddock, outside!"

They slowly stood and walked toward the door. Yates stood as well. "Councilmember," Brown said, "you should stay here and talk to no one until I return."

A dozen people had gathered in the outer office. Brown said to Yates's chief of staff, "I'd like the room." Once everyone filed out the door and clustered on the sidewalk, Brown said, "Now, what in the hell do you two think you're doing?"

"Investigating a murder," Sinclair said. "That's what I'm paid to do."

"Don't be flip with me, Sinclair. You know better than to interrogate a sitting city councilmember without running it up the chain of command."

Sinclair wanted to ask him where in the manual of rules that was written, but decided his best chance for keeping his job rested with a logical explanation. Brown listened for ten minutes as Sinclair laid out the facts that led them to Yates. The rage left

Brown's face, and by the end of the story, he was shaking his head in disbelief. "So Yates was keeping the girl as a mistress and they had a love child together?"

"Yes, sir."

"And shortly before her murder, she was planning on asking him for greater child support?"

"That's what it looks like."

"But you don't think he killed her?"

Sinclair shrugged his shoulders.

"Wait here," Brown said, and he disappeared into the room with Yates.

Fifteen minutes later, Brown came back out just as Maloney burst into the room out of breath. "It's about time you got here," Brown said to the homicide commander.

"Chief, I—"

Brown waved his hand to quiet him. "Last weekend, Yates was in Long Beach with two commissioners from the Port of Oakland for a conference. I know it's possible that he had someone kill your victim, but it's doubtful he did it himself. The councilmember will be in my office Tuesday at five o'clock. He will have copies of all of his bank and cell phone records. Come prepared with a list of questions you have for him. He will be there without a lawyer and will answer anything related to your murder investigation."

Sinclair nodded his approval.

"This stays among us." Brown made eye contact separately with each of them, and then locked his gaze on Sinclair. "If I find any of you leaked this to the media or said a word to anyone—and I mean *anyone* . . . I don't even need to finish that sentence, do I?"

Maloney, Sinclair, and Braddock all shook their heads in unison.

"Personally, behavior of this sort by a government official disgusts me, but I try not to impose my morality on others. The politics of this situation are well above your pay grade. Don't involve yourself. That's not just advice; it's an order. Leave the politics to me."

★

Skyline Boulevard ran for twenty miles along the Oakland Hills from the border with Berkeley to the end of Oakland's city limits in the east. Dozens of pullouts offered panoramic views of the Oakland flatland, the Bay Bridge, and on clear days, as far as San Francisco, Alcatraz Island, and the Golden Gate Bridge. William Whitt's house sat on the south side of the winding two-lane road, high above toney Montclair Village and the city of Piedmont.

After Brown had finished with Maloney and his two investigators, Maloney had taken Sinclair and Braddock outside to add to the chief's ass-chewing. Sinclair felt bad for putting his lieutenant in the chief's line of fire by keeping him in the dark, but had he asked for permission to interview Yates, he would never have gotten it. When Sinclair told him of his plan to next interview William Whitt, Maloney gave him permission under the condition that he and Braddock keep it low-key and non-confrontational unless clear evidence of Whitt's involvement in the murder surfaced. If he received another call from the chief, Maloney promised them there'd be hell to pay.

Whitt opened the door dressed in a cardigan sweater, tweed slacks, and leather slippers. "Sergeant Sinclair, I'm surprised to see you again so soon."

"Do you have time to talk?" Sinclair asked.

"Sure." He held the door open and led them through the foyer to the living room. "I was just downstairs in my office reading a bunch of boring reports."

Built into the downward slope of the hill, the house seemed as if it had been constructed upside down, with the main floor at street level and bedrooms below. Windows covered the entire back of the house and offered what was literally a million-dollar view. This part of Skyline was above the blanket of fog that lay over Oakland and San Francisco.

"Beautiful place," said Sinclair, "but I'd always be afraid it would slide down the hill."

Whitt chuckled. "I've lived here for thirty years and felt the same way for the first ten or so, but when it was intact after the Loma Prieta earthquake, I knew it could weather anything." Whitt offered them seats in the living room overlooking the fog bank that was rolling in across the bay. "Sitting up here, I've become a weather watcher. Although it's calm right now, you can see the weather coming our way."

"They say we need all the rain we can get," Braddock said.

"Yes, but not this kind." Whitt walked to the window and looked out. "The meteorologists say we're going to get hit with the bottom edge of a Pineapple Express system. Do you know what that is?"

Sinclair wanted Whitt to talk and relax, so he prompted, "Tell me."

"It's an informal term for a strong flow of moist air coming from the waters around the Hawaiian Islands. It usually brings warm torrential rain. This one's pointed at Portland. We're just getting a few inches. It's bad news for the snowpack and skiers, since rain's expected all the way up to six thousand feet."

When Whitt turned from the window, Sinclair said, "We came here to talk to you about Dawn Gustafson."

"I figured as much." Whitt sat in an upholstered Queen Ann chair that looked uncomfortable. Sinclair and Braddock sat in two swivel chairs across from him. "I was heartbroken to hear of her death. She was an extraordinary young woman."

"Can you tell us how you knew her?"

"Since you're here, you already know the answer to that. I saw her profile on the website for Special Ladies Escorts, called the service, and requested her. That was probably seven years ago."

"How many times did you see her?"

"Detectives, I know the way this makes me look, but the reality is, after my wife died, I was lonely. I'm not particularly good-looking and I don't have the time nor skill to do the bar scene. Where does a man meet a woman these days? I don't like to mix business with pleasure. You know the old adage about not dipping your pen in the company inkwell. You're probably thinking I'm a dirty old man or a sex fiend. She's just a few years older than my son, after all. But she made me feel good about myself. I would arrange to see her weekly. Sometimes all we did was talk. She was a great listener."

"Can you give us an estimate, Mr. Whitt?" Braddock asked.

"In the hundreds. About five years ago, she quit the agency. I tried other escorts, but none were Dawn. She called me when she returned to the agency, and we began seeing each other again. She was trying to change her life. We talked about her business plan and I fully supported it, so when she quit the agency, I was the first in line to sign up for her personal finance business. It allowed me to still spend time with her, and her hourly rate was much lower."

Braddock picked up a framed photo from the coffee table of a young man dressed in a tuxedo. "Is this your son?"

"Travis." Whitt smiled. "He had it rough after his mother died, but he turned out okay. Finally."

"Losing a mother must've been hard on him," Braddock said.

"He was ten, maybe eleven, when his mother died. The year before she died was difficult as well. I'm sure you'll find out. It's all out there, so I might as well tell you. I had an affair with Travis's fourth-grade teacher. Susan, my wife, found out and filed for divorce. It was public and messy. I entered counseling, did everything she asked of me. We were reconciling. It's all in the court records."

"The teacher's name?" Sinclair said.

"Lisa Harper. That was a huge mistake for both of us. I haven't heard from her in years, but I imagine she's still teaching at the Caldecott Academy. When Susan made my indiscretion public, the school terminated Lisa. She was teaching at the public elementary school then. I helped her get the job at Caldecott and, out of guilt and a sense of responsibility, I paid the difference in her salary and benefits for a number of years."

"How'd your wife die?" Braddock asked.

"Car accident. Drove off the road on Grizzly Peak Boulevard. The car ended up three hundred feet down the cliff."

"Where were you?" Sinclair asked.

"It was all investigated and I wasn't there. But I'm still responsible."

Sinclair raised his eyebrows.

"I told you we were reconciling," Whitt said. "Well, it was a process. Susan put the divorce proceedings on hold and I was going to move back into the house at the end of the month. I was staying at the corporate apartment. Cal Asia had two at the time, mostly for overseas partners who were engaged in lengthy business here. Sunday morning I came to the house to take Travis for the day. She threw down a bunch of photos. It seems she had hired a PI to watch me, and they got photos of Dawn entering the corporate apartment. I tried to explain it was a one-time thing—a relapse. I had called my therapist the day after it happened. Susan was angry. I don't blame her. I left with Travis. Took him canoeing at Lake Chabot. Later that day, the police called and said she ran off the road over a cliff. She had a temper and was known to drive crazy when she was mad. Probably took one of those hairpin turns too fast."

Sinclair looked at the photograph of Travis. Tall, thin, good-looking kid. "Where's Travis now?"

"It was tough at first, raising him alone. When he graduated from middle school, I sent him to a college prep school in Connecticut for his high school years. Great school with plenty of direction. He was accepted to MIT from there, and got a degree in computer science and engineering. He's been working as a software designer at Google down in Mountain View for the last three years. I think he still holds me responsible for his mom's death."

"If we wanted to talk to him, how do we reach him?" Sinclair asked.

Whitt recited his cell number. "If he doesn't answer, text him. Kids never listen to their voicemails today."

Sinclair thanked Whitt and signaled to Braddock that it was time to go.

When they started down the hill, Braddock said, "I had some more questions for him."

"I want to dig a bit deeper into Mr. Whitt before we talk to him again, maybe check out the court file on the divorce, pull the traffic collision report, and talk to Lisa Harper. See if everything in his story matches up."

"He appeared pretty up-front."

"Yeah, he's really good at appearing that way."

Chapter 27

Once in the guesthouse, Sinclair stripped off his coat and tie, pulled on a fleece jacket, and walked to the main house with an umbrella. It was only six o'clock, but the house was quiet. Sinclair got a cigar from Fred's humidor in the library and walked out the side entrance, where a portico covered the driveway and service entry.

He sat on a step and typed a text to Alyssa:

Was up all night with a break in case. How are you?

All day at niece's BDay party. How R U?

Tired but I'll be ready for a run later this week.

Sounds fun. Let me know.

OK. Good night.

Nite.

Sinclair put his phone away and heard the door behind him open. He looked over his shoulder to see Walt.

"You want some company?" Walt asked.

"Sure." Sinclair lit his cigar and waited for Walt to shut the door. "What do you think about men who engage the services of prostitutes?"

Walt buried his hands in his jacket pockets. "I look at the place and time when it occurred and try to understand the emotional and spiritual condition the man is in."

Sinclair took a few puffs on his cigar and looked out at the rain pelting the driveway. One thing he liked about sitting with Walt was that periods of silence weren't awkward. Sinclair was searching for a simple answer, not a "depends on the circumstances" response. But Walt seldom gave simple answers to such questions.

"Times have changed," Walt continued. "When I was in Vietnam, most soldiers used prostitutes at one time or another. It was accepted. We can't judge men in the past by our standards today."

"What about the men who pay for escorts?"

"It's the same, except those men have more money, and the girl receives greater compensation. That makes it more palatable to some people. But the reasons are the same. Some do it to try to fill an emptiness within them. Some enjoy the power that their money can buy."

"Did you ever?"

Walt sat down on the step beside Sinclair. "In Vietnam. When I reflected back on it as I got older, I felt nothing but shame. What about you?"

"I've never paid for sex." Sinclair puffed on his cigar and stared at the rain.

Walt glanced at him. "However . . ."

"I don't know how you can always tell when there's more to the story."

Walt smiled.

Sinclair had heard people in AA say, "You're only as sick as your secrets," and he'd been holding this one in too long. "I'd been back from Iraq less than a year, and Jill started on my case again to open up and talk about it."

"Jill, your ex-wife?"

"Yeah. I thought I was fine. War changes you. You know that. It doesn't mean you have PTSD or are about to go postal. Anyway, that's what I thought at the time. Finally, her nagging got to be too much and I moved out for a while. One of the guys in CID had converted his uncle's garage in Alameda into an apartment and rented it out short-term to fellow officers going through the suitcase drill with their wives. It was available, so I moved in. I'd been there about a week when I got a call from Dawn. She was scared, but wouldn't tell me of who. Wouldn't tell me the details other than she couldn't go back to her apartment and had no one to turn to for help. I'd never done this before—taking someone from my work life into my house—but I gave her a spare key to the apartment and told her to stay there until I got home."

"Are you the first police officer who brought someone like her into their home?" Walt asked. "In AA we do it all the time."

"We had this sergeant years ago who was a born-again. He and his wife took plenty of prostitutes into their home to try to save them. But that was different. Everyone knew his intentions were pure."

"And yours weren't?" Walt asked.

"I gave her the couch and I slept in my bed. She said she was in trouble and it was because of the choices she had made. She didn't want to discuss her past or concern herself with what she was going to do in the future for now. She didn't ask me to talk about my past either. It was as if we could both exist fully in the present and use the opportunity to take a breath before we had to figure out what to do next. We took walks on the beach, held hands, drank wine, and talked late into the night.

"She'd been there almost a week when I heard her sobbing one night. I sat on the couch next to her as she cried. She said she'd have to make a decision soon about her situation and was afraid it would be the wrong one. I didn't pry or try to give her advice. I just sat with her until she fell asleep and then went back to bed. A little bit later, she knelt next to my bed and said she didn't want to be alone. She slipped into bed with me. I held her and after a while, one thing led to another."

"Two people clinging to life by its threads made love and took comfort in each other," Walt said. "Is that wrong?"

"I think I had fantasized that because she was a *professional* she would do things to me that no woman had ever done, that it would be the most mind-blowing sex in the world. It wasn't. It was soft, quiet, and, if a man can use that word, sweet. We slept together the rest of her time there. We made love as soon as I got home from work every day and again before we went to sleep. It was as if we couldn't get close enough to each other. She pulled me into her as deep as she could, but it was never far enough. Yet at the same time, we gave each other everything we could. When I came home from work one evening, she was gone. She left a note."

"What did she say?"

"She thanked me for being there for her and saving her from herself. Said I was the kindest and most loving man she'd ever met. And she had met a few. She added a smiley face. She said she made her decision, knew it was the right one, and what we had was special. She ended by saying she had never loved a man as much as she loved me and hoped that I would find that kind of love myself someday."

"Did you ever try to find her?"

"No, it didn't seem right. Not long afterward, Jill filed for divorce and I got caught up in that and then work stuff, and of course my drinking took over. I'd thought about her occasionally and hoped she found happiness. I ran her name a few times and was glad when I never found her in the system. I figured she left Oakland for good. And then I saw her hanging from the tree."

Chapter 28

"How's your shoulder?" Braddock asked when Sinclair arrived at the office Monday morning an hour late.

He had called earlier and told her that the shoulder he was shot in years ago was acting up and he needed to see his physical therapist on the way to work. At least the part about seeing a therapist was the truth. In his session with Dr. Elliott, he had gone through the ambush in Baghdad again and begun talking about his brother's death. He felt a bit lighter after bringing that incident to the surface.

"It'll be okay," he said to Braddock. Another thing he'd lied to her about.

She headed over to the court building to pull a copy of Whitt's divorce proceeding, while Sinclair went downstairs to beg a police records specialist to pull a sixteen-year-old traffic collision report. Sinclair found an empty desk, opened the dusty accordion folder, and pulled out the collision form. It listed Susan Whitt as the driver and William Whitt as the registered owner of the 1998 BMW 750i four-door sedan. The incident time was listed as between 1300 and 1500 hours, and it was reported at 1510 when a passerby saw the car upside down in a canyon. The report prepared by the traffic accident investigator described the laborious process by a fire department rescue team to get to the wreckage and pronounce the driver dead.

In multiple pages, it detailed the recovery of the body and the recovery of the car, which took most of the following day.

Sinclair turned to a series of diagrams that indicated an absence of skid marks on the road but a set of tire tracks in the dirt leading from the roadway to the edge of the cliff. The traffic investigator concluded the vehicle was airborne for more than a hundred feet and then rolled and slid an additional 130 feet down the hillside until it came to rest. A statement from a firefighter stated the driver was still in the driver seat area, but the vehicle was crumpled in around her when his team reached the car. Her seat belt was unfastened.

A report by a vehicle inspector found no evidence of brake failure or steering malfunction, but due to the condition of the vehicle, he could not be 100 percent certain it hadn't been tampered with.

Sinclair poked his head into the admin sergeant's office and asked about the investigator who handled the scene. He had retired thirteen years ago, a year after Sinclair came on the department, and was working for an insurance company as an accident reconstruction investigator. Sinclair called the phone number the admin sergeant gave him and the retired officer answered on the first ring.

"Yeah, I remember that one like it was yesterday. Not every day we get that kind of crash."

"Any suspicions about the husband?" Sinclair asked.

"I remember they were going through a divorce and just had a spat earlier that day, but the husband had an alibi. Besides, cutting brake lines or tampering with steering only works in the movies. Ya know what I think?"

"That's why I called."

"I put down the speed as sixty, but that's the minimum. I think she was doing closer to eighty. She couldn't have taken the previous curve at much above thirty, so I think she punched the pedal to the metal when she came out of that turn, pointed the car at the cliff, and rocketed off into space."

"You think it was suicide?"

"I'd seen it before. People with terminal diseases who smash into a tree at seventy. I would never put that in a report unless I could prove it, because it messes up people's insurance settlements and stuff. Some strict priests won't even bury suicide victims in a Catholic cemetery. But the woman had lived there for years. She knew those roads like the back of her hand. The visibility was perfect, the road was dry, there were no indications of mechanical issues, and no skid marks or debris to indicate someone ran her off the road."

"Did you look for a suicide note?"

"Nothing in the car. I asked the husband and he denied it. It's not like a homicide. We don't get a warrant to search a house and stuff like you guys do. Single vehicle accident, no one at fault other than the driver who's dead. Case closed."

Sinclair went back to the office, and Braddock returned a few minutes later with an inch-thick stack of paper.

"This is a copy of the entire court file," she said. "I skimmed through it, and it looks like Whitt was being up-front with us. His wife's lawyer put him through the ringer. They deposed Lisa Harper, who was only twenty-six back then, and asked her about every lurid detail of the affair, which amounts to about twenty pages of questions about their sex life."

"Sounds unnecessarily cruel to me," Sinclair said.

"Yeah, but pissed-off wives love to use their divorce lawyers to beat up cheating husbands. What better way to punish him than to ridicule the girlfriend?"

"Anything else interesting?"

"Susan wasn't employed outside the home. The financial assets report put his net worth around five million, not too shabby for back then. She was asking for the house, half of all investments, forty thousand a month spousal support for the rest of her life, full custody of their son, and another twenty grand a month child support."

"Hell, if she were our murder victim, I know who would've had plenty of motive to kill her."

Sinclair called Harper's school, found out her class had the early lunch period, and decided to make another run at NorCal in the meantime. They drove the six blocks to the city center complex, parked their car in a loading zone, hung the radio mic off the mirror to prevent a ticket or tow, and took the elevator to the top floor of the twenty-four-story building. They were bounced from person to person for an hour, finally landing in an office with a window. A fiftyish woman wearing a high-necked white blouse sat behind a desk with a nameplate reading Alice Chan. Sinclair told their story for the fifth time.

"NorCal developed that property and sold all of the condominiums in the building about ten years ago," Chan said.

"Unit four-nineteen is still owned by NorCal," Sinclair said.

"Who told you that?"

Sinclair told her again about the two maintenance workers employed by NorCal entering the unit to clean it out.

She picked up her phone, spoke softly, listened, and hung up. "You're right, maintenance was dispatched there."

"NorCal still owns the building, right?" Sinclair asked.

"Yes, but each unit is individually owned."

"Every condo owner must pay a homeowner's association fee to you to maintain the building and common areas, right?"

"Of course."

"Who here has the list of those condo owners?"

"That would be the property management office."

"And who can I speak to there?"

"I'm the assistant department head for property management," Chan said.

Sinclair would've laughed if his business weren't so serious. "Where do you keep the list of condo owners, Ms. Chan?"

"The information is on our computer server."

Sinclair felt as if he were speaking to a child. "Do you have access to that data?"

"I do."

"May I see it?"

"That's confidential information. You need a court order."

Sinclair took a deep breath and exhaled loudly to show his frustration. "There's nothing confidential about a business owning property. These aren't medical records or something of the sort. If you are refusing to cooperate with the police, it's because you're hiding something. Is NorCal listed as the owner of four-nineteen?"

"Yes."

Chan's performance reminded him of his first few times being cross-examined in court, when the DA instructed him to only answer what was asked and offer absolutely nothing more.

"Ms. Chan, I'm pleased that we're making such progress," Sinclair said. "Since we're in agreement that NorCal owns it, my next question is who in NorCal is in charge of the unit? Now remember, I told you a woman was murdered there, so I need to find out who it is that gave my murder victim permission to live there."

"I don't know."

Sinclair believed her. "Who at NorCal would know the answer to that?"

She sat there passively.

"Let me phrase this another way. Is there anyone besides Sergio Kozlov that would know the answer to my question?"

"I don't know."

"I'd like to see Mr. Kozlov."

"You'll have to call his personal assistant to arrange that."

Sinclair had Chan dial the number. A pleasant woman answered the phone and said Mr. Kozlov was unavailable, but she would take Sinclair's name and number, confer with Mr. Kozlov, and call back to arrange an appointment. Sinclair doubted he'd ever get a call.

When they got on the elevator, Sinclair pressed eighteen.

Braddock said, "That was bizarre."

"I've known CIA officers who were more forthcoming."

When the elevator opened on the eighteenth floor, Braddock looked around the lobby and fixed her eyes on the long marble reception desk where two people were seated. "Why are we here?"

"You remember Fred Towers, the man who owns the estate where I live?"

"Fred? Sure."

"This is his company."

A receptionist led them down a corridor lined with offices to a corner office with an open door. Fred was sitting at a round table in the corner of the spacious room, the sleeves of his white shirt rolled up two turns. When Sinclair and Braddock entered, the three men who were seated with him rose.

"Let's meet again at four, and you can show me what you came up with," Fred said to the men as they filed out of the office. "Coffee?" he asked Sinclair and Braddock.

They both accepted, and the receptionist turned and left. Lake Merritt and the Oakland Hills were visible through the window beyond the massive mahogany desk and credenza centered toward the back of the wood-paneled room. Fred led them to the opposite corner, where a leather sofa and three chairs surrounded a low mahogany table.

"To what do I owe this unexpected pleasure?" Fred asked.

Sinclair recited his experience at NorCal.

Fred chuckled. "NorCal owns this building and a number of other ones throughout the Bay Area. They're also in the development phase for a half dozen other properties, the most significant being the Global Logistics Center on the site of the old army base. Every other property management company I know selects one of the lower floors for their offices. The top floor always commands the highest rent, so it makes financial sense to lease that to a paying client and one with significant name recognition. Sergio Kozlov took the entire top floor for himself."

"It sounds like Mr. Kozlov is more concerned with prestige than the bottom line," Braddock said.

"Prestige, ego, power: those are all words that other business leaders in Oakland bandy about when they discuss Sergio," Fred said.

"How do I get in to see him?" Sinclair asked.

"He emigrated from Russia in the nineties, so nothing American police can do scares him, and he has plenty of lawyers at his disposal. His reputation, however, is important to him, so if someone in a high place, such as your police chief, were to ask him nicely, he'd probably respond."

"If he was giving a politician a perk, such as a free apartment, would he admit it?" Sinclair asked.

Fred laughed. "Not to you, but he might hint around to the old boys club that he was doing so. Who do you think he has in his pocket?"

"I shouldn't say," Sinclair said. "Is he the kind of businessman who would buy off politicians?"

"Matt, you're talking such shades of gray. If you're asking whether Kozlov and his company support the city and probably get more access to elected officials as a result, well sure. So does my company. Is he a little more direct in his dealings with local government? I'm sure he is. Would he come right out and tell elected officials he'll give them X in exchange for Y? I don't think he's that dumb."

"Is there anyone in Oakland City Hall who comes to mind that Kozlov has especially close ties with?"

Fred leaned forward with his elbows on his knees. "You know I respect your oath and love you like a son, but I have to do business in this city."

"I didn't mean to put you in a tight spot," Sinclair said. "I'd never mention your name or directly use anything you told me. This is only background so I can navigate through terrain that's totally foreign to me."

Fred leaned back in his chair. "You spoke to him at the fundraiser. I'm sure that's why Bianca introduced you."

"Preston Yates?"

Fred nodded.

"How about William Whitt?" Sinclair asked. "Is he close to Yates?"

"William's an old-school businessman. He glad-hands all the elected officials, but he'd never buy a politician."

"Would he and Kozlov know each other?"

"Sure. Their companies have been negotiating for years over the Global Logistics Center. Kozlov is developing it, and Cal Asia hopes to be their primary tenant."

Chapter 29

Sinclair wasn't surprised to encounter locked doors at the entrance to Caldecott Academy. Although private schools were not as frequent targets of school violence as public ones, they were not immune, and even though the school was nestled in the redwoods not far from Montclair Village, the crime and violence that plagued the Oakland flatlands were only a ten-minute car ride away. He and Braddock stood in a covered alcove facing two reinforced glass doors. To their left was a thick glass window similar to what many inner-city banks place between their tellers and the customers. A tall, thin woman wearing large, black-framed glasses smiled at them. "May I help you?"

Sinclair pulled his badge from his belt, held it up to the window, and said, "Sergeants Sinclair and Braddock. I called about seeing Lisa Harper."

Sinclair pulled open the door when it buzzed and made an immediate left into the office. A waist-high counter separated a waiting area with six chairs from an open office area with three desks, behind which were two closed doors, labeled *Headmaster* and *School Counselor*. "Mrs. Harper's expecting you. Make a left out the door, take your first right, and follow the hallway to room fourteen."

The hallway was empty but filled with a steady din of laughing and screaming kids coming from the direction they headed. "Tell me again why we're talking to Harper?" Braddock asked.

"To verify Whitt's story."

"Tell me again why we're focusing on Whitt?"

Her questions caused him pause. They had originally interviewed Whitt not because they thought he was the killer, although Sinclair couldn't rule him out, but because they thought he knew Dawn better than her other clients and could provide useful background. Although they hadn't talked about it, Sinclair figured Braddock shared his suspicions. After they were stonewalled at NorCal, Sinclair grew more suspicious of Kozlov, and once Fred explained how Whitt, Yates, and Kozlov were intertwined, his suspicions grew. Now he wondered if he had gone off on a tangent when the real trail to the killer was elsewhere.

"Can you just bear with me while we talk to her?" Sinclair asked. "When we're done, we'll head back to the office and figure out what direction we want to head in."

"It's your case, but if you shared with me what you were thinking occasionally, maybe I could help."

She was pissed off. He'd worry about it later. Sinclair pushed open the door to room fourteen. Four rows of desks took up the center of the room. Windows on one wall. A wall of whiteboards filled another. Bulletin boards covered with bright artwork, posters, letters, and other stuff covered the other two walls. A trim woman with long, blonde hair, deep-blue eyes, and a wide smile sat behind a desk in the front of the room.

"Hi, I'm Lisa Harper. Pull up a desk. They're a bit small, but it's all I have." Harper described her affair with Whitt much as Whitt and the court documents had. When she finished, she said, "There's no excuse for what I did. Getting involved with a parent is bad enough, but what was worse was the impact it had on Travis and my other students. In my profession, it's all about the children, and I had forgotten that. Once the shock of what I had done wore off, I entered therapy. It turned my life around. I married a solid man twelve years ago and have two wonderful children." She paused and smiled. "In addition to twenty-three wonderful fourth graders."

"I understand Mr. Whitt subsidized your salary after the incident," Sinclair said.

Harper brushed a strand of hair behind her ear. "He gave me two thousand dollars a month to make up for the lower pay. It was a nice gesture and much needed for a while, but I was responsible for my choices. A few years ago, I mailed a check back to him and told him to stop sending them. My husband does very well, and quite honestly, I don't teach for the money."

"Have you had much contact with him?"

"After the divorce hearings were finished, I never saw him or spoke to him again. At the suggestion of my therapist, I wrote him a letter as a sort of closure and apologized for my part in the affair. He wrote something back. Except for a short note when I returned his check, that's the last contact I had with him."

Sinclair pulled a photo of Dawn from his folio. "Do you know her? Her name's Dawn Gustafson."

Harper shook her head.

Sinclair pried himself out of the student desk and walked toward the door with Braddock. Harper followed and said, "The girl you showed me—is that who was killed?"

"Yeah," Sinclair said.

"Do you think William was involved?"

"Do you think he's capable of it?"

"I don't know. I try not to psychoanalyze others, but William was never violent and never even exhibited a temper."

On a bulletin board by the door were a series of black-and-white photos of a young woman in various ballet moves. In one, the ballerina's right leg was stretched high and her head was turned to the side and looking upward. The similarity to how Dawn's body was posed in the park was uncanny. Below were color photos of Harper, wearing leotards and surrounded by grade-school-age girls in dance clothing. "Is that you in the black-and-white photos?" Sinclair asked.

"Yes." Harper smiled. "In my teens, I dreamed of being a professional ballerina, but I wasn't good enough. Instead, today I share that dream with young girls by teaching them the joy of dance."

Harper continued as Sinclair grabbed the doorknob: "My biggest regret is the damage we caused to Travis. His father's affair and his mother's suicide were hard on him. Like many kids, he blamed himself."

"Who told you it was a suicide?" Sinclair asked.

"Travis thought for the longest time it was an accident, but he recently found out she intentionally killed herself."

"You're in contact with Travis?" Sinclair asked.

"My therapist suggested I write a letter to Travis as well. When he turned eighteen, I did. He wrote back, and we corresponded for a year or so, and about a year ago, he called me—just to let me know he was doing well. I keep in touch with many of my students. Travis and I have since talked on the phone several times. He's a computer engineer and doing well professionally. He's had therapy himself, and he told me he's in a nice, healthy relationship with a girl his age and has reconciled with his father."

Chapter 30

When Travis Whitt's cell phone went straight to voicemail, Sinclair sent him a text requesting he call him back. He threw a sandwich wrapper in the trashcan next to his desk, ripped open a small bag of chips, and looked at his partner. "What are you so pissed about, Braddock?"

She forked a cube of melon and popped it in her mouth. "Men like William Whitt and Yates use women as sex toys with no repercussions. Their money gives them a free pass to do as they wish. Meanwhile women's lives are destroyed, some permanently."

"We're working to hold them accountable."

"For murder," she said. "Assuming one of them's involved. But what about for the ruined lives?"

"Cathy, we can't fix the world. We can't even fix this tiny piece called Oakland. All we can do is solve the murders we're assigned and bring those responsible to justice."

"I started getting frustrated when it became clear that Whitt and Yates had nothing to do with the murders and would get away with what they did to those women."

"You're sure they're innocent?"

"Come on, Matt, there's not a bit of evidence that points to them. You're trying to concoct a motive out of thin air, but it's all conjecture. We've been speeding down the wrong road and need to turn around and find the right path."

"Did you see the photo of Lisa Harper in her classroom?"

"Yeah."

"Just like how Dawn was posed in the tree," Sinclair said.

"Matt, hanging a woman by her neck and tying up one leg is not a ballet pose."

"What about Travis telling Harper his mother's death was a suicide? Doesn't that make you wonder why his father lied to us?"

"Aren't you the one who told me that everybody lies?"

Just because someone lied, it didn't make him a killer. Whitt had obviously figured out his wife had committed suicide just as the traffic investigator had, and at some point told his son.

Sinclair's desk phone rang. It was John Johnson, the *Oakland Tribune* reporter. "Have you seen the video of your murder?"

"What video?" Sinclair asked.

"On YouTube."

"I don't know what you're talking about."

"I just sent you the link," Johnson said. "Check your e-mail. This thing's going viral. Call me back after you see it. I need a quote."

The video was dark, but he immediately recognized the tree at Burckhalter Park. The camera zoomed in, showing a tall, slender person in a black mask lifting an inert, naked female body.

Sinclair turned on the speakers. Braddock stopped what she was doing and wheeled her chair alongside his. The video shifted to another man, shorter and stockier, also wearing a black mask. He was pulling a rope downward as if he were hefting a weight on a pulley. The video shifted back to the tall man and showed the rope around Dawn's neck. The tall man lifted her a few feet and let go. The rope suspended Dawn's body as the tall man grabbed her at the waist and lifted again. The video jumped forward. The person shooting the video had either stopped filming or edited out parts. The tall man was now standing next to Dawn's body, which was hanging from the tree exactly as Sinclair saw her a week ago. A long piece of cloth dangled from her groin area.

A young, excited male voice, which probably belonged to the videographer since it was loud and clear, said, "Watch here as we barbecue a hooker just like on GTA." The tall man lit a disposable lighter and held it next to a can of hairspray. The videographer said, "Flame on!" followed by a childish laugh. Flame shot two or three feet from the hairspray can. The tall man directed the flame toward Dawn, and the cloth that had been inserted into her vagina burst into flames. The fireball illuminated Dawn's face for a few seconds. Then the video stopped.

Sinclair yelled for the lieutenant and played the video again as Maloney and five other investigators crowded around his computer. When it finished, Maloney asked, "Is there any way to trace this?"

Sinclair shrugged his shoulders.

Behind him, Sergeant Lou Sanchez, the unit's resident computer guru, said, "Lemme see."

Sinclair got up, and Sanchez took his seat. After a few clicks of the mouse, Sanchez said, "It was posted an hour ago by someone with a username of G-G-four-thirty-eight. It has over three thousand views already. The profile was created today. The only information listed on the profile is gender—male. This is the only video or any other content the user's posted."

"Is there any way to identify him?" Maloney asked.

"YouTube is part of Google, and anyone can create an account with Google," Sanchez said. "You can use any name you want. Some people have dozens of profiles and use different ones for different things. I could create one right now under the name of Donald Duck if I wanted to. But I'm sure someone already has that name."

"So there's no way to trace him?" Maloney asked.

"Google won't just release information," Sanchez said. "If we did a search warrant, they'd be compelled to give us what we ask for. But unless this guy's an idiot, he didn't use his real name or personal info. In theory, they should have a record of the IP address of the computer the person used when he created his account and the IP address when he posted this video."

"That could tell us where he lives or works," Maloney said.

"Only if he used an Internet connection there. He could've sat outside a Burger King that had a Wi-Fi connection."

"Can we get this taken down?" Maloney asked.

Sanchez chuckled. "YouTube is into freedom of speech in a big way. But if we tell them this is an actual murder someone posted, they might."

"Do it," Sinclair said. "Our victims and their families don't need this shit blasted to the world."

"I'll get on it, but it could take a while." Sanchez returned to his desk and went to work at his computer.

Even though it would take more than a week to get anything back, and the chances of the results leading anywhere was a longshot, the video was still their best lead to the identity of the killers, so Braddock volunteered to start the search warrant paperwork.

In the blink of an eye, the video changed everything Sinclair had assumed about the murder. The voice sounded young, early twenties or so. Not the profile of someone who would normally employ an escort. The reference to GTA was about the video game Grand Theft Auto, the five versions of which were some of the most violent games ever marketed. In one, there was a scene where gamers could kill a prostitute with a flamethrower. Opponents of these games, claiming there was a connection between violent video games and real-world violence, frequently cited that scene as an example. Sinclair had never gotten into video games, not even in Iraq, where many of his fellow soldiers spent hours of their off time mesmerized by them.

The video, as disturbing as it was, gave Sinclair hope. It showed three people involved in the murder. One man could keep a secret, but three couldn't. They sounded proud of what they'd done and might brag more about it.

His phone rang. "Well?" asked John Johnson.

"Well, what?"

"Is that the way you figured the murder went down?"

"I guess it doesn't matter what I thought before," Sinclair said. "The video pretty much shows it."

"You believe this is real?"

Sinclair chose his words carefully. "What I saw in the video is not inconsistent with what the crime scene and autopsy showed."

"Do you have a suspect?"

"All I know is what you saw on the video."

"Can't you ID them from that?" Johnson asked.

"We just had that discussion in the office, but the short answer is you can't trace a YouTube video unless the person posting it uses his real name. The video isn't very clear, and I don't imagine anyone could recognize masked men."

"Any thoughts on the motive?"

"Come on, John, you saw the video the same as me."

"I can't write an article about what I think the motive is."

"I don't want to speculate."

"Looks to me like people killing a prostitute for the fun of it."

"I need to know a lot more before I'm willing to say these killers fit into the thrill-killer mold," Sinclair said.

"But it is a possibility?"

"Sure, but the victim's background opens all kinds of motives."

"Okay. I'll check back later."

Sinclair hung up and walked into the lieutenant's office. "The *Trib* already called," he said. "The rest of the media will be on it before long."

"Any benefit to you talking with them?"

"Just a distraction."

Maloney picked up his phone and pushed four buttons. "I'll tell the PIO this is his to handle. Tell Connie the same," he said, referring to the unit admin.

Sinclair's phone rang again as soon as he sat down. "Homicide, Sinclair," he barked.

"Matt, it's Phil."

"Did you call to apologize?"

"Not exactly," said Roberts. "A source of one of my guys just called and told him to look at one of the websites set up by a fringe Occupy Oakland group. It has a video of your homicide posted on it."

"I just saw the same thing on YouTube."

"This includes some comments about who the people might be. Let me give you the URL. Look at it and call me back. I might be able to help you identify these people."

Sinclair punched the web address into his computer and brought up a blog. The top banner read, *Black Lives Matter. So do brown, red, yellow, and white lives. All lives matter except blue ones and 1%ers.*

The top entry showed a photo of a line of OPD officers in riot gear in front of a police car with all its windows shattered, probably from one of the most recent demonstrations. Under the photo was a long tirade about how cops work for the one-percenters to oppress the working class. The video was attached to a comment posted by GG438 that read, *A slave to the elite meets her maker.*

Other comments followed:

OCCUPY JLS: The voice in the video sounds like Gothic Geek. Geek is that you?

GG438: Flame on!!! More fun than burning dumpsters or pig cars.

OCCUPY JLS: Were you the torch?

GG438: I was the cameraman.

OCCUPY JLS: I'll bet your bud, Anarchist Soldier, was the flamer.

GG438: Flame on . . . LMFAO.

Sinclair called Roberts. "Do you think suspects in my murder are occupiers?"

"What do you know about the Occupy movement?" Roberts asked.

"Probably as much as most cops. I've stood in many a skirmish line and had rocks and bottles thrown at me."

"Most of the people in those protests are normal people. They believe in the cause and attend what they consider to be rallies. Then there's the professional demonstrators, who come to yell and scream. It doesn't matter whether it's for animal rights, gay rights, police brutality, or the environment. Some of them are the hard-core anarchists. Those are the ones that cause most of the trouble. They burn cars, break business's windows, and toss Molotov cocktails at us."

"Under what category do my murder suspects fall?"

"It's not like these groups have lists of members. They might just be hangers-on. There's no real hierarchy, and the leadership is vague and fluid. But we've heard of Gothic Geek and Anarchist Soldier. Their names first surfaced during the protests in Oakland over Ferguson."

Sinclair, like every able-bodied cop in Oakland, had been assigned to work uniform after the Ferguson grand jury decided not to charge an officer for the death of Michael Brown. OPD stopped a crowd of thousands from marching onto the freeway and shutting down traffic. Later that night, they arrested dozens of demonstrators when the crowd began breaking storefront windows in downtown Oakland. The protest moved to Berkeley the next night. The protesters were hoping for a kinder, gentler police force, but when the crowd blocked the entrance to the freeway and started fires, Berkley PD called for mutual aid. OPD was one of many departments that responded.

"Are they anarchists?" Sinclair asked.

"Their names pop up in anarchist circles and are also associated with the By Any Means Necessary group."

Sinclair remembered one of the anonymous leaders of that group being quoted in a newspaper as saying, "You can never replace the lives of Michael Brown and Eric Garner, but you can always replace broken windows." The group's website said aggressive actions were justified whenever police killed a black man with impunity.

"You didn't get this from me," Roberts continued, "but for the last few years, one of my guys has been working these groups nearly full-time. They've cost the city millions of dollars, not including the millions in lost business revenue when they shut down streets and businesses. They blocked access to the Port of Oakland last year because two Israeli flagged ships were supposed to dock. The cost estimate from that disruption to the supply chain was over fifty million. We're working on the identity of Anarchist Soldier and Gothic Geek, and I'll let you know the second we get something."

As soon as Sinclair hung up, Braddock picked up her phone and dialed an inside number. She summarized the video and the information Roberts had told them, and then she listened and wrote notes on a legal pad for a few minutes. After she hung up, she said, "That was the investigator for the protest task force."

"I didn't know we had a protest task force," Sinclair said.

"Last summer the department decided to assign an officer full-time to handle all the offenses stemming from the protests since the same players' names were coming up over and over. She noticed a trend beginning last summer with some fringe troublemakers showing up at protests that identified themselves with gamer screennames."

"Gamer?" Sinclair asked.

"Yeah, young people who play online video games. She has a felony vandalism warrant for the arrest of Sean Garvin, who goes by Evil Tildor, for firebombing a police car and a downtown store during the Occupy Oakland protest in October."

"Is Garvin associated with Gothic Geek or Anarchist Soldier?"

"She's never heard of them," Braddock said. "But it sounds like they're gamers, so Garvin might know them."

"Do we have an address?"

"She went to his father's address back in October and struck out."

"Maybe we'll have better luck," Sinclair said.

Chapter 31

A half hour later, Sinclair and Braddock met two uniforms in front of Garvin father's house on Rawson Street in Oakland's Maxwell Park neighborhood. A cold, steady rain fell, and Sinclair pulled his raincoat closed but left it unbuttoned so he could quickly access his gun. A four-foot fence surrounded the nicely maintained single-story stucco house, painted an olive-brown color. A green Ford Fusion sat in a newly stamped concrete driveway. Sinclair's computer research had shown the house was built in 1922, was 1,400 square feet, and was valued at just over five hundred thousand. Even though the house was old and small, Sinclair still couldn't afford to buy it.

Sinclair briefed the officers on the warrant and Garvin's description: male, white, twenty-five, five-foot-ten, 160 pounds, brown hair, hazel eyes. Garvin had some minor arrests and a number of traffic tickets, the most recent on a seven-year-old Hyundai. Sinclair reminded the officers that three people were involved in the hanging and burning of his victim. Since they had worn masks, Garvin could be one of them.

Barton, the older officer of the two, made his way around the back, while the other accompanied Sinclair to the front door. Braddock stood at the front of the driveway, where she could cover the right side of the house as well the front in case Garvin squeezed out a front window as Sinclair entered. A man in his late fifties with thinning brown hair and dressed in jeans and a denim shirt answered the door. "We're looking for Sean Garvin," Sinclair said.

"I'm his father. Like I told the other officers, he doesn't live here."

"Do you know where I could find him?"

"The boy doesn't much tell me anything these days."

"When did you last see him?" Sinclair asked.

"Sometime last summer."

Had Mr. Garvin been more forthcoming, Sinclair might have believed his son wasn't there, but he sensed the man would have no problem lying to the police. "We have a warrant for his arrest, and this is his listed address, so we need to come in and check."

Mr. Garvin stepped aside. "You got the guns. I ain't fool enough to try to stop you."

Sinclair and the uniformed officer walked inside and through a small living room, formal dining room, and kitchen. Neat and clean. They followed a narrow hallway to a master bedroom so small the queen-size bed barely fit and into a second bedroom with two twin beds. The closet was filled with women's clothes. When the kids had moved out, Mr. Garvin's wife probably started using it as an overflow for the miniscule closet in the master. Both bathrooms were empty.

At the front door, Sinclair handed Mr. Garvin his card. "If you were to call me with his whereabouts, we wouldn't need to keep on tromping through your house."

Garvin grunted and slammed the door.

The four of them regrouped in the street. Sinclair saw a window curtain in a house across the street move and a face in the window quickly disappear. "Why don't your guys knock on two or three doors each way on this side of the street," Sinclair said to the uniformed officers. "See if anyone knows anything about Sean. We'll take the houses on the other side."

The officers didn't look too thrilled about knocking on doors in the rain, but they kept it to themselves and trudged down the street. Sinclair and Braddock crossed the street to a yellow stucco house about the same size as Garvin's. A short black woman with white hair opened the door before they knocked. She leaned on a cane with her left hand.

"Come in, officers," she said. She shuffled into the living room and lowered herself into a rocking chair next to the front window. "Mr. Garvin's an ornery old man, isn't he?"

Sinclair removed his hat. "He didn't seem to like the police too much."

"In the thirty years he's lived in the neighborhood, I don't think he found anyone he liked."

"Do you know his son?" Sinclair asked.

"You must mean Sean. The other boy—his name escapes me—he went away to college years ago and never came back."

"Yes, Sean. Have you seen him lately?"

"Last week maybe. He comes by the house every week or two. Mostly when his mom's home and Mr. Garvin's at work. I don't think the father likes Sean much."

"Does he come alone?"

"Oh, yeah. His friends aren't welcome there. Haven't seen any of them in years."

"Do you know any of them by name?"

"No, it's been too long, and I'm not good with names anymore."

"Does he have a car?"

"A little one. Gray. I'm not very good with car makes anymore either. They all seem to look alike these days. Did the boy do something wrong?"

"We'd just like to talk to him," Sinclair said. "What brings him around the house if he and his father don't get along?"

"Walks in with a heavy garbage bag. Walks out with shirts and pants on hangers and a box of neatly folded underwear. You'd think a boy his age could do his own laundry."

"Is there anything else you can tell us about Sean?"

"He was a nice boy when he was little. Used to ride his bike on the street with the other boys his age. When he got older— maybe about high school—he got real quiet. Seemed lost. Lots of boys that age try to figure out the world and where they fit in. Didn't seem like he ever did. Couple years after he graduated, he moved out. Mrs. Garvin said he wanted to be on his own. I think she misses him, being alone with her husband. Now that I think about it, doing Sean's laundry's probably a good thing for her. Lets her see her son on a regular basis."

"You wouldn't happen to know where he moved to, would you?"

"Sorry, officer."

"When will Mrs. Garvin be home?"

"Right at five thirty-five. Sharp. Monday through Friday. Mr. Garvin leaves for work at three forty-five. Their marriage probably works best when they don't see each other much."

Sinclair made a mental note to come back later to see if Mrs. Garvin was more cooperative than her husband was. "Is there anyone else in the neighborhood who might know where we could find him?"

"He's always at the Mills Café. You know—over on MacArthur, across from the college. My girlfriends from church and I go to lunch a couple times a week. Sometimes there. Seems like Sean's always sitting there with his computer, drinking coffee."

Sinclair jotted down her name and contact information and left his card, asking her to call if she saw him.

Both officers were sitting in their cars when Sinclair and Braddock crossed the street.

Barton lowered his window halfway, obviously trying to keep the rain from soaking the interior. "We went three houses down both ways. Only one resident home. She knew nothing."

Sinclair told him about Garvin frequenting the Mills Café.

"I've been there," Barton said. "Years ago it was a real dive, but since the hipsters started moving into the area, it's gotten better."

After Barton described the layout of the café, Sinclair briefed a quick plan where Barton and the other officer would cover the two doors while he and Braddock entered casually to see if Garvin was there. Sinclair followed the two marked cars to Mills Café, less than a mile away. It was located in a decrepit building on the corner of MacArthur Boulevard and Seminary Avenue next to a liquor store and nail salon. A new blue awning stretched along the front of the café, and four metal tables with chairs were arranged outside, waiting for a sunny day. Across the street was Mills College, a private women's liberal arts school that was highly ranked among colleges in the western United States. But Sinclair always wondered why parents would spend over forty thousand dollars a year on tuition to send their daughters to college in the middle of one of the most dangerous cities in the nation.

Sinclair and Barton approached the front door, and Braddock and the other officer went around the side to the back. Sinclair left Barton and stepped inside. He scanned the room. There were about twenty round tables surrounded by chairs crowded into the dining area. A counter where customers placed orders and picked up their food covered the back wall. Behind it were a swinging door and an open window that led to the kitchen. Every table was occupied. A dozen people stood in line at the counter. The customers, a mix of black, white, Hispanic, and Asian men and women, most under the age of thirty, reflected the diversity of the student population and that of the surrounding neighborhood.

Sinclair saw Braddock enter the back door and begin looking over the crowd. The plan was for them each to walk through the café looking for Garvin and go out the opposite door if they didn't see him. Sinclair slowly walked toward the back door, looking closely at the face of every white male, hoping to recognize Garvin from a driver's license photo from four years ago. Sinclair weaved between two tables and spotted a man wearing a baseball cap, his face buried in a laptop computer. The man glanced up. Sinclair stopped.

A look of surprise and panic shot across Garvin's face as he made Sinclair for a cop. Garvin's hands dropped to his lap. He slowly and deliberately rose from his chair, a black handgun in his right hand.

Sinclair swept back his raincoat and suitcoat and grabbed his Sig Sauer P220 while simultaneously yelling, "Police! Freeze!"

Garvin had the drop on him. All he had to do was raise the pistol and pull the trigger while Sinclair was still clearing his holster.

Sinclair didn't think. Thinking took too long. He reacted as he'd been drilled in similar scenarios hundreds of times. Draw the gun from its holster. As it's coming up, punch the gun forward to meet the left hand, which locks onto the right hand. Continue to bring the gun forward to eye level and pull the trigger the microsecond the front sight aligns on the target's torso.

Sinclair felt as if he were moving in slow motion. Front sight on the target. He took up half the slack in the double action trigger and stopped.

Garvin's gun was still at his side. Sinclair was locked into a strong Weaver shooting stance, both hands on his pistol, the sights aligned on the suspect's sternum.

Four girls sat at a table between him and Garvin. Even though Sinclair didn't take his eyes off his target, he knew the faces of each girl showed sheer terror. He prayed they wouldn't leap up into his line of fire. Beyond Garvin were more tables of people and more still at the counter. Some customers rose from their tables. Sinclair heard screams as people rushed toward the back door.

In his peripheral vision, he saw Braddock fighting her way toward Garvin through the throng of people pushing to get out the back door. Although it had been drummed into him and every Oakland cop to always consider their backstop—where their bullet would end up if it missed their target—Sinclair was only slightly concerned about the people behind Garvin. The best way to avoid hitting them was by putting any rounds he fired in the center of Garvin's chest.

Garvin's gun hadn't moved. Still, Sinclair knew Garvin could raise it and shoot faster than Sinclair's brain could tell him to pull the trigger and send the requisite command to his index finger.

"Garvin, drop the gun!" Sinclair bellowed. "Now!"

Garvin didn't move. His face was frozen. His mouth gaped open.

Braddock slipped through the crowd of people to a position behind Garvin.

Sinclair saw Braddock holster her Glock and wondered what the hell she was doing. Her right hand reached across her body, under her coat, and came out with her ASP. With a backward flick of her wrist, the eight-inch expandable baton snapped out to its full twenty-one-inch length. She swung it down across Garvin's forearm with a loud crack.

Garvin's gun flew across the floor. Braddock threw her arm across Garvin's shoulder, trying to drag him to the floor. Sinclair pushed through the four girls in front of him and holstered his pistol. Grabbing Garvin's coat, he pulled him to the ground, landing Braddock on top of him. Barton scooped up Garvin's pistol while the other officer jumped on top of the suspect and handcuffed him.

The two uniformed officers pulled Garvin to his feet and shoved him through the crowd to the front door. After a thorough pat down, they crammed him into the backseat of a patrol car.

Barton slammed the door and turned to face Sinclair. His nostrils flared as he obviously fought to control his breathing and the adrenalin still coursing through his veins. "Why the hell didn't you shoot?" Barton yelled. "You had the shot. He had a gun." Barton took a breath and half-turned as if he was walking away. Then he turned back, faced Sinclair again, and yelled, "Why the fuck didn't you shoot?"

Sinclair said nothing. He was wondering the same thing.

Chapter 32

When Sinclair and Braddock entered room 201, Garvin was sitting in the corner with a cast covering his right arm from the knuckles of his hand to just below the elbow. Sinclair had Garvin sit between him and Braddock at the small metal table.

"What did the hospital say?" Sinclair asked.

"The bitch cop broke my wrist." Garvin glared at Braddock. "They said I need to come back next week for surgery."

"You're lucky I didn't shoot you," Sinclair said.

"It wasn't even a real gun," Garvin replied.

After Garvin had been safely confined in the patrol car, Sinclair examined the gun. It was a Crossman pellet gun, designed to look like a Colt .45 Model 1911. From a distance, no one could tell the difference.

"You're very lucky an experienced police officer like my partner was there," Braddock said. "It sure looked real, and most police officers would've shot. What are you carrying a BB gun for anyway?"

Garvin shrugged his shoulders.

"To shoot out windows and engage in other acts of vandalism with your anarchist friends?" Braddock said.

He shrugged his shoulders again.

"Right now, you're under arrest on a warrant," Sinclair said. "But that's not why we picked you up."

"I figured that."

Sinclair and Braddock had discussed the interview strategy before coming into the room. There was a great deal that Sinclair didn't know about the murder, and Garvin could be one of the suspects from the park. It was even possible that the three men in the park weren't the ones who choked and shot Dawn but were instead the cleanup crew.

Sinclair slid the Miranda form from his folio and read it verbatim.

Garvin looked up at the camera in the corner of the room. "Lawyer," he said.

"Suit yourself." Sinclair took out a blank arrest form and filled in Garvin's name and birthdate. "What's your home address?"

"Lawyer," Garvin said.

"You're required to provide this information," Sinclair said. "If you don't, you'll sit in the booking cell until you do."

Garvin recited his parent's Rawson Street address.

"Bullshit," Sinclair said. "We've been there and searched the house. You don't live there."

Garvin shrugged his shoulders.

"Right now, there's a relatively low bail on your warrant. Even if you can't make it, a judge will probably release you on your own recognizance when you go to court tomorrow. But only if you have a valid address that shows you're a responsible and permanent member of the community."

"Twenty-seven-oh-one High Street."

"Apartment number?" Sinclair asked.

"Twenty-three."

"Who do you live there with?"

"I know what this is about," Garvin said. "I was working that night."

"What night are you talking about?" Sinclair asked.

"Saturday night. The night that whore was killed and strung up in the tree."

"Since you're bringing it up, work address and occupation is another box I need to complete on this form."

"I work at Best Buy."

"The one in Oakland?" Sinclair asked.

"Yeah, by Emeryville."

"Best Buy closes at nine. The woman was probably killed after that. So if you think you've got an alibi through work, you're wrong." Sinclair was on rocky ground, because if Garvin said something in response to Sinclair's comment that incriminated him in the murder, a judge might rule that Sinclair induced him to continue talking even when Garvin clearly asked for a lawyer. But Sinclair didn't care.

"Three of us did inventory after hours that night. I was there from closing until six the next morning."

"If I can verify that, we can disregard the Miranda stuff. I just want to know who was at the park that night. I understand you know them."

"The whole world knows some bitch shot off her mouth on the Internet about who it was, and then one of those stupid fucks chimed in."

"Then you know the police saw the same thing on your anarchist website. I'm trying to figure out who Gothic Geek and Anarchist Soldier are."

He shrugged his shoulders. "Just send me to jail. I'm not saying anything else without a lawyer."

"Have it your way. We have your phone and laptop. If you give us permission to search them, I can return them to you by the time you're released from jail. If you make us get a warrant, the technology in both will be obsolete by the time you get them back."

"Fuck you."

Sinclair and Braddock left the interview room, finished Garvin's paperwork, and took him to the jail. Before he turned Garvin over to the jailers, Sinclair shoved his card into Garvin's pocket in case he changed his mind after a few hours.

Sinclair and Braddock drove through the rain-soaked city to High Street, about a mile from Garvin's parents' house. Two uniformed officers were waiting out front when they arrived.

Sinclair instructed one of the uniforms to stay outside in case someone jumped out a window. Sinclair, Braddock, and the other officer approached the front of the three-story building. An occupant coming out held the door for them. Sinclair rang the bell and knocked on the door of unit twenty-three. Having the manager open the door for them would've been the easiest approach, but they didn't have the legal exigency to do so. At the same time, they didn't have sufficient probable cause to get a warrant based on anonymous Internet chatter and sources the intelligence unit wouldn't identify. He sent Braddock to the manager's office to see if they had information about Garvin, his roommate, and any friends. Meanwhile, he sent the uniform down the hall one way to knock on doors, and he went down the hall the opposite way.

A petite Hispanic woman in her early twenties with a small boy clinging to her leg answered the first door Sinclair knocked on. Sinclair showed his badge. "Do you know the man who lives next door? We think his name's Sean Garvin."

"Yes. My husband know him," she replied in somewhat broken English.

"Is your husband home?"

"He stop work at five. Then come home."

"Does Sean, the man next door, have a roommate?"

"Ed."

"Do you know Ed's last name?"

"Edgar is his proper name. I do not know surname." She nervously shuffled her feet, looked back into her apartment, and then back at Sinclair. "Come in. You must see."

Sinclair followed her into a small, basic apartment filled with mismatched, used furniture. She led him down a hallway into a bedroom with a full-size bed and a particleboard dresser. She pointed to a mirrored closet door. Sinclair looked closely and saw a hole in the middle of the shattered glass. Across the room in the opposite wall—part of the common wall with Garvin's apartment next door—he spotted a small hole and loose plaster in the drywall.

"When did this occur?" Sinclair asked.

She looked at him confused.

"When did you first see this?"

"When I came home today. About three o'clock."

"When was it all okay?"

"My husband and I leave today at seven in morning. He go work. I go where I work day care—watch children."

"Why didn't you call the police when you saw this?" Sinclair asked.

"I tell husband when he come home. He do."

Sinclair phoned Braddock and asked her to bring the manager with a key to Garvin's apartment. Shining his flashlight into the closet, he searched for the path the bullet would have taken after it went through the door. There was no hole in the back wall, so the bullet probably hit the tightly packed clothes in the closet. He'd let the techs search for it later.

Sinclair met Braddock outside Garvin's apartment and told her about the bullet hole.

"Sounds like plenty of exigent circumstances to me." She put the manager's key in the lock and pushed open the door.

Sinclair yelled, "Police, anybody home?" He drew his gun and entered. Braddock and the uniformed officer followed.

Sinclair took two steps inside and stopped.

A body lay on the living-room floor in front of him. Thick blood soaked the dirty, worn carpet under the man's head. A two-inch piece of skull was missing from the back of his head, and brain matter had oozed and congealed in his hair. Checking for a pulse was a waste of time.

They swept through the rest of the apartment looking for other people—dead or alive—but it was clear. The officer used his radio to request a field supervisor, an evidence technician, and additional units. Sinclair also had him request an ambulance.

Even though there was no doubt the man was dead, as long as the victim's head was still attached to the body, no one wanted the police making the official determination.

The victim was lying on his side, looking like he collapsed in a heap when the bullet entered his brain. Sinclair gloved up and lowered himself to the ground, careful to avoid getting blood on his pants. The victim's right eye socket looked like it was filled with grape jelly. Probably the bullet entrance. Once he made sure the officer was out of the room, Sinclair removed the victim's wallet from his back pocket and pulled out a driver's license, copying the name Edgar Pratt and a DOB that made him twenty-four into his notebook. Sinclair returned the wallet to his pocket so the coroner wouldn't be the wiser.

"That's the roommate according to the rental agreement," Braddock said. "Both Garvin and Pratt work at Best Buy. There's not much more on the application than that."

Sinclair discovered a hole in the living-room wall about five and a half feet high. He walked back to the body and pointed his hand toward the hole. Looking to his right, he got down on his hands and knees and peeked under a worn maroon upholstered chair. He located what he was looking for—a shiny brass shell casing. "It's a three-eighty," he announced to Braddock.

"Wasn't that the caliber of the slug they recovered from Dawn?" Braddock asked.

"Sure was. We'll need to find the slug in the neighbor's apartment for a comparison, but I'm sure it'll be a match."

"I can't believe the bullet traveled that far," Braddock said.

"I can. It looks like it entered Pratt's head through the eye socket, so it might have entered the brain without hitting bone. It would still have plenty of energy when it came out of the back of the head. It took nothing to punch through two pieces of sheetrock—one at this wall and one at the neighbor's wall. As long as it didn't hit a stud, it had enough energy to smash through the glass and the particleboard closet door."

"Check this out," Braddock said as she crouched next to a series of shelves that held a large flat-screen TV, cable company receiver, and dozens of cords. Braddock held up a wireless controller in her gloved hand. "These are the DualShock controllers for PlayStation Four."

"I didn't take you for a gamer."

Braddock laughed. "When that husband of mine had his knee surgery last summer, he was confined to the house and spent hours a day on the couch playing different SWAT and military games. He claimed he was honing his professional skills."

"Where's the box?"

"See this clean spot," Braddock said, pointing to rectangular area on the shelf surrounded by thick dust. "This is exactly the size of the PS Four console."

"The killer took the box?"

"That system is more than just a box," Braddock said. "It's a computer. They cost around four hundred without any accessories, so they could've taken it for its value. But more likely, they took it because of the data that's on it—player names and a record of any chat messages between players. You can even e-mail or Facebook message through it. When people play online together, they're often chatting via text, and the system would probably have a record of that."

"So that box might've told us who the other suspects in Dawn's murder were and who killed Edgar Pratt," Sinclair said.

Chapter 33

By the time Sinclair returned to the scene with the signed warrant, the body was gone and Braddock was in the living room with the evidence tech. "Coroner deputies pointed out some tattooing around the entrance wound," Braddock said. "Means the gun was close—maybe within inches—when it was fired. Nothing else remarkable about the body. No signs of a struggle or forced entry to the apartment. Pratt must've let the killer in."

"I called Phil and gave him Pratt's name when I was driving back to the PAB. He just got back to me and said one of his Intel officers showed Pratt's photo to a source, who confirmed Pratt is Gothic Geek."

"Is Phil's source someone inside the anarchists?"

"He didn't say," Sinclair said.

"There's a lot our old partner isn't saying."

Sinclair nodded in agreement.

"The videographer is down," Braddock said. "Two more to go. Why would someone kill both Dawn and Pratt?"

Braddock was obviously assuming Pratt and the other two suspects in the park were the only ones involved in Dawn's death. Sinclair wasn't as sure. "Maybe Pratt's associates didn't like him blabbing about what they did. Wouldn't be the first time partners in crime knocked off the weak link."

"Looks like we're worse off than we were this morning."

"I wish we got to Pratt before his friends did, but the fact that they felt it necessary to kill him says a lot," Sinclair said. "These guys can't keep their mouths shut, and that could be to our advantage."

★

Sinclair's watch read 8:30 when he and Braddock knocked at the door of Garvin's house for the second time that day. The remaining search of the apartment hadn't yielded much of value. A dresser drawer in Pratt's bedroom was filled with old bills and receipts. Among the papers, Braddock found a pen-and-ink drawing of a medieval castle with the words *Gothic Geek* across the top, which corroborated the assertion by Roberts's informant that Pratt's username was Gothic Geek. What they didn't find were any computers, cell phones, or any papers with names of friends or associates.

A stout woman with bottle-blonde hair opened the door. Mrs. Garvin invited them in and sat behind a can of Coors at the kitchen table. "My husband said you came by earlier, and Sean just called from the jail asking me to make bail for him."

"Will you?" asked Braddock.

"I love my son, but he needs to face the consequences of his actions."

Braddock told her what happened at the Mills Café and what they discovered at the apartment.

"Edgar's dead?" She shook her head, took another swig of her beer, and wiped her mouth with the back of her hand. "I knew him since he was little. He and Sean went to school together and have been best friends ever since."

Mrs. Garvin didn't seem too surprised by the death of her son's best friend. Sinclair asked, "What about any other friends?"

"Sean doesn't talk about anyone in particular. I know he has some friends from work—other kids he plays his video games with. He's been at Best Buy for years. He talks about the Occupy Oakland and Black Lives Matter stuff that he's involved in, but he has no understanding of the politics behind it or any real interest in the cause. To him, it's just a thing to do."

Sinclair and Braddock spent another twenty minutes with Mrs. Garvin but gained nothing useful. They drove four blocks to the address the coroner's office gave them for Edgar Pratt's parents. The coroner had already made the death notification to Edgar's father, and Sinclair hoped the shock had dulled a bit. According to the coroner, the parents had been divorced for ten years, and Edgar's mother was now living in Fresno. Parked cars choked the street in front of Pratt's house. Sinclair double-parked and flipped the switch to the flashing yellow light on the rear of his car.

A thirty-something brunette woman dressed in a Cal hoodie and jeans answered the door. Sinclair identified himself and flashed his badge. "I'm Trish, Ed's sister." She opened the door and led the way into the living room where fifteen people were talking, laughing, and crying. "Dad," she yelled over the noise. "The homicide sergeants are here."

Mr. Pratt was white, about six-foot-two, and appeared to be about sixty years old. He rose from a chair in the corner and pushed through the crowd. He and Trish led Sinclair and Braddock through a kitchen crowded with people to a bedroom converted into a TV room with a small sofa and recliner.

"I'm sorry for your loss, Mr. Pratt," Sinclair said once everyone found a place to sit.

"The coroner didn't say much other than Edgar was shot inside his apartment," Mr. Pratt replied.

Sinclair figured there was no reason to withhold the details about the video, so he explained that he came across the YouTube video filmed by Edgar when he was investigating Dawn's murder.

"Edgar's into computers," Mr. Pratt said. "He plays those shooting games, but he'd be afraid of a real gun. I can believe the stuff about him attending protests. That's what young people do.

Hell, I marched in Berkeley when I was young. But a murder? I can't accept that."

"I saw the video, Dad," Trish said. "It's Ed's voice."

"How'd you hear about the video?" Sinclair asked.

"It's gone viral," Trish said. "Everyone knows about it."

Sinclair continued to look at her until she continued.

"My dad called me as soon as the coroner left, so I texted a few old friends to see if anyone knew what Ed's been up to. They told me about the video."

Sinclair jotted down the names and phone numbers of everyone who texted or called her. He'd have to talk to each of them and find out how they heard about the video, hoping one of them might lead him to a direct source.

"I moved to Castro Valley ten years ago," Trish said. "So I don't know much about Ed's life today, but he's always been a nerd. He's not into girls and would never pay for a prostitute. Getting involved with an escort makes no sense. He prided himself on his Gothic Geek persona. Except at work, he always dressed in black. I can't see him being dragged into something like a murder."

Families of murderers were usually the last ones to accept their loved ones were capable of killing. "What about other friends besides Sean?" Sinclair asked.

Mr. Pratt shrugged his shoulders. "He moved out of the house a year after he graduated from high school. He never brings friends around anymore."

"I'm seven years older than him," Trish said. "He was just my dorky little brother when we were growing up. When I moved out, he was still in middle school."

"You've got a house full of people," Sinclair said. "Are any of them Ed's friends?"

Mr. Pratt pulled a blue bandana from his pocket and wiped his eyes. "Some are relatives and others are from my work or neighbors."

"Would any of them have had recent contact with Ed?"

"I doubt it," Mr. Pratt said.

"I can ask around," Trish said. "If so, they're more likely to talk to me than you."

"I appreciate it." Sinclair handed several business cards to Mr. Pratt and Trish. "If you could, pass around a pad of paper and collect names and phone numbers of everyone here and anyone else who calls or comes by. You can tell them it's so you can let them know about funeral arrangements."

"I can do that," Trish said.

On their way out, Sinclair and Braddock looked over the people in the house. None fit their image of a young geek, Goth, or anarchist.

Once they were out of the Maxwell Park neighborhood and on the 580 Freeway, Braddock said, "The involvement of these anarchists and gamers sure throws a twist in our theory that Dawn's death was connected to her escort work."

Sinclair heard Braddock's subtle *I told you so* in her comment. "I can't see Dawn having anything to do with this stuff. Tomorrow, we'll dig more into Garvin and Pratt and see what else they were involved in when they weren't gaming or protesting."

★

The digital clock on Sinclair's bed table flipped to 5:30. He'd been watching it jump minute by minute for the last hour. It had taken him an hour to fall asleep after he went to bed around midnight, his mind churning through the latest murder and trying to fit it into the one involving Dawn. Too many pieces didn't fit. When he finally drifted off, it was a fitful sleep, punctuated by a dream of him standing in the Mills Café and watching bullets exit Sean Garvin's gun and punch through him. He woke drenched in sweat. He changed into a dry T-shirt and boxers and crawled back into bed. But sleep never came.

He finally showered, dressed, and padded to the kitchen. He was about to hit the button to the coffee grinder when he saw the kitchen lights in the main house come on. The decorative lights guided him around the pool and down the path to the mansion. He opened the back door without knocking.

"Good morning, Matthew," Walt said. "Coffee'll be ready in a minute. You got in late last night."

"Yeah, we had another murder." Sinclair gave him the basics.

Walt poured two mugs of coffee and handed one to Sinclair. "Peet's Sumatra."

Sinclair took a sip of the gutsy, dark roast blend. Walt took a seat at the kitchen table, and Sinclair pulled out a chair and sat across from him.

"Didn't sleep well, huh?" Walt said, undoubtedly seeing the fatigue written on his face.

"Trying to figure out the murders."

"Is there something more personal you're also trying to figure out?"

Sinclair set his cup on the table. "You cut right through my shit, don't you?"

Walt smiled. "Sometimes we need to tell our friends what they need to hear and not just what they want to hear."

"You remember when I started therapy with Dr. Elliott and you mentioned that until I can risk a chink in my armor, I'll never be able to have a deep and meaningful relationship with anyone?"

"Yes, although the metaphor may not be perfect. What I meant is that like most people, you likely developed defense mechanisms over the years; however, yours were reinforced by traumatic incidents in your life. These defenses allowed you to protect yourself from getting hurt. Avoiding pain is good, but when the fear of getting hurt emotionally becomes your driving force, it prevents you from getting close to people. By opening up a little bit and risking emotional pain, you also make yourself available to all the pleasures of close human contact."

"Dr. Elliott mentioned this stuff again the other day. When I started therapy, I told her one of my concerns was that if I started to feel too much, I'd lose my edge at work. I'd start feeling at the wrong time, and in the worst case scenario, it could get me killed."

"Feeling is not weakness, Matthew, it's the opposite. Only the strong are capable of the full range of emotions."

"Yeah, well this therapy that's putting chinks in my armor or allowing me to drop my shield, or whatever the fuck analogy you want to use, almost got me killed yesterday."

Walt raised his eyebrows and was ready to say something when Betty, Walt's wife, came down the back stairway into the kitchen.

"Matthew," she said, opening her arms.

Sinclair got up and received her hug. She was a year or two younger than Walt, heavyset, and with the kind of rosy, wrinkle-free face that women in their forties wished for.

"How about some breakfast?" she said.

"I've really got to—"

"Matthew, you look gaunt," she said. "When did you last eat?"

Sinclair thought about it. It had been a sandwich at lunch-time yesterday. "I'd love some breakfast."

"I'm sorry I disturbed you boys. You go back to your discussion, and I'll stay out of your hair." Betty went to the other side of the kitchen, put two large pans on the commercial-grade gas stove, and began unloading the refrigerator onto the counter.

"Would you like to tell me what happened?" Walt said once Betty focused her full attention to cooking.

Sinclair told him about the incident with Garvin at the Mills Café.

When he finished, Walt asked, "Why didn't you shoot?"

"Maybe I froze. I should've shot. He had a gun. He could've brought it up and fired in a split second—faster than I could've reacted."

"But he didn't," Walt said. "And it wasn't a real gun."

"You can't tell a real gun from a replica in that kind of situation, and I can't read someone's mind and figure out what they intend to do. I need to act based on what's in front of me."

"But you did know." Walt grabbed their cups, walked across the kitchen to fill them, and returned to the table. "You picked up on something in the way that young man acted or the way he looked. You knew he wasn't going to shoot you with that gun— that he wasn't a threat to you. That's why you didn't shoot."

"My fellow officers think I've lost my nerve. They'll think I'll freeze again and get one of them killed because I won't drop the hammer when it's necessary."

"I have to reach back a few years, but I remember when I was a young soldier in 'Nam. No one wanted to be around a soldier who was a coward. There was nothing more important than having my buddies know I'd have their backs in a firefight. Could it be that you're less concerned about others thinking you lost your nerve than you are about you thinking so yourself?"

Chapter 34

Sinclair was sitting at his desk, filling out his overtime slip from the previous night, when Maloney walked into the office a few minutes before eight. He plopped an *Oakland Tribune* on Sinclair's desk. Underneath a headline reading *THRILL KILL* was a grainy photograph, obviously a still from the video, of Dawn hanging from the tree with a fireball surrounding her abdomen.

Maloney crossed his arms. "The story says a source close to the investigation believes the murderer may fit the thrill-killer classification."

Sinclair swiveled his chair around to face his boss. "John asked what I thought the motive was, and asked if it could be a thrill kill. I said I didn't know enough to rule it out."

"That's all the confirmation he needed," Maloney said. "The article goes on to quote some retired FBI agent theorizing about the psychological profile of the kinds of people who would do this. The chief isn't going to like this. With the media fanning the flames, it'll get the community all riled up about some more psychopaths on the loose in Oakland."

Even though the media feeding frenzy over the Bus Bench Killer had been more than a year ago, Sinclair recalled vividly how much it distracted him from his work. "I'll bet that FBI agent never stepped foot in a crime scene with a body still present, but he's lectured at Quantico about thrill killers. You know I can't control who the media talks to or what they print."

Maloney took a deep breath and sighed. "I'm just venting before I head to the eighth floor and face the music. Anything new on the murder of the anarchist?"

Sinclair had called Maloney last night after he left Pratt's house and brought him up to speed on the case. "Nothing since we talked."

"Let's keep his connection to the girl's murder in house. The media will figure it out soon enough."

★

Two hours later as Sinclair returned from the coroner's office, Braddock hung up her phone and said, "Phil needs to see us ASAP."

"What's up?" Sinclair asked.

"I don't know, but he sounded excited, and it takes a lot to get him excited."

On their way to the intelligence office, Sinclair briefed her on the autopsy results. The pathologist had confirmed the presence of tattooing—particles of unburnt gunpowder—in the tissue below the eye where the bullet had entered. Besides the bullet wound, there were no other wounds or injuries. Sinclair pictured one of the men in the video—either as punishment for posting the video or to ensure he never named his coconspirators—visiting Edgar's apartment, immediately pulling out his gun, pointing it at Edgar's face, and pulling the trigger. No talk, no discussion, just bang—the weak link eliminated.

Roberts shepherded Sinclair and Braddock into his office as soon as they buzzed, and then he shut his office door. "One of my contacts from another agency noticed this," he said as he jiggled the mouse to wake up his computer.

Sinclair and Braddock moved around his desk and studied a Twitter feed for a group named @BLM415. Roberts scrolled down a few entries and clicked on a photo to enlarge it. It showed Edgar Pratt sprawled on the floor of the apartment exactly as they had found him yesterday. The only difference was the pool of blood was smaller and brighter red in the photo.

"This must've been taken right after he was shot," Sinclair said. "Who posted it?"

Roberts closed out of the photo and returned to the Twitter feed. Sinclair read the message poster's name: Deathtowhores. The message read, *Police snitches should lie in ditches.*

"The profile was created yesterday," Roberts said. "Probably just to post this."

They both knew the difficulty in tracing social media posts. With a series of search warrants and a month or more of time, they could eventually track it to an IP address, but unless someone posted from his home Wi-Fi or used a cell service in his name, it would be a dead end.

Braddock sat down on the couch. "What's B-L-M-four-fifteen stand for?"

"Black Lives Matter," Roberts said. "The four-fifteen stands for San Francisco's area code. It's a Bay Area group that formed after the Ferguson shooting to bring attention to so-called unjustified police shootings of black men."

"I don't get it," Sinclair said. "Why are anarchists and Black Lives Matter activists interested in killing a white woman who worked as an escort? And what's this crap about death to whores?"

Roberts chuckled. "You have to stop thinking of these social media networks as traditional organizations. The same people who post stuff on sites connected to the Occupy movement post on the anarchist and Black Lives Matter sites. They're activists and rabble-rousers. The organizations are nebulous, often no more than a cause that people attach themselves to. Some of the people at the last protest organized by B-L-M-four-fifteen were the same people who attended the Occupy protests. They don't care about the cause, as long as it's against the status quo. Some of their social media postings are about reasonable concerns, however . . ."

Roberts got up from his desk and gazed at his wall of plaques and certificates. "As a black man myself, I understand racial profiling is a problem. But as a cop, I know we stop blacks at a higher rate because blacks commit crime at a higher rate. People with their own agendas attach themselves to one or more of the causes to advance their own interests. Last year, a group of anarchists that called themselves the Black Bloc smashed the windows of fifty downtown businesses. Meanwhile, they looted the stores—not of food or necessities, but of two-hundred-dollar sneakers and electronics. The group Anonymous posted a video asking people to stop the vandalism and looting. Was that representative of Anonymous? Who knows? A half dozen of those arrested that night were first busted at the Earth First protests back in the eighties."

Sinclair looked up from his notepad. "The old environmental group?"

"Right," Roberts said. "They show up at whatever cause is popular at the time—environmental, animal rights, nuclear power in the eighties and nineties, and income inequality and police brutality today."

"So the people involved in my murders could be some middle-aged radicals," Sinclair said.

Roberts shrugged his shoulders. "Who knows? This isn't a full-time job for these people. And don't forget, the vast majority of the people involved in the protests are righteous citizens. We're focusing on a small minority."

"So, where's this leave us?" Sinclair asked.

"If I were in your shoes," Roberts said, "I wouldn't worry too much about this social media chatter. Our friends at the state and federal level spend their days monitoring it, and even they don't have a good handle on who's involved in what and how they're connected. If something comes up, like when Gothic Geek and Anarchist Soldier were named, I'll let you know."

"What about this guy's account name of 'death to whores'?" Braddock asked. "Is this a new cause connected with the anarchists?"

"It's the first we've seen it," Roberts said. "It could be disinformation."

"Someone trying to throw us off the right track?" Sinclair said.

"I've seen it before," Roberts said.

Sinclair and Braddock left the intelligence office and drove to the Best Buy store, where they met with the manager, a short, pudgy white man in his fifties with horn-rimmed glasses. He wore a short-sleeved white shirt with a clip-on tie and black leather shoes that he'd probably never polished. The manager had already heard about Edgar Pratt's murder and was over his shock—if the murder of an employee actually shocked someone more comfortable around computers than people. He set up Sinclair and Braddock with a copy of the employee roster in a back room that he called their training room, though it seemed to double as a break room based on the clutter of empty energy drinks and candy wrappers on the tables.

By two o'clock, they had interviewed eight young men who were assigned to the Geek Squad and compiled twenty pages of handwritten notes. No one knew Garvin or Pratt outside the store, they all played computer games, but not with Garvin or Pratt, and no one had any idea why someone would kill Dawn or Pratt. The detectives took a break and walked through a steady rain to a sandwich shop in the same mall where Best Buy was located. Sinclair ordered the Italian special and Braddock had grilled chicken in a spinach wrap.

"This is the part of investigations I hate," Braddock said.

"You and me both," Sinclair said. "We could talk to a hundred people here over the next week and no one will know anything."

"Or some will know something, lie about it, and we won't be able to tell."

"We're too good to let that happen." Sinclair winked.

His cell buzzed. He didn't recognize the number.

"Is this the detective investigating the murder of Dawn Gustafson?" The voice was male and sounded white and young.

"Yes, this is Sergeant Sinclair."

"Do you want her computers—the one from the apartment by the lake and the one from the condo downtown?"

Sinclair waved to get Braddock's attention and cracked the phone from his ear so that Braddock could hear. "Absolutely," Sinclair said. "Do you have them?"

"I can get them for you if you want to meet me."

"Sure, give me your address."

"No, this has to be anonymous. Meet me at Peet's Coffee Shop on Lakeshore in a half hour."

"Okay. How will I recognize you?"

"I'll recognize you," the man said before hanging up.

★

Peet's Coffee was located between a burrito shop and health food store in the trendy Lakeshore business district, just north of Lake Merritt. There was an empty handicapped space in front, but even a homicide car didn't get a free pass to park there unless a dead body was lying next to it. Sinclair parked halfway down the block and walked with Braddock in the steady rain, dodging a few pedestrians whose heads were covered by umbrellas. Despite the rain, a man with long hair hanging out of a fedora similar to Sinclair's sat on a wooden bench outside the door smoking a cigarette and drinking coffee from a paper Peet's cup.

Inside the store, Sinclair removed his hat and shook off the water. Every seat was taken. Sinclair's mind immediately flashed on his encounter with Garvin at the Mills Café four days earlier. He scanned the crowd—about thirty people, six or seven white males in the age group of his caller. Two of the workers behind the counter fit that description as well. No one gave him a second look. They were ten minutes early, so Braddock got in line to get drinks while Sinclair found a wall to put his back against and watch the door.

Braddock handed him a small cup of black coffee and shouldered in beside him. He popped off the top and sipped the dark French roast. She sipped her frou-frou coffee, something with a head of white foam. Sinclair couldn't imagine anyone not making them for cops. His phone rang, and he dug it out from under his raincoat. The same number. "Sinclair," he said.

"It's too crowded in there, and I don't want you to drag me downtown for questioning, so I'm leaving them on the top deck of the parking garage behind Peet's. They'll be in a black backpack by the far stairs."

"Let's talk a minute," Sinclair said, but the line was already dead.

They walked through the parking lot next to the CVS Pharmacy to the parking structure. People under umbrellas or with turned-up collars and hunched shoulders rushed between cars and stores. Most of the spaces on the covered ground floor of the garage were full. Sinclair led the way up the concrete stairs to the open top deck. Nearly a hundred cars could park here, and on a nice Saturday afternoon, it would be full. He counted six cars parked by the stairs. Twenty empty stalls away was a single dark car parked by the far stairway. Braddock started toward it.

"Hang on," Sinclair said.

Braddock stopped and turned.

"This doesn't feel right," he said. "Let's check out these cars."

They peered into each car, checking the front and back seats for occupants, but they were empty. They continued their march toward the far stairway, passing the ramp to the upper deck and one going back down.

The rain rolled off the brim of his hat. His unbuttoned raincoat flapped in the wind, and a gust flipped his tie over his shoulder. Halfway across the parking lot, Sinclair stopped and looked back at the stairway from where they came. He thought he saw movement, but couldn't be sure with the rain and wind. There was no one there now.

"Why don't you wait here," he said to Braddock. "Watch my back and keep an eye on the car ramps and the far stairway. I'll check out the car."

She nodded. He walked toward the lone car. The wind whipped his coat open, and the driving rain soaked the front of his shirt and pants. He ignored it. He walked around the far side of the Ford sedan and peered into the windows. The car was empty. He walked around the rear of the vehicle and spotted a black backpack on the top step of the stairwell.

A memory from Iraq flashed in his mind. *Riding shotgun in the middle Humvee of a three-truck convoy. Up ahead, alongside the road, he spotted a military rucksack—one of the old ones, OD green in color. He grabbed the radio mic and yelled for the lead vehicle to punch it and for his driver and the rear vehicle to reverse. Seconds later, the rucksack exploded with all three trucks just barely outside the kill zone.*

Sinclair turned. Braddock was watching him. Beyond her, at the top of the other stairwell, stood the man who had been smoking the cigarette outside Peet's. He pulled out a cell phone and held it in front of his face.

Sinclair pointed at him and yelled to Braddock, "Run!"

Sinclair crouched and sprinted toward Braddock. She turned and ran toward the man. Sinclair ran as fast as he could, the leather soles of his shoes slipping with each step on the rain-slick concrete.

The explosion sounded in his ears at the same time the blast wave hit him. The air around him moved. Instead of shoving him forward, as he thought it should, it felt like it picked him up and pulled him, as a rogue wave does to a surfer just before erupting over him and smashing him into the ocean floor.

Chapter 35

At six o'clock, Sinclair and Braddock walked up the same concrete stairs they had ascended three hours earlier. Sinclair grimaced with each step and limped slightly from where the doctors at ACH ER had dug a piece of concrete out of his right hamstring and closed the wound with five sutures and surgical superglue. The rest of his body felt like it had just gone ten rounds with a heavyweight champ. His thick raincoat protected most of his body after he went airborne and landed on the asphalt, where he slid, tumbled, and rolled for another twenty feet. Still, he ended up with road rash on his left hip where the surface of the parking deck tore through his wool pants, as well as oozing abrasions on his left arm and chin.

A canvas canopy the size of a small circus tent covered the far end of the parking lot where the device had exploded. Maloney waved at Sinclair as soon as he stepped under a smaller canopy that had been set up as a break area for the scores of officers and agents from a variety of local, state, and federal agencies. "I thought I told you at the hospital to go home when they released you," Maloney said.

"I figured it was a suggestion," Sinclair replied.

Maloney shook his head and sighed. "I take it the MRI found your brain wasn't too badly rattled."

Sinclair turned his head to the left, since the ringing in his right ear drowned out all but the loudest sounds. "No more than normal."

"What about you, Cathy?" Maloney asked Braddock.

"I was a lot farther away, so the blast didn't even knock me down." She was almost yelling even though Maloney was only a few feet away. "Other than a slight headache from the noise, I'm good, but the bomber got away."

"You stayed with your partner," Maloney said. "That's the right decision."

Sinclair poured himself a cup of coffee and pulled a cigar from his pocket, bit off the end, and pulled out his Zippo. Immediately, a man in an FBI windbreaker rushed from the other side of the tent, yelling, "You can't smoke here! This is a crime scene."

Maloney turned toward the man and held up his hand like a stop sign. "This is Matt Sinclair, the man who was nearly blown up. Correct me if I'm wrong, but the crime scene and all the evidence is under the other tent."

Sinclair lit his cigar.

The man in the FBI windbreaker introduced himself as the San Francisco Field Office assistant special agent in charge for counterterrorism. ASAIC Lee said, "You're a very lucky man, Sergeant. They tell me if you were much closer, you wouldn't be standing here right now."

"No luck involved, sir," another man with a weightlifter's build said. He was wearing an ATF windbreaker, for the Bureau of Alcohol, Tobacco, Firearms, and Explosives. "I just read the sergeant's statement from the hospital. He recognized the backpack as an IED, saw the bomber preparing to trigger it with a cell phone, and hauled ass out of the blast radius. Only a fucking warrior knows to do that."

Sinclair puffed on the cigar to get it started, drew a mouthful of smoke into his lungs, and exhaled. From the way the ATF agent talked, he had to be prior military, but Sinclair didn't have the energy to swap military service and unit assignments with him. "Are you guys doing the scene?" he asked.

"Us and the FBI's evidence response team," the ATF agent said.

"What was the device?" Sinclair asked.

The ATF agent looked to Lee, who nodded his approval. "A simple pressure cooker bomb filled with black powder and set off remotely with a cell phone triggering device that was attached to a blasting cap in the lid. The bomber didn't fill it with shrapnel—you know, nails or ball bearings—like the Boston Marathon bomber and most other bombers do. Still, the concussion would kill anyone within twenty feet, lots more in an enclosed area. Some fragments of the pressure cooker became airborne projectiles, too. If one of those would've hit you or your partner, even from across the parking lot, you'd be in for a big hurt."

"Does that mean the bomber was an amateur?" Braddock asked.

"Not necessarily," the AFT agent replied. "He probably figured you would pick up the backpack, at which time he'd detonate it. No need for fragmentation projectiles at that distance. Amateur, professional, who knows. Anyone with an Internet connection can learn how to make a pressure cooker bomb."

"Anything on the cell phone yet?" Sinclair asked.

"The lab will have to examine it, but it looks like a cheap flip phone, probably a prepay."

Lee added, "We traced the number that the subject called you from. It's a TracFone, part of a batch that was distributed to Bay Area convenience stores. It'll take a while to trace it to a particular store. Eight minutes after the second call to you, precisely at the time of the explosion, the phone made an outgoing call to a number that's part of that same batch of TracFones."

"Which would be the phone used as the detonator," Braddock said.

Sinclair drifted to the far end of the tent and looked through the rain to the large canopy on the other side of the parking lot. Thirty or forty people, most dressed in white coveralls and yellow booties, scurried about with cameras and evidence bags. The Ford sedan was a twisted carcass of metal and broken glass. Twenty feet of the parking structure's concrete railing was missing, obviously blown apart by the blast. Sinclair felt a hand on his shoulder and turned.

"Glad you're okay, partner." Phil Roberts was dressed in an OPD baseball cap and a blue windbreaker with yellow OPD letters on the front and back.

Sinclair pulled a cigar from his pocket and handed it to Roberts. Roberts cut the end with a pocketknife and lit it with Sinclair's Zippo.

"The FBI labeled this an act of terrorism and think it's connected to the anarchists' video of your murder," Roberts said. "That's freeing up all kind of resources. They'll be able to track the movement of the cell phone the bomber used through its GPS, which might provide some leads to his identity. They'll trace any cell phones nearby his and look for connections. That might give us associates. Your killer has to be among them."

"Do the Feds have anything that directly links this to the anarchists?" Sinclair asked.

"Earlier today, the cell phone's GPS put it at one of the cafes frequented by Occupy Oakland types. At the same time, three other cell phones they've linked to known occupiers were there."

"Do these guys have names?"

"Matt, an investigation like this expands tenfold every eight hours as more and more data are linked. This is what the FBI excels at. They'll work up files on everyone. When the time's right, agents will interview them. Analysts, who combine it with phone, e-mail, and financial records, enter the details from every interview and surveillance into a computer program. That will show the relationships between hundreds of people and thousands of pieces of information, more than we can possibly keep in our heads. Most of the time it's best for us to just stay out of their way and not muddy the waters."

Sinclair didn't deny the FBI's ability to amass enormous resources to collect and compile massive amounts of information in complex investigations. But he had worked with the Feds on drug cases before, where numerous people continued to die in the drug wars and tons of dope continued to flow onto the streets while he waited for them to act. "When are they going to reveal what they learned?" Sinclair asked.

"They're talking about holding a briefing tomorrow, after which they'll divvy up responsibilities for the investigation."

"What about my murders?"

Roberts tapped the ash off his cigar. "Should be one and the same."

"What if it isn't?"

"We'll have to see where the evidence points. They collected three cigarette butts outside the coffee shop. The manager said most people obey the law about no smoking within twenty-five feet of the doorway, so one of them might belong to our guy. This is a priority, so they could have DNA results within days. Can you remember anything else about the bomber?"

When Sinclair first saw him on the bench outside Peet's, he didn't give him a second glance. A fedora hid his face, and it was impossible to accurately gauge the size of someone sitting. Sinclair told the agents at the hospital he thought the man was in his twenties or thirties, probably between five-eight and six-two, thin to medium build, with dark-brown hair that hung over his ears. Besides a fedora-style brown hat, he wore a navy-blue parka similar to what you'd see in an REI or North Face store, dark jeans, and dark hiking boots. He was too far away for Sinclair to pick up any other details about him in the split second he saw him later across the parking deck, and Braddock only caught a glimpse of him before he disappeared into the stairwell a second before the explosion.

"What about the car that was blown up?" Sinclair asked.

"Belongs to an employee at Petco. She parks there every morning and walks down those steps and into the back door of the store. She's clean."

"When will I get a copy of the client list from the escort service?"

Roberts puffed on his cigar and blew a smoke ring that hung above him for a few seconds before dissipating. "You're not giving up on that, are you?"

"What would it hurt to feed all those names into the big FBI computer in the sky with everything else your Fed friends are collecting and see what it spits out?"

"I'll talk to them," Roberts said. "We'll probably be here the rest of the night. Why don't you get some rest? Nothing for you to do unless you want to crawl around on your hands and knees looking for bomb fragments."

Chapter 36

More than a hundred people filled the briefing room at 450 Golden Gate Avenue in San Francisco when Sinclair, Braddock, and Maloney arrived a few minutes before nine. Sinclair was ushered to a long table at the front of the room. Standing at the back of the room were Linda Archard, Mark Cummings, and the two agents that were doing surveillance in the Waterfront hotel bar during the escort service undercover operation. The briefing began with an introduction by the San Francisco FBI special agent in charge, and was followed by a succession of ATF and FBI agents who flashed hundreds of photos on the monitors and discussed minute details of the bombing scene, an overview of the anarchist and Occupy movements and the local Bay Area groups associated with them, and a summary of Dawn's and Pratt's murders.

When the final slide appeared on the screen, Lee quickly took over the podium and said, "The joint terrorism task force and field intelligence group will be overseeing the investigation and handling fusion of all information out of this field office. For those outside the bureau who don't know your assignment, see your team leader in the JTTF or your supervisory special agent. The Oakland RA will operate a twenty-four-seven op-center as well, and all local and federal agencies located in the East Bay will operate out of there. Areas of responsibility and assignments have already been given out to team leaders and case agents."

A short woman wearing a blue polo shirt with the FBI patch on her chest whispered something in Lee's ear. "This just came in," Lee said, glancing at the monitor behind him.

The monitor showed a computer screenshot of a blog that read, *Soon we'll strike a blow to the 1%ers. More fun than blowing out windows on Wall Street. We will hit at the old white men of the privileged society. The 1%ers will realize their worst fears.*

"We'll send out updates through JTTF channels as we get them," Lee said. "There's a new sense of urgency. Let's stop the next attack."

People rose from their seats and gathered in small clusters or headed for the door. Sinclair stepped in front of Lee as he started for a back door. "Why was everything about the escort service's clients cut from the briefing?" Sinclair asked.

Archard walked to Lee's side, while the two agents who'd been sitting next to her remained a few feet away. "I don't see how it's pertinent," Lee said.

"Yates, Whitt, and Kozlov," Sinclair said. "You're absolutely positive they have nothing to do with any of this? Nothing to do with the murders?"

Maloney and Braddock joined Sinclair, facing Lee and his entourage.

Lee crossed his arms across his chest. "It's a separate area of investigation that most people in this room are not cleared for."

"I'd like to talk to whoever's running that *area of investigation*," Sinclair said, making eye contact with Archard and then back to Lee.

"To what purpose?"

"Maybe I'm just a dumb local cop, but it seems to me they might know something that'll help me solve my murders or tell me who the hell tried to blow me up."

"Agent Archard is the case agent for the investigation into the escort service," Lee said. "She'll keep you abreast of any developments that relate to your murders."

Archard stood there stone-faced.

"Funny thing," Sinclair said. "I was told Ms. Archard worked in your organized crime unit, but I talked to buddies of mine at OPD and SFPD who know all the agents who work organized crime, and none of them have heard of her."

★

The Oakland FBI office, officially called a resident agency, was housed in a high-rise office building at Twenty-First Street and Webster and fell under the control of the San Francisco field office. Sinclair had worked with many of the agents over the years on one kind of investigation or another, and most knew him. He and Braddock were escorted past the security doors to the home of the working agents, a large room filled with cubicles, each about four times as large as the space allotted to a homicide investigator in the PAB's cramped quarters.

Upton Bellamy, known as "Uppy" to his fellow agents, was a former Detroit cop who had been hired by the FBI when he was thirty-three. He spent his first ten years in the New York field office before coming to Oakland two years ago. He worked in the bank robbery squad and had been assigned to work with Sinclair on the murder of a check-cashing teller six months ago when the MO fit that of a string of bank robberies the bureau was working.

"Sinclair, glad you didn't get blown to smithereens," Uppy yelled as he strode across the room. He grabbed Sinclair and gave him a half hug. He then took Braddock's hand and kissed the back of it.

"I'm still married, Uppy," Braddock said.

"I'm still the first one you'll call when you leave that husband of yours, right?"

Braddock laughed.

Sinclair and Braddock spent the next two hours swapping information with the agents in the room. When Sinclair pulled the Best Buy employee list from his case packet and showed it, Uppy disappeared down a hallway. Moments later, he returned with the word that the brass would detail a team of agents from another squad to conduct backgrounds and interviews on the rest of the eighty or so employees. What would've taken Sinclair and Braddock more than a week, the FBI would do in a day.

Sinclair swiveled his chair around in the FBI cubical to face Braddock. "The Feds have everything else covered. Other than tagging along with them when they talk to the third cousin of someone who once watched an Occupy Wall Street protest on TV, I don't have any ideas other than going back after Yates and Whitt."

"What the heck, let's go for it." Braddock flipped to a clean page of her legal pad.

"You're not gonna talk me out of it?"

"The only reason I'm not arguing about it is because you almost got blown up yesterday."

"Don't get all sentimental on me now, partner," Sinclair said.

Sinclair called Maloney and reminded him that Yates was to have come to the chief's office last night. Since the bombing obviously changed everyone's plans, Sinclair wanted to know if the chief could arrange for Yates to come in today. Maloney said he'd ask, but Sinclair shouldn't expect it.

Sinclair called Bianca, who answered on the first ring. "I've been wondering how you were. The news said you were treated and released from the hospital, so I guess . . . How are you?"

"I'm fine," he said, not mentioning that he could barely hear out of his right ear, had a steady, dull pounding in his head, and felt as if he'd been hit by a freight train when he crawled out of bed that morning.

"Glad to hear it. I imagine the escort service is no longer a priority after what happened."

"Not exactly. You said Whitt and Yates were Dawn's most frequent clients, right?"

"That's right."

"Did Preston Yates ever use the agency for other girls after he had the affair with Dawn?"

"After he settled with the agency for stealing her away, they never heard from him again."

"What about Whitt? Did he continue with other girls after Dawn left the agency?"

She put him on hold and came back on the line a minute later. "William still orders an escort weekly. Usually different girls. His last time was Saturday."

Sinclair thanked her and hung up.

It was a short drive to the City Center, and as the elevator took Sinclair and Braddock to the sixth floor, he wondered if it were a coincidence that Whitt's office was in the same building as Kozlov's and Fred Towers's companies. The receptionist tried to fulfill her gatekeeper role, but when Sinclair told her it was about the bombing yesterday, which wasn't a complete lie, she escorted them to Whitt's office. It wasn't a corner office and it was only a quarter the size of Fred Towers's office, but it was still nicer than all but the one the police chief had in the PAB. Whitt sat in a leather executive chair behind a glossy black desk. A window that faced Broadway Street and other high-rises was behind him.

Whitt looked up from a desk strewn with papers. "I heard about the bomb. Was this the work of domestic terrorists as the news is saying?"

"We're looking into it," Sinclair said. "We spoke to the officer who investigated your wife's death."

"What's that have to do with anything?"

"He thinks your wife committed suicide."

"Why would he say that?"

"Why do you think?" Sinclair walked around the desk and stood over Whitt.

Whitt swiveled his chair to face him. "Would you like to take a seat?" Whitt motioned to a guest chair in front of his desk.

Sinclair wanted Whitt to feel uncomfortable. "I'm fine."

Whitt leaned back in his chair and looked up at Sinclair. "I suspected the same thing. Susan knew the road, and I can't imagine she'd just miss the turn."

"The traffic officer actually shared his thoughts with you and asked if she left a note, didn't he?"

"It's been a long time. I don't remember."

"That's not something a man would forget."

Whitt was silent for a few counts, obviously weighing how much truth he'd have to reveal. "I believe he did. Susan didn't leave a note. She was angry when I left, but not distraught. What difference does it make whether it was an accident or suicide?"

"Did you ever mention it to Travis?"

"Never," Whitt shot back without hesitation. "Even if I believed it, I'd never breathe a word of it to my son."

"Then why would he say that to Lisa Harper?"

The look of surprise on Whitt's face couldn't be faked. Sinclair asked, "Did you know he was in contact with Ms. Harper?"

"Why would they be talking?"

"Why would Travis think his mother's death was a suicide if you didn't mention it?"

"I have no idea," Whitt said. "He has no business talking with that woman."

"He doesn't respond to that phone number you gave us, but we still need to talk to him."

"For what purpose?"

"To ask him the same questions you probably want an answer to—why he thinks it was a suicide and why he's in contact with Ms. Harper."

"What's this have to do with Dawn's murder and the bombing?" Whitt asked.

Sinclair's patience was worn thin by Whitt answering each of his questions with a question, so he shrugged, "Why don't you leave the police work to us."

Whitt picked up his desk phone, dialed, and then slammed it down. "He never answers when I call, either." Whitt slid a cell phone from his pocket. Sinclair stood over his shoulder and watched as Whitt tapped out a text: *Call me. It's an emergency. The police are here with questions.*

"Where is Travis?" Sinclair asked.

"I told you. He works in Mountain View with Google. He shares an apartment down there with someone from work."

"Where's the apartment?"

"I've never been there. It's not like kids invite their old man to their apartments."

"Stop lying to me," Sinclair said. "Where's he living?"

"The truth is he's never forgiven me for his mother's death, so I don't pry into his life."

"When did you last see him?"

"A few weeks ago, I guess."

"Where?"

"At the house. He was visiting some old friends in the area and stopped by."

"What did you talk about?"

"Nothing much. You know: 'How are you? I'm fine. How's work? It's fine. How's that girl you're seeing? It's not serious. She's fine.' Travis has a genius-level IQ, but socially he's somewhat inept. He comes across as knowing he's the smartest person in the room, which makes other people quite uncomfortable. Most young men think they're smarter than their old man. Travis knows it for a fact."

Sinclair backed up a step. "After Dawn stopped her escort work, did you hire other escorts?"

"Why's that relevant?"

"It tells me more about you and whether you've been truthful with me."

"Yes. I'm not ashamed of it, so yes."

"How often?"

"Since you're asking, you probably already know."

Sinclair furrowed his eyebrows and locked eyes with Whitt.

"Three, maybe four times a month."

"Do you know Preston Yates?"

"He's the councilmember for my district. I've supported him. He's a member of the Claremont Country Club, as am I, but it's not like we're friends or anything."

"Sergio Kozlov?" Sinclair asked.

"Of course. He owns this building. He's developing the Global Logistics Center, so we're in negotiations with him to become the primary tenant."

"You get along with him?"

"Sergio is a shrewd businessman. No one gets along with him, but if you want what he has, you must try to."

"Do you know other men who saw Dawn when she was escorting?"

"That's not something gentlemen talk about, so I don't bandy it about, and neither would the men I associate with. If one of them was seeing her, I wouldn't have known it."

Sinclair glanced at Braddock. She shook her head to indicate she had no questions for Whitt.

"Anything back from your son?" Sinclair asked.

Whitt looked at his phone and shook his head.

"If he calls, I want to know about it immediately. I need to talk to him, and I'd rather not broadcast a 'be on the lookout for him' to all my brothers in blue to make that happen." Sinclair wrote his cell number on the back of his card and handed it to Whitt. "If I need to talk to you later tonight, where will you be?"

"Here or home."

Sinclair checked his notebook and verified he had Whitt's office, home, and cell numbers. "Thank you for your time," Sinclair said, and then he walked out the door.

Chapter 37

It was quarter to four when Sinclair merged onto the 580 Freeway heading east. He hated making a drive to the South Bay during commute hours, but he had a gnawing feeling Travis was more than merely the genius son of a sex-addict businessman. He tasked Braddock with finding someone at Google who could locate Travis and securing a place where they could interview him, while he plugged in his headset and listened to his office phone voicemails.

The crime lab had left a message saying they matched the slug from the Pratt case to the one from Dawn, as they'd anticipated. The lab entered the second bullet into the system and still got no hits, which wasn't a surprise, since they'd never suspected the gun was a pass-around as was common with drug and gang murders. Traffic slowed for a few miles in Hayward but soon started flowing at normal speed. Braddock was still busy on her phone, so Sinclair called Maloney.

"Any luck with getting the chief to bring Yates in?" Sinclair asked.

"He wants you to prepare a list of questions for the councilmember, which the chief will ask."

"Come on, boss, you know that doesn't work. I need to be able to ask follow-up questions and to call bullshit when the little prick lies."

"I'm just the messenger, Matt. I don't think the chief is too excited about Preston Yates right now, especially considering the FBI and homeland security has issued a red alert for an imminent but unspecified terrorist threat with Oakland as the primary target."

"Yates might be related," Sinclair said, and was immediately sorry he had.

"How?"

"I don't know. But it all ties together. I just don't know exactly how yet."

"When you figure it out, let me know, and I'll get you an audience with Yates," Maloney said. "What are you doing now?"

"Just running down leads with the Feds," Sinclair said. "Pure grunt work." Maloney would be pissed if he found out Sinclair lied to him again, but if nothing materialized on the Travis Whitt angle, they didn't need to tell him. If it did, Maloney might be grateful Sinclair didn't put him in a position where he'd have to rein Sinclair in—at least, that's what Sinclair hoped.

"Okay," Maloney said. "Give me a heads-up if anything develops."

Sinclair was halfway across the Dumbarton Bridge when Braddock put down her phone. "I talked to this guy who's a retired captain from San Jose PD and now works as the number two or three at Google security. He confirmed that Travis works there. Like most employees, he's a contract worker, so another company handles recruitment, hiring, and all human resource functions. By the time we get there, he'll know what division Travis works in, and he can find us a place to interview him."

Traffic slowed again as they approached the exit for the Shoreline Amphitheater and Googleplex, the corporate headquarters for Google, with more than three million square feet of office space.

Braddock's phone rang. "You're kidding," she said. "Three months . . . okay . . . well, thanks anyway."

"That didn't sound good," Sinclair said.

"The security guy apologized for wasting our time, but Travis left Google three months ago. Travis was exhibiting behavior problems consistent with drug abuse, and when confronted about it, he resigned. They later learned that Travis was prescribed Ritalin for ADD, which is common for these computer whizzes, but he was buying extra from others in his work group, crushing it up, and snorting it. His employee file listed a residence not far from here and the same cell phone that we already have."

"I wonder if we could talk to his supervisor and coworkers," Sinclair said.

"The security guy said he'd do that himself tomorrow. Says he can low-key it and get more than we could. Besides, Google isn't real keen on cops on their campus unless it's an emergency."

"Investigating a series of murders probably doesn't qualify," Sinclair said wryly. "Let's see if he's home."

The address on North Rengstorff Avenue was less than two miles away. They pulled into a 1960s apartment complex of basic three-story buildings surrounding a center courtyard with a pool. They found the apartment number, rang the doorbell, and knocked. No answer. So they found a door marked *Manager.* A fortyish man with a ruddy complexion and receding hairline invited them into a small cluttered office.

"He moved out," the manager said after they identified themselves and inquired about Travis Whitt.

"When was that?" Braddock asked.

"Couple months ago."

"Can you be more precise?" Braddock asked.

The man opened the bottom drawer of a metal file cabinet, pulled out a manila folder, and opened it on his desk. "October thirty-first," he said.

"May I see that?" Braddock asked.

The man shrugged his shoulders and handed her the file. Sinclair and Braddock looked over the rental application, which was dated three years ago. It listed Travis's employment with

Google, a monthly salary of eight thousand dollars, his father as an emergency contact, and checking and credit card account details, which Sinclair recorded in his notebook.

"Did he leave a forwarding address?" Braddock asked.

"The same as his emergency contact, his father in Oakland."

"I heard he had a roommate," Sinclair said.

"He lived alone," the manager said. "If someone was staying with him, I didn't know about it. It was only a one bedroom, so if he did have a roommate, someone was on the couch or they were sharing a bed."

"Did he have any friends here?" Braddock asked.

"I don't pay attention as long as they pay their rent and don't do nothing that causes complaints from other tenants. Most of the Googlers don't do much other than sleep here."

"A lot of your tenants work at Google?" Braddock asked.

"The unit Whitt moved out of—a six-hundred-fifty-square-foot one bedroom—was advertised at thirty-one hundred a month, and I had a dozen applications within two days. You have to work at Google or one of the other high-tech places to afford that."

"You mind if we knock on some doors, see if anyone knew him?" Sinclair asked.

"You're the police. You can do what you want, but most of these computer nerds don't roll back home until nine or ten. With the cafeterias there that feed them for free, these kids eat a bag of chips in the morning, wash it down with an energy drink, and go to Googleplex until it's time to go to bed."

Sinclair and Braddock knocked at twenty or thirty doors. The few people who answered had no idea who Travis Whitt was, which confirmed the manager's assessment that the tenants didn't do much beyond sleep here.

On their drive back to Oakland, Braddock called back to homicide and had Jankowski run out Travis. He had no arrest or criminal history record and nothing in LRMS, which meant he had never been listed in a report taken by OPD. DMV showed a valid driver's license with the Mountain View apartment as his current address and a three-year-old Toyota Prius registered to him.

Sinclair called William Whitt's office and, as he expected, got the corporate voicemail saying the office closed at five. He called Whitt's cell, but it went directly to voicemail. "Let's stop by his house," Sinclair said to Braddock.

"Do you think he's lying about his son?" she asked.

"Among other things."

Wind-driven rain slapped Sinclair in the face when he exited his car in front of Whitt's house. He turned his head into the wind to keep it from blowing his hat from his head and marched to the front door with Braddock on his heels. He rang the doorbell. The house was dark and quiet. He rang again. Still no answer. He dialed Whitt's cell phone. It went straight to voicemail. He called the home phone number and heard it ringing inside, but no one answered. "You feel like doing a canvass of the neighborhood to see if anyone's seen Travis around?"

"In this weather?"

Sinclair smiled.

"Damn you, Sinclair," she said, stepping off the porch into the rain.

The first two houses to the left were dark, and no one answered the door. A frail woman leaning on a walker answered the door to the third house. She knew the Whitts but hadn't spoken to Mr. Whitt in years. She was vaguely aware of a son named Travis, but that was about all. No one answered the door at the next house. Sinclair and Braddock knocked on the doors of three houses on the other side of Whitt's home to no avail.

Back inside their car, Sinclair grabbed a handful of paper towels from the glove box and dried his face and hands. His pants were soaked from the knees down. Water had run down his neck and soaked his shirt collar. He was back to wearing his old London Fog raincoat, which wasn't as waterproof as the Burberry trench coat Walt had loaned him and which the FBI now had as evidence. Sinclair wondered if he'd ever get it back and whether it was even repairable after what it endured during the explosion.

Rivulets of water rolled from Braddock's hair and down her face. Her wide-brimmed hat didn't keep her head any drier than Sinclair's hat with rain coming in sideways. She dabbed her face with a paper towel. "I'm going to have to start wearing water-proof makeup when working with you. Should you call your buddy, Uppy, and tell him Travis is in the wind?"

"The FBI's only worried about the bombing and how it relates to terrorism, and we have nothing more solid that connects Travis than when we talked to Uppy earlier."

"Yeah, but Travis Whitt is causing the hairs on the back of my neck to stand up. Maybe we can put out a comm order on him and his car for questioning in connection with our one-eighty-sevens."

He was glad Braddock's gut was starting to feel the same as his. "Go ahead, but limit it to OPD and specify he's only a witness to our murders and we're only looking for his where-abouts. We don't want some rookie thinking he's a suspect and getting into the shit arresting him without probable cause, or worse." Sinclair didn't need to say the *worse* could mean a situation escalating into a shooting, which would require a whole lot of explaining as to why they put out a want on him.

Chapter 38

Sinclair's watch showed 9:30 as he sat on his couch wrapped in a thick fleece robe, listening to the rain pounding outside. When they had returned to the office from Whitt's house, Sinclair called the numbers he had for both William and Travis again. He then called the Oakland FBI office on the off-chance they'd agree to track their cell phones, but the duty agent refused, since Sinclair was still unable to provide a clear nexus to the terrorism angle. There was nothing meaningful for them to do, and Braddock said it would be counterproductive to sit in the office all night waiting for a call from the FBI or OPD on a break when their phones would ring as clearly from their respective bedrooms.

The Tylenol-Motrin combination that Sinclair had washed down with cold coffee in the office did its trick. His headache had dulled, and the rest of his muscle aches subsided to more discomfort than outright pain. Even though his body was so weary he didn't even have the energy to get up from the couch and go to bed, his mind was racing with all the possibilities the murders presented.

When Sinclair had first seen Dawn's burned, naked body hanging from the tree, he sensed the killer's anger—an anger that stemmed from something sexual. And when they found Edgar Pratt's body, Sinclair was convinced the killer or killers eliminated him to keep him quiet about Dawn's murder. Then there was all the Internet chatter about thrill kill, anarchists, and the Occupy movement. Everyone else was pulled in that direction, convinced that was what the murders were about. With the bombing and the subsequent threat conveyed in radical Occupy-type language, it made sense. Or the killers wanted the police to think that.

He was now certain they were wrong. The killers were gamers. They intentionally threw a red herring into the pack of badge-and-gun-carrying hounds. Obviously, the killers were somehow associated with the anarchists and occupiers, but as Phil Roberts continually reminded him, they were loosely affiliated and no one was in charge. Dawn's and Pratt's murders had nothing to do with that affiliation. The man who killed Dawn and Pratt hijacked a few of the radicals involved in the movement and used their skills and hatred for his own purpose.

Sinclair's phone buzzed with a text from Alyssa: *R U still up?*

Sinclair's mind immediately went to the sexual connotation, but he answered as if his thoughts weren't always in the gutter. *I'm wide awake.*

A few seconds later, she called. "Cathy said you ignored the doctor's bed-rest advice and went back to work."

Alyssa had been on duty when Sinclair and Braddock came to the ER after the explosion, and after the initial exam by the trauma team and a CT-scan, she cleaned and dressed his wounds and prepped the one in his leg for suturing. Her demeanor was cool and professional as she probed every inch of his body and pulled up the hospital gown to expose his entire butt and wash the dirt and debris from the road rash on his left hip. When he glanced over his shoulder as the doctor worked on his hamstring wound, she gave him a smile so warm he hardly felt the pain.

"I should probably lay off running for a while, but would you like to meet for coffee before work tomorrow?"

"I'm teaching a Pilates class at seven, then doing a career presentation on nursing at a grade school."

"Are you recruiting future nurses?" Sinclair asked.

"One of the women in my yoga class is a teacher, and her school has someone in a profession talk to their students once a month. A doctor was supposed to do it tomorrow, but she cancelled at the last minute, so I'm filling in."

"The boys will all fall in love with you."

"They're fourth graders, so I'll be gentle with their little hearts," she said. "How are you feeling?"

"Better."

"Cathy said you were in a lot of pain."

"She exaggerates."

"Get some rest," Alyssa said. "I'll check on you tomorrow afternoon."

★

At eight o'clock, Sinclair and Braddock were seated in a conference room at the Oakland FBI office listening to the morning briefing. Agents had conducted background checks on hundreds of people and interviewed dozens of them, but they still had no likely suspects in the bombing.

ATF briefed that preliminary analysis of the pressure cooker, black powder, and blasting cap showed the bomb had been identical to one that was set off at the Occupy rally in San Francisco last year, and the blasting cap appeared to be commercial grade, rather than U.S. or foreign military. Analysts at the San Francisco field office were still working to trace the phone numbers and computer IP addresses of Sean Garvin and Edgar Pratt to identify their associates and try to link them to the bombing.

After the meeting was over, Sinclair and Braddock cornered Uppy in his cubicle.

"Can you locate a cell phone for me?" Sinclair asked.

"Not Travis Whitt again?" Uppy said. "Whatever happened to OPD's Triggerfish?"

A Triggerfish was a device that mimicked cellular base stations to allow law enforcement officers to track cell phones. Since the device didn't collect actual voice communications, courts determined police didn't need a warrant to use it. "The city cut our funding, so we lost it."

"Connect Travis to some kind of federal crime, even if it's littering on federal property, and I'll locate him. But give me something."

Chapter 39

Sinclair took over an empty cubicle and called William Whitt's office number from a desk phone. Having *FBI* displayed on the caller ID probably got him connected immediately with Whitt's assistant, who said he was working from home this morning. Sinclair called his home and cell phones, but both rang through to voicemail. Sinclair called homicide, and Jankowski answered the phone.

"I need a favor, Dan," Sinclair said.

"You always need a favor," Jankowski said.

"Can you run someone out for me? This guy's avoiding me and if I can find a warrant—I don't care if it's for a ten-year-old expired meter—I'm gonna kick in his door and drag his ass downtown."

"Gimme his name and horsepower," Jankowski said. "And you owe me."

Sinclair read off Whitt's full name, date of birth, and address. A moment later, Jankowski said, "No wants or warrants. DMV shows a Jaguar XJ registered to him at the address on Skyline you gave me. Six years ago, he got a stop-sign ticket in a Mercedes. Nothing in CRIMS. LRMS shows he made a four-fifty-nine locked auto report four years ago. His car, the Mercedes, was broken into at Jack London Square. That's it. He looks like a model citizen."

"How about any firearms registered to him," Sinclair said.

"Lemme see." Sinclair pictured Jankowski punching Whitt's information onto his keyboard with two fingers. "Here we go. Looks like he bought a Walther PPK/S back in 2002."

"A thirty-two or three-eighty?" Sinclair asked.

"Three-eighty," Jankowski said. "And there's no record of sale or transfer, so he should still have it."

"Lunch at a place of your choice," Sinclair said to Jankowski before hanging up.

Braddock's ears had perked up when Sinclair said .380.

"Whitt owns a Walther PPK," he said to Braddock as he headed for the door. "Same rifling characteristics as our murder weapon."

"Shouldn't we get a search warrant?" Braddock asked.

"We still don't have enough, but it doesn't matter because the asshole's gonna voluntarily open the door and either show us his gun or explain what the hell happened to it."

Sinclair took the 24 Freeway to 13, got off at Broadway Terrace, and followed it as it wound through the hills to Skyline Boulevard. Braddock requested a marked unit meet them there. Neither of them thought Whitt was the killer, and he didn't seem the type to put up a fight. But having a uniformed officer present would make their actions appear less reckless if he decided to go the hard way. The marked car was parked a few houses away and pulled in behind Sinclair and Braddock as they passed by.

"What'cha got, Sarge?" The first officer asked as he climbed out of the marked unit. Officer Buckner had graduated a few academies before Sinclair and worked in special operations with him more than ten years ago. He'd been a field training officer, or FTO, for the past six years, while his rookie partner looked as if he'd gotten out of the academy yesterday. After taking the last five exams, Buckner finally got on the sergeant promotional list, so he was keeping his nose as clean as possible and hoping to get his stripes before the list expired.

Sinclair filled him in and rang the doorbell. Buckner pulled out his baton and rapped on the door with it, the sound reverberating through the house. Still no response. Sinclair called Whitt's cell and home phone, but no answer. The only visible window, which a curtain covered, was by the front door. The other windows were down the steep slopes on the sides of the house or faced the Oakland flatlands below and would require a helicopter to look into.

An SUV drove into the driveway next door and slid into the garage. Sinclair told Buckner to stay at the door in case Whitt came out. He and Braddock walked next door and into the open garage just as a woman with two armloads of groceries slammed the passenger door of a white Audi Q7 with her hip.

Sinclair stayed back to avoid startling the woman, and Braddock took the lead. "Ma'am, we're with Oakland PD, can we ask you a few questions?"

The woman looked up. Midfifties, white, brunette, wearing a tan raincoat over jeans and boots. "Sure," she said. "Come on in so I can put this stuff down."

Braddock grabbed an eco-friendly reusable bag filled with produce and followed her through a laundry room into a kitchen.

The woman set the bags on the counter. "I was waiting for the rain to let up before going to Safeway, but we're out of everything."

"Do you know the Whitts next door?" Braddock asked.

"Sure, we've lived here going on twenty years. He's been here longer."

"Do you know if he's home now?" Braddock asked.

"I don't have a clue. I mostly see him if we're both going in or out at the same time. It's not like we have a front yard to hang out in." She looked at her watch. "He's probably at work."

"His office said he's home," Sinclair said.

She shrugged her shoulders and opened the refrigerator.

"What about his son, Travis?" Sinclair asked.

"If he's home, you'd probably hear him." She began unloading plastic bags full of vegetables and fruit into the refrigerator.

"Have you seen him lately?"

"I saw him about an hour ago with a bunch of his weirdo friends. One of them was blocking my driveway, and I had to wait until he moved to go to the store."

"Can you describe him?" Sinclair asked.

"The one driving?"

Sinclair nodded.

"Shaved head, in his late twenties, about Travis's age. A few inches taller than you. Muscular."

"There were other friends of Travis's with him?" Sinclair asked.

"One that I saw. I didn't get a good look at him, but he wasn't as tall and a lot thinner."

"What were they wearing?"

She closed the refrigerator and opened a cabinet next to the sink. "Black raincoats and black pants. Everything black. Travis, too."

"And the car?"

"An old Bronco. The big truck-like ones. It looks like it was painted with cans of spray paint. An ugly mud-brown color."

"Did you see them leave?"

"Travis came up to the muscular one, said something, and he got into the Bronco and pulled it into the Whitts' driveway. That's when I left for the store."

"Was Travis's car there?" Sinclair asked.

She put a jar of peanut butter and boxes of pasta into the cabinet. "His little green Prius was in the driveway when I left."

"When did you last see Travis before this morning?"

"It's not seeing him, it's hearing him," she said. "He's been back home for the last two or three months. It's better now that it's raining, but when the weather was warm, he'd leave the slider open on the bottom level and blast his music. I don't even know what people his age listen to these days. I though rap was bad, but this stuff . . ."

"Have you talked to William?"

"Several times, but it only goes on during the day when he's at work."

Sinclair copied her name and numbers into his notebook, thanked her for her help, and returned to the Whitts' front porch. Sinclair noticed Braddock adjusting her belt under her coat, unconsciously touching her holster and other gear. He didn't have to tell her the trail to the killer was getting hot.

While Braddock told Buckner and his rookie what the neighbor reported, Sinclair called Bianca. "I'm at William Whitt's house. His office says he's home but he won't answer the door or his phones. Do you think he'll answer for you?"

"I can try," she said. "What's happening?"

"I can't get into it, but I need to talk to him and Travis now."

"Is Travis there?"

Sinclair hated being the one answering questions right now, but he needed her help. "He was here, but I think he's gone off with some friends who are about to get into major trouble. They may have a gun."

The phone was silent, and Sinclair looked at it to ensure there was still a connection. "Bianca, are you there?" Sinclair switched the phone to speaker so Braddock could hear.

"Matt, when William and I were seeing each other, I took an interest in Travis. He was a troubled young man who needed a mother figure. He would talk and I would listen. I hadn't heard from him in a year or more until maybe a month ago. He called me and said he knew his mother didn't die by accident and that his father was screwing whores again. I talked to William about it, and he, of course, denied it. He said he'd talk to Travis but everything was fine. Let me call him. He'll pick up for me."

A few minutes later, the deadbolt retracted and the door opened. William Whitt appeared, dressed in gray slacks with a white shirt and tie. Sinclair's hand rested on his Sig Sauer, holstered under his coat.

"Put your hands up and turn around," he ordered.

"What's going on?" Whitt asked.

"Do it!" Sinclair barked.

Whitt complied and Sinclair guided him into the living room and patted him down. "You can put your hands down. Where's Travis?"

"He's not here."

"Where is he?" Sinclair asked.

Whitt was sweating profusely. "I don't know."

Sinclair's phone vibrated. He looked at the screen. It was Uppy. "Watch him," he said to Buckner as he stepped into the kitchen with Braddock to answer the call.

"We identified Anarchist Soldier. His name's Andrew Pearson, male, white, twenty-eight, six-two, two hundred, shaved head. He's active in the Occupy protests, busting windows and throwing firebombs. He's usually masked, but we IDed him by some distinctive tattoos. We linked him to Garvin and Pratt through cell phone records and Internet messages on the gaming websites."

"Have you got a location on him?" Sinclair asked.

"Not yet. The bureau's surveillance team's set up on the addresses we have for him, but he's a no-show so far. His phone's off. But get this, Matt, he was in the Marines and got kicked out with a bad conduct discharge after six months. Until a month ago, he worked for JB Construction doing road work in the Sierras."

"Let me guess," Sinclair said. "He had access to explosives."

"The company said it was highly likely."

"A guy fitting his description was seen with Travis Whitt at the Whitt's house less than an hour ago. Can you do your magic with Travis's cell phone?"

"Sarge," shouted Officer Buckner from the living room.

"Let me call you back," Sinclair said to Uppy as he returned to the living room.

"I heard you mention it on the phone," said Buckner, "so I asked Mr. Whitt if he had any guns in the house, and he said he has a Walther PPK in his study."

"Show me," Sinclair said, and he followed Whitt down a set of stairs and through a door into a large wood-paneled office. Beyond the window stretched a balcony with the same view of the city as the living room ten feet above. Whitt moved around to the back of a black lacquered desk and opened a drawer.

"Hang on," Sinclair said, grabbing Whitt and pulling him aside. "I'll get it."

"The key's in the drawer. It opens a cabinet where the gun is."

Sinclair slid the desk drawer out and removed a brass key from the pen tray. He followed Whitt across the room to a solid wood cabinet situated between two matching bookshelves. Sinclair unlocked the sliding panels in the middle of the cabinet and slid them open. On the shelf were several binders, boxes of checks, and three bound journals, two black and one pink and yellow. "Where's the gun?" Sinclair asked.

Whitt looked inside. "It's gone." The surprise in his voice was genuine.

"When did you last see it?" Sinclair asked.

"It was here the first of the month. I went in here to get a new book of checks for Dawn."

"That was two days before she was killed," Sinclair said.

"Yeah, she came over to drop off some spreadsheets and pick up the checkbook and some bills that came to the house."

"And you're just mentioning this now?"

Whitt lowered his head. "Sorry," he whispered.

"Was Travis here at the time?" Sinclair asked.

"He was downstairs in his room."

"Does he know you keep the key—oh hell, never mind. He'd have to be a moron not to know there's a key in your desk drawer. Is anything else missing?"

"Oh my god!" Whitt said.

"What is it?" Sinclair asked.

"It's nothing."

"Whitt, what is it?" Sinclair asked again.

"Nothing."

Travis had obviously seen Dawn that night in his father's study. Sinclair pictured Travis listening outside the door when William and Dawn talked about their past. Or maybe he was conveniently in the living room when William walked her to the front door, forcing an introduction. Or maybe Travis waited by her car, where he could talk to her alone. It might have been a casual, polite conversation, one where he did nothing more than gather information about her to use later. Or maybe Travis didn't meet her at all that night, but followed her to her apartment so he could visit her later with the gun.

"Show me his room," Sinclair ordered.

Whitt led them down the stairs to the lower level. Three doors faced them at the bottom of the stairs. Whitt pointed at one door. "He keeps it locked. To show I trust him, I don't go in."

Sinclair didn't waste his breath telling Whitt what a fool he was for ignoring all the warning signs. Sinclair turned his back to the door, looked over his shoulder, and using a mule kick, smashed his right heel into the doorknob. The door splintered. He felt a stabbing pain where the hospital had stitched him up, but nothing wet rolled down his leg, so he probably hadn't ripped out the stitches. Sinclair shoved the door open and entered. Braddock, Whitt, Buckner, and his rookie followed.

The room's blueprint was a copy of Whitt's study a level above, twenty by thirty, with a balcony that overlooked the city. A bed and dresser were in one corner. A door on that wall led to a bathroom. Buckner and his partner swept through it to ensure no one was there. In the opposite corner were two leather couches facing a seventy-inch flat screen, a gaming console, and several handheld controllers lying on the floor.

Photos printed with a home printer on letter-size paper were taped to the wall. Sinclair stepped over two empty pizza boxes to get a closer look. One photo was of Dawn in a lace negligee, the same image Sinclair saw a few days earlier on the Special Ladies Escorts website. Another was of Lisa Harper in a ballet pose similar to what he saw in her classroom. Whitt stood beside Sinclair with his mouth gaping open.

"There were things in that cabinet more dangerous than the gun," Whitt said. "Susan's diary, where she described my affair with Lisa in detail and my use of escorts. Her last entry talked about taking her own life. If Travis read it . . ."

Sinclair wanted to slam him against the wall, first for lying to him, and second to knock every ounce of truth out of him. But he took a deep breath. "What else?"

"Journals that my therapist told me to write." Whitt looked down at his wingtips. "About my feelings and my struggles with . . . you know."

"Your struggles with sex addiction?" Sinclair said.

Whitt nodded.

"Sinclair!" Braddock yelled from the other side of the room, where she was crouched inside a closet.

Sinclair crossed the room and looked over Braddock's shoulder: a dozen empty black-powder containers and empty ammunition boxes labeled *7.62x39*—the rifle cartridge designed for the Russian and Chinese AK-47 and SKS rifles.

Sinclair's phone rang. It was Uppy. "We located Travis Whitt's cell phone. It shows at an address on Thornhill Drive, not far from his father's house. Get a pen and I'll give you the numbers."

Sinclair reached in his pocket as Uppy continued, "We just brought the address up in the mapping program. It's a school by the name of Caldecott Academy."

Chapter 40

"We found bomb-making materials and empty boxes of ammo," Sinclair said to Uppy. "They're planning a school massacre. Get your SWAT people and every agent you can muster there."

Sinclair hung up before Uppy could respond. He turned to Buckner's police trainee. "Detain Whitt and secure this room. No one touches anything until an OPD command officer tells you different."

The kid's eyes lit up. "Yes, sir."

"Let's go," Sinclair yelled to Braddock and Buckner as he sprinted up the stairs, taking them two at a time.

As Sinclair rushed out the front door, he looked over his shoulder to see Braddock and Buckner on his heels. He yelled to Buckner, "You know the fastest way to the school?"

"It's my beat, I should."

"Lead the way," Sinclair said as he jumped in his Crown Vic and cranked the engine.

Buckner spun a U-turn and sped up Skyline Boulevard. Braddock fastened her seat belt and reached for the radio microphone as Sinclair took off after the black-and-white SUV. Buckner and Sinclair had both been around long enough to know they didn't want to alert the suspects they were coming. Straight-line distance, the school was only a mile away, twice as far via the winding mountain roads, so neither turned on their sirens—not that there was any traffic ahead of them to clear.

"Thirteen-Adam-Five, code thirty-three," Braddock said into the mic.

"You have the air, Thirteen-Adam-Five," the dispatcher replied.

"We're responding to Caldecott Academy on Thornhill with the FTO half of One-John-Thirteen on a possible school shooting in progress."

The dispatcher echoed the information for all units, "Thirteen-Adam-Five and half of One-John-Thirteen are responding to a possible school shooting in progress at the Caldecott Academy on Thornhill Drive. Any further details, Thirteen-Adam-Five?"

Buckner made a sharp left onto Elverton Drive, the Police Interceptor Utility taking the corner without a hint of body sway while Sinclair's big sedan fishtailed on the wet road at the same speed. In the background, he heard Braddock providing a description of the suspects and the likelihood that three or more men were armed with AK-47-type weapons and one or more bombs similar to what detonated on Lakeshore Drive two days ago. Sinclair took a quick left switchback, which normal drivers would take at ten miles an hour, at twice that, throwing Braddock against the passenger door. He accelerated down a straightaway, trying to keep Buckner in sight and praying no one would pull out of a driveway in front of him.

The radio screamed in Sinclair's ears with units advising they were en route to the school. The nearest one was coming from Forty-First and Telegraph, which would probably take just under ten minutes at code-three speed. The Oakland Hills were blessed with the lowest crime rate in the city, which meant their police coverage was bare bones, but when they did have a significant crime in progress, the nearest officer was often a long way off and his nearest cover officer even farther.

"Advise all responding units," Braddock said over the radio, "to shut down lights and sirens at least a mile away."

The dispatcher relayed the instructions for all other units on the channel.

When Buckner crossed Beauforest Drive, the Caldecott Academy appeared ahead. Sinclair and every officer in Oakland had been trained how to respond to active shooter incidents. Traditional police tactics that included a slow, methodical, cautious approach and waiting for SWAT teams did nothing but give these kind of shooters more time to kill. Even though the risk to responding officers was great, the only way to stop an active shooter was to rush through the scene toward the gunfire and engage him.

Buckner stopped his vehicle at the far end of the parking lot. Sinclair pulled alongside and popped the trunk. He and Braddock stripped off their coats, threw them in the trunk, and pulled out their Kevlar vests. Although Sinclair wished for a heavy tactical vest—one that would stop 7.62x39 rounds—and the M4 rifle he had when he was on the SWAT team, they only had two choices. They could wait for more officers with the right equipment to gain a tactical advantage or rush toward the sound of gunfire and screaming children to eliminate the threat with what they had.

Buckner held a Remington 870, the standard shotgun mounted in every marked Oakland police car. He worked the pump action and racked a round into the chamber. He then slid another 12-gauge round from the carrier on the shotgun's stock and fed it into the gun's magazine, giving him five rounds of double-ought buckshot in the gun and four more rounds in the carrier. Sinclair and Braddock gave him a thumbs-up to indicate they were ready. There was no need to discuss who would take point—the officer in uniform with the biggest gun was the logical choice. Buckner took off on a slow jog toward the front door, with Sinclair falling in behind him and Braddock taking up the rear.

Gunshots echoed from inside the school. Two, then three more, followed by a pause, and then a succession of shots too numerous to count. The shots were sharp and loud, as Sinclair had feared, undoubtedly coming from rifles such as AK-47s or SKSs. Armed with only handguns and a shotgun, they were significantly outgunned.

Buckner squeezed his lapel mic and said, "Shots fired inside. We're on the scene and approaching the front door."

Sinclair gripped his .45 Sig Sauer with both hands at a low ready as his eyes scanned the parking lot and the front windows of the school for any movement. The rain beat down on him, rolling off his head, down his face, and soaking his shirt. He ignored it. In the right side of the parking lot, he spotted the mud-brown Ford Bronco parked next to a green Prius.

A couple rows down, a familiar red Mazda Miata was parked—Alyssa's car. This was the school where she was doing the career presentation. He felt his heart skip a beat. But he forced himself to return to the present. *Mission focus*, he reminded himself.

They reached the alcove by the front doors where Sinclair and Braddock had stood two days ago. The reinforced glass in the doors was shattered, a few shards of glass still hanging from the doorframes. A sledgehammer lay on the ground on top of the broken glass.

They stepped through the doorframes. Two adult women were sprawled on the floor in pools of blood inside the main office. One was moaning and writhing in pain; the other, a tall, thin woman, remained motionless. A pair of large black-framed glasses lay in the puddle of blood.

The harsh reality in active shooter incidents was that to save the most people, you sometimes had to leave people to die. Rendering first aid had to come later. The hardest part for Sinclair and any officer responding to a school shooting was seeing injured and frightened children, knowing they'd have to bypass them to stop the killers.

They flowed through the office, Buckner leading the way with his shotgun. The door to the headmaster's office was open. No one was inside. She was likely the woman lying wounded on the floor.

Sinclair tried the other door. Locked.

"Police," Sinclair said. "Anyone inside?"

The door squeaked open. A heavyset woman, her arms wrapped around three small children, peered out. Her eyes froze on the women lying in front of her.

"How many are there?" Sinclair asked.

"Are they alive?" The woman's face was white. Obviously in shock.

"They'll be fine," Sinclair lied. "Help's on the way. How many armed people did you see?"

"I saw two, announced lock-down on the PA, then pulled the children in here and locked the door. Then I heard voices. More than two. They asked where Mrs. Harper's classroom was. The headmaster wouldn't tell them. Then I heard gunshots."

"Stay here," Sinclair said. "Lock the door."

She pulled the kids inside. The lock clicked. Through the door, she said, "All the third and fourth graders are in Mrs. Harper's classroom for a presentation by a nurse. You have to get there before those men do."

Buckner spoke into his radio mic, "One dead, one wounded in the front office. Teacher and kids barricaded in a room. We're headed toward the classrooms."

Even with the volume on Buckner's radio turned low, Sinclair heard the dispatcher acknowledge and one unit announce he was five minutes out. Men armed with semiautomatic rifles could kill a lot of people in five minutes.

They stepped into a short hallway. Fifty feet ahead, a longer hallway turned right. Sinclair remembered from Monday that it was a long corridor, maybe two hundred feet long, with Harper's classroom near the end. Beyond it, another hallway turned right and led to more classrooms, an auditorium, and a cafeteria.

They marched forward, Sinclair and Buckner in front, shoulder to shoulder, with Braddock in the rear, glancing back every few steps to ensure no one attacked from behind.

Suddenly, a man jumped around the corner in front of them. Black trench coat, black ski mask. He held an SKS rifle at his hip and fired.

Buckner's shotgun roared. Sinclair brought up his pistol and shot. The SKS rifle barked again, and again. Sinclair continued to shoot. He didn't know how many times Buckner shot or how many rounds the man fired. He focused on his front sight and the man beyond it, and he continued firing until the man dropped and Sinclair's slide locked back.

He depressed the magazine release, and the empty magazine rattled to the ground. He inserted a fresh magazine of eight rounds, guiding it into the pistol's butt with his left index finger touching the top round and slamming it home with the heel of his hand in one smooth movement. He thumbed the slide release, which slammed a .45 cartridge into the chamber, and scanned the hallway.

The shooter was down, but so was Buckner.

Braddock was still standing. She went to Buckner and Sinclair went to the shooter, lying in the open area where the two hallways intersected. Rule number one in a gunfight: it's not over until you're certain the threat is neutralized. Sinclair pulled the SKS rifle from the shooter's hands and ripped open the man's trench coat, revealing a ballistic vest similar to what he was wearing. A dozen or more projectiles were embedded in the Kevlar fibers. Half of his throat was missing, blown out by one or more .45 slugs or .33 caliber pellets from the shotgun. Sinclair flipped him over. The back of his skull was gone. The exit wound from a .45.

Sinclair glanced to his right. Two men in black raincoats came out of an empty classroom halfway down the long hallway. Their guns came up. A third man took up prone position at the end of the hallway, pointing a rifle down the corridor. Sinclair leaped back around the corner as they fired.

Sinclair duck walked backward to where Braddock was attending to Buckner. Buckner's face was pale and coated with sweat. Braddock had stripped off his vest to reveal an entry wound just below his right breast. The Kevlar vests they wore weren't designed to stop rifle bullets. Sinclair rolled Buckner on his side. The bullet had exited near his kidney, creating a bloody hole an inch in diameter.

"Is it bad?" Buckner asked.

"Hell, brother, ACH will patch you up good as new," Sinclair said, hoping Buckner would believe him.

Braddock shook her head. She knew it was bad. Sinclair had seen wounds like this in Iraq. They couldn't do much for him here. The internal bleeding could only be handled by opening him up in an operating room. In the meantime, he needed bandages, direct pressure, and an IV to counteract the blood loss and to keep his body from going into shock until the trauma surgeons at ACH could do their magic.

Sinclair grabbed Buckner's shoulder mic. "Thirteen-Adam-Five, we have an officer down. GSW to the chest. We need paramedics to the front door now."

"Thirteen-Adam-Five," the dispatcher said. "Ambulances and fire are staging one block south waiting for the scene to be secured."

Screw radio procedure. "Damn it!" Sinclair yelled into the microphone. "An officer's going to die if we don't get him out now. Send them to the front door. It will be secure."

Buckner forced a smile. "So it's worse than you said."

"Don't you fuckin' give up," Sinclair said. "You're gonna make it."

It wasn't fair that police ignored wounded civilians in an active shooter scenario but would stop and aid a fallen officer. But that's the way it was. Just like with soldiers on a battlefield, cops don't leave a fallen officer behind.

Sinclair said to Braddock. "Drag him to the front door. If you don't see the paramedics or fire department, keep dragging him. All the fucking way to ACH if you have to."

Tears began welling in Braddock's eyes.

"There's no time for that," Sinclair said. "Buckner's gonna make it if you get him out of here."

She blinked away the tears. "What about you?"

"I'm gonna go and get those assholes."

"Alone?"

"Don't worry about me. Save Buckner." Sinclair watched as Braddock grabbed Buckner under the armpits and dragged him down the hall.

Chapter 41

Sinclair picked up Buckner's empty shotgun, loaded the four rounds from the buttstock carrier into the magazine, and racked a round into the chamber. He peeked around the corner. Only the man proned-out with the rifle in the hallway was visible. The other two were probably searching classrooms for children. Sinclair peeked again and pulled his head back just as a bullet zinged past him.

The man securing the hallway was two hundred feet away. Too far for a pistol shot but an easy target for someone with a rifle. To enter the hallway and get to the men searching the classrooms, Sinclair had to take out the rifleman.

He knew the spread of the shotgun's pellets was about an inch for every yard of distance, so at this range, the nine pellets would spread half the width of the hallway. A short-barreled shotgun with buckshot wasn't designed for this distance. A man could stand right in the middle of the pattern and remain unscathed as pellets hit all around him. A man lying on the ground offered an even smaller target.

Sinclair stuck the shotgun around the corner with one hand and fired. The recoil nearly ripped the gun from his hand. Two rifle bullets pinged into the wall behind him. The man wasn't a skilled rifleman, but at this range, he didn't need to be. Even an amateur could keep his sights on the corner from where Sinclair would next appear and get a round off within two seconds.

Sinclair did another quick peek. The man was still there. Two seconds later, a gunshot rang out. Sinclair's shot obviously didn't hit him or frighten him into giving up his position. Sinclair was capable of hitting a man-sized target with his pistol at two hundred feet, but it required careful aiming and three or four misses for every hit. The rifleman would nail him before he got off the first shot. A shotgun with rifled slugs would've been a game changer, and although some officers carried them, Buckner didn't.

Although the man presented a small target by lying in the prone position, he had obviously never learned about ricochet shooting or grazing fire, as they called it in the military. When a bullet is fired at a surface at an acute angle, it has a tendency to skip along the surface, much as a flat rock can be skipped along the surface of a lake. The Army taught machine gunners to keep their fire low when engaging enemy forces. Rounds that don't hit the personnel directly and miss low will graze along the ground, often bouncing a foot or two high, much like a skipped rock.

It had taken two seconds for the rifleman to get off a shot. If Sinclair appeared at a location different from the corner of the hallway where the man was now aiming, the rifleman would have to shift his aim, thus giving Sinclair another second. If Sinclair could get his first shot directed at the floor halfway down the hallway within that time, one or more pellets, skipping along the floor, might hit the target. Even if he missed, Sinclair might get close enough to upset the rifleman's aim and give him time to fire the last three rounds. He had a good chance of hitting the rifleman if he could put thirty-six pellets downrange.

Sinclair quick peeked. Two men were disappearing into a classroom near the end of the hall. Lisa Harper's classroom couldn't be much further. The rifleman was still in position.

Sinclair checked the shotgun. One round in the chamber, three more in the magazine. He got a running start and dashed into the hallway, immediately dropping to his knees and sliding halfway to the far wall. The shotgun's stock was already against his shoulder. He twisted his body and fired. Without waiting to see the results, he pumped the action and fired again, and again, and again.

Sinclair dropped the empty shotgun and drew his pistol. The rifleman was motionless. He hadn't gotten off a shot. Two men in long, black raincoats and ski masks exited a classroom and pointed guns in Sinclair's direction. One was an SKS rifle, the other a pistol. Sinclair sprinted back around the corner out of their field of fire as a barrage of bullets struck the wall behind where he had been standing.

Although he had taken out one target, Sinclair wasn't much better off than before. He was pinned down once again. The only way forward was through open ground defended by a man with a rifle.

Sinclair looked in front of him. The dead man's rifle lay ten feet into the exposed kill zone. Although he had never fired an SKS, he'd handled them as evidence on numerous occasions. Years ago, Oakland was flooded with thousands of Norinco SKS rifles. At two hundred dollars each, the Chinese-made rifles were a favorite drive-by shooting choice of drug gangs for several years. Crudely built, marginally accurate, but utterly reliable, the SKS was a military rifle designed by Russia during World War II. Because it didn't match the characteristics of an assault rifle, it was legal to purchase even in California.

Sinclair had survived one sprint into the long hallway, and he hoped his luck would hold out again. If the two remaining gunmen were skilled at hitting a moving target, as were many hunters, he was a dead man. He dashed into the corridor and grabbed the SKS. His leather-soled shoes provided little traction on the slick floor, and he nearly fell. Bullets pinged around him as he dove back to safety around the corner.

He pulled the SKS's bolt to the rear and ejected a live cartridge into his hand. The internal box magazine, which could hold up to ten rounds, was empty. The dead man had fired them during their brief gunfight. Sinclair wished the body wasn't in the kill zone because the man's pockets surely contained stripper clips of ammo, but he didn't dare risk searching the body while exposed to gunfire. He pressed the single cartridge into the magazine, released the bolt, and watched it load into the chamber. He had one shot. If he was lucky, he could take out the man with the rifle, close the distance to the final man, who was armed only with a handgun, and finish the fight.

He quick peeked around the corner. The muscular man had a crowbar in his hand and was trying to pry open a classroom door at the end of the hall—Lisa Harper's room. His rifle lay at his feet. The other man, tall and thin, stood nearby holding a pistol in his hand. Both wore black backpacks identical to the one Sinclair saw in the parking garage just before it detonated.

Sinclair shouldered the rifle and stepped into the hallway. He pointed it at the thin man and walked forward. If the muscular man went for the rifle, Sinclair would shift to him, put the sights on his chest, and take the shot. He'd then drop the rifle, draw his pistol, and engage the thin man. Sinclair was confident he was a better handgun shooter than his adversary, and even with the time it took to drop the rifle and transition to his pistol, he had a decent chance of prevailing. He was now 150 feet away. The man with the crowbar looked up at him. The other just stood there and watched him advance. An easy rifle shot, but still far for a pistol. Sinclair continued to close the distance, moving slowly to maintain his balance and shooting stance.

The muscular man, who Sinclair suspected was Andrew Pearson, put down the crowbar and began to reach for the rifle. Sinclair shifted to him and prepared to pull the trigger. He thought of yelling, "Police! Freeze!" but it seemed ridiculous under the circumstances.

"I've got this handled," the thin man said to Pearson, and he pulled the ski mask off his head with his gun hand.

Sinclair immediately recognized Travis Whitt from the photos he'd seen. He shifted the rifle back to him, settling the sights on his chest while watching Pearson in his peripheral vision.

"Keep working on the door," Travis said to Pearson. He then pulled his left hand from his pocket and held a small black box the size of a garage door opener above his head.

"What're you doing?" Pearson shouted to Travis. "I thought the plan was to hightail it out of here before you pulled that out!"

"Just get the door open," Travis said.

Pearson shoved the straight end of the crowbar into the gap between the door and the frame and pulled backward. It slipped out and he jammed it in again.

Sinclair took a few steps closer. He pictured all the third and fourth graders huddled together in the back of Mrs. Harper's classroom, surrounded by teachers hushing them in hopes the gunmen would think the room was empty and move on. He imagined Alyssa in the middle of the huddle, trying to comfort the terrified children while hiding her own fear from them.

"Put the triggering device down, Travis," Sinclair said. "You know I'm not letting you get in that classroom."

"Prostitutes destroy families," Travis said. "You, if anyone, should know that. They deserve to die."

"Even if that was true, why the innocent kids?"

"That's the only way the one-percenters take notice."

It was futile to argue with crazy men armed with guns and explosives. They only understood one thing. He shifted the sights to the imaginary triangle between Travis's eyes and nose. A bullet there would kill him and short-circuit his brain before he could trigger the explosives.

"I know what you're thinking," Travis said. "Kill me and no big boom. But what I'm holding here is a dead man's switch. I've already pressed one button. If my finger comes off it without depressing the other button first, both backpacks explode."

"Wait a fucking minute," said Pearson. "I'm not part of any suicide mission."

"Just open the door," Travis said. "The cop knows if he shoots us, he'll die with us. Besides, cops don't kill unarmed men." Travis crouched down and set his handgun on the floor.

Travis might have been right about the explosion killing Sinclair as well as them. He was forty yards away, more than twice the distance from the last bomb. But this was an enclosed area, which would contain and direct the explosive force to the areas of least resistance, one of which was down the corridor where Sinclair was standing. He wondered if people inside the classroom would survive an explosion in the hallway, and whether the bombs packed more explosives than the last one, and whether they were filled with nails or other shrapnel that would rip through his flesh like a wall of high-velocity bullets.

His only other option was to back down the hallway. But he couldn't do that. One bomb inside the enclosed classroom would surely kill everyone inside. Maybe Travis was bluffing about the dead man's switch. But suicide was often the final step in many school shooters' plans.

There were too many unknowns with too many possible outcomes, but one thing was for certain: Sinclair had no doubt he could pull the trigger. It didn't matter if a gun was in Travis's hand or on the ground. Any uncertainty he had when he faced Garvin in the Mills Café a few days ago had vanished the moment he'd stepped into the school.

"Last chance, Travis," Sinclair said. "Put down the detonator."

"You won't shoot me. You wouldn't shoot an unarmed man."

Sinclair squeezed the trigger.

Everything began to move in slow motion. He felt the recoil of the rifle against his shoulder and heard the report of the gunshot. Travis's head jerked backward. Red mist sprayed from the back of his head. Pearson looked at Travis, an expression of shock and surprise on his face. Sinclair released the rifle and went for his pistol on his right side. His eyes shifted to Pearson—his next target. Sinclair's hand touched his Sig Sauer. In another second, it would be in his hand and at eye level, pointed at Pearson. In a split second, he'd decide whether to pull the trigger or not.

Since he was still alive and hadn't been blown to kingdom come, the thought that Travis had been bluffing flashed through Sinclair's mind as his fingers curled around the butt of his pistol and began to lift it from the holster. Simultaneously, a brilliant flash of white light blinded him, a deafening roar filled his eardrums, and a shock wave smashed into his body.

Chapter 42

Sinclair fought to open his eyes. They felt glued shut. He tried to reach his hand to his face to separate his eyelids, but it had ropes or something attached to it. He tried his other hand. It took all the strength he had to move it. He touched his face. It was scratchy. He was sure he had shaved this morning. Familiar voices sounded as if they were at the end of a tunnel. They were coming closer. Or was he moving through the tunnel toward them? He rubbed his eyes with his free hand.

"I think he's waking up."

The voice sounded like Maloney.

"Matt, are you awake?" Braddock asked.

Sinclair opened his eyes. He was in a hospital bed. A blurry shape that he made out to be Maloney stood on one side of his bed. With great effort, he turned his head and recognized Braddock on the other side. All around him were machines attached to wires and tubes that were running into him. Braddock pressed a button on a box, and the back of Sinclair's bed rose until he was sitting up. She held out a glass and put a straw in his mouth.

He sucked on the straw. Tasted something cold and sweet. Apple juice. That confirmed he was in a hospital. No other place served apple juice to adults. He tried to raise his left hand again, but saw a thick IV tube stuck in his forearm. He had so many questions, he didn't know where to start. He tried to speak, but his voice cracked. He swallowed more of the juice.

Maloney turned and spoke to a uniformed officer seated outside his room. "Tell a nurse he's awake."

"You don't need to talk," Braddock said. "You're in the ICU at Highland Hospital. You're going to be okay."

Braddock's voice sounded distant, even though she was beside him. Sinclair stuck a finger in his ear, hoping to clear it. He ran his right hand down his chest and tried to move his legs. His feet moved the blanket that covered him.

Braddock laughed. "Every body part is accounted for."

"What about the kids . . . are they . . . ?" Sinclair began in a hoarse whisper.

"They're all alive," she said. "The blast blew out part of the cinderblock wall that separated the hall from the classroom. A few were injured by debris, others had minor concussions, but nothing life threatening. The last child was released from Children's Hospital today."

"Today?" Sinclair said, trying to form a complete thought in the mud in which his brain seemed to be immersed.

"It's Saturday, Matt," Braddock said. "You've been unconscious for two days."

"Two days?"

"You came around a bit yesterday," Braddock said. "You mumbled something, thrashed about, and tried to pull out your IV. The doctor gave you some more pain meds and you drifted off."

"Alyssa?" Sinclair asked.

"She's fine. She and the other teachers were checked out at ACH and released. She's been one of your most frequent visitors." Braddock smiled and took his hand in both of hers. "I called her when you started coming around. She's on duty downstairs in the ER and will be up to see you soon."

The final moments before the explosion were slowly coming back to him. "What happened?"

"Cathy was getting Buckner onto a gurney when the next officer arrived," Maloney said. "He ran inside. How do you stop an officer from rushing toward the gunfire? He got to the corner of the hallway where Bucker had been shot just as Travis pulled out the detonator. The officer thought if he rushed down the corridor to cover you, one of them might panic and start shooting or press the button. His body camera was on, so we have a full video and audio recording of everything that happened. When you shot Travis, the officer instinctively ducked around the corner. There was a full-second delay between your shot and the explosion."

"Buckner?" Sinclair asked.

"He's alive," Braddock said. "Two paramedics and three firefighters arrived. The doctors don't know if he'll fully recover and return to duty, but he'll live. The bullet went through a lung and other stuff, so he'll be in for a long time."

"The trauma surgeon said that if he got here two minutes later, he'd be dead," Maloney said. "Cathy was a warrior. The paramedics weren't exactly waiting at the front door for her. She dragged Buckner across the parking lot and was getting ready to head down the street when the paramedics and firefighters finally decided to ignore the staging order from their bosses and ran up."

Braddock gripped Sinclair's hand harder. "He wasn't going to die in my arms because I sat at the front door waiting for help."

"Bucker's body camera was on," said Maloney. "The chief's office edited it and released it to the media. It's great PR to show the heroic actions of the three of you, but they did have to add a bleep when you told Cathy to drag Buckner all the fucking way to ACH if she had to."

"I'm proud of you." Sinclair squeezed her hand. Buckner was well over two hundred pounds with his gear on, so dragging him nearly a quarter mile was no easy task even for a large, muscular man. But he had no doubt Braddock wouldn't have quit until she got Buckner into the hands of the paramedics.

"Me? Shit, Matt, you blew yourself up to save those kids. You can't turn on the news without hearing your name."

A nurse walked in, checked Sinclair's vitals, and shined a penlight in his eyes. "How's the pain?" she asked.

"I feel fine," he said.

"I'll talk to the doctor and see if we can cut back on the pain meds. We'll probably run another MRI later. Can I get you anything?"

"Coffee," Sinclair said.

"That's not on the approved list for patients, but I'll see what I can do." She stopped at the door and smiled back at him. "We have some good stuff at the nurse's station, and I won't tell if you don't."

"ATF brought in their big team from back east to work the bomb scene," Maloney said. "Both devices were pressure cookers just like the last one, but with twice as much black powder. ATF said that if even one bomb had gone off inside the classroom, everyone would've died. Not that they even needed the bombs. Both Pearson and Whitt had twenty loaded magazines for their nine millimeters. They had four hundred rounds and only needed a few seconds to change magazines. Shooting kids and teachers huddled in corners is no more difficult than shooting tin cans at the dump."

The nurse brought Sinclair his coffee. He felt his head begin to clear at the first sip. "Was this all over Travis's father and his affairs?" Sinclair asked.

"I don't know if we'll ever know the full answer," Braddock said. "I read his mother's diary and William's journals. We have to assume Travis did, too, and that's what set him off."

"What's the connection between him and the anarchists?" Sinclair asked.

"The FBI pulled out all stops and processed every bit of evidence at both of Dawn's apartments and the one where Edgar

Pratt was killed," Braddock said. "Coupled with e-mail and cell phone records, it looks like Travis went to Dawn's apartment alone and killed her. He returned later with Edgar Pratt and another anarchist by the name of Justin Dixon to move the body. Dixon was the man you and Buckner shot at the school. Travis, Pratt, and Dixon took her body to the park. I have to think that was all Travis's idea. Andrew Pearson came into the group and accompanied Travis and Dixon when they went to kill Edgar Pratt. Then a fourth guy, an anarchist friend of Pearson, joined them at the school. He was the rifleman you killed with the shotgun. Travis apparently had all these guys convinced they were mounting a noble attack on the establishment, when in effect, it was just personal. I think he planned to go out in a huge bang that his father had no choice but to notice."

"Is Yates connected to this at all?" Sinclair asked.

Sinclair noticed a conspiratorial look between Maloney and Braddock.

Maloney nodded to Braddock, obviously giving her permission to continue. "William Whitt knew Travis lost his job three months ago, and he and Councilmember Yates were actually closer than he let on," she said. "Yates needed someone in his community outreach office to revamp their computer network and website, and William recommended his son. Yates hired Travis to work twenty hours a week, but it was like hiring a master chef to flip hamburgers at McDonalds. Travis met scores of political activists while working there, some of whom were connected to the anarchist, Occupy, and Black Lives Matter movements."

"How do you know Yates didn't put him up to killing Dawn?" Sinclair asked.

Braddock shrugged her shoulders. "We talked to Yates's staff. They acknowledged that Yates and Travis had talked together privately at times, but everyone assumed it was about computer stuff. Since the chief thinks we're the biggest heroes in OPD history, he let the lieutenant and me interview Yates. The man is smooth and convincing. If he and Travis conspired to kill Dawn, he never let on, and their secret died with Travis."

"So he gets away with it?" Sinclair said.

"We can't prove he did anything," Maloney said.

"What about other evidence that connects them—phone records, e-mails?"

"The FBI gave us all of Travis's cell phone and e-mail records," Braddock said. "There were calls to and from Yates's offices. All of that is explainable by Travis working there."

"What about the ties between Yates and Kozlov?" Sinclair asked. "How does Yates explain Kozlov giving him a condo for his mistress?"

"He took the fifth on that," Maloney said. "Kozlov's attorneys won't let him talk to us about it either."

"And that's it?" Sinclair said.

"Look, Matt, we're the murder police," Maloney said. "We solved both homicides. All of the suspects are dead, so nothing's going to trial. It's up to others to investigate political corruption and bribery."

"It's not right," Sinclair said.

"I know," Maloney said.

"What about William Whitt?"

"Jankowski and I interviewed him for hours," Braddock said. "He's guilty of protecting his son, but that's about it. His life is in shambles. He resigned from Cal Asia and has already listed his house for sale. He's talking about moving to Florida, where he has a sister and can start a new life."

"I'm sure they have escort services down there," Sinclair said.

"I spoke to Dawn's parents and both of her sisters numerous times over the last few days," Braddock said. "No one understands why Dawn was so fixated on leaving home and living out here. I explored the possibly that she was abused as a child, but both sisters were adamant such a thing never occurred."

"It's probably impossible to look at someone else's life from the outside and figure out why they took a particular path," Sinclair said.

Braddock looked at him funny, squinting with one eye. She wasn't used to him being so introspective.

She continued, "One thing's for sure: Madison couldn't be in a better home. Just this morning, I got a call from Dawn's father. He received a notice that the brokerage account that was sending the checks will begin sending five thousand dollars every month and will deposit another two thousand into a college fund, both until Madison turns twenty-five."

"Guilt money to make Yates feel better, or hush money so Dawn's parents let it go," Sinclair said. "That's all it is."

"Dawn's parents would love to talk to you once you're better, and they want Madison to meet you when she gets older."

"I'd like that," Sinclair said. He thought for a moment about meeting the boy whose parents he couldn't save outside the movie theater years ago, and now planning to meet Madison, whose mother he also couldn't save. Maybe by the time those meetings happened, he'd be in a place where he no longer felt that he had failed them.

"I don't intend to let this stuff with Yates go," Sinclair said.

"Get yourself better," Maloney said. "We'll talk about it more later."

The nurse pushed a wheelchair into his room. "We have a reservation for you in radiology. Do you feel up to taking a ride?"

Chapter 43

Walt drove Sinclair home from the hospital Sunday evening in the big Mercedes sedan. Sinclair sat up front and watched the full moon light up the city through a clear sky. A few hours ago, a physician who specialized in traumatic brain injuries had explained that even though his physical injuries—mostly bumps and bruises from being thrown twenty feet by the blast—were minimal, the pressure wave passing through his brain probably disrupted its functioning to some degree. Even though the latest MRI showed no permanent damage, the doctor wouldn't approve Sinclair's release because he lived alone and there would be no one to notice if he experienced convulsions or seizures in his sleep. When Walt assured the doctor that either he or his wife would remain with Sinclair overnight, he reluctantly agreed to release him.

Sinclair had lost count of the number of visitors who stopped in to see him over the last two days. The police chief escorted the mayor to his bedside to tell him that he and Braddock would be awarded the Medal of Valor once he returned to duty. U.S. Attorney Campbell and District Attorney O'Brien visited together to praise him for his actions. O'Brien assured him that the DA office's investigation into his officer-involved shooting was just a formality, and his office and the police department would together announce his shooting was justified as soon as he was up to giving his formal statement. Campbell told him, with a wink, that he was glad Sinclair hadn't followed his admonishment to tread softly. Countless police officers and federal agents, many of whom Sinclair didn't know by name, passed through his room, most only to shake his hand and wish him a speedy recovery.

Alyssa came by when she got off shift. She stayed with him most of the evening and never lost her smile even after getting up for the twentieth time so other visitors could come in. Sinclair wanted to talk about whether their relationship had changed after what happened at the Caldecott Academy. But every time he tried to talk to her, another well-wisher showed up in the doorway. She had mentioned that Christmas was eight days away, but he was afraid to ask about her plans. He was afraid she might laugh and remind him that they were only friends, or worse yet, he was just her patient, and that spending Christmas together was something couples did. How could he rush toward multiple suspects armed with rifles and bombs, yet be afraid to risk rejection from a woman?

Walt parked the car next to the kitchen door of Sinclair's guesthouse and walked him inside. "If you're hungry, Betty stocked your refrigerator with all kind of goodies, and I can have her make whatever you want."

"I ate just before they signed me out," Sinclair said. "What I want first is a shower. Hospital sponge baths don't cut it. Then I just want to sit in my chair, watch the Raiders finish losing their eleventh game of the season, and sleep in my own bed."

"While you're showering, I'll park the car and grab a pillow and blanket so I can camp out on your couch tonight."

"That's really not necessary."

"Matthew, the doctors said you should not be left alone tonight, and we will obey the doctors."

Sinclair knew it was useless to argue with Walt, so he headed toward the shower.

He had just hung up his towel when he heard a knock at the French doors that led from his living room to the pool area.

It wasn't like Walt not to carry his keys. Sinclair pulled on his robe and went to the living room to let him in.

On the other side of the door stood Alyssa, wearing a fleece jacket over a sweater and skinny jeans. Sinclair opened the door. "This is a surprise," he said.

She stepped inside. Sinclair looked past her to see if Walt was there. He wasn't. Her long, sleek hair was down and the corners of her mouth turned upward. Her entire face was smiling.

"I was going to wait until Christmas morning to give this to you," she said, holding up a shopping bag. "But I couldn't stand it. I couldn't wait to see the expression on your face." She reached in the bag and pulled out a Burberry trench coat, a brand-new version of the Westminster classic that was destroyed in the first explosion.

"Jeez, Alyssa, this is way too much."

She draped the coat over the back of his sofa. "When I went to the Burberry store in San Francisco and told them who it was for and what happened to your last one, the owner came out and . . . well, he almost gave it to me for free."

"I don't know what to say."

"Say nothing. You're my hero." She reached up and kissed him softly on the lips.

Was she also giving him the gift early because she had separate plans for Christmas? Sinclair swallowed hard. "Christmas . . . so what are you doing for Christmas?"

"It's crazy with my family. Dinner Christmas Eve, the following morning at my parent's house with my brothers and sisters and their kids. Food flowing all the time. Children laughing. Adults talking over each other while engaged in multiple, simultaneous conversations. Italian families are loud. I hope you can handle it."

"So . . ."

"If you don't have any other plans, that is. Everyone's heard so much about you, and they're dying to meet you. Oops, that was probably a poor choice of words to use around a homicide detective."

Sinclair laughed. "I can't think of any place I'd rather be."

"But we can also fit in any plans you have with Walt and Fred, or Cathy and her family."

Sinclair felt enormous relief. He didn't need to ask her to define their relationship. It just was what it was.

"How are you feeling?" she asked.

"A little sore, but otherwise fine."

"Walt told me the doctors insisted you not be left alone, so I volunteered to take the night shift." She took his hand, led him toward the leather recliner, and picked up the TV remote. "It's the third quarter and the Raiders are down by three touchdowns. Make yourself comfortable, and I'll fix you some hot tea and a snack."

He settled into his recliner and smiled as he watched Alyssa walk into the kitchen. Remembering the view of her hiking up a trail years ago and her jogging ahead of him a few days ago, he thought she looked pretty damn good in jeans, too.

Acknowledgments

It's been a hell of a ride this past year watching *Red Line* make its way to readers while writing *Thrill Kill*. The list of those who helped me along the way includes fellow writers, active and retired police officers, and others who provided support, advice, and expertise to make this story and its characters as authentic as fiction can be: Andy Alexander, Dana Bottenhagen, Robert Chan, Jane Cleland, Bob Crawford, Wendy Cross, Christian Cruz, Carol Healy, Pam Kelley, Jack Kelly, Mike Martin, Lou Norton, Steve Paich, Dan Pope, Don Snyder, Emerson Thrower, Rachael Van Sloten, Shirley Whiddon, and Lynn Wilcox. I apologize to those I missed.

I'm blessed to be represented by the world's greatest agent, Paula Munier, who holds my hand when necessary, kicks me in the butt when I need it, and teaches me how to write better. I'm doubly blessed to have the greatest New York publisher, Crooked Lane Books, whose editorial director, Matt Martz, and his talented team of editors, Maddie Caldwell, Heather Boak, and Sarah Poppe, made this book and me as a writer many times better, while publicists Dana Kaye and Julia Borcherts helped spread the word about *Red Line* and the Detective Matt Sinclair Mystery Series.

I'm especially grateful for my lovely wife, Cathy. Without her support, understanding, and patience, none of this would be possible or worthwhile.